4

The Wilder Side of Life

THE WILDER SIDE OF LIFE

Diana Stainforth

C

CENTURY

LONDON SYDNEY AUCKLAND JOHANNESBURG

First published in Great Britain in 1992 by
Random Century Group
20 Vauxhall Bridge Road, London, SW1V 2SA

Century Hutchinson South Africa (Pty) Ltd
PO Box 337, Bergvlei 2012, South Africa

Random Century Australia Pty Ltd
20 Alfred Street, Milsons Point, Sydney, NSW 2061
Australia

Random Century New Zealand Ltd
PO Box 40–086, Glenfield, Auckland 10
New Zealand

The catalogue data record for this book
is available from the British Library

Typeset by Deltatype Ltd, Ellesmere Port
Printed in Great Britain by
Mackays of Chatham plc, Chatham, Kent

Acknowledgements

When I started to research this book I had never played poker. By the end, I'd played in Las Vegas!

But the background to my story doesn't only concern poker. *The Wilder Side of Life* is equally situated in the cut and thrust of the legal world and the fast pace of a greyhound track. In every area, people gave up their time to help me. I thank them all. Some have asked not to be named. I respect their wishes.

In the legal world, I am indebted to: Michael Stimpson, for two years of good-humoured answering of my queries; His Honour Judge Ryland; all those at the Inner Temple, Lincoln's Inn, the Bar Council, and the Lord Chancellor's office who provided me with the minutiae to give credibility to my story.

For my forays into greyhound racing, I thank: Sue Bunn and her dogs; Tony James, formerly General Manager of GRA's Wimbledon Stadium; Norah McEllistrim, NGRC trainer, and her many dogs, but especially Fred, on whom I have based my blue dog.

For their knowledge of Dallas and for their hospitality, I thank Ray and Carolyn Giles.

For her medical information, I am grateful to Joan Mahon.

As for poker, for their assistance and their insights into Las Vegas, I am very grateful to: Jim Albrecht, poker room manager at Binion's Horseshoe Casino, for his knowlege of the World Poker Series; Jeff and Cora Fadigan and Jeff Vanderlip of Binion's poker room. In London I received help from: Bill Slate, poker room manager of the Victoria Casino; Group Captain Richard Stephens, formerly of the British Casino Association; Freddy Moyle.

I pay tribute to Anthony Holden's terrific book *Big Deal*. It was my guidebook to Las Vegas.

Finally, I thank Edward Twinberrow for my first poker lesson, and all those friends with whom I played before leaving for Las Vegas. They were convinced I'd lose. Had they been wrong, I might never have come home to finish this book!

Diana Stainforth
30 December 1991

One

Until that spring, Francesca had managed to convince herself that she was no more unhappy than anyone else. Then everything came to a head. It started that March afternoon.

The magnolia trees were coming into flower in the Inner Temple Gardens as she hurried along the uneven pavement towards Makepeace Buildings. She tried to walk faster, cursing as her high heels caught in the gaps between the flagstones. She was always about to be late. If only she had more time to concentrate on her cases, she might become a better barrister. If she could concentrate on William, she'd be a better wife. At least, he said she would.

At the top of King's Bench Walk, two barristers crossed her path, heading for the library. One was Rupert Barbour, the best-looking of her male colleagues in chambers. He nodded. She smiled. Not that she particularly liked him. He was pompous and a snob, but one had to be professional. His companion gave her a broad grin, then murmured something to Rupert, who hissed, 'Don't be a fool. That's Eastgate's wife.' Francesca directed a second smile at Rupert's companion. What did a smile cost? One never knew when people were going to be useful. That was William's philosophy.

Francesca was a strange dichotomy of rebel and madonna. Her glossy mahogany hair, which could have been a rippling mane of seductive curls, was scraped back into a subdued schoolgirl plait. Her teddy-bear eyes, so soft and warm and brown, frowned from beneath straight, serious eyebrows. Her skin was very pale, almost too pale. When she was anxious, it turned purple in the hollows around her eyes. She was unadventurous with make-up, using merely a touch of mascara and a hint of pinkish lip gloss. Her scent was lemony and light, and unsuggestive. But her black work suits, the uniform of all female barristers, exposed an underlying

1

sensuality. She preferred moulded jackets and tight skirts. When she walked, it was with an easy grace, but if approached, especially by strangers, she held herself very straight and slightly prim. They thought her haughty. Only if amused did she reveal her other side. Then she would throw back her head to give a deep, throaty, raunchy laugh.

She shared a set of chambers with ten other barristers in Makepeace Buildings, named after Thackeray who'd had rooms near the Inn. The buildings were of dark red brick, which on that afternoon was turning slowly to an ochre gold, whilst the glass panes in the white-painted sash windows liquified in the firing of the dying sun. The light caught the delicate pink petals of the magnolias as they reached through the iron railings to lift their candelabra of blooms. It cast cold shadows across the pavement where their luscious petals lay squashed on the flagstones. Francesca loved this hour. The Inn and the gardens beyond had a tranquil painted quality, from which not even the roar of the traffic along the Embankment could detract.

She ran up the stone steps and through the shiny black door. All the doors along Makepeace were painted black, with a white board on the adjoining wall and each barrister's name listed on it, handpainted in elegant black lettering. To see her name always gave her a surge of pride.

Her chambers were on the third floor, occupying the rooms on both sides of the staircase. She'd joined them after her pupillage. Or rather, after her marriage. Head of chambers, with his name at the top of the list, was Geoffrey Culmstock, QC, a huge, charismatic Yorkshireman with a bloodhound face. He had a way of looking as if he were about to cry which extracted the truth from the most reluctant witness. His room was the largest. Desmond, their small, dapper, charming second head of chambers had the second-largest office. Most of the other barristers doubled up to reduce overheads. Debonair Rupert shared with the pompous and very overweight Hugo. Melanie Llanellen, Francesca's closest friend, shared with James, who was kind and quiet and worked mainly out of town: he had a cottage in Suffolk. Abrasive Thomas divided a gloomy back room with horsy, well-connected Charlotte Regan-Walker. Sanjiv, who was Indian and never said a bad word against anyone, had his own room. So did

2

Francesca. Hers was one of the nicest; small, but at the front, with a view over the gardens. But then Francesca received preferential treatment, or so Charlotte and Thomas complained behind her back.

Mr Nailsworth, their chief clerk, looked up from his desk as she entered the reception. Called 'Old Nailbag' but only behind his back, he was a former sergeant major whose father and grandfather had also been clerks; the position was one of unspoken nepotism. His task was to liaise with solicitors, to allocate briefs, and to chase fees. He took a percentage of each barrister's earnings. 'Your client's waiting,' he told Francesca, glancing pointedly at his watch.

'Thank you, Mr Nailsworth. I'll ring when I want him shown in.' She collected the messages from her pigeon-hole, determined that she wasn't going to bullied by her clerk. The trouble was, old Nailsworth didn't approve of female barristers. William said she imagined it. But she was right.

In her office she flicked through her messages, then reached for the telephone, quickly tapping out a number. 'Dining and Wining? This is Mrs Eastgate. I need a starter for tonight. For ten. Yes, I know it's short notice. I'm sorry, I thought I'd have time to make something. Mackerel pâté? Well, if you've nothing else it'll have to do. I'll pay on collection. Don't send me a bill!'

She was so hungry she felt faint. She'd had nothing to eat since six o'clock that morning, when she'd laid the table for tonight's dinner party. From her briefcase she took a half-eaten Mars Bar. Resting her elbows on her desk, she gazed out of the window at the dying day, and slowly chewed her way through the stale chocolate. She tried to remember what William had told her not to say at dinner, but her mind was blank. She couldn't even remember who they'd invited. She just wished that for once they were to spend an evening at home, alone, talking.

Her intercom buzzed. 'Your client is becoming impatient,' barked Nailsworth.

Francesca choked on the Mars Bar. She'd forgotten all about her client. Forgotten everything, except the dying light and how tired and hungry she was. No wonder William complained.

She was surprised to see that it was Mr Atterbury, of Allport & Atterbury, and not a junior partner, who ushered in Lex Gunter, a pug-faced thug accused of assault. Francesca had been instructed by the firm before, but never by Atterbury himself.

The thug was short and thickset, with a junk-food complexion and on his upper lip pale fluff which he was trying unsuccessfully to grow into a moustache. He stared sullenly at Francesca. 'I didn't know I was getting some woman.'

'I am your counsel, Mr Gunter' she answered crisply. 'But if you wish another barrister to be instructed, that's perfectly all right with me.'

Atterbury had turned scarlet. 'I apologise, Mrs Eastgate. So does my client.'

'Oh, you'll do.' Gunter sat down heavily and rested his thick forearms on her desk. He had very hairy wrists which made Francesca think longingly of William's smooth ones.

She skimmed Atterbury's brief. In an ideal world she would have read it before the conference, but Atterbury, like many solicitors, hadn't sent the papers till the last minute. In an ideal world she'd have eaten lunch, and wouldn't now be surreptitiously trying to remove the chocolate which clung to her back teeth. 'Richmond Greyhound Racing Stadium!' she read out, surprised. 'I didn't realise it was still in use.'

'It ain't. The old bloke who owns it can't afford the upkeep.'

'You mean . . . Marius Charlwood, the man you are said to have assaulted?'

'I plead not guilty. He's the only witness.'

Francesca closed the papers with relief. 'I cannot represent a client who admits culpability but insists on pleading innocent. It's against the rules.'

'I didn't hit 'im. I just threatened 'im, that's all. He must've fallen later. I didn't even 'ave to break the fence to get in. The place is fallin' apart.' A look of cunning came into Gunter's eyes. 'A shame to 'ave all that good building land not in use, what with the need for 'ousing and young couples desperate for an 'ome. Rich young couples!' He laughed and, without asking her permission, lit a cigarette, gazing insolently at Francesca through the smoke. 'Mr Marmintoll is paying my defence. He said 'e'd see me right.'

'Mr Marmintoll of Marmintoll Construction?'

The thug laughed. 'That shocked you. But where there's money, darlin', we're all villains. An' you lawyers are the worst.'

4

Darkness had fallen by the time Francesca left chambers. The light from the wrought-iron gas lamps outside each doorway threw its white radiance against the hoary night. William's chambers – where he was a QC, and second head – were three doors away from hers. Francesca could see the light in his room was on. He was still in conference. She hoped he wouldn't reach home before she did. He'd find the kitchen piled with unpeeled vegetables and open recipe books, and would panic that dinner would never be ready.

She cut through the narrow alley beside the library and crossed the courtyard between the Hall and the Temple Church. There was a scholarly mellowness about the Inn which reminded her of the courtyards at Oxford. Not that she'd been to Oxford. But William had. Francesca had joined the Bar School straight from school, one of the last to be accepted without a university degree: the following year the rules had changed.

Francesca could never pass the Temple Church without thinking of her wedding day, especially late in the evening, when there was no one around and she had the courtyard to herself. It took her back to that wintry Saturday afternoon when her stepfather had escorted her up the aisle to become Mrs William Eastgate, whilst the organ played Bach and the sunlight danced through the stained-glass windows, casting a kaleidoscope of colours over the white brocade of her bridal gown. She'd been so nervous, and so proud.

Within an hour of leaving chambers, Francesca was home in the bright white kitchen of their smart Islington house, transferring the mackerel pâté from Dining & Wining's foil dish to her own elegant silver platter. On the windowsill Jaws, her goldfish, swam furiously up and down his tank. She'd bought him on impulse last summer, when he was barely an inch long and living in a small bowl. Since the arrival of the tank he'd done nothing but eat and grow. She hoped he wasn't offended by the mackerel pâté.

The front door opened and William stepped into the hall. She smiled and called, 'I'm in the kitchen,' wondering how he managed to remain so smart and unruffled all day whilst she became hot and tired and creased.

When Francesca had first seen William she'd thought he looked like a poet, or as a poet ought to be: tall, fair, handsome and aesthetic, a man who possessed a sense of beauty. She'd been dining in Hall. All students had to 'keep terms' – to dine at their Inn of Court three times a term for eight terms before they were called to the Bar. It was part of the ritual, the induction to the life of the Inn. Nervous and excited in her black gown, Frankie had been seated at one of the lower tables. At a higher table was William Eastgate. Her neighbour had pointed him out as the most brilliant barrister of his decade. Francesca had watched him talk, while all those near him listened. He never noticed her.

But William's appearance was deceptive, as she later discovered. He was no dreamer. His chiselled face had a stubborn jut. His grey eyes were piercing and determined. His voice was modulated, he seldom raised it. He didn't need to.

'Everything under control?' He glanced at the chaos.

'Almost.' She kicked the Dining & Wining bag underneath the Welsh dresser. 'I was late back. I had a conference.' She sliced a lime and decorated the mackerel pâté with half twists, alternating with mint and lemon. 'I'll have to withdraw from the case. My client's accused of assaulting old Marius Charlwood, the owner of Richmond Greyhound Racing. What a coincidence!'

'But you haven't been near the stadium since you were a child.'

'My father lives there. At least, I suppose he does. Marius was his closest friend. I can't accept instructions where I have a personal connection with the opposing side.'

'Francesca, if you were going to withdraw, you should have returned the brief after you'd read it, before the conference.'

She sighed. 'I didn't read it. I didn't have time.'

'How could you be so unprofessional?'

'Atterbury delivered late. It happens to us all.'

'Not to me.' He watched in silence as she quickly watered the Busy Lizzies lined up beside Jaws's tank. She wanted to cry with tiredness and rage and guilt, because of course what she had done was wrong. 'If you pull out now,' he went on, more gently, 'you'll have to explain about your father. That wouldn't help either of our careers.'

She looked doubtful. 'I suppose you could be right.'

'I am, darling. Believe me.'

She dug around in the bottom of the fridge looking for another

6

lime. 'I want to cut back on criminal law. It bugs me to use my brain to defend a thug who's clearly guilty.'

'Everyone deserves legal representation.'

'When we first met, you often said how immoral it was that rich villains could afford top counsel.'

'Did I?'

She smiled. 'It was one of the things I admired about you.'

'But I don't do criminal law, except as a favour to my commercial clients. If I were a criminal advocate, I wouldn't be considered as a High Court judge' He watched her, frowning. 'We're having two judges and both our heads of chambers to dinner tonight. So for God's sake don't go blabbing your scruples in front of them.'

She was stung. 'William! Please! I'm not criticising.'

'Good. Because I haven't noticed you object to our lifestyle. You don't say no to St Moritz or Barbados. You can hardly pass a shop without buying something.'

'Maybe I'm compensating.'

'What do you mean?'

'Nothing.' Afraid to go further in case she reached a point from which she couldn't return, Francesca picked up a handful of carrots and went out into the garden. It was freezing outside. Big Ears, her enormous black and white rabbit, was at his hutch door, waiting for her, his fur all fluffed up. As she approached, his nose twitched in anticipation. She'd found him two Christmases ago, hiding in William's parents' garden after he'd escaped from the nearby rabbit farm. As she approached, his nose twitched in anticipation. One by one, she fed the carrots into the cage, then, before returning to the house, she tickled the spot between his ears, as he loved her to do.

Back in the kitchen, she washed her hands and checked the *boeuf en croute*, sticking a long-pronged fork into an uncovered corner. Blood oozed from the still raw meat. 'Don't hurry them into dinner,' she said. 'This won't be ready till ten.'

He clicked his tongue in annoyance.

'I can't help it. Not if you want me to hold dinner parties when I'm working all day and you won't hear of me hiring a cook.'

'If you didn't have that stupid goldfish or those house plants or that greedy rabbit, you'd have plenty of time. Adults don't keep rabbits in London gardens.'

7

'I'm not getting rid of Big Ears.' It was an old argument.

'What you need's a baby. You used to long for children. It was I who said you were too young. But I want an heir, Francesca, an Eastgate son.'

'Oh, we've plenty of time.' She carried on preparing dinner. William was right. She had wanted children, lots of them. Once. He watched her, infuriated. Every suggestion he made, she questioned. She never used to. Eventually Francesca said, in a normal, friendly voice, 'You know what really makes me sick? Guess who's paying Gunter's legal fees?'

'I don't think we should discuss it.'

'Marmintoll! Your major client.'

He was shocked, and she was glad. 'Why should they go to another chambers?' he demanded, unwilling to believe her.

'Because this is a small, dirty case.'

'They know you're my wife.'

'Perhaps they want you involved but not involved.'

'Maybe.' He paced up and down between the kitchen and the breakfast room. Then he turned. 'Nevertheless, it's unethical of you to divulge this information. Even to me!'

She faced him. 'If I can't confide in you, who can I turn to? And I want to confide in you, William, I want you to confide in me. After all, we are married.'

He picked up the silver platter and sniffed its contents. 'Mackerel pâté! But I wanted salmon. This is an important dinner, Francesca, not a student bottle-party. Can't you ever do anything right?'

Francesca threw the remaining mint on to the table and ran out of the kitchen and up the stairs, her head bent so that he couldn't see she was crying.

Twenty minutes later she walked back down, bathed, scented, dressed in cornflower-blue silk, her hair in a smooth plait. William was in the drawing room, pouring a gin and tonic for Geoffrey Culmstock. She could hear him saying, 'I must show you my new Alexander Pope. I bought it today, a first edition. I'm quite in love with it. My antique bookseller knows of another. I'm thinking it over. Of course I don't read them, I don't have time. I just like to possess beautiful objects.'

As Francesca reached the bottom step, she clenched her fists and prayed that William wouldn't belittle her in front of Geoffrey.

He turned when he saw her, and hurried across the room. She tried not to flinch as he raised his arm. 'Frankie, darling, you look lovely,' he said, slippng it around her shoulders. 'I'm a lucky man, aren't I, Geoffrey?'

'The luckiest.' Geoffrey raised his glass. 'To the Bar's golden couple.'

Francesca forced a smile, but inside she felt sick. She wanted to scream. Do you mean it now, or did you mean it in the kitchen? Am I useless, or do you love me?

Two

Francesca was delayed by a previous case, so she couldn't be in court when Gunter appeared before the magistrates to have his case committed to the Crown Court. Melanie stood in for her.

Gunter came straight from the court to Francesca's chambers, barging into her office before Old Nailbag could stop him. He banged his fist on her desk. 'You think I'm muck, don't you?' he accused. 'That's why you weren't in court.'

'I explained my absence. Your solicitor was happy. Miss Llanellen is most competent.' Francesca raised her voice. 'Thank you, Mr Nailsworth. You can show Mr Gunter out.'

'You cold bitch!' Gunter swept the papers from her desk on to the floor.

A bright-red mark appeared on each of Francesca's cheeks. Nailsworth and a junior clerk hurried to protect her. They seized Gunter by the arms, but he shook them off with ease, as if they were flies. 'It's all right,' he sneered. 'I'm leaving. But get something straight, darlin'.' He pointed a stubby finger at Francesca. 'You ain't goin' to be absent at my trial. Mr Marmintoll wouldn't like that.'

She stood up. 'I'll be in court, Mr Gunter, because that's my professional duty, not because of your threats. Now, get out!'

He went. Francesca, Nailbag and the junior listened to his retreating footsteps on the stairs. Then Nailbag turned to her, puce with embarrassment. 'I'm sorry about that, Mrs Eastgate. Don't know how he evaded me.'

'It mustn't happen again, Mr Nailsworth.' She exacted retribution for his decade of ill temper.

'It won't, I promise.' He half saluted. 'Mr Eastgate would be proud of you.'

She waited a full ten minutes, to be sure Gunter had left the building, before she ran up the street to William's chambers.

He was sitting behind his massive leather-topped desk, surrounded by neat piles of law books. When Francesca burst in, unannounced, he looked up in amazement. 'What is wrong?'

10

She sank on to the chair in front of him, moving his papers very slightly, in order to lean her elbows on his desk, but not enough to annoy him. 'Gunter threatened me. Nailbag had to evict him.'

'Don't take things personally. Be more detached. Don't you remember anything I taught you during your pupillage?'

'William, he said I was a cold bitch.'

'And you'd give an uneducated bully the satisfaction of having riled you?'

She longed for him to take her in his arms. 'I'm your wife. Doesn't it anger you?'

'All right! Calm down! Next time we have dinner with Marmintoll, we'll drop a hint that you don't want to act for people like Gunter. But I can't fight your professional battles, Francesca.'

She felt flat and very tired. 'I'm not asking you to. I just want you to . . . show you care.'

'You're being childish again. Of course I care. But chambers is not the place to show it.' He opened a law book. 'Naturally, Gunter will now expect you to lose his case.'

'I ought to withdraw. There's still time.'

'And have him think he's got the better of you?'

'William, my father might accompany Marius Charlwood to court.'

'He won't. He'll be drunk – or in gaol.'

She flushed. Into her memory came her father's laughing blue eyes, his voice, soft like the Kerry mists, the smell of whisky on his old tweed jacket, his nicotined fingers holding her small, childish hands as he taught her how to deal a pack of cards, and how to cheat when she dealt. 'Please don't talk of him like that,' she said. 'He's still my father.'

'Darling, you haven't seen him for twenty years. You chose not to. He's nothing but an embarrassment, you've always said so. Of course, if you'd read the brief before the conference, as you should have done, you could have withdrawn easily. Now, Marmintoll would want an explanation. You'd look foolish, and we don't want that. So just win the case, and forget about it.' He smiled. 'I want to be proud of you, Francesca. You're a very good barrister!'

'Am I really?' she asked, pleased by the unexpected compliment.

'When you keep your emotions in check.' He reached across the desk and patted her hand, which wasn't better than nothing. It was worse, it raised a hunger in her. She wanted so much more from him.

William and Francesca spent Saturday night with his parents, Mortimer and Audrey Eastgate, at Kingly Grange, a cavernous early-Victorian mansion which dominated the small Kent town of Kingly. Grey and angular, the house rose like a disapproving scowl from the gentle, undulating countryside. William's parents had inherited it from an uncle. They couldn't afford to live there in comfort but they refused to sell. The enormous drawing room and dining room were adorned with gilt-framed portraits of past Eastgates, all judges, rectors or army officers. They had the frozen look of people who'd spent their lives sitting on uncomfortable chairs in cold rooms.

The house had twelve bedrooms, all icy and unwelcoming. The beds were hard, the carpets threadbare. The drawers in the chests always stuck because the wood distended in the damp. At night, water gurgled through ancient pipes. In the morning, when Francesca ran her bath, it gushed out at her, rusty and not very warm. When William had first brought her to meet his parents, she'd been impressed by the grandeur of Kingly Grange. Now she suffered its discomforts for his sake.

They arrived in the morning to find her father-in-law practising his serve on the tennis court. Below his baggy shorts, his long, skinny legs were magenta with cold. Her mother-in-law was pruning roses. She was wearing a wool jersey dress, hitched up so its muddy hem rested on the tops of her muddier green Wellington boots. She had another dress the same; she ordered them, two at a time, from the Army & Navy. A battleship of a woman, with steely grey hair and foghorn voice, she never read letters, but answered as she saw fit. Other people's comments didn't alter her reply. When invited to join the church bazaar committee, she accepted the post of chairwoman.

'William,' she boomed, 'your father wants to play tennis. And you, Francesca, bring me the willow basket for the daffodils. I want to talk to you.' She waited until William was out of earshot before adding, 'William tells me you don't want children any more.'

Francesca flushed. 'I never said anything of the sort.'

'Good, It's time you started a family. You need an heir for Kingly. You've been married nearly ten years.'

'We have plenty of time.'

'*You* may have, but William's almost two decades older than you. He wants to enjoy his offspring.' Audrey paused and gave a deep sigh. 'Oh dear! Now I've upset you again. You're so touchy, Francesca.' She bent to snip, and the bright morning sunlight caught the grey bristles of her moustache.

Francesca dropped the basket on the ground and stalked back across the lawn, her boots making silvery footprints on the dew. She spent her time at Kingly Grange trying not to argue with her mother-in-law. Sometimes she wondered why she bothered.

Inside the house, it was freezing. The Eastgates, unlike her own mother, never lolled around in the daytime. They were propelled by puritan guilt. The only warm room was the conservatory, where a weak early-spring sun heated the glass roof and an ancient boiler melted the icicles which hung on the inside. She wrapped herself in a rug and stretched out on the chaise-longue, with the newspapers and a cup of coffee. But Audrey's words wouldn't go away.

When William came in from the tennis court, she said, 'Your mother's been on at me. She seems to think I don't want children.'

He looked sheepish. 'I never said that. Not exactly. But you know what she's like.'

Francesca gave him a sympathetic smile. 'She's a bully.'

He touched her shoulder, very briefly. 'That's why I married a woman her complete opposite.'

She reached up for his hand, but by that time he'd removed it.

That night, in the creaking spare-room bed, Francesca turned to William, sliding her arms around his neck and nestling against the warmth of his body, which felt lean and hard through his silk pyjamas. 'Am I cold?' she asked him.

'Of course not.'

'Are you sure?'

'Darling, what a silly question.'

'You're the only man I've known, so who else can I ask?'

He drew her closer. 'Make love to me.'

She slid her body on top of his, moving rhythmically up and

down him, not pressing down on him but with her weight taken by her arms, as he'd taught her. Her breasts stroked him. The crêpe de Chine of her nightdress whispered over him like a caress. He slipped one silken strap from her shoulder and kissed her bare flesh. Then, slowly, he rolled the material down her so that she was naked from the waist upwards, riding astride him, never altering her rhythm, until he gripped her buttocks with his hands and dug his fingers into her flesh. As he climaxed, she rode him harder, faster, trying desperately to seize her own pleasure in that brief moment before he stopped her, gripping her by the hips and groaning, 'Don't move!'

She sat still, as he'd taught her to do, although every animal instinct in her cried out to carry on.

After a few moments, he moved her to one side. 'You're perfect. We're perfect.'

He fell asleep quickly. He always did. She lay awake, staring at the ceiling. The thug was right. She was cold, but William was too kind to tell her. She thought of men who'd seemed interested in her, then shied away. And it wasn't just because she was married. Listening to a distant train hurtle through the sleeping country-side, she wondered who'd want her if William left her. The room screamed, 'No one!'

She woke at dawn and lay recalling her first date with William. The pupillage vacancy in his chambers had been advertised in the *Bar News*. Francesca had applied, as had many others in her year, because William Eastgate had a reputation as a brilliant advocate. He, together with four colleagues at his chambers, had interviewed her. The sun had been shining through the window on to William's very fair hair. She remembered thinking how handsome he was, with his narrow face, his grey eyes and his long, slender fingers.

'Pupils are a nuisance.' he'd said haughtily. 'But I feel obliged to do my duty to the Inn. You're the most amenable of the promising applicants. I can't work with people who are difficult. Try not to get in my way.'

For a month he'd scarcely spoken to her. She'd scuttled behind him, carrying his books, or looked up references which he seldom used, or drafted pleadings he barely read. She began to wish she'd chosen a less brilliant pupilmaster; someone who had more time for her.

14

One afternoon, she overheard William on the telephone. He was saying, 'I only bought the tickets because you wanted to go, Rebecca.' A moment later, he called Francesca to his office. 'Busy this evening? No? Good. You're coming to the opera. Go home and put on a smart dress. I'll meet you in the foyer. Don't keep me waiting!'

During her two years at the Bar School, Francesca had had several boyfriends but no one serious. They were all fellow students with little money, who took her to pubs or for cheap Indian meals. She liked them, but not as she yearned to love her first lover. When she wouldn't let them make love to her, they moved on to more willing partners. The opera with William was her first grown-up date. In the interval, when he enquired what she'd like to drink, she was too nervous to reply. At dinner, he ordered for her. He talked. She listened, and wondered who Rebecca was.

On the following morning, Francesca stuttered her thanks for a lovely evening, hoping he'd invite her again. For several weeks after that, William didn't even speak to her. Then he invited her to the theatre, again at the last minute, which made her suspect that Rebecca had let him down once more.

During dinner, he suddenly begun to talk about Rebecca. 'I met her at Ascot,' he said. 'Her ex-husband was a racehorse owner. She was wearing a hat with a veil. I've always liked women in veils.'

'Are you going to marry her?' Francesca asked, miserably picturing a sophisticated vamp.

He laughed. 'Good God, no! I'd never trust a woman with a past. My mother would never accept a divorcee. There's never been one in the Eastgate family.'

'My parents were divorced,' Frankie told him. 'I'm determined that will never happen to me.'

He nodded. 'I agree. Marriage is for life.'

The next time he took Francesca out to dinner, he said, 'I wont be seeing Rebecca any more.'

Francesca had glowed with hope and happiness.

It all seemed so long ago. She glanced at William sleeping beside her. She recalled the night they became lovers. She was nervous. He was patient. He hurt her, and she cried, not from pain but from emotion. She remembered waking up next morning and wondering where she was. He brought her up a cup of tea. She sat in his bed, flushed and embarrassed, his duvet clutched under her chin, whilst he lay beside her, calmly reading the *Financial Times*. The following weekend he brought her down to Kingly to meet his parents. Nine months later they were married. She'd been so in love – at least, she thought she was. So impressed that someone like William Eastgate wanted her.

Suddenly, a crucifying loneliness rolled over her, bringing tears to her eyes. She brushed them away and rose abruptly, hurrying through the cold house to the bathroom.

She was subdued at breakfast. William didn't comment. But as she was clearing the plates away, he took her in his arms and held her tight against him. 'People are jealous because we have everything,' he said. 'They look for cracks. Don't listen to them.'

She leaned against him, savouring the warmth of his body through his thick sweater, feeling happier than she had for months.

'You mustn't let things upset you.' He stroked her hair. 'You hardly said a word at dinner the other night.'

She stiffened at his criticism. 'I'm sorry if it was so noticeable.'

'Develop more small talk. You'll have to when I'm a judge. We'll be entertaining constantly.' He kissed her on the forehead as if she were a child.

She wanted to say, If you hadn't belittled me in the kitchen I might have been more talkative, but she didn't want to start another argument.

They drove to her mother and stepfather for Sunday lunch. Francesca took the wheel. She usually did, so William could sit in the back and work. Or that's what they said. In reality she was a better driver, though this was never said. She loved the power of the big BMW. As she accelerated hard away from the Eastgates, the tyres spat wet gravel at her mother-in-law.

White Oast was a charming oast house built of warm, rounded Sussex flint. It was on the edge of the village of Rockhurst, which was set in the green rolling fields and soft woods to the south of Tunbridge Wells. Until the turn of the century, the oast house had been used to store hops. Now the hop fields had become a golf course and the rounded oast room was used by Steven as a study.

Francesca had been ten the first time she'd come here. She'd been wearing her only smart dress, red velvet with a stiff lace collar, and her only good pair of shoes, buckled ones from Clarks in Kensington High Street. The house had been more formal then, the home of a careful widower. The garden had been regimented, without the beautiful, lazy drifts of blue larkspur and pale pink lupins which her mother had planted.

But clearest of all, when Francesca looked back, was her memory of the night before that first visit, when her mother had said, 'We're going to the country tomorrow to stay with Mr Hartington, the solicitor who helped me with my divorce. He has a son called Robert, about ten years older than you. Robert's mummy was killed by a bomb in the war. I want you to be very good because Steven . . . Mr Hartington is going to be your new daddy.'

'But I have a dad.'

Her mother had held her tight. 'Frankie, for both of our sakes you mustn't talk about him any more. And you mustn't talk about greyhounds or gambling or cards in our new life. People won't like us if you do.'

At the time they were living in the small, dreary flat near Shepherd's Bush. Her mother worked in a dress shop, Francesca went to the local school. They knew no one, except for Madame Natasha, an elderly Russian émigrée who lived above them in decaying gentility. Each day after school, whilst her mother was still at work, Francesca climbed the uncarpeted stairs to Madame Natasha's flat to do her homework. Compared to the excitement of life with her father, and the bustle of the dogtrack, it was a lonely existence.

That night before their first visit to White Oast, Francesca had lain awake listening to her mother move softly around the second room. Finally, she'd risen, drawn by the light still shining beneath the door. She'd turned the handle and opened it, wanting to ask more about this stranger who was to become her father. Her mother hadn't heard the door. She was stretched out on the sofa, crying softly into a cushion.

As Francesca and William drove up to White Oast, her mother stepped from the French windows. An elegant woman, with blonde streaks in her greying hair, Dominique Hartington had a

17

golden smartness which made her look forever unEnglish. Her mother had been French and, although Dominique had lived in England for most of her life and spoke the language with no trace of accent, there was something intrinsically Continental about her. In the way she walked, her mannerisms. In the way she handled men.

'I'm so glad you've come, William.' She laid a hand on his arm. 'You're so good at saying the right thing. Poor Steven needs support. The vicar's being boring about the church spire and I don't want to have to offer him lunch.' She dismissed William with a wave towards the house and turned to kiss Francesca on the cheek. 'Let's walk around the garden. We never seem to be alone. We never talk.'

'What do you want to say?' Francesca tried not to sound stiff.

'Oh, everything and nothing.'

They followed the gravel path between the rosebeds and the herbs. There was a peppery smell from the neatly clipped box hedge. Every tree and plant and shrub was on the threshold of spring, pale green just apparent in tight-closed buds, life waiting to burst forth. It was up this path that Francesca had walked on her first visit, a young girl alone, crunching through the wet gravel whilst inside the house her mother had talked to a funny, whiskery little man who looked like an elderly hamster.

'You look exhausted,' said her mother. 'I wish you'd come for a whole weekend, not just lunch. I wish you'd come on your own and let me pamper you. We used to be so close when you were little. Now, sometimes, I feel as though I'm speaking to a stranger, not to my daughter.'

Francesca didn't want to talk about the past. She was afraid that once she began other things would come out: things she didn't yet want to face.

Her mother went on, 'Only this morning I was talking to Father John. He says remarriage is a sin and you've never forgiven me for it. Is that true? But we were destitute. Steven offered me love and security.'

Francesca raised her eyes heavenward. 'Mother, you're always guilt-ridden on Sundays.'

'I know. But I can't help it.'

'Then don't blame me. Or Steven. He's been good to me. He

18

sent me to private school, encouraged me to take up law. He even paid for elocution lessons to get rid of what he called my ruffian accent.' She hesitated. 'Why are you bringing all this up now? You must have a reason.'

'Because you're unhappy and I blame myself,' said her mother sadly. 'Is it William? I've always thought he was too old for you. You only married him because you wanted a father figure.'

'Mother! Please! I'm tired, I work hard. So does William. We don't have as much time alone as we'd like. That's all.'

'Trust my Frankie to shut her eyes. But you must be practical, darling. Is the house in your name?'

'What are you talking about?'

'You and William.'

'Oh, for goodness' sake! One minute you're scared of hellfire, the next you're calculating alimony. There's nothing wrong with my marriage!'

'And even if there were, you'd be too obstinate to admit it. Just like your father!'

Francesca pulled away. 'I am not like my father! He's a drunk and a gambler.'

Three

Francesca sat at the front of the courtroom, listening as the prosecution put its case in the Crown versus Lex Gunter. She sat sideways on the bench, the folds of her black robe draped like wings across her body to her knees. Frowning, she made a note, adjusted her wig, then sucked on her pencil. Behind her, Atterbury whispered to his articled clerk. Gunter was at the back, in the dock, dressed in the sombre grey suit which she'd instructed him to wear. He still looked like a man who mugged old ladies on Sunday afternoons.

She'd vetted the jury as best she could, objecting to two 'flog 'em all' ex-colonels and one aristocratic do-gooder. The remainder were innocuous. Twelve men and women good and true, sitting upright as though in church. From time to time they glanced at Gunter, their mouths pursed in disapproval.

She wondered what Marius Charlwood looked like now. So many years had passed. Would he recognise her? Did he know that she was a barrister? She wished the case were over. She wished that she were not about to come face to face with her childhood.

Counsel for the prosecution was in full swing. His voice boomed around the courtroom. 'This is a vicious case of a young man breaking into the property of an elderly one, threatening him, and assaulting him,' he told the jury. 'I shall produce photographs of the victim's injuries, a statement from the doctor who treated him, and a statement from the police constable who was called to the scene. But first I shall call the victim of this unprovoked assault. Mr Marius Charlwood.'

There was a noise at the back of the courtroom. Solid footsteps came up the aisle between the wooden benches. Francesca tried not to turn her head, but she couldn't help it. She had to look. Bearing down on her was a compact and agile man, with short white hair like someone growing out a crewcut, a weatherbeaten face, a pair of very blue eyes, and a goatee beard. He walked straight past her,

20

his eyes not even flickering when they met hers. But then, of course, she was wearing a wig.

He took the Bible in his right hand and read out, loud but slightly hoarse, 'I swear by Almighty God to tell the truth, the whole truth and nothing but the truth.'

The prosecution said, most sympathetically, 'Mr Charlwood, are you the proprietor of the Richmond Greyhound Racing Stadium?'

'That's correct. And no one's going to scare me into selling. Not unless they kill me.' He glared across the courtroom at Gunter.

'Please tell us in your own words what happened on the night in question.'

'Well, it was like this.' The old man laid his hands on the front of the witness box and flexed his knotted fingers. 'I was on my own in the house, watching television, when I heard a noise. So I went outside and shouted, "Who's there?" And that bloke came out of the shadows. He had a piece of wood in his hand. He'd pulled it out of the fence. I gave him the benefit of the doubt and said, "Put it back, son, and we'll say no more about it." He ain't the first young ruffian I've found at the stadium, but I always reason with them. I tell 'em this ain't life's dress rehearsal. This is real. Don't waste it inside prison. The lad who drove me here today I caught stealing lead pipes a year or two back.'

'Very commendable, Mr Charlwood,' said the judge. 'But what happened next?'

'He hit me. Over and over again. He never said a word, as if this were a job he'd been hired to do. Then I knew that scum was one of *them*.'

'One of who?'

'Marmintoll. They've been harassing me to sell the track because they want to build more bloody houses.'

The words were barely out of his mouth before Atterbury handed Francesca a note. 'Object. Marmintoll don't harass.'

She rose, cursing herself for not having withdrawn from this case. Even now she could have said, 'Your Honour, I find myself professionally embarrassed.' But William would be furious. 'Your Honour,' she began, 'Marmintoll are a respectable City firm. There is no evidence to suggest they had threatened the witness.'

Before the judge could reply, the old man cut in. 'You asked me

21

to swear to tell the truth and that's what I'm doing. Marmintoll want my land. First they offered me money. Then they send that.' He pointed at Gunter. 'I'm seventy-five but I can still defend what's mine. Come to my place again, boy, and they'll be arranging your funeral. I'm not alone any longer.' He sat down heavily. 'I don't suppose I can smoke my pipe in here?'

'No, you cannot!' The judge hid a smile behind his hand.

Francesca's task wasn't going to be easy. Marius Charlwood had the jury eating out of his hand. He was a human being bullied by a faceless corporation, he was old age abused by youth. She felt a tap on her shoulder. It was a note from Gunter: *You're not just a cold bitch but a fucking useless one.*

It was her turn to cross-examine the witness. She stepped towards him. 'Mr Charlwood.' He looked up. For a moment she thought he recognised her. 'Is it not a fact that you were once known as Mark Wood?'

He stared at her, astonished.

'And that under that name you ran an unlicensed card room?'

'Well . . . I . . . what about it?'

'I was merely establishing your credentials as an honest witness.'

There was an uproar of objection from the prosecution. But Francesca had made her point. The jury were looking doubtful.

The old man spoke quietly. 'That was nearly thirty years ago. I don't believe there's anyone in this room who has nothing he'd prefer to forget. We all have. Even a judge. Even a barrister.' He stepped from the stand. 'Forget the case. I'm going home. This ain't justice. I came as a witness, I'm treated like a thief.'

'Mr Charlwood, sit down!' ordered the judge.

'I am ill.'

'Then you should ask for an adjournment.'

'I'm asking.'

The case was adjourned for three weeks. As soon as the judge left the courtroom, Marius Charlwood hurried out. Francesca rose to follow him, but was delayed by Atterbury's congratulations. By the time she reached the crowded corridor outside, the old man had disappeared. She sank on to a bench in a secluded window alcove near the stairs, removed her wig and shook her hair. She felt dirty.

'You've got guts, lady,' said Gunter, pushing in front of her. 'I owe you a drink.'

She looked at him with disgust, and was disgusted at herself.

A side door opened and Marius Charlwood stepped out. 'I don't know who you are or where you found your information,' he told Francesca, 'but you should be ashamed of yourself, defending scum.'

Francesca wanted to say she was sorry. To explain that she'd thought her means of discrediting him were justified by her duty to her client, only now she'd realised she was wrong. But before she could formulate her words, he'd stalked off down the corridor, searching through the groups of people as though expecting someone. As he reached the exit stairs, a powerful, black-haired man strode up them, taking the steps two at a time. He towered over Marius.

'Sorry I'm late,' said the man, in a voice which had more than a touch of the East End in its mixture of late nights and night streets. 'Is it over? You look ill.'

'I'm better now you're here, Jack.' Marius Charlwood lowered his voice, and the stranger bent to listen. Then he turned to look at Francesca and Gunter.

He wasn't handsome, not like William. His cheekbones were too pronounced. His jaw was hard. His eyes were brilliant blue, but hooded. He looked tough. He was tough. Power exuded from him and yet, when he smiled, he had a boyish, unrepentant charm. His hair was so black that it was almost blue; a colour her mother called kingfisher black. A rogue lock fell forward into his eyes and caught on his eyelashes. He flicked it back and bent again to Marius, his face soft with sympathy for the older man.

But for Francesca and Gunter, he had only cold dislike. 'I don't forget the enemies of my friends,' he said with an eloquence which was at odds with his street-life accent. Then he took Marius's arm and ushered him gently down the stairs.

Behind Francesca, Gunter hissed through his teeth, 'I'd never have gone near the fuckin' track if I'd known Jack Broderick was out of prison.'

Four

Francesca sat on her own at one of the long refectory tables in the Inner Temple Hall. She toyed with a plate of lasagne as she waited for Melanie, glancing at the door every few minutes, hoping that her friend wouldn't be too busy for lunch. Above her, on the wood-panelled walls, portraits of former judges frowned down from their gilded frames. Around her, barristers hurried through lunch, talking with their mouths full as they argued points of law before speeding back to the afternoon court session.

'Sorry I'm late, Frankie,' Melanie called out as she tapped across the floor in very high heels. She always wore high heels because she was short and plump and longed to be taller. 'I was acting for the father in a custody case and – can you believe it – the mother never turned up! She's on legal aid. I think she should damn well have to pay the court's expenses herself.' Melanie sat down, ruffled her short blonde curls, and leaned her elbows on the table, forcing her black jersey dress to strain even tighter across her matronly bosom. 'So, what's new?' She grinned. She had a pretty, cherubic face dotted with freckles, and very large cornflower-blue eyes. 'Tell me before you burst.'

'I've done something unforgivable.'

'You've seduced the Lord Chief Justice?'

'It's not funny! I used private information to discredit a witness. I can't tell you the details. I wish I could. Every time I think of it, I feel sick.'

'What does William say?'

'Oh, I haven't discussed it with him.'

'Then it can't be serious. You always confide in each other.'

'Do we?'

'You told me so when we first met. I remember, because I thought how lucky you were.'

Francesca felt a lump begin to form in her throat. Quickly, she changed the subject. 'How's Simon?'

Melanie turned pink with excitement. 'Tonight is our second

date. I couldn't believe it when he rang. I told you, I was sure I'd put him off with my rabbiting. But he doesn't seem to mind. He says his mother talked the hind leg off a donkey right up to the day she died. Rupert never let me chatter. It's funny, I've never fancied a man who wears glasses before.' She paused. 'You haven't told William that I'm seeing Simon?'

'Of course not.'

'They're in the same chambers. I don't want Simon to know I gossip.'

Francesca threw back her head and gave her throaty, rauchy laugh. 'Which, of course, you do not!'

They walked back through the Inn to chambers. The morning drizzle had given way to a mild, sunny afternoon. People were in the gardens, pacing the gravel path in groups of two or three. She and Melanie had chosen to join the Inner Temple for the same reason. They were attracted by its beautiful buildings, its gardens, and its history: its sense of 'feet in ancient times.' The Knights Templar had had a hall on the site of the present Hall. All barristers had to belong to one of the four Inns of Court: Inner Temple, Middle Temple, Lincoln's Inn or Gray's Inn. The Inns were governed by benchers, judges and Queens Counsels – silks as they were known – who ensured that the Code of Conduct, as set down by the Bar Council, was adhered to.

'Does Rupert know about Simon?' asked Francesca, reverting to the soap opera of Melanie's life.

'We've hardly spoken since he dropped me, after I took him home to meet Mother. The Llanellens just weren't grand enough. And I don't want a man who snubs my poor widowed mother.'

'Simon's much nicer.' Francesca hesitated as she selected her next words.

'Don't add the obvious. I know! He's four years younger than me.'

'I was going to say that he seems very serious.'

'That's because you're William's wife and William is his hero. Come to the wine bar on Friday. So long as we don't fall out tomorrow, he'll be there with me. You'll see. He can be very funny.'

'I'd love to come but we have another dinner party. Two QCs and a judge.

'How grand!'

Francesca flushed. 'It's hard work, Mel.'

'Frankie, you live in a cocoon. Handsome, clever husband. Own career. Lovely home. Expensive holidays. Money. Security. You and William are the Inn's golden couple. You should try being single. I'm thirty-five and thirteen months. Freedom's delicious but I've had enough. I want to settle down before all that are left for me are the walking wounded.'

'Freedom's a dream when you don't have it.'

Melanie was shocked. 'You don't mean that.'

'William never talks to me.' Francesca looked bleakly down the sloping car park outside King's Bench Walk. 'If I speak of work, he says I'm unethical. If I talk of us –.' She frowned. 'I never do. The only way I can reach him is by endlessly entertaining people twice my age to further his career.'

Melanie laid a sympathetic hand on her arm. 'I'd no idea you were unhappy. You never confide. I wish you would.'

Frankie pulled a face. 'I learned to be secretive when I was very young. If your father drinks as mine did, you have to pretend it isn't happening.'

'Does William realise?'

'You're joking. He notices nothing, unless I've done something wrong. You know, we married in the Temple Church. Sometimes I want to go inside and kick the pews. William's more wedded to his poetry books than he is to me. They don't answer back, they don't need affection or praise or even the odd kind word.'

'Does he read them?'

'No. He just likes to possess them.'

Back in her office, Francesca couldn't settle. She stood by the window, looking down on the lawns of the Inner Temple Gardens. On the far side, William and Rupert were deep in conversation, pacing the gravel-path perimeter beneath the trees. She imagined him saying, 'Unfortunately, Francesca will not be an asset as a judge's wife.'

That was unfair of her. William was too loyal for that. Feeling guilty, she made a telephone call. Then she wrote him a note: *I've invited Sir Giles and Lady Henrietta to dinner on the 16th. Who else would you like?*

She had to force herself to concentrate on her next case, the

26

highly publicised affair of an accountant accused of embezzling money from a children's charity. Several million pounds had been raised through a masked ball, fun runs, a charity polo match, and several celebrity appearances. Only one million had been handed to the actual cause. Francesca studied the accountant's statement, checked copies of accounts, and made notes on her pad. She was appalled by the extent of freeloading by the organisers, the chauffeured limousines, hotels, bouquets of flowers, expensive meals, champagne, all paid for with money donated to the charity. The accountant was pleading innocent. He was a weak, vain, easily flattered man. She suspected he was guilty, not of theft as charged, but of turning a blind eye whilst others partied.

The sound of the front door banging and the click of high heels brought her back to the present. She hurried to the window and forced it up. 'Mel!'

Melanie turned to look up.

'I'm sorry I moaned about . . . you know. Things aren't so bad. I'm just tired.'

'What are friends for?' Melanie smiled and waved, and hurried on towards the library.

By the spring in her step, Francesca knew she was thinking about her date tonight with Simon. She imagined them walking together. Simon tall and thin, Melanie short and voluptuous. She pictured Melanie's small, soft fingers linked in Simon's bony ones, and she tried to remember the last time William had reached for her in public.

She felt trapped by loneliness. Home was a prison, William her gaoler. She wished she could disappear for a few weeks, to step outside her life and her marriage, and decide what there was for her in them. What existed, and what she was afraid to admit had died.

In this frame of mind, she took the car and cut down into the rat race of the Embankment. The traffic swept her west, towards Richmond. It was twenty years since she'd been to the stadium. She could have returned any time, but she hadn't wanted to. She wasn't sure if she wanted to return now, but curiosity drove her onwards. Curiosity, and something much stronger than nostalgia.

She turned up Queen's Road, which swung her round under large budding trees to the narrowing hill where the houses were older and more beautiful. She remembered the afternoon of her sixth birthday when she had run home from school, up this hill, her knee socks falling about her ankles, racing to see what her father had bought her. She remembered the anticipation – and the disappointment. He didn't come home for a week, and when he did he was broke.

Before the park gates Francesca turned again, following a rough road. It dipped and turned, loose earth shooting from beneath her tyres. Just as she thought she must have made a mistake, the road panned out into the large, uneven car park which flanked the stadium. There were two vehicles parked side by side, a dark-green Land Rover and an ancient, gleaming black Bentley.

The stadium was surrounded by a high brick wall, in the centre of which was a sweeping arch of sculpted iron greyhounds. The words *Richmond Greyhound Racing* were picked out on it in gilt. Except that the gilt had flaked and the *g* in *Racing* was missing.

Francesca hesitated. She must be mad to come back. There was nothing for her here, except distorted memories of a childhood which at the time had seemed exciting because it was wild, but later had become something to feel ashamed of. She remembered her first day at private school when an older girl had asked, 'Francesca, is that old man your father?'

'No. He's my stepfather. My father's dead.'

Something prevented her from leaving now. She crossed the car park to the rusted iron door and knocked. The noise rumbled like cannon fire. She waited, nervously clenching and unclenching her chewed fingers into the palms of her hands.

She tried the handle. The door wasn't locked. Gingerly she pushed it open. It creaked and swung back, and she stepped inside, on to the wide terrace in the centre of what had once been the main grandstand. In front of her the oval sanded track of the greyhound circuit was still apparent in spite of the long grass, the broken benches, and huge sectors of the roof which had been blown down.

For a moment she stood perfectly still near the railings, allowing the past to roll over her. She had stood here when she was too small to see above the railings, peering through the iron bars to watch the dogs trial around the arena, whilst her father leaned on the top rail. He'd been standing like that, telling her which dogs ran well and which had no stamina, when the three men arrived, the ones whom he'd cheated at cards. Francesca would never forget the sickening crunch of his nose as they smashed his face down on to the railings, and the crack of his right thumb as they pulled it back, saying, 'That'll teach you not to deal with the "mechanic's grip".' His blood had spattered on to Francesca's pink dungarees, and she'd screamed. Marius had come running. He'd scooped her up and carried her away, whilst she shrieked, 'Don't hurt my dad!' From that day onwards, she was terrified by violence. It was a fear she shared with William.

'Mr Charlwood!' she called, her voice echoing around the stadium. It bounced across the track to the far side, where the cheaper open terraces stood bereft of all protection. It reached the rambling red-brick Paddock House, the half house, half office.

No one answered.

She picked her way down the tiers where diners had once sat to watch the races, out through the vacant casing of a huge plate window, and over the rubble of broken glass and flagstones to the edge of the circuit, where the starting hutches still stood, broken and rotting. It was desolate, and yet there was something perversely beautiful in the way the late afternoon sun caught the twisted metal. In the long shadows, the sadness, the silence.

'Mr Charlwood?' she called again.

'What do you want?'

'I'm sorry, I didn't hear you . . .' She turned. But it wasn't Marius Charlwood. It was Jack Broderick.'

He was standing on the edge of the terrace, blocking her exit. Leashed to his left hand were two greyhounds, one black, one fawn, their ears pricked. He looked rougher and older than he had at the court. He wore scruffy jeans and a battered brown leather flying jacket. His black hair was ruffled as if he'd just got out of bed. A cigarette dangled from the fingers of his right hand. His blue eyes were flat with dislike. She couldn't think why she'd found him attractive.

She wanted to ask for her father but was unwilling to explain her reason, so she said, in her courtroom voice, 'I'd like to see Mr Charlwood.'

'He wouldn't want to see you, and I protect him from those he doesn't want to see.'

'He can be the judge of that.'

29

'He isn't here.'

'Is . . . anyone else here?'

'Why? Are you afraid of me?'

'Of course not.' She squared her shoulders. 'I shall wait for Mr Charlwood. I'm sure he won't be long – if indeed he *is* out!'

Jack Broderick looked her up and down, slowly, insolently, smiling cynically at her orderliness – her career-girl suit, her high heels, her elegant, smoothed-plaited hair – all set against the backcloth of the devastation which was the stadium. 'I had fourteen years of insults from the likes of you, but I'm not in prison any more. Get out!'

He unnerved her, but she refused to show it. 'Fourteen years? If you're Jack Broderick, the gold bullion robber, you only got ten, with a further two for trying to nobble a juror! We studied your retrial in law school.'

'I executed the man who grassed on me. Perhaps you'd left law school by then. It was four years later.' He gave a mocking laugh. 'Though I'm surprised you don't know. Geoffrey Culmstock prosecuted. I've him to thank for my extra sentence.'

She turned pale. She remembered now. It had happened the first spring she was married, after she'd finished her pupillage with William and before she joined Geoffrey Culmstock's chambers: it was an unwritten rule that husbands and wives didn't share chambers. She'd taken a month off to move into the house in Islington. She'd been far too wrapped up in her new role as William's wife to be aware of much outside.

'They transferred me to the same prison as the grass,' he went on. 'A bureaucratic error. Or maybe it wasn't. He begged for Rule 43 but there was a slip. No one respects a traitor, not even the screws. They called it manslaughter.'

Again his eloquence surprised her. Not just the words he used, but the way he used them, as if he'd trained in the verbal jousting at the Bar. 'But you murdered him,' she said.

'Rats deserve to die.'

'No one does.'

'Because it's against the law?' he mocked.

'Yes.'

'The same law which allows you to defend a thug who beats up an old man?'

'Even Gunter deserves a fair trial.'

'You played dirty.'

'If guilty, he could go to gaol.' She raised her chin. 'Criminals deserve prison. Especially murderers. Whatever their excuse!'

His eyes narrowed. 'Aren't you afraid to say that to me? You should be.'

She'd gone too far but he'd provoked her. Now she had to get away. Turning on her heel, she walked towards the exit, controlling an urge to run. He followed, the greyhounds at his side. She walked faster. He walked faster. When she reached her car, she nearly jammed the lock in her panic to get the door open. She jumped inside and tried to force the key into the ignition. But her hands shook so much it wouldn't fit.

She hadn't locked the door. He opened it, reached inside and took her trembling hand in his, prising her fingers from the ignition key.

'Let me go!' she cried, her voice rising in fear.

He twisted the key from her grasp, stepped away and, laughing, tossed it from one hand to the other.

'Give it back to me!'

He tossed it higher. 'Only if you say please.'

'Please!' She spat out the word.

'Nicely.'

She gritted her teeth. 'Please.'

He bent to take her hand in his, turning it over, palm upwards, cupping it inside his own large hand. Slowly, he let the key drop into her palm, turning up her fingers to close them around it. Then he stopped, frowning, holding the bitten half-moons of her fingernails to the light. 'I'd never have expected Mrs Eastgate to bite her nails,' he said gently.

He was looking at her from his hooded blue eyes. She stared back at him. A current passed between them, through her skin, magnetised to his. Suddenly, she realised what was happening. Jack Broderick was holding her hand, and she was allowing him to do so. More than that, she wanted him to do so. She blushed and snatched it away, slotted the key into the ignition, and drove out of the car park.

Five

Francesca almost cried with relief as she fitted her front-door key into the well-oiled lock and collapsed into the safety of her own home. The lights were on. Mozart played softly through the stereo system. William was at his desk in his book-lined study, working his way through a neat pile of papers.

He smiled vaguely. 'Hello, darling.'

'I'm so glad to be home.' She kicked off her shoes and ran, to him, hugging his straight shoulders and bending to kiss the soft skin at the corner of his eye.

He moved the papers so that she didn't disarrange them. 'Had a bad day?'

'Horrible. I went to . . .' She stopped. The image of Jack Broderick rose up. *I executed the man who grassed on me.*

'You went where, darling?'

She patted his shoulder and stepped away. 'I went to Harrods to buy your mother's birthday present.'

'But her birthday isn't till August!'

'I know but I thought . . .' She gave a light laugh. 'Anyhow, I couldn't park so it was all a waste of time. Would you like a gin and tonic?'

He tapped the glass on his desk. 'I've already had mine.'

'Then I'll start dinner.' She walked through to the kitchen. Mrs MacDougall had been that morning. The house was sparkling. It smelled of polish. She felt secure in its order and its normality.

William followed her. 'Don't you want to eat out? Last month you complained you were too tired to entertain.'

She opened the fridge. 'I enjoy cooking when it's just the two of us.'

He came and stood behind her, linking his arms around her waist, drawing her to him. 'I'd much prefer an evening at home.'

'So would I.' She leaned into his warmth.

'I've a lot of work to do. This tax fraud case is a nightmare.'

She snuggled closer. 'Do you have to work tonight?'

'Unfortunately, yes.' He released her.

Francesca leaned her forehead on the fridge door and told herself she was unreasonable to feel rejected.

From the doorway, William said, 'I know your birthday's not till June, but would you like to go to New Orleans that weekend as your present. It's not my sort of place but you've always wanted to go, haven't you?'

'Yes.' Her face lit up, not for New Orleans but for his thought behind it.

That night, as William folded his silk dressing gown on to the back of his chair, he said, 'I've made a list for dinner.'

Francesca was sitting up in bed, propped against the pillows, her hair brushed and her teeth tart with peppermint. She was trying not to think about the stadium or Jack Broderick.

'Your note,' William said, as she stared blankly at him. He slipped into bed beside her. 'We ought to invite the Treasurer and his wife. And we'll ask Rupert. You'll have to dig up a girl for him. Someone glamorous.' He slid the strap of her silk nightdress from her shoulder and kissed her bare flesh.

She snuggled against him. 'We can't ask Rupert. I've invited Melanie.'

'The Welsh piglet!'

'Oh, don't call her that. She hates it.' Francesca paused. 'It's time we had Simon Rosenmann again.'

William clicked his tongue. 'Melanie's good company. I'll put her next to Sir Giles. Better warn her he has wandering hands. But we can't have Simon, darling. He's too intense. Last time he never said a word. He may be my colleague and an excellent advocate, but he's a social death.'

Francesca linked her arms behind his head, and lied, 'I'm sorry, I've already mentioned it to both him and Mel.'

Gunter's case hung over Francesca. She tried to regard it with detachment, as just another case, as William so often told her to do, but it undermined the security of her life. Her visit to the stadium had brought back memories. They would not be driven away.

On a bright spring morning she arrived at court, consoling herself that by lunchtime it would be over. She would never face

Marius Charlwood again. She would never see Jack Broderick. As for her father? What could they have in common after all these years?

Francesca took her place on the front bench. The judge entered and the court rose. Counsel for the prosecution approached the bench. 'Your Honour,' he said, 'Marius Charlwood, the Crown's only witness, has written to say that at the age of seventy-five he doesn't have time to waste in coming to court when the accused will only receive a suspended sentence. He suggests your Honour brings back the lash.'

Francesca stifled a giggle. Good old Marius. She stood up. 'Your Honour, in the absence of the sole witness, I ask for the case against my client to be dismissed.'

The judge sighed. 'Many will sympathise with Mr Charlwood. Case dismissed!'

Francesca couldn't get away from Gunter quickly enough. He made her feel unclean. 'Of all my clients to get off, that thug is the least deserving,' she told Melanie, as they walked back to chambers after lunch. She stopped, then added in a half sad, half amused voice, 'Today is the anniversary of my first date with William.'

'Is he taking you out to dinner?'

'Oh, no. He's forgotten.'

They went up the stone stairs to their chambers. Melanie walked ahead into Francesca's office. 'You're wrong,' she called. 'Look at this!'

On the desk was a beautiful red rose nestling in folds of white satin. 'I don't believe it!' Francesca gave a little happy laugh as she opened the accompanying envelope. Then she turned scarlet. On the card was written, *Why do you bite your fingernails?*

'Mel,' she said quickly, take the rose.'

'Don't be silly. William will be hurt.'

'It isn't from William.' Francesca tore the card into tiny pieces. 'Don't ask me to explain. Just take it. Please!'

She was horrified that Jack Broderick had contacted her. She relived that moment of terror when she'd fought with the car door, and that other, inexplicable moment when he had cupped her hand in his and she had been enveloped by his warmth and his tenderness.

34

He telephoned in the late afternoon. When Nailsworth put him through, she said, in a voice made more aggressive by her own fears, 'Mr Broderick, I don't want your flowers and I don't want to hear from you.'

'Mrs Eastgate,' he replied, 'Your husband is a shit. I thought you were different. I was wrong.' He replaced his receiver before she had time to cut him off.

Francesca buried herself in work and tried to forget about the stadium and Jack Broderick. The embezzling accountant had changed his plea to guilty to one charge; a free weekend for himself and his wife in Paris. This was to have been a raffle prize at a ball which had been cancelled. He claimed that two members of the committee had told him to take the prize. They denied it. Francesca believed him. Mild, frightened and without important friends, he'd clearly been selected as the scapegoat. His defence lay in proving that two of the titled and powerful members of the committee were the real villains. It wasn't going to be easy.

At her request, Nailsworth began to allocate her less criminal work and more family cases. She found the work interesting, though often very sad.

'I know both parents should have access, but I have a case where it's making the child more unsettled,' she confided to Melanie over their lunchtime sandwiches on the lawn of the Inner Temple Gardens. 'He spends a week with his mother, a week with his father, but doesn't feel he belongs to either.'

Melanie stretched out on the grass and lifted her freckled face to the spring sunshine. 'That's better than one parent dropping out of their life completely. Oh, Frankie, I'm sorry I shouldn't have said that.'

'My father didn't drop me. I refused to see him.' Francesca helped herself to another sandwich, and changed the subject. 'How's Simon?'

'I'm beginning to think he doesn't fancy me. He holds my hand and kisses me goodnight but he still hasn't tried to make love to me.'

'Don't worry. I'll lace the dinner party with aphrodisiacs.'

Melanie sat up. 'I'm so grateful to you and William for inviting us together, Frankie. It gives us the Eastgate seal of approval. That's important to Simon.'

35

*

On the morning of the dinner party Francesca rose before six, laid the table whilst eating her toast, whisked cream into the vichyssoise as she drank her coffee, rearranged the blue irises in a white vase, and phoned Dining & Wining from the secrecy of the bathroom as she dried her hair. It was nine when she reached chambers. She was exhausted.

On her desk was an envelope from the Bar Council marked 'Private & Confidential'. She slit it open. Inside was a letter from the Secretary of the Professional Conduct Committee.

Dear Mrs Eastgate,
We invite your comments on the attached complaint.

She lifted the top page. Underneath was a piece of notepaper with '*Richmond Greyhound Racing Stadium*' arched across the top in large gold letters. She read the scrawled handwriting:

Dear Sirs,
Marius Charlwood is a prosecution witness. Surely it is wrong
for the defending counsel to approach him? In my world, this
is called harassment.

It was signed by Jack Broderick.

Francesca stared at the page. The words fuzzed together.

Melanie stuck her head around the door. 'What are you wearing tonight?'

Francesca looked up.

'You're white as a sheet. Is something wrong?'

'I'm fine.' Francesca refolded the letter. 'I'll see you later.' She waited till Melanie's high heels clattered back to her office, then ran downstairs and up the street to William.

He was standing by his desk, sorting through his reference books. 'I can't stop now. I'm due in court,' he said, irritated at her sudden, unplanned arrival.

'I've been reported to the Bar Council.' The words choked her. She held out the letter.

He read it quickly. 'Jack Broderick! Not the gold bullion robber who nobbled the jury, cost a fortune in retrial fees, then killed an informer? I thought he was still in prison.'

'He's out now. He's a friend of Marius Charlwood.'

36

'But I don't understand. Surely you didn't approach Charlwood on behalf of Gunter?'

'Of course not! But I did go to the stadium.'

He stared at her incredulously. 'What the hell for?'

'To tell Marius I was sorry for discrediting him. I realise now it was a mistake. But I just had to go.'

'In the middle of the trial when he is a prosecution witness and you're acting for the defence? You fool!' William threw the letter at her.

It fell to the ground. She bent to pick it up, her fingers slipping clumsily on the paper. 'I also wanted to see my father,' she whispered.

'And you couldn't wait till after the trial?' William shouted at her. 'Don't you realise what your stupidity will do to my chances of becoming a judge? Or maybe you don't care, Francesca.'

Tears brimmed in her eyes. 'William, I'm terribly sorry. It was unethical of me to go. I should have waited. You're right. But I never saw my father. Or Marius. So I certainly didn't harass him.' She took a deep breath. 'Please help me. How shall I answer the Bar Council?'

'I haven't time.' He picked up his gown and wig. 'If you weren't so stupid, you'd have withdrawn from this case at the start.'

'Don't you think I wish I had?' Her voice rose in despair. 'But you persuaded me not to.'

'I did nothing of the sort.' He called his pupil on the intercom then walked to the door, leaving his brief and books to be carried by his clerk and pupil. 'You must cancel dinner,' he said. 'Pretend you're ill.'

'Why? I need the distraction. I need support. Your support!'

'Sir Giles is a High Court judge. I don't want him embarrassed by an invitation to my house when my wife has been reported for unethical behaviour.'

At eight o' clock, Sir Giles and Lady Henrietta arrived. Francesca greeted them with a bright smile. 'I'm afraid William's not back yet.'

Sir Giles gave her a whiskery peck on the cheek. 'Ah, these hard-working young barristers. I remember when I started at the Bar . . .'

The door bell interrupted him. It was Melanie and Simon. 'William's late,' Francesca explained. 'Simon, could you help me with drinks?' She longed to confide in Melanie, but her friend was looking so happy and the truth would ruin her evening. Francesca dashed into the kitchen to check the poached salmon. Then she hurried into the dining room to light the candles. As she crossed the hall, the front door opened and William stepped inside. He looked from her to the dining room. She raised her chin and stood her ground. He closed the door, very quietly.

'I told you to cancel.'

'I told you I needed support.'

'You've made a bloody fool of me.'

Before Francesca could reply, Sir Giles burst out of the drawing room. 'There you are William, my boy. Your wife's been looking after us marvellously. I was just telling young Simon Rosenmann here that it's time he got married.'

'I agree.' William smiled at his guests. He turned to Francesca, but did not look at her. 'Everything all right in the kitchen, darling?'

'Yes.' She swallowed. 'Thank you.'

Dinner was a nightmare for Francesca. She felt too sick to eat and was afraid to drink in case it went to her head. At his end of the table, William was talking courteously. She prayed he was enjoying himself.

None of the guests left until after midnight. As Melanie slipped on her coat, she winked at Francesca. 'I won't be in chambers early.'

Whilst William locked the front door, Francesca hovered nervously in the hall, clenching and unclenching her fists, waiting for him to speak. But he said nothing. He walked straight past her and up the stairs.

She followed. 'William, please. I'm sorry you're angry, but can't you understand that I'm upset too? After all, it's my career. I'm the one who's been reported.'

Without replying, he went into their bedroom. She watched as he collected his silk pyjamas and dressing gown. Still in silence, he opened the spare-room door.

'Where are you going?' she asked unhappily.

'I'm too ashamed of you to share a bed with you tonight.'

38

'But I need you. Please.' Her voice choked on her words. He shut the door in her face.

By six, Francesca was up and dressed. As she smoothed her hair into its plait, she could hear William lift the kitchen telephone. When she came downstairs, he was at the breakfast table in the conservatory, glancing through the headlines in the *Financial Times*. The dining room was still littered with dirty plates, but the glasses, his special Waterford glasses, were carefully lined up, still dirty, on the Welsh dresser.

'I'm sorry about last night,' she said, as she poured herself some coffee.

He lowered the paper and looked at her without expression. 'I think you need a few days' rest.'

She wanted to believe in his concern. 'You're right. I'm tired. That's why I let that awful man Gunter get to me.' She sat down opposite William. 'But I can't take a break this week. My embezzling accountant case starts today.'

'I've told Nailsworth you're ill. Sanjiv is taking over.'

She lowered her cup. 'What!'

'There's no need to shout.'

'William, you can't cancel my case.'

'You're not suggesting Sanjiv's not capable? He's as good a lawyer as you. In fact, better.'

Francesca flushed. 'That's not the point. The accountant is my case. He has confidence in me. I've been working on his defence for weeks. You accuse me of being unethical, but your interference is contrary to all Bar rules.'

'Then call Nailsworth and explain.'

'I will.' She reached for the phone.

He clamped his hand over hers. 'So you'd make me look a fool in front of your clerk?'

She stared at him, her face rigid with anger.

'I've arranged for you to go to Mother till Sunday,' he went on, still gripping her hand. 'I told her you're suffering from stress. She's expecting you for lunch.'

Francesca yanked her hand away and kicked back her chair. 'You'd better cancel her,' she snapped. 'Because I'm going into chambers. I'm going to defend my career against Jack Broderick.

And if our marriage means what it should to you, you'll support
me.'

Six

Francesca was still shaking with rage when she arrived at Makepeace Buildings. She ran up the steps to the first floor, then stopped to catch her breath, wiping the perspiration from her forehead with the back of her hand before proceeding.

Old Nailbag looked up from his desk as she burst into the reception. 'Mrs Eastgate! I thought you were ill. Sanjiv's taken your case, he's already left for court. Your client has been advised of the change.'

She thought of the wretched little accountant. She felt bad about letting him down. He'd believed in her. But much as she wanted her case back, she knew she was in no state to give it her best. 'Let Sanjiv continue,' she said.

'Mr Eastgate said you were ill,' Nailbag repeated. 'I only did as he asked.'

'I'm better now.' She went into her room and closed the door. She had twenty-one days in which to answer the Secretary's letter. If her explanation satisfied the Committee, the matter would go no further. If not, if they decided there was a prima-facie case of professional midconduct, she would be called to a disciplinary tribunal. She could be reprimanded. She could be suspended. She could even by disbarred.

Settling at her desk, she began to list the events of that unwise afternoon. Why she had gone to the stadium. What she had said. What she had intended to say. She pictured herself standing with her back to the ruined arena, wanting to ask for her father, but asking instead for Marius Charlwood.

The morning dragged. She chewed on her thumbnail as she drafted and redrafted her reply. No one came near her room. She wondered if people already knew she'd been reported for approaching a witness. The proceedings were in secret, but people had a way of picking up on these things. The word 'approaching' had unpleasant connotations, such as harassing or nobbling. Surely her colleagues wouldn't believe she was capable of that.

41

When she went to the coffee machine, the doors to all the other offices were closed. She couldn't remember if this was usual, but it increased her sense of being an outcast. She was tempted to telephone William, to apologise for her outburst, not because she felt she was in the wrong, simply to talk to someone.

In the middle of the afternoon, oppressed by solitude, she went down into the gardens, now deserted of lunchers, to walk alone across the grass beneath the trees. By the pond she halted, hands dug deep into her jacket pockets, and read the quotation by the statue of the young boy: 'Lawyers were children once.' She wished she were a child again. To begin again, and do things differently, and hopefully better.

On her return to her chambers she found a note from Sanjiv: *Your accountant got nine months, with three suspended.* She pictured the little man facing his first night in prison, and blamed herself.

She went home punctually, determined to make peace with William. Everyone had arguments. It was good to clear the air. Driving up the Gray's Inn Road, she thought of the times she'd shied away from speaking her mind. That was a mistake. She switched on the radio. The thudding beat of 'Night Fever' came out through the speakers. It had been popular that summer when she and William had bought the house in Islington. She turned up the volume.

The song took her back to the sunny afternoon when they'd first looked at the house. They'd only been married a few months and were still living in William's sterile bachelor flat in Holborn. On that day they had seen eight houses, all too dark or too small. But the Islington house was large and airy. Sunlight had been streaming in through the drawing-room windows. They both liked it. Frankie recalled their first dinner party, a family dinner. She spent two days making a summer pudding, but when she turned it out on to a plate, it collapsed in a mushy heap. How they had laughed. She remembered too their first serious argument. It was a winter Sunday morning. They were still in bed when she heard the front door open. 'That'll be Mother,' William said, sliding out of bed. 'Has she a key?' 'Why not? She's my mother.' 'But this is our house. I don't want her turning up unannounced. She bullies me.' He turned white with anger.

'Don't insult my mother.' For days he didn't speak to Francesca. In the end, miserable, she begged forgiveness, even though she believed herself to be right. That had been her mistake. It had set a precedent from which she was still battling to escape. The only difference was he now admitted his mother was a bully.

The house was tidy. Mrs MacDougall had cleared up. Only the special Waterford glasses waited for Francesca. William wouldn't allow Mrs MacDougall to touch them.

There were three messages on the tape. 'Hi, this is Mel. Thanks a bundle! 'Hello, this is Simon. Thanks so much. I did enjoy myself.' 'Frankie, this is Mel. Sorry to hear you're ill. Do you need any help? Call me!' She rewound the tape and played it again, in case she'd missed William's message. He hadn't rung. She dialled Melanie's number. The answerphone cut in on the fifth ring. Without speaking, she replaced the receiver.

William frequently worked late. It was nothing for him to return at nine or ten, or even midnight. But he always telephoned. She fed Big Ears and Jaws and watered her plants. Then she opened the fridge. It was full of last night's leftovers: cold poached salmon, cold mangetout, cold Duchesse potatoes. She picked at the mangetout. Then she washed up the Waterford glasses, put two potatoes in the oven to bake because William disliked cold potatoes, and laid the table with particular care. At eight, she arranged the salmon prettily on another dish and made a salad of tomatoes and fresh basil. At nine, she watched the television news, one ear listening for William's taxi.

Footsteps walked down the street – and walked on. Cars drove up, but not to her house. She alternated between thinking he was still angry and worrying that he'd had an accident. She picked up the phone to see if it was out of order. It wasn't. She wondered if she should call Geoffrey or Rupert, but decided against it.

Unable to sit still, she paced the drawing room through the weather forecast and the south-east news. Three years earlier they'd had the room redecorated in shades of lemon and palest turquoise, with a specially woven geometric carpet and elaborate draped, glazed chintz curtains. Exquisite, dainty Virginia Culmstock had advised them.

Suddenly the perfection of the room irritated Francesca. She felt chained by its symmetry, as William constrained her. She

43

bunched his favourite ornaments on the marble mantelpiece, tossed the cushions in random piles and kicked the sofas out of line. She'd come home prepared to compromise. Not any more.

Returning to the kitchen, she switched off the oven, and helped herself to last night's leftovers straight from the serving dishes, an action which William regarded as disgusting. Rolling a lettuce leaf around a Duchesse potato, she made an eclair from which the piped mashed potato and tiny green petits pois oozed on to her fingers as she ate it.

At midnight William returned. She lay in bed, listening to his footsteps in the hall. He came up the stairs. She closed her eyes, pretending to be asleep. He reached the landing. She tried to breathe normally, waiting for the click of the door and the shaft of light as he came in. A door clicked, but it wasn't hers. He went into the spare room. Not long afterwards she heard him turn out the main light. From the house next door came the muffled sound of her neighbours. She could hear murmurs, then sudden, happy laughter. The sound brought acute loneliness. She buried her face in her pillow, and cried.

Even with blusher on her cheeks, Francesca knew she looked like a walking corpse. Her face was pale and sickly. Cold perspiration gathered on her forehead. Her eyes were sunken. The area round them had turned purple as if she'd been punched.

Melanie was sitting at her desk, swinging her legs backwards and forwards, high heels dangling loose from her toes. She was thinking about Simon. Her skin glowed from his lovemaking. Her limbs felt stretched. She'd never have imagined he would be such an affectionate lover. He didn't look like it. He was too tall and gangly and intense. Smiling, she put on her reading glasses and opened the brief on her desk.

Franesca tapped on her door. 'Busy?'

'There you are. I've been trying to phone. Thanks so much for a wonderful dinner.' Melanie giggled and pushed up her glasses. Then her eyes focussed. 'Frankie, you look terrible. Sit down! What's wrong?'

Francesca nodded towards James's empty desk. 'Is he away?'

'He's in Suffolk.'

'Thank goodness!' She slumped on to a chair. 'Mel, I've been

44

reported to the Professional Conduct Committee for trying to approach a witness.'

'I don't believe it.'

'It's true. Only I didn't approach him. Not for the reason they think.' Francesca leaned forward, laid her arms on the edge of Melanie's desk and buried her face in them. 'Don't tell anyone. Please! Not even Simon.'

'Of course I won't. Oh, you poor thing. Stay here. I'll make you some coffee.' Melanie bustled from the room. When she returned, she said, 'Drink this. You'll feel better. Now, tell me what happened.'

Francesca raised her head. 'I told you that I never see my father. I haven't, since my mother remarried. But when I was little, I loved him more than anyone. More than my mother. He was wild and charming, like a rebellious older brother, not a father. He took me dog-racing and horse-racing, telling my mother we were going to the park. He drank, he gambled. He taught me to play poker. I had to win my pocket money. If I lost, I received nothing, he made no concessions. When mother found out, she was angry. But I took his side. At six, I could riffle my chips like a professional.

'But there was a dark side to my father. We lived in a series of cheap rented flats. Not in the smart streets on Richmond Hill with views of the river, but in lower side streets, in houses which had yet to be modernised. We were always behind with our rent and were constantly harassed by landlords. But my father didn't care. He was totally irresponsible. He would rifle my mother's bag for money and disappear for days. I'd wait, convinced he'd gone because of something I'd said or done. Often he was in gaol, arrested for drunkenness. Other times it was petty theft. Or doing card tricks in Oxford Street to fleece gullible tourists. "Spot the Lady" I think they call it, when you have to choose the queen from three face-down cards. Invariably he came home broke. But I still loved him.

'When my mother remarried, I was heartbroken. I've always denied that to her, but it's the truth. Until then I believed that one day we'd go home to Father and everything would be fine. Not that he had a home. Instead, I found myself living in rural Kent, in a village where people didn't drink and gamble to excess, at least not visibly. We became respectable. I was warned not to talk of greyhounds or poker games. Especially as my father was doing two months for loading dice! So I told the girls at my new, private school that he was dead. When he sent me letters, I returned them unread. I pretended he didn't exist. I refused to invite him to my wedding. I really believed I never wanted to see him again – until Marius Charlwood came back into my life. Since then, I've felt deeply ashamed. That's why I went to the dogtrack. You see, I traded my integrity to win Gunter's case just as I traded my father in order to be acceptable.'

Melanie was astounded. 'I knew your father drank but I didn't realise he was . . .'

'A continual offender? A recidivist?' Frankie smiled. 'Yes, he is. But minor offences. Two months is his longest sentence. Mostly it's overnight, till he sobers up. Every time I go to a magistrates' court, I'm afraid I'll meet him. He appeared so often at one time that even the clerk called him Ben!'

Melanie laughed. 'What a character!'

'So long as he's not your father.'

'But I don't understand where the Bar Council comes in. Did this Marius Charlwood report you?'

'No. An ex-criminal. His name's Jack Broderick.'

'Not the gold bullion robber! I studied his case at law school. He nobbled half the jury and killed the police informer. Geoffrey prosecuted on that count. My God, Frankie, I'm surprised he didn't murder you too.'

'He's killed off my career instead.' Francesca stood up. 'Thanks for listening.'

'Where are you going?'

'To draft my reply to the Committee.'

'Is William helping you?'

Francesca shook her head.

'Oh, I know most people wouldn't want their spouse to defend them, but he is the best.'

'William's so angry with me he won't even discuss it,' said Francesca.

'It's your right to have counsel. You're too emotional to put your own case.' Melanie reached for her notepad. 'So if he won't defend you, I will. I'm not as brilliant, but I'll do my best. And if you think I want a fee, you've already paid – the dinner which brought me Simon.'

Francesca swallowed back tears. 'Oh, Mel, what would I do without you!'

The week dragged. William continued to sleep in the spare room. He ate out every evening. She lay in bed, listening until he came home. One night she waited up, unable to bear his silence any longer. 'William, please talk to me.' She tried to control the desperation in her voice.

'I am too appalled by your behaviour.'

Her face crumpled as he walked past her.

In the daytime Francesca forced herself to concentrate on her cases. She owed it to her clients. She read papers, held conferences, and stood up in court. She attacked her work with cold detachment. This was how William approached the law.

Old Nailbag passed her a brief concerning a five-year-old boy, Alexander Swaffield, whose parents claimed had been brain damaged during an operation to remove his tonsils the previous year. A scan showed slight brain damage. The most likely cause would be lack of oxygen, but the hospital denied any fault. They claimed that Alexander was backward prior to the operation. Because he was so young, it was going to be hard to prove otherwise.

'Just look at these drawings, Mrs Eastgate,' said Mr Swaffield, an articulate businessman. 'Before the operation, Alexander could write his name. Now he can barely draw one letter. He could count. Now he can't.'

Mrs Swaffield was trying hard not to cry. 'They say he must have been like this from birth. I know he wasn't. He was bright. We don't want revenge. Doctors and nurses work long hours. Everyone makes mistakes. All we want is an apology, some sympathy, and our son's future needs assured.'

At any other time, Francesca would have relished such a case.

She was falling apart. Beneath the brittle surface of her behaviour, she was in small, broken pieces. She started going into chambers late so as to avoid her colleagues. She took briefs home and did not answer the telephone, even to Melanie. If Jack Broderick wanted to destroy her, he was doing a good job.

On Sunday, William went alone to Kingly Grange. Francesca

stayed at home. Her mother rang during the morning. 'Something's wrong, isn't it?' she said. 'I can hear it in your voice.'

'I'm fine.'

'Where's William?'

'Gone to buy the Sunday papers.'

'I thought you had them delivered.'

'The newsagent forgot.'

That night, William didn't come home at all.

Francesca went into chambers even later than usual. Except for Old Nailbag, the reception was deserted. She helped herself to coffee from the machine, then hurried to the safety of her room. The door was shut. Coffee and briefcase in one hand, she freed the other to open it.

William was standing at the window, his back to the door. He turned. She could not speak. Her legs began to tremble, and she dropped the coffee on to her desk. It slopped. He saw the mess and frowned.

'Nailsworth signed for this.' He handed her a sealed envelope. 'I presume they intend to proceed with a disciplinary tribunal.'

Her wild hope disintegrated. 'I suppose so.'

'In your reply, did you admit to going to the stadium?'

'Of course. But I said I went for personal reasons.'

'They must think you're mad.' He walked to the door, careful not to brush against her as he passed. 'Do you intend to defend yourself?'

'Melanie's helping me.'

He hesitated, his hand on the doorknob. 'It's unusual for a man to defend his wife, but it is legal. Why didn't you ask me?'

'How can I if you won't speak to me?'

He seemed surprised by the deep anguish in her voice. 'Of course I'll help you – that is, unless you prefer Melanie. We don't want outsiders knowing what a black sheep your father is, do we?'

Francesca felt weak with relief. The storm was passing. At the same time, part of her longed to tell him to stuff his advice. But she didn't. 'Mel will understand,' she said. 'You're the best. She said so herself.' She took a tentative step towards him.

He opened the door. 'I have to go. I'm due in court. Bring all the papers home tonight. I'll see you at eight.'

Everything began to go right. An adoption case for a Brazilian baby which had seemed so complicated fell into place. Her argument clarified. She saw the parents with their solicitor. She felt confident. They became confident. They thanked her warmly. She was still smiling when she went home.

She laid the dining-room table and arranged a bowl of freesias in its centre. Then it occured to her that William might bring her flowers. Quickly, she transferred the freesias from their silver bowl to a glass one so as to have the silver free for roses.

She sliced the smoked salmon, which he loved, and marinated the steaks in brandy with a touch of garlic. She remembered to open the claret in good time and to check the glasses bore no fingerprints. Then she arranged the tribunal papers on the far end of the dining-room table, placing them in date order, as William had insisted when she was his pupil and he her pupilmaster. With an hour to spare she fed Jaws and Big Ears and watered the Busy Lizzies, all of which irritated William. Then she drew a bath, loaded it with bath oil, washed her hair, replaited it, rubbed moisturiser into her legs, and dressed in a yellow linen culotte dress William particularly liked.

By eight o'clock she was hovering between the dining room and the kitchen. At eight fifteen she began to feel sick. At eight thirty she stood in front of the telephone clenching and unclenching her fists, willing it to ring.

The front door opened and William walked in. There were no flowers. How silly she was to hope. He settled his briefcase on his desk and came through to the kitchen to stand in the doorway, looking at her, neither approving nor disparaging. She walked towards him. He reached for her hands and lifted them up, turning them over, palms down. 'You've been biting your fingernails again, Frankie,' he said.

'What do you expect when you ignore me?'

Again he seemed surprised by her deep anguish. He put his arms around her and drew her close, kissing her forehead as if she were a child. 'We must see how we can get you out of this mess,' he said. 'But you'll have to trust me if I'm to help you. You must do exactly as I say, with no arguing!'

She buried her face in his shoulder and hugged him, too choked to speak.

After dinner, William read through her papers. The envelope

from the Professional Conduct Committee contained a charge sheet and copies of all documents. Francesca was charged with professional misconduct under paragraph 145 of the Code of Conduct, which stated that it was an offence for a barrister to communicate directly or indirectly with a witness, whether or not the witness was her client, once the witness had begun to give evidence until his evidence had been concluded. If Gunter's case had been dismissed at the first hearing, she'd have been all right.

Included in the envelope was an affidavit signed by Jack Broderick. His statement had been taken the previous week, at the stadium, by an investigating officer. William read it twice before he spoke. 'Broderick says you arrived at four o'clock. Surely you were in chambers that afternoon?'

'I left early.'

'How did you get there?'

'I took the car.'

He flicked back through his diary. 'The day you told me you went to Harrods?'

She nodded.

He poured himself another glass of claret. If you've told me other lies, Francesca, you had better admit them now.'

She couldn't keep still with him watching her. She got up and walked around the dining room. 'Jack Broderick sent me a rose. It arrived at chambers. Then he telephoned, and I told him not to contact me.'

William stared at her. 'A criminal sends a rose to my wife! This is monstrous. Frankie, why didn't you tell me?'

'Because then I'd have had to explain about my visit to the stadium.'

'Anyone would think you were frightened of me.'

'I'm frightened of the loneliness when you ignore me.'

He made no reply but picked up the charge sheet. 'The fact remains that you went to the stadium. Are you sure you didn't mention your father to Broderick?'

'I purposely didn't.'

'It would be better if you had done.' He closed the papers into a file. 'We'll go through everything again tomorrow. It's time for bed.'

She wanted to ask if he was going to sleep with her but she didn't like to. Whilst he locked the front and back doors she went up, turned on both bedside lights, cleaned her teeth, washed the make-up from her face and tapped scent behind her ears and about her neck. His footsteps came up the stairs. She heard them on the landing. She turned, smiling. But he went straight into the spare room.

His rejection was worse because she had not expected it. She slumped on to the end of the bed, feeling both wounded and angry. She'd done everything she could to make amends, including accepting more blame than was her due.

'Aren't you getting into bed?' William stood in the doorway. He was wearing his silk pyjamas. 'Come on, Frankie. It's late.'

Her face lit up. 'I thought you'd gone next door.'

He climbed into bed. 'Next time we have a row, you can sleep in the spare room.'

She laughed with the relief of him being there, kicked off her shoes, and rolled over to him. 'Maybe there won't be a next time.' She kissed the soft skin around his eyes, travelling down with her mouth to his lips, then his throat, and back again to his mouth.

'You'd better take off that dress,' he murmured. 'I don't want it ruined. It's one of my favourites.'

'I thought you hadn't noticed.' She slid it down over her hips.

His arms tightened around her. He kissed her gently, tenderly, unwinding her hair from its plait, spreading it over her bare shoulders in a mahogany cascade of rich curls. 'Just because I don't say things it doesn't mean I don't feel them,' he said. 'Because I do.'

She pressed her face into the hollow of his neck. 'I need to hear. I need reassurance.'

'But you know how I feel about you.'

'No, I don't, William,' she said. 'Often I really don't. Sometimes I think you feel nothing. Occasionally you act as though you dislike me. I need reassurance. Maybe I'm weak, but I'm different from you. I need to know I'm loved.'

Seven

It was hot. It was summer. People talked of holidays. Although none of the Inns of Court closed during August, as they had done in earlier times, most barristers took the month off. As the weather grew warmer, the atmosphere in the alleyways and courtyards became reminiscent of the end of a school term. Only Francesca could not think of holidays. The disciplinary tribunal was set for July.

Her birthday approached. William made no further mention of the promised weekend in New Orleans. Instead, he took her out to dinner, with Melanie and Simon. She tried not to feel disappointed.

On the day of the Inner Temple garden party, three weeks prior to the tribunal, William was called to attend the direction hearing on her behalf. A directions judge was to preside whilst William and the counsel for the Committee argued what evidence and witnesses were to be admissible at the tribunal. William wouldn't allow Francesca to be present. 'You're far too emotional. You might ruin our defence,' he told her firmly. 'Go to the garden party with Simon and Melanie. I'll join you there.' He paused, then added more gently, 'Try not to look as if you're about to be executed.'

She gave him a brave smile. 'That's exactly how I do feel.'

She wore a dress of scarlet crêpe de Chine. It had a soft, swirling wrapover skirt which slithered around her body in fluid and sensuous folds. Her hat was large, of black straw, with three flat red buttons placed diagonally across the cartwheel brim. The effect was simple yet stunning. On any other day she would have enjoyed dressing up in chambers with Melanie, giggling like teenagers as they adjusted their hats and glossed their lips. Today she could think of nothing but the hearing.

The party was held in the Inner Temple Gardens, inside the black wrought-iron railings on the sweeping velvet lawn where she and Melanie often ate their lunch. It was packed with members of the Inn, their wives and friends. Waiters proffered champagne, whilst waitresses moved between the guests with trays of smoked salmon canapés and dainty sausage rolls. To one side, a table covered with a heavy white damask tablecloth groaned beneath bowls of strawberries and cream.

Francesca stayed close to Melanie and Simon. She needed their protection. She tried not to fidget, but it was difficult when her heels kept sinking into the lawn. And she tried not to fiddle with her champagne glass, but the cold drink and the heat of her hands made the glass slip about between her fingers.

Sanjiv joined them with Deepa, his beautiful wife in her exquisite pink sari. Charlotte bounced up in her mother's Ascot hat, talking nineteen to the dozen. She was followed by Rupert, whose new girlfriend looked remarkablay like Melanie. Small, dapper Desmond was accompanied by his wife. As untidy as he was neat, she bred spaniels and always smelled of dog biscuits. James was absent, in the country, as usual. But Hugo was there, with a bored-looking girl. And Thomas, who'd had too much to drink, was trying to chat up Charlotte, who was more interested in Rupert. Francesca wished she could join in the banter and laughter, but words would not come.

'Everything's going to be all right,' whispered Melanie, reading her mind. 'Who's going to believe the word of a man who did fourteen years for armed robbery?'

Francesca saw William leave the Treasurer's office. He walked slowly towards her, neither smiling nor frowning. She longed to run to him, but knew how he would hate the lack of control. So she forced herself to wait.

'You look gorgeous, darling.' He bent under the brim of her enormous black hat and kissed her cheek.

'That's just what we've all been telling her.' Geoffrey Culmstock clapped William on the back. 'Come on, you lot! Let's have some more champagne.'

'What happened?' Francesca asked William, as soon as she could draw him to one side.

'I've demanded that Jack Broderick appear in person.'

'No, William! Please!'

'Your defence is a clear-cut case of a rejected admirer. Whilst searching for your father, you met Broderick. He made advances to you. When you rejected him, he decided to get his revenge by complaining that you had attempted to hassle Charlwood. It's quite simple.'

'But it's not true.'

'Do you want to be disbarred?'

'Of course not!'

'Then trust me. You promised you would.' He drew her hand through the crook of his arm and patted her fingers. 'Ah, here come Sir Giles and Lady Henrietta. Smile, Frankie!'

She did as he asked because she wanted to please him. As with the girls at school, she longed to be acceptable. But part of her screamed, 'What's wrong with the real me?'

Francesca buried herself in work to keep her mind off the tribunal. In the case of Alexander, the hospital continued to deny negligence but made an offer of twenty thousand pounds without prejudice. Mr Swaffield ws incensed. It was nowhere near enough to assure the boy's future needs. Francesca suggested that the solicitor obtain statements from the family doctor, an independent paediatrician, and the boy's former playschool teacher.

She was the first to arrive at chambers each morning, and the last to leave at night. She seldom stopped for lunch. She existed on coffee and sandwiches and Mars Bars. On a hot weekend in early July, while Becker won Wimbledon and Live Aid rocked Wembley, Frankie was at her desk. The only afternoon she took off was to visit William's antique bookseller to buy the edition of Alexander Pope's poetry which he coveted.

Melanie gave up suggesting lunch to Francesca. 'I hope you're taking a holiday,' she said one evening.

'It depends on the tribunal.'

'You'll need a rest, whatever happens. Why don't you and William come to Crete with Simon and me? We've taken a villa. It sleeps four. We'd have a lovely time.'

When Francesca mentioned it to William, he gave a deep sigh. 'We can't go swanning off to Crete, not after the time I've spent on your defence.'

On the morning of the disciplinary tribunal, Francesca dressed with special care in her smartest black suit. William ate a full breakfast. She was so nervous she couldn't even manage a slice of toast.

'Do I look all right?' she asked him, hovering in the study doorway as he sorted the papers into his briefcase.

He glanced up. 'Perfect – so long as you don't chew your fingernails.'

'I haven't. Look! They're growing.' She held out her hands to him.'

He didn't take them, as she hoped he would, but gave her a brief smile. 'Come along. We mustn't be late.'

It was hot. The sun beat on the car roof as they crawled down the Canonbury Road in heavy traffic. Lorries belched black, fetid exhaust into the summer morning. Car radios blared a mix of news, music and traffic updates, advising drivers to avoid the roads on which they were already trapped.

Perspiration rolled down Francesca's face. Her hands were wet on the steering wheel. Her heart was thudding so fast that she felt faint. She longed for a glass of water. She longed to lie down and close her eyes, and wake up when this nightmare was over.

They parked at the top of King's Bench Walk. Somehow Francesca's legs carried her across the tarmac to the modern red-brick Treasury Office. At least it was modern by the Inn's standards, having been rebuilt after the Second World War.

'Now remember to answer only the question you're asked,' William instructed. 'The judge is very heavy on professional misconduct. If you irritate him, you've had it.'

Her eyes were hollow with anxiety. She longed for the feel of his arm around her shoulders. Or even for his smile, his briefest smile. 'I'll do my best,' she said.

'That's my girl!' He exuded a quiet confidence. It was contagious. She lifted her chin and squared her shoulders. She understood now why all William's clients praised him.

The disciplinary tribunal was held in a room just inside the entrance to the Treasury Office. William and Francesca took seats outside, in the hall. From behind the closed door she could hear low murmuring from the panel as they assembled. Chairs scraped. Men coughed.

William glanced through his notes. Francesca did not interrupt him. Beside her was a spare chair, on which she rested her briefcase. Then suddenly she realised the seat was for Jack Broderick. She moved to the far side of William.

A clerk stepped out of the tribunal room. 'Please come in,' he said.

They followed him into a small, wood-panelled room, from whose walls portraits of long-dead judges frowned down on a T-shaped table. The five members of the panel sat along its top, horizontal bar. They were a circuit judge, three barristers and a lay respresentative – in this case a leathery retired brigadier. The prosecuting counsel sat on the far side of the downward stroke of the T. William and Francesca were ushered to seats opposite him. Everyone stared at her. She felt a red flush rise from her chest to travel up her throat and encompass her whole face. In her time at the Bar she'd seen many defendants step into the dock, but until that moment she'd had no idea what it meant to be the accused.

The judge introduced the panel. Each member nodded as his name was called. Francesca tried to concentrate, but had she been asked, a moment later, which name belonged to which person, she could not have answered, even though she already knew the three barristers by sight. Her mind was frozen. Her tongue stuck to the roof of her mouth. Mel was right. She could never have defended herself.

The clerk asked Francesca to stand. She did as she was told, conscious of her knees knocking against each other and of William, rigid and stiff in his chair. He then read the charge: 'Francesca Eastgate, you are charged with professional misconduct in that, contrary to paragraph 145 of the Code of Conduct, you approached Marius Charlwood, a prosecution witness in a case where you were the defence counsel. Would you say whether you admit or deny the charge?'

'I deny it.' Her voice was loud and firm.

William gave her his quick smile. She was suffused with her gratitude and love towards him.

The prosecuting counsel rose. 'Your Honour, I find myself embarrassed. The witness has not yet arrived. We are assured he will do so. May I proceed?'

'Very well. But there's no need to stand. I can't bear people bobbing up and down.'

Before the prosecution could proceed, Francesca heard a

scrape as the door behind her opened. She clenched her fists and steeled herself to face Jack Broderick.

'Excuse me, Your Honour,' said a woman's voice. 'A letter has been delivered for the prosecution.'

The room was silent with expectation as the prosecuting counsel slit the envelope. He read the contents, frowned, and turned to the judge. 'Your Honour, Mr Broderick declines to attend. He gives no reason. We cannot oblige him. In the circumstances, I offer no further evidence.'

'In that case the charge is dismissed.' The judge glowered down the table. 'This has been a waste of time for everyone present, not least for myself!'

They scrambled to their feet as he stormed from the room. Francesca swayed and clutched at the table, unable to believe the nightmare was over. She felt light-headed, almost drunk. She wanted to both laugh and cry.

William collected his papers into his briefcase, thanked the panel and the clerk, and walked out of the room. She was so surprised by the suddenness of his departure that for a full minute she remained, leaning against the table. Then she hurried out, muttering her thanks. By the time she was free of the building, William was halfway across the tarmac.

'Wait for me!' she called, racing after him. 'Oh, William!' She laughed as she caught up, linking her arm through his. 'I don't know what I'd have done without you. I'm so grateful. Tonight we're going out to dinner, wherever you wish. It's my treat.' She stood on tiptoe to kiss his cheek, not caring that he might be embarrassed. 'I love you.'

William halted. 'We have nothing to celebrate, Francesca. Broderick's absence does not alter the fact that you contravened the Bar Code by visiting the stadium. If I defended you, it was merely to limit the disgrace to my name.' He unlinked his arm from hers and walked away.

She watched him, stunned. She felt as if he'd punched her in the face.

'You didn't deserve that.'

She turned. Jack Broderick was watching her from the front seat of his Land Rover.

'What the hell do you want?'

He swung down and came towards her. 'To tell you why I pulled out of the tribunal.'

'Oh, I know that. It was easy to complain about me behind my back. All you had to do was write the letter. You even managed to sign the statement. It must have seemed hilarious to put me through weeks of anguish and worry. But facing me's another matter.'

'I withdrew because when I checked you out, hoping to discredit you as you discredited Marius, I discovered your maiden name was Tiernay. You're Ben's daughter.'

'So my father made you back down?'

'No one puts pressure on me, not even the dead.'

'What do you mean by . . . the dead?'

'You must know.'

'I don't.' Her voice came out in a hoarse whisper.

'I presumed you did.' He spoke gently now. 'Your father died in February, of lung cancer.'

'I don't believe it.'

'I'm sorry. It's true.'

Francesca wanted to cry, though she told herself this was ridiculous when all these years she could have seen her father had she wanted to. Or maybe that was why she felt near to tears. It was now too late. Too late to say she was sorry.

She remembered her fourth birthday when he'd given her her first rabbit. The first Big Ears. He'd woken her early and, still in her dressing gown, had taken her down into the small garden behind their flat. There, in a smart new hutch with a spacious run, was a black and white rabbit. He'd shown her how to feed it. How to clean its hutch. How to hold it in the crook of her left arm with her right hand firmly on its ears. Even now she could hear him saying, 'Never love a person who doesn't love animals, Frankie.'

'Do you want to sit down?' Jack was saying. 'Come on! You can rest in the Land Rover. I'll drive you home.' He took her by the elbow.

'No . . . thank you.' She was conscious of the pressure of his hand under her elbow, and of herself leaning against him. She noticed that the skin beneath his eyes and across the bridge of his nose was not coarse but very fine. His forehead was smooth, his eyelashes curled. He no longer seemed so tough. Or perhaps he was, and she needed toughness against a world which was becoming increasingly cruel.

She sensed that he was truly sorry that she was distressed about her father. His tenderness extended to his voice, to his smile. It was impossible to believe that he was the same person who had reported her. A criminal. A murderer.

He had thought her bigger and tougher. At court, in a black gown, with her hair scraped back, she'd appeared very tall and haughty. In the stadium she'd seemed earthy and aggressive, until that moment in the car park when she had suddenly become vulnerable. Now, leaning on his arm, she seemed different again. She was slight, almost too thin, and her face was very pale with dark purple rings beneath her soft brown eyes. He could feel her heart thudding against his elbow. She took short breaths as if about to hyperventilate.

'I'm surprised your mother didn't tell you about your father,' he said.

'Perhaps she doesn't know.'

'Oh, she does. She visited him every day at the end. Marius told me. And I saw her at the funeral. He pointed her out.'

Francesca shook her head vehemently. 'You're wrong.'

'I was released from prison that morning,' he said, in a voice which still carried the emotion. 'It was my first day of freedom. There's no detail I could ever forget.'

'But my mother never saw my father again after she remarried. I know she didn't. She'd have told me.'

Jack didn't answer.

Francesca pulled away from him. 'What are you insinuating?' she demanded. 'My mother wouldn't deceive my stepfather. She couldn't have driven up to Richmond every day without him wondering where she'd gone.'

'Believe what you like. But if you love someone and they're dying, nothing's going to stop you from being with them. Except prison!' He walked back to the Land Rover.

'But she didn't love him. Not any more.' Unaware of the people walking past, Francesca shouted after him. 'I don't know why you're making all this up. Why are you trying to undermine everything I care for? First my career. Now my mother.'

'You've forgotten your husband. Or don't you care for him?'

She flushed.

'I don't blame you.' He stepped up into the Land Rover, turned on the ignition and revved up the engine hard. The sound bounced off the high buildings of the Inn. Jack laughed aloud in defiance. 'He's a shit. You deserve better.'

'My marriage is none of your concern, Mr Broderick,' said Francesca, taking cover behind primness.

He lowered his voice, so that it was soft, as it had been in the car park when he'd cupped her hand in his and the magnet had held them. 'Don't play games with me, Mrs Eastgate.'

Eight

After Jack drove away, Francesca decided not to go into chambers. She wanted time alone, to think about her father. She went home.

If, even six months earlier, anyone had asked her if she'd be sorry when her father died, she'd have answered crisply, 'I'm indifferent to him, so I'll feel nothing.' But now that he had gone beyond reparation, she was deeply sorry. He rose up before her, more alive now that he was dead. She remembered funny incidents, like the day he'd won five thousand pounds at poker. He'd come home dressed to kill, in a hired limousine piled high with presents. Dresses for her mother, clothes and toys for herself. The most beautiful present of all, or so it had seemed to her, was a brown-haired walkie-talkie doll almost as big as herself, wearing a beautiful crimson velvet dress trimmed with white lace. As her father stepped from the limousine, the bailiffs had appeared, chasing one of his many debts. Grandiosely, he'd paid them off in fifty-pound notes. Afterwards, how he and Marius had laughed.

Francesca wished she had a photograph of him, but long ago she'd torn them all up. It added to her remorse that although she could remember many details, she couldn't recall exactly what he looked like. Her memories were of his presence. The rough stubble on his chin when he'd been out all night and was still too drunk to shave. His hands cupping hers as he showed her how to hold her cards. The excitement of seeing her pocket money on the table between them. His voice saying, 'Remember, Frankie, poker's a game of bluff and skill.' And her mother shouting at him. Her mother pacing the floor. Her mother waiting. Her mother crying when he didn't come home.

Dominique Hartington crossed the sun-dappled garden at White Oast to the silver birch, in whose shade Steven slept in his favourite deck chair. The *Rockhurst Times* was balanced on his lap, his spectacles were folded in one hand. Around him buzzed the sounds of a summer garden.

She kissed his whiskery cheek. He woke, and reached quickly for the newspaper, pretending he hadn't been asleep. He always did. She laughed, but did not say she knew his tricks. 'We'll have lunch out here, if you like,' she said.

'That would be lovely, my dear. Can I help?'

'Oh, no! You carry on with your paper.' She walked back towards the house.

Steven watched her glide across the lawn. He heard her go upstairs. She was singing *Je ne regrette rien*. The words drifted down from an open lattice window. He wished he knew if it were her marriage to him or the earlier years of poverty and passion which she didn't regret. But he was afraid to ask.

Francesca spun her car into the driveway and parked it untidily outside the front door. On the far side of the lawn she could see her mother and Steven eating lunch at the table beneath the silver birch. They turned at the sound of the car.

'Frankie!' her mother called out. 'Darling, we didn't expect you. Is everything all right?'

'No, it is not!' Francesca strode across the lawn. She ignored her stepfather's shy greeting and spoke only to her mother, whose smooth gold hair appeared too brassy, her slim gold wristwatch too expensive. 'Is it true my father died in February?'

Her mother hesitated, then gave a helpless shrug. 'Yes.'

Steven looked surprised.

'Did you visit him when he was ill?'

'Yes.'

'Why didn't you tell me he was dying? I had a right to know.'

'Because you'd only have visited him out of duty. I had to protect him from that.'

'Oh, so it was all my fault?'

'No, darling. Mine. You were my beautiful rebel and I made you afraid to be different. I allowed my own insecurity to make you ashamed of your father.' Suddenly Dominique became aware that Steven had left the table. He was walking towards the house, his head bowed, his shoulders hunched. Tears filled her eyes. 'Hurt me, Frankie,' she said, 'but don't hurt Steven! He doesn't deserve it.' She hurried across the lawn and followed her husband into the house.

62

Francesca stood beneath the silver birch, unsure what to do next. The anger which had propelled her down from London evaporated. She'd wanted to wound her mother. And she had. But she'd also wounded Steven, who didn't deserve it. The thought reminded her of Jack Broderick saying she didn't deserve William.

Too emotionally drained to drive straight home, she lay down on the grassy bank at the far end of the garden. It was where she used to sunbathe in her teens, a gawky teenager wondering if she would find love, if her breasts would grow, if anyone would ask her to dance at the school disco.

The sun was hot. The garden buzzed with honey bees. They hovered over the succulent pink tongues of the honeysuckle. She closed her eyes.

At teatime her mother carried out a tray and arranged cups and plates on the garden table. Steven joined her, and they sat side by side on the bench in the shade of a large parasol. Francesca slept on.

'The rest will do her good.' Steven laid a kindly hand on his wife's arm. 'Don't be upset, my dear.'

'I'm upset for you. I should have told you about Ben.'

'Not unless you wanted to.' He picked up the *Rockhurst Times* and pretended to scan the headlines, waiting for his wife to elaborate. She didn't.

Francesca woke to find her stepfather shaking her arm. 'A cup of tea, dear?'

'What . . . what time is it?'

'Nearly five.' He smiled. 'You must have been very tired.'

She sat up. 'I'm sorry I hurt you.'

'Oh, don't worry about me. It's your mother who's upset.'

Frankie drank her tea, whilst around her the garden buzzed with honey bees and the shadows began to lengthen. An odd blackbird warbled from the top of the silver birch. She wondered if he was the same one who'd sung there every summer since she could remember.

She went into the house. It exuded calm, as it had done each afternoon when she'd returned from school. She stood at the bottom of the stairs, listening to its familiar noises; the muffled creaks from the woodwork, and the gurgle of water running through the pipes.

Her mother was in the kitchen, a pinafore tied neatly over her navy linen dress as she marinated mushrooms. Francesca hovered in the doorway. 'I'm sorry I attacked you. I've had a terrible week. I know that's no excuse.'

'Who told you about Ben?'

'Jack Broderick.'

'How do you know that man? Oh, Frankie, do be careful. I know Marius thinks the world of him, but he's dangerous.'

'I don't know him and I don't want to!' Francesca slumped down at the kitchen table and told her mother about the disciplinary hearing, finishing with the words, 'I thought William was helping me because he loved me. I was wrong. He doesn't give a damn about anything but his career.' She took a deep breath, trying to keep the tears out of her voice. 'I don't want to divorce, but I'm so unhappy.'

'You can always come here.'

Francesca walked over to her mother and put her arms around her. 'I'd like to stay tonight.'

'You used to hug me like this when you were little,' said her mother softly. 'You haven't done so for years.'

Francesca went to bed straight after supper. As she opened the door to her childhood bedroom, it greeted her with its familiar smell of fresh cotton. She touched the pink and white striped curtains. They were newly ironed. The ornaments on the shelves were as they had always been. The books – *Heather the Exmoor Pony*, *Anne of Green Gables* – had been recently dusted. Above them all, on the very top shelf, sat the walkie-talkie doll in a crimson dress, souvenir of the day her father won five thousand pounds.

Francesca sat on the edge of the narrow single bed, looking out at the darkened garden, listening to the sounds of the summer night, as she'd done so often as a child. Only she wasn't that child now. She was an adult running away from the choices she'd made. The Francesca Tiernay who used to sleep in this bed didn't exist any more. And the woman she'd thought her mother was had never existed.

Dominique Hartington was the only child of an English doctor and his much younger French wife; it was from her that Francesca and her mother inherited their very brown eyes. The doctor died unexpectedly, when Dominique was twelve, and she was sent to live with her grandparents, who owned a small hotel in Provence, whilst her mother took a job in Paris. She was happy at the hotel. Her mother visited every weekend, until one Friday night when she failed to arrive. She'd been crushed by a falling tree. Her death destroyed her parents. They sold the hotel and sent Dominique to stay with her English cousins, children of the doctor's sister. On the deck of the Dover ferry, Dominique met Ben Tiernay.

In the morning, the peace and sunshine of White Oast enveloped Francesca. She lay in bed listening to her mother and Steven talking above a background of Radio 4 news. Up the stairs wafted the smell of toast and fresh ground coffee. Then the telephone rang and she heard her mother say, 'I'm sorry, William, Frankie's asleep. She had a difficult day. She discovered her father died in February. Yes, I'll tell her you rang.'

At breakfast Francesca said, 'I'd like to stay till Thursday, if that's all right.'

Her mother reached across the table to squeeze her hand.

They went shopping. Once away from the house, her mother talked more openly about her father. 'When Marius phoned to tell me Ben had cancer, I couldn't refuse to see him,' she said. 'Oh, I hated him at times. We were so unsuited. He was irresponsible, I'm practical. But even when I hated him, I was never indifferent. I'm much happier married to Steven, but a part of me belongs to Ben. I can see him now, that first time we met. He was leaning on the rails, looking down at the sea, laughing. I never did find out why. He had such a magnetic smile.' Her mother gave a chuckle. 'By the time we reached Dover, I thought I couldn't live without him.'

Francesca laughed too. She couldn't imagine her serene mother being swept up by madness and passion.

She spent the days lying in the garden, and the evenings playing Scrabble with Steven. She thought about her father, although they talked of him no more. She didn't speak to William: she merely left a message that she'd be back by the weekend. She didn't telephone chambers. She didn't open her briefcase, or even read a newspaper. The world beyond White Oast did not exist.

But it did exist. Try as she might, she could not forget her problems. William. Work. And Jack Broderick. When the sun warmed her cheek, she remembered his touch. When she lay on the rug, she recalled the intimacy of his hand beneath her elbow. When she closed her eyes, she heard him say, 'You deserve better.'

She didn't leave on Thursday. Her mother didn't ask why, and Francesca simply stayed on, lying on her rug until it was too late to go. On Friday, Steven withdrew tactfully after lunch, leaving Francesca and her mother to linger over their empty plates, neither of them wanting to finish the meal, the day, the week.

'You don't have to go,' said her mother gently.

'If I stay, I'll never face up to him again.'

'Don't walk out in a fit of rage, or you'll end up destitute.'

'I'm not planning to leave William. I want to make our marriage work.'

Her mother watched the grains swirl in the bottom of her coffee cup. 'Everyone should know great love once. Your father was mine. Seeing him didn't alter my affection and commitment to my husband.'

Francesca shook her head in disbelief. 'Are you telling me to find a lover?'

'I'm telling you not to do anything rash. You're so like Ben that it makes me afraid.'

For once Francesca did not deny her father. 'Do you have a photo of him?' she asked.

It was her mother's turn to look shocked. 'Not here! Not in Steven's house! That wouldn't be proper. If you want one, you must ask Marius.'

When Francesca left White Oast, her plan was to go straight back to London, but by the time she hit the M25 she'd changed her mind. She turned west, to Richmond.

Jack's Land Rover was in the car park. She was appalled by her reaction to it. Until that moment she had not realised or, perhaps, admitted to herself, her longing to see him.

The big iron gate was unlocked. She stepped inside and looked for signs of life. The arena appeared deserted. The only movement was a loose metal sheet banging against a crossbar. She hesitated, running her fingers through her mahogany curls, free for once of their restraining plait. She called out. No one answered. She crossed the grandstand and the terrace, wishing that her red shorts didn't ride up and her white T-shirt wasn't so tight.

The front door of the Paddock House was open. She stepped into the black and white hall where, as a child, she had played hopscotch. From behind the door of what had been the card room, she could hear the honky-tonk piano of *The Entertainer*. She knocked.

A muffled voice called, 'Come in!'

Francesca opened the door. There was no sign of Jack. Marius Charlwood sat alone at the old pine table, playing with a plaster model of the stadium as it used to be. In his mouth was a pipe, which had long gone out, though he didn't seem to notice. 'I thought you'd come,' he grunted. 'Jack said you wouldn't. But you always were a nosy little monkey.' He looked her up and down. 'Frankie Tiernay! No wonder you knew my shady past.'

'I shouldn't have used that information.'

'It was a dirty trick. Your father'd have been ashamed.'

'I'm sorry.'

He grunted again. 'Sit down. I'll make some tea. Do you still steal the sugar lumps when no one's watching?'

She threw back her head and laughed, a mixture of relief and memory.

'You look just like Ben,' he told her as he shambled across the hall to the ill-fitted kitchen, where piles of washing-up crowded on the same, ancient wooden draining board of her childhood. 'I can see him in your laugh. Ben used to throw his head back as you do. He laughed even when he shouldn't have, when he was arrested, when he was in the dock. Suddenly, he'd laugh. There was no way to stop him. The worst was, he made everyone want to laugh with him.'

Francesca was torn between wanting to hear more about her father and the anxiety that Jack Broderick would arrive. Or that he wouldn't arrive. She no longer knew which. She listened for his footsteps on the stairs. She glanced out of the window. There was no one there. But she sensed the power of his presence in the card room, in the hall, in the whole house, although there was nothing she could categorically say did not belong to Marius.

It was over twenty years since she had been in this house, but it had changed little. It was merely shabbier. The dark red curtains hung from a broken pole, beer cans which served as ashtrays overflowed with cigarette stubs, and the same old sagging sofa was pushed into the window alcove. The last time she had been here, her father had lain stretched out, drunk, along that sagging sofa, whilst her mother shouted, 'I've had enough, Ben. I'm going.'

'Did he live here all the time after we left?' she asked Marius.

'Whenever he wanted to.'

'Did he die here?'

'Upstairs.'

'May I see his room.'

'You can go up, but you won't find anything of him. There's nothing to see. We cleared everything away. Not that he had much.'

'I'd like to see, all the same.'

He nodded. 'It's the little one overlooking the track, next to mine. I used to leave my door open so I could hear if he called out.'

Francesca climbed the bare wooden stairs to the first floor. The house was darker than she remembered. The cream paint bore traces of many dirty fingermarks. She wondered which of them belonged to her father. She opened his bedroom door and stepped inside, steeling herself for a wave of nostalgia. But Marius was right. There was nothing of her father in the small, bare room. His spirit was on the track, in the grandstand, downstairs in the card room, amid the bustle and the people.

By the time she came downstairs, Marius had made her a cup of tea. They returned to the card room. 'Could I have a photo of my father?' she asked.

'I don't have one.'

'Mother thought you did. She told me to ask you.'

'Oh, maybe I can find something.' Frowning, he reached inside the table drawer and scuffled amongst various papers. 'Will this do?' He produced a small black and white photo.

Francesca was prepared for her father to look ill and gaunt, but the face which stared up at her was firm, oval and bright with life. He was sitting at that very table, a cigarette in one hand and a pack of cards in the other. He was half smiling, half apologetic. It was how she remembered him best, when he was being charming, when her mother would berate him and he would tease his way back into her good books. 'When was it taken?' she asked.

68

'Oh, a month or two before he died.'

'I thought he'd look ill and old and . . .'

'He didn't.' Marius picked up his pipe and started to suck on it.

Francesca remembered that that was his way of announcing he wished to be alone. Reluctantly, she rose. 'Can I come again another day?' she said.

'Don't wait another twenty years or I'll be dead.'

She kissed him on the cheek and wished him goodbye. As she did so, she thought she heard footsteps on the stairs. The sound made the blood rush to her face, where it seemed to freeze, tingling, beneath her skin. Clutching her father's photograph, she hurried from the room, through the empty grandstand to her car. She felt as if she had reached one hand towards a furnace and only pulled it back just in time.

Nine

William was in his study, sorting papers into his briefcase. Francesca was surprised to find him home so early. He frowned at her. 'Is something wrong? You look flushed and dishevelled.'

Determined not to be provoked, she answered pleasantly, 'I'm fine. Much better, thanks.'

'I said all you needed was rest.' He closed his briefcase and turned out the desk lamp.

'Where . . . where are you going?'

'Kingly Grange.' He locked his desk. He always did that when he went away, but somehow today it had more significance.

'I'll pack my case.' She bounded up the stairs. 'I won't be long.'

'It's a bridge weekend.'

She halted. 'You mean, you don't want me with you?'

'You'd be bored.' He walked through the hallway to the front door. Now she saw his weekend bag, which was hidden under the table. At least, it seemed to her that he had hidden it.

'William, I came back to spend the weekend with you. If I'd known you were going away, I'd have stayed at White Oast.' She tried to keep her voice steady. 'We have to talk about us.'

'I haven't time now. I'll be late for dinner.'

'William! Please! This is important.'

'Then why did you run away? We could have talked all week. You see, Francesca, you never think.' He opened the front door. 'You forgot to take my suit to be dry-cleaned. It's on our bed. Don't forget the Culmstocks are expecting us on Sunday. I'll see you there at three. I told them you weren't well enough to play tennis.' He looked her up and down. 'Wear something more suitable. Those shorts are for holidays.'

'I am on holiday! I'm taking a month off. You can work if you want to, but I need a break.' She marched up the stairs. In the top drawer of her dressing table was the slim leatherbound volume of Alexander Pope, beautifully wrapped, waiting to be presented. She pushed it to the back of the drawer.

William drove away. She listened to his hesitant revving as he turned out of their street. Then the silence of the house enveloped her. She felt desperately, acutely lonely. He hadn't even mentioned her father.

Some fifteen minutes later, the telephone rang. She grabbed it, hoping William had changed his mind. It was Melanie. 'William said you were at White Oast but your mother tells me you're in London. Is something wrong? I haven't heard from you since the tribunal.'

'I'm fine.'

'Let's all go out to dinner. We'll celebrate your acquittal.

'No! No!' She could not face the loneliness of other people's pity.

Unable to keep still, Francesca paced the rooms. She pictured William dining with his parents. Was he telling them his marriage was over? Was it over? If she could feel such attraction for Jack, it must mean she didn't love William. She imagined a For Sale board outside the house and other people moving in. Strangers living, eating, bathing, and making love where she and William had lived. The ground beneath her feet had been whisked away, put back, then whisked away again. As the hours passed, she returned to blaming herself. She bit the thumbnail of her right hand to the quick. Then the left. The flesh beside her nails became swollen and sore.

The phone rang for the second time. She nearly didn't answer, and only grabbed it on the eighth ring. 'Hello?'

'Why did you avoid me at the stadium?'

'Who's that?'

'You know who it is.'

She swallowed hard. Her heart was pounding in her ears.

'I want to show you my greyhounds,' Jack Broderick went on. 'Will you come on Sunday and take them for a walk?'

'How did you get this number? We're ex-directory.'

'I have friends in low places. I'll expect you around three?'

'No! You mustn't ring me again.' She slammed down the receiver.

But now she paced the house with a different type of nervousness. Jack Broderick's voice was in her ears and in her mind. It vibrated through her body. It brought guilt, fear, and desire.

Saturday was hot. The sun blazed down on the windless, dusty streets of North London, wilting the flowers in small back gardens. Francesca cleaned Jaws's tank and moved him out of the bright sunlight. Then she aired Big Ears's hutch whilst he hopped in and out of the plants. Finally, she stretched out, naked, to sunbathe in the secluded doorway of the conservatory, her Walkman clamped to her ears to drown out her neighbour, Mr Riddle-Longman's attempts at using a Black & Decker. The heat on her body made her think of Jack. She thought of him now as Jack, not Jack Broderick. She recalled his hand on her elbow. She remembered the fine skin beneath his eyes.

Her mood seesawed. It was William's fault if she turned to Jack: he shouldn't neglect her. She didn't want to be unfaithful but she was starved of cherishment, if there was such a word. She'd tried to be a good wife. If her marriage had problems, Jack was not the reason but a symptom. Not the cause but the catalyst.

A car came down the street. She waited for it to stop, but it drove on. She heard footsteps on the pavement. They kept walking. Someone was dropping leaflets through the letter boxes. Her neighbour's dog barked. Big Ears scuttled towards his hutch. The telephone rang. She raced naked into the kitchen to answer it.

It was her mother. 'I bumped into Audrey Eastgate. She told me William's at Kingly Grange.'

'It's a bridge weekend. I decided to stay here.'

'On your own?'

'I'm perfectly all right,' Francesca snapped. Then she remembered that they were a new, closer mother and daughter, and added quickly, 'Thanks for asking. Thanks for everything.'

She was furious with William. He was driving her away. She opened one of the special bottles of Krug from the case he'd been keeping to celebrate becoming a High Court judge and poured it into one of the Waterford champagne glasses he wouldn't allow Mrs MacDougall to touch. She slipped on her bikini and returned to the garden, where she lay in a deck chair, alternately sipping champagne and spooning cold baked beans straight from the tin. Solitude enveloped her. She relished it, and wondered if she'd be happier living alone.

She dreamed of Jack and woke in the middle of the night. Sleep would not come again. She imagined him beside her, with her, around her. In the darkness, the side of her which found him so attractive could admit to it, whilst her other side lay dormant. But with the grey light of dawn came the reminder of reality. She was a barrister. Jack Broderick was a criminal, a man who'd done fourteen years for armed robbery. A murderer!

For tea at the Culmstocks, Francesca wore the yellow linen culotte dress which William liked. She plaited her hair so that every strand was off her face. Her make-up was minimal, her lipstick a touch of pink gloss, her scent lemony and light.

Geoffrey and Virginia lived near Windsor, in a luxurious mock-Tudor house set in acres of manicured woodland. Francesca stopped the car in the drive. Through the rhododendrons she could see Rupert and Charlotte, but not Simon or Melanie. Geoffrey came out of the house. He was followed by William, who bent to flatter Virginia Culmstock. Francesca watched him. He looked very fair and handsome, upright and well bred. She knew that when she drove up he would smile and call out, 'Hello, darling. How lovely you look,' and everyone would think how lucky she was. But tonight, at home, he would ignore her.

She slipped the car into reverse and backed out of the Culmstocks' drive.

The Paddock House reeked of new paint. Francesca could smell it as she crossed the terrace. She found the doors and windows wide open, although the ground floor was deserted. From somewhere upstairs came the honky-tonk of *The Entertainer*. She followed the music, up the uncarpeted but freshly painted stairs, past Marius's bedroom, to what used to be the attic storeroom. Her heart was thumping in her ears again, adding a bass line to the piano. She felt sure it must be audible. As she reached the top step she took a deep breath and clenched her fists extra hard. What was she doing here? What was she going to say? She must be mad.

The dirty old attic had been transformed into a bright, white-raftered space which stretched in each direction to sloping windows. Jack was standing in the centre, covering a bare double bed with architectural drawings, laying them carefully so that each sheet of paper just overlapped the adjacent page. 'You're late,' he said, as though it hadn't occurred to him she wouldn't come. 'I want to tape these drawings in sequence so old Marius can't put them out of order. Work starts on the stadium tomorrow.' His face was bright and boyish with enthusiasm. 'Do you want to hold or stick?'

'I'll hold.'

Of all the things Francesca had imagined doing with Jack, attaching architectural drawings was not one of them. She faced him across the width of the bed, bending to hold one sheet of paper on top of the other.

He measured a length of Sellotape. To do so he had to bend his face near hers and touch her hands with his fingers. She felt his skin on hers, and flushed, hoping he wouldn't notice. But she knew he had. 'Stop shaking,' he said softly.

'I can't help it.' She looked at him from under her very straight eyebrows. 'I'm not used to this . . . sort of thing.'

He straightened up, the length of sticky tape still taut between his hands. 'You're doing no wrong.'

'I'm wrong even to be here. I'm married. William's my husband and my first lover. My only lover. I don't want to break that.'

He relaxed his arms. 'We all have daydreams. Do you think mine were to go to prison?'

She looked at him, hesitating. Then she gave a nervous giggle. 'You've twisted the tape around your wrists. It looks like a pair of handcuffs.'

'I swore I'd never wear them again.' He pulled it off. 'Do you know, when I was a kid, I used to wrap this tape around my fingertips so as not to leave prints.'

'You must have been a right little rogue.'

'I was. A villain in the making. But I never beat up old ladies. I had my pride!' He winked. 'Come on! Hold the page. And don't wobble.'

His face was near Francesca's. She could feel his breath lightly on her cheek. When he removed the joined pages, he touched her fingers. His touch felt natural. She wanted it. She wanted more. As she bent to hold each page, she had to press her knees into the side of the bed to prevent them from trembling. She was conscious that this was a bed, his bed. In one of the corners of the attic was a chair, with a duvet and pillows tossed over it. She hadn't noticed them at first. She peeped up under her eyelashes and found Jack watching her.

74

She backed away as soon as he had attached the final page. 'I must go.'

'You haven't met my dogs,' he said.

'I saw them before.'

'Not properly. You didn't pat them.'

'I'll meet them now.' She was halfway down the stairs by the time he caught up with her. He did not touch her, but his warm breath was on the back of her neck where her plaited hair laid the skin bare.

He led her to the Paddock Kennels behind the Paddock Bar, where on racing days the dogs used to be kept in small, numbered kennels built around a covered courtyard. The two greyhounds, the big black dog and the dainty fawn bitch, had been sleeping on an old blanket in the courtyard. When they heard Jack's footsteps, they raced to the door, jostling for his attention.

'This is Golden Delicious.' Jack patted the fawn. 'I named her after the apples. They remind me of my aunt Phoebe. Every Saturday she used to go to the market, just before it closed, when the fruit was cheapest. She always bought apples. She spent her life in grinding poverty, cleaning City offices and dreaming of winning the pools. She did win once. Two pounds! Just enough to stand a round at the pub on Friday night.' He gave a tough, sad smile. 'Poor Phoebe! The first time the police came looking for me, she told them I couldn't possibly have stolen a lorry because I was only nine.'

'Had you?'

'Oh, no!' His eyes danced with unrepentant charm. 'I couldn't reach the pedals, so I'd paid another boy to drive it.'

'Didn't I say you were a rogue?'

'Just like Jet.' He stroked the big, ugly black dog who was pushing up against their legs. 'He's a thug. If he likes you, he'll sit on your feet and run his cold nose up your leg.'

'Is that what you do when you'd like someone?'

'Are you flirting with me?'

She blushed and raked her mind for a quick response. But there was no need, Jack had turned back to the dogs. 'I'm going to mate them,' he said. 'Goldie should come into season at Christmas. She'll run her best race just before. Bitches often do that.'

'Will you race her here, at Richmond?'

'We won't be open by then.' He closed the dogs back into the kennels. 'We'll be lucky to be in business by Easter. This place is going to take a lot of work – and a lot of money. But when it's ready, it'll be the best.'

'And where will you get the money from?'

His mood switched. 'Will you make love with your husband tonight?'

Frankie flushed.

'You see.' He moved towards her in the gloom of the deserted grandstand. 'There are questions you and I must not ask each other.'

She knew he was about to take her in his arms and that she would not be able to prevent her mouth from parting beneath his. She craved him about her, with her, in her. She was appalled by herself. She dreaded his approach. She longed to run away but her legs wouldn't move. She dreaded tomorrow, and every day afterwards, when she would be overwhelmed by guilt. And yet, she knew she would not resist him.

'You'd better go home,' he said quietly, and turned back to the Paddock House, leaving her perplexed and humiliated, but slightly relieved.

Ten

William was in the drawing room, studying a catalogue of a forthcoming rare book sale. He lowered it as Francesca burst through the front door. 'Why weren't you at tea?' he demanded.

'I didn't feel well. I went to see Melanie. It's disgraceful that they didn't invite her.'

'They did. She's packing for Crete. If you saw her, you'd know that.'

'I didn't see her. When I reached her street I remembered she'd be busy.' Francesca escaped upstairs.

'You made me look a bloody fool,' he shouted after her. 'You're not to go to bed till you've apologised to Virginia.'

'I'll do it tomorrow.' She leaned over the banisters. 'I am not a child, so stop treating me as one.'

He didn't reply. In the hall mirror, she could see he'd returned to his catalogue: she was too far away to see he was holding it upside down.

Although Francesca was on holiday she went into chambers next morning, not because she wanted to work but to avoid the temptation of returning to Richmond. She studied law reports which she never normally had time to read, wrote to Virginia, wrote to her accountant, and wrote to other people where a phone call would easily have sufficed. Anything to keep herself away from the magnet of Jack.

In the case of Alexander Swaffield, the hospital had refused to increase their offer, so the matter was now in the preparatory period leading up to a hearing. But there was little Francesca could work on until September, because the child psychologist and the paediatrician, booked to give independent reports, were on holiday. So were the boy and his parents. So was the solicitor, whose articled clerk had failed to trace the playschool teacher.

She heard nothing from Jack for three days. Then, on the first day she chose to stay at home, he telephoned. 'Eamonn O'Donnell, the old dog-trainer, wants to see you,' he said.

'He's expecting us this afternoon.'

'Jack, I can't. Listen! Please . . .!'

'Two o'clock!'

Of course she shouldn't go. She knew that. But she couldn't stay away. And it was more than pure attraction. There was something in Jack, and in the stadium, which liberated her. As she walked through the deserted grandstand, she felt feisty and punchy and happy. She was free from the mental constraints of her existence with William.

'You're late again!' Jack called from the card-room window when he saw her approach.

'You're lucky I came at all.'

'Didn't your learn timekeeping in law school?'

'Don't you know good things are worth waiting for?' She pushed open the card-room door, and exclaimed, 'Good heavens!' Jack was sitting at a double desk, with a computer on one side and a battery of telephones on the other. The dirty, dingy card room was now a gleaming chrome and glass office of Anglepoise lamps and filing cabinets. The chaos of magazines had been tidied on to glass shelves. The beer cans and coffee mugs had been cleared away. The torn curtain had been replaced by black wicker blinds. Only the sagging sofa remained from the old days. Francesca was glad.

'Do you like it?' Jack asked, bright with enthusiasm.

'Oh, yes.' She could not tell him that she found it brash. 'Where's Eamonn?'

'At his kennels.' Jack picked up his car keys. 'Marius!' he shouted up the stairs. 'Are you coming?'

'No.' The older man appeared on the first-floor landing. 'You two be sensible. Frankie's a married woman, Jack, and her father was my friend.'

'She's not married today.' Jack's eyes met hers. 'She's with me.'

'No, I am not! I came to see Eamonn. I thought he'd be here. I wouldn't have come if I'd known otherwise.'

'Then don't come.' Jack sauntered out of the room, tossing the car keys from one hand to the other.

His footsteps crossed the terrace and disappeared into the grandstand. Francesca looked up at Marius. He sighed. 'Don't make your mother angry with me.'

'I won't.'

She refused to run after Jack, but walked slowly, telling herself she didn't care if he went without her. He was waiting in the Land Rover, with the passenger door open. Jet and Goldie were in the back. Francesca climbed in and fastened the seat belt, her eyes fixed straight ahead and her knees tight together.

At the first set of traffic lights they had to stop. Jack leaned across and kissed her very quickly and very lightly on the corner of her mouth. 'You look beautiful,' he said. 'Wild and beautiful.' Then the lights changed. He drove on as if nothing had happened, whilst she sat beside him, her fists clenched on her bare knees.

Eamonn O'Donnell's kennels were on the edge of the North Downs. A narrow road led through the back of a village, past a pub, to a gravel car park. As they arrived, the other dogs started to bark.

'Little Frankie Tiernay!' Eamonn hurried forward, a tiny, tubby man in a flat hat and a dark blue jacket. He was as she remembered him, like an elderly baby with chubby cheeks and a permanently smiling bland face. The dogs bounded out of the Land Rover and threw themselves at Eamonn. Clearly, they loved him.

'I'm sorry about your father,' he said as he led the way into the kennels. 'He was a real character. Of course he wasn't a greyhound man. He liked poker. Now I like a good game meself but cards don't rule my life. It wouldn't 'ave mattered if he'd kept off the bottle. Sober, I've seen him win five grand in one night.' He grinned at Francesca. 'You were a mean little player yourself.'

'When I was seven! But not since. I hate all gambling.'

Eamonn was a professional National Greyhound Racing Club trainer. He'd been attached to the Richmond Stadium until its closure. Not that his dogs had simply run there, it was where he'd chosen to trial them; where Marius had graded them. His kennels had the warm, sleepy, doggy smell Francesca remembered from her childhood. The dogs were kennelled in pairs, usually a bitch and a dog. They lolled together on raised wooden beds filled with clean shredded paper, their bright eyes following the kennel-girls who crossed and recrossed the yard between the office and the kitchens.

Eamonn placed Goldie and Jet in a spacious outdoor run.

'When's Richmond going to open?' he asked Jack. 'I've space for seventy but I've kept thirty kennels free for Richmond dogs, as you asked me.'

'I told you to phone me if you needed anything.'

'I'm not talking money, Jack. You've given me enough already. I love greyhounds. They're the happiest dogs, always smiling. I just hate to see an empty kennel.'

Jack patted the little man's shoulder. 'We'll open by Easter. Then you'll soon fill up, I'll make sure of that. And you'll have Goldie's puppies by then.'

'Not till they're reared. I'm a trainer, not a breeder, and don't think you can get round me. Puppies are 'ard work.'

Jack smiled at Francesca. 'Eamonn's like a greyhound. All yap and no bite. He looked after Goldie's mother whilst I was inside, never charged me a penny, and kept her till she died.'

'Because Marius asked me to. He told me a sob story about the bitch having no home. But I'm not doing it again, so you'd better keep out of prison.'

Jack didn't reply but stood perfectly still. Francesca saw Eamonn pale. He started to apologise. Then, suddenly, Jack laughed. 'Oh, Frankie will make sure I stay out.'

'I thought she was married.'

'I'm a barrister,' said Francesca quickly. 'That's what Jack means. He's counting on me to advise him.' She gave Jack a bright smile, then turned to Eamonn. 'It's been lovely to see you again, but we must go. My husband is expecting me.'

They drove back to London in silence. When Jack dropped Francesca by her car, he said, 'On Sunday I could have made love to you in the grandstand. I could have lain you down on the concrete and you wouldn't have refused. Today I could have stopped in a secluded gateway and you wouldn't have tried to prevent me. Oh, maybe a little. But I could have won you over. Don't deny it! You were mine for the taking. You were ripe. But I didn't take you, because when we make love I don't want you to regret it. Only never, never play your hypocrite games on me.' He walked across the empty car park towards the stadium.

'I'm not playing games,' she yelled after him. 'But I am married. And I don't want you making out to all and sundry that there is something between us.'

'If there isn't,' he shouted over his shoulder, 'why the hell are you coming here?'

'That's what I ask myself.' She shrugged helplessly. 'I'm crazy. I'm risking everything.'

'You haven't done anything yet – except argue with me in various car parks.'

'I have, by coming here.'

'And all for a man with a criminal record?'

She lowered her voice to a whisper, but he could still hear it. 'Yes.'

He made no move to return to her. 'Do you think I choose to want another man's wife?'

'Perhaps it's because I'm married to William that you want me. I'm a barrister married to a Queen's Counsel. What sweeter revenge could you have on the law?'

'Maybe that's true. In which case, you'd better stay away.' He disappeared into the stadium.

This time Francesca didn't follow him. She was too afraid she was right.

Eleven

When William arrived home he found Francesca in the garden, retying the jasmine to the back wall whilst Big Ears hopped around her feet. 'You weren't in chambers today,' he said, accusingly.

'I'm on holiday.' She continued tying the jasmine.

'I like that white dress. Is it new?'

'You bought it for me in Barbados.'

'Of course. I forgot.' He paused. 'We must go there again.' He was trying to make amends in his stiff, stilted way, but Francesca could think only of Jack.

She walked past William into the house, careful not to touch him, and started to prepare supper. He watched her.

That night, he reached across the bed and drew a tentative hand down her bare arm. She lay still, with the hairs on her arm standing on end. 'It's a long time since we made love,' he said.

'I'm tired.'

'Is that all, Francesca?'

She was jolted by his question. She stared into the darkness, his words hanging between them. Then she replied, 'Of course.'

He drew her close. 'You've been different lately. A bit sharp. Perhaps you miss having Melanie to gossip with. Or maybe you have a new friend?'

She thought of Jack. 'No, I don't.'

He kissed her neck. 'When I've finished the groundwork on this fraud case, I'll take a few days off. We might go to Paris for a weekend.' He slid her silken nightdress up her leg. 'You like Paris.'

This was the nearest he could bring himself to an apology. Francesca turned her face to him and opened her arms, blotting out the face of Jack Broderick. William was her husband, this was her life. Everything else was fantasy.

In the morning she gave him a volume of Alexander Pope.

He gave a small cry of pleasure when he unwrapped it. 'Darling, it's the most perfect present.' His long, slender fingers stroked the leatherbound volume. Then he kissed her tenderly on the forehead. 'Thank you.'

Again she told herself she was greedy to want more.

If only Melanie hadn't been away, Francesca could have talked Jack through and out and, with luck, over. She tried to keep busy and out of the house. On the days she didn't go into chambers, she visited her mother or went shopping in the sales, buying clothes she neither wanted nor needed. William was detached but companionable. If it were not for the occasional lovemaking, they could have been flatmates. If Jack had not obsessed her body and her mind, she could have been relatively happy.

Old Nailbag allocated her a couple of new cases. She could have hugged him. She didn't care that they dealt with minor crimes. They kept her sane. They took her back into the real world.

Lindsay Dault was one such case. She was a twenty-five-year-old mother of three who had violated a suspended sentence by stealing a video of *Pinocchio* from Woolworths. Small and thin, with straggling mousy hair and mascara smudged under her eyes, she could have had an elfin prettiness had she not been defeated by the tiredness of poverty.

She was accompanied by her solicitor, a gangling redhead called David Jarrow, who had the threadbare untidiness of a perennial student. Francesca had never heard of the small, struggling firm in Brixton where he was a junior partner. Her kind of chambers seldom took instructions from that sort of practice. She categorised David Jarrow as a failed idealist, although she liked his engaging, freckly grin, which was more than she could say of his sulky client with her South London whine.

'You stole the goods when on a suspended sentence,' she told the young woman. 'You'll be very lucky to escape prison.'

'I couldn't 'elp it.' She lit a cigarette and took a long drag on it, inhaling the nicotine into every pore of her thin body. 'I 'ad to buy my kids a present. Their dad was meant to take them to the pictures, but 'e never showed. The bastard! What could I do? I 'ad no money. I only get the minimum and the rent takes most of it.'

'What about maintenance?'

'Derek's meant to pay but 'e never does.'

'We've done our best,' David Jarrow interrupted. 'There's an affiliation order against him but he keeps changing addresses.'

'And women,' Lindsay cut in.

Francesca glanced at the brief. Lindsay Dault's home was a council flat on the seventh floor of a tower block. Surprisingly, she was only a month behind with her rent. She'd been in prison once, when she was eighteen, for receiving stolen goods. The social worker reported she was a good mother but a bad picker of men. Francesca thought of Jack. She frowned and closed the brief.

'I'm caught in a trap.' Lindsay ground her cigarette into the ashtray. 'If I go to prison, I'll lose my kids. They'll be taken into care, 'cos there's no one to look after them. My mum can't cope. Welfare will 'ave to feed, clothe and house them. But if only Welfare 'elped me get the money from Derek, I wouldn't have to steal in the first place.' She stood abruptly. 'But you don't care. No one does.'

Francesca picked up her pen. 'How do you know I don't care?'

'I can read your face.'

'You're wrong.' Francesca turned to a new page in her notebook. 'But I can't help you if you stand there yelling at me.'

Lindsay sat down on the edge of her chair. 'Sorry.'

'How long were you married?'

'We weren't.' She blushed and gave a girlish giggle which transformed her into the young woman she could have been. 'But my mum thinks we were. She's a strict Catholic.'

'So is mine. At least, she was brought up that way,' said Francesca with understanding. 'Married or not, Derek is still the children's father and they are his responsibility.' She smiled encouragingly. 'Now, tell me exactly what happened.'

After David Jarrow and Lindsay Dault had left, Francesca tapped through to Nailsworth. 'Was this case meant for Miss Llanellen?' she asked. 'It's more her area.'

'No. Mr Jarrow asked for you in person.'

'How peculiar! I've never heard of him.'

When she next spoke to David Jarrow, she asked, 'How did you know my name?'

'Marius Charlwood recommended you. He knows my sister.'

It was the excuse Francesca needed to return to Richmond.

*

84

The building work was well under way. Francesca was impressed by the progress. The rubble had been cleared, the arena had been ploughed and rolled. Workmen swarmed up the stands, erecting a powerful steel frame to reinforce the overhanging roof. The whole place echoed with the noise of their hammering, sawing, welding and drilling.

Jack and Marius were playing poker in the newly appointed card room when they heard tentative footsteps approach. They glanced at each other, but continued talking as Jack dealt the next hand. Their only change in position was that Jack swivelled his chair so that his back was better protected by the wall.

Francesca took a deep breath before opening the door. The two men looked up, as though surprised by her intrusion. 'I came to thank you for recommending me,' she said to Marius.

'Ah, Nicoletta's brother.' Marius laid down his cards. 'A true champion of the underdog.'

'Just like you, old man,' said Jack. He turned to Francesca. 'Tell me, Mrs Eastgate, do you always visit those who recommend you. Did you visit Lex Gunter?'

'Of course not!'

'Stop fighting! I'm old and I want peace.' Marius stood up. 'You're like a couple of scrapping puppies.'

He left them alone. Jack faced Francesca. 'I was afraid you wouldn't come back.'

'I was afraid you meant what you said.'

He reached for her hand.

She drew away. 'No, Jack.'

'Then why did you come?'

She gave him the helpless, vulnerable shrug he found so endearing. 'Because I wanted to see you.' She was both relieved and appalled by her admission.

'I want to make love to you,' he said, very gently.

She backed away, out into the hall. 'I've tried so hard to make my marriage work. I never wanted it to come to this.'

She'd backed so far she was right out on the terrace. Now she started along the wide concrete steps where rows of broken bucket-seats were riveted to the concrete floor. The sun glinted through the roofless structure which curved upwards into the sky. It cast strange shadowed shapes between the iron struts and through the vacant, glassless window frames. Jack paced below her, on the sand where one day the dogs would run. She climbed higher, as far away from him as she could go.

'We'll be extending the grandstand dining room right along this side,' he called up to her, talking normally as if nothing had happened between them. 'People who dine want good food, drink, a trackside table, and enough glamour to impress the girlfriend.'

'And elegant surroundings?'

'You mean, for your friends? Oh, no! They of all people want to see the glitter of dubious money. They like to watch a man with gold rings on every finger lose ten thousand pounds without batting an eyelid. They love stories of dog-doping. They want the sport to be rough. It makes them feel daring and macho. Then they can go to their City offices and say, "I rubbed shoulders with a big-time hood." That's part of the attraction. If not, they might as well be at Ascot.'

Yet again she was impressed by his articulacy. 'You have us all worked out,' she said, looking down at him, her hair ruffled by the breeze.

'Not you.' He held out his hand. 'Come here.'

She walked down the wide steps, unsure and unsteady like a young colt. But even then she did not take his hand. She stood a few feet away, clenching and unclenching her fists.

'I missed you,' he said.

'I missed you too.'

'Yet when we meet, we fight. I'm angry at you because you have to leave.'

'I'm angry at myself for coming at all.' She glanced at her watch. 'Now I'm angry because I have to go and I'm late. And William will be angry because he'll have been kept waiting.'

He took her by the shoulders and drew her near. He cupped her face in his hand and brushed her mouth with his. He kissed the dewiness from her lips. She reached up, clinging to him, wanting to be enveloped by his powerful body, knowing she should pull back but unable to do so. 'Come tomorrow,' he whispered.

'I'll try.'

She drove home unaware of the road, the other cars, or the pedestrians. She could think of nothing but Jack. She craved him as though he were a drug.

86

William was in the study. He often worked at home these days. For an awful moment she wondered if he suspected something.

'Hello, darling,' he called. 'There's a card from Simon and Melanie. They're staying on an extra week. And your mother phoned. Your stepbrother and the Ageing Bimbo have arrived unexpectedly.'

'Robert and Priscilla!' She was sure he didn't suspect.

'I promised we'd go down tomorrow to help entertain them. Your mother and Steven are exhausted already. You know what Robert's like, he never draws breath. I invited them to stay with us next week. You'd better book theatre tickets. Not *Cats*. Dancing bores me. Choose something you'd like to see.'

Francesca went into the kitchen, opened a bottle of wine, and gulped down two glasses. She wished they had a dog so she had an excuse to get out of the house and use a public telephone. But William didn't like dogs. He said they were dirty.

Robert was the son of Steven's first wife, an American who had been killed in a car crash. By the time Francesca and her mother came to live at White Oast, Robert was in his first year at university. Her most vivid early memory of him was at her mother and Steven's wedding, when he'd roared up to the registry office in a battered purple Mini with 'Let's Spend the Night Together' blaring from every broken window. To Frankie, he'd seemed everything an older brother should be: tall, dark, handsome and daring. When he'd emigrated to America, she'd taken his departure as a personal rejection. It was four years before he returned. She'd rushed home from school to see him. In the drawing room she'd found a very precise, stocky young man, now several inches shorter than herself in spite of his cowboy boots, talking nineteen to the dozen in a phoney American accent. She'd been bitterly disappointed.

Now they arrived to find Robert pacing the garden, talking loudly and without pause to Steven. 'Hi there! How's my little sister?' He rushed over to Francesca and hugged her. 'I want to hear all your news.' He said almost exactly the same to William.

Francesca escaped inside the house to use the upstairs telephone, only to be cornered by Priscilla on the landing. The Ageing Bimbo was an effervescent toothsome blonde with a permanent

Californian suntan, damned for ever at White Oast by the nickname William had bestowed on her. 'The kids are just dying to meet you,' she prattled, clasping both of Francesca's hands. 'And I'm dying to know you better. It's a shame you can't come to San Francisco before we leave. We're relocating to Dallas in the fall, so we'll be there when you visit.'

'I'm sure we'll come over one day.'

'William just told Robert we'd be seeing you at New Year.'

'He did?' From the window she could see William walking along the gravel path between her stepfather and Robert, his ear bent patiently to the staccato of one, his arm proffered to the old age of the other.

'Didn't you know? Oh dear, maybe it was meant to be a secret. Why did I open my big mouth? Don't tell Robert, he'll be furious with me.'

'I won't.' Francesca felt sorry for Priscilla. She was friendly and harmless, but somehow she always got things wrong. 'I'll join you in the sitting room,' she said. 'I want to talk to my mother.'

Priscilla watched Francesca hurry through to the back of the house. There had been a hint of, 'I want to talk to my mother alone,' as if implying that she would push herself in.

Priscilla disliked her husband's relations, except for Steven. On her first visit to White Oast, aged twenty-one, just engaged, and on her first trip outside the US, she'd been so excited and so eager to please. The old oast house had seemed cute, and Steven such an old-fashioned darling. Priscilla could still recall the warmth with which he'd welcomed her into his family. Then Dominique had walked downstairs, immaculate in navy linen with one small bar brooch on her left shoulder and a matching clasp at her neck. Priscilla had been expecting someone like her own mother, warm, overweight and mumsy. What's more, she'd sensed laughter in Dominique's eyes but hadn't understood the reason.

Then the front door had been flung open by a schoolgirl with a long brown plait. 'Robert!' she'd cried. Then she'd caught sight of Priscilla, hesitated, and burst into giggles. Francesca was wearing her school uniform; a grey pleated skirt, white blouse and white knee socks. It was exactly the same as Priscilla's carefully chosen outfit.

Dominique was basting chicken breasts with a mixture of fresh

88

lime and butter when Francesca appeared in the doorway. 'I'm so glad you could come,' she said. 'Robert's exhausting. He talks like a machine gun. William's wonderfully patient with him.' She lowered her voice. 'How are things?'

'Up and down.' Francesca hesitated. 'I want to use the upstairs telephone.'

'Jack Broderick?'

Francesca blushed. 'How did you know?'

'Marius telephoned me. He was so pleased to see you again.' Her mother lowered her voice. 'But he's worried about you and Jack. He says you're playing with fire. Darling, do be sensible. Broderick's a dangerous man, whatever Marius swears to the contrary.'

'This is no game,' said Francesca. 'It would be much easier if it were.'

She'd never telephoned Jack before. Until now there had been no direct link, no explanations. That had allowed her to pretend it was Marius, as much as Jack, whom she visited at Richmond. But whispering down the telephone to Jack from her mother's bedroom there could be no more pretence. From the window she could see William settle her stepfather on the garden bench. They had ten years of marriage, of families, of mutual friends, of living together. Her clandestine telephone call to Jack was the first step to betrayal. Away from him, she was no longer so sure she wanted to take that step.

Robert and Priscilla kept Francesca busy for most of the following week. They went to see *The Mousetrap*, ate out in Covent Garden, trailed around the Tate Gallery, and shopped till they dropped in Harrods. As the days passed, Francesca became increasingly restless. William sensed that. Even when they made love, he felt a part of her was elsewhere. But he didn't confront her – that wasn't his way. He watched.

On the morning of Robert and Priscilla's departure, she drove them to the airport. Her plan was to go straight to Richmond, to see Jack, but as she came back on to the motorway, she was assailed by the same doubts she'd had at White Oast. Ten years of marriage couldn't be dismissed. Instead of going to Richmond, she went home to furiously clean the house, scrubbing the tiled kitchen floor on her hands and knees as if she were doing penance. At midday the front doorbell rang. She froze. It rang again. Still she didn't move. The letter box was forced open and Jack shouted, 'Frankie! Open this door!'

She stood in the hall and called out, 'You mustn't come here.'

'Open up or I'll break the door down! If you don't want to see me again, have the guts to tell me to my face.'

She slid back the bolts but kept the chain in place. 'I want to give my marriage a chance.'

'You let him make love to you last night. I can see it in your eyes. In the way you can't look straight at me.'

'Jack, he's my husband.'

'That's not an answer.'

Clarissa Riddle-Longman drew up in her Volvo estate car. 'That's my nosiest neighbour,' Francesca hissed. 'You must leave.'

'Either let me in or come to Eamonn's. The dogs are in the car. I have to take them back to him.'

'Jack, don't tempt me. Please!'

'But I want to tempt you,' he said in a voice which made her weak. 'I'll wait five minutes. Then I'll go. And that'll be the end.'

She gave him her helpless shrug. 'Fifteen.'

'Ten – and not a second longer.'

She rushed upstairs, ripped off her dirty clothes, showered, and pulled on a pair of clean jeans and a T-shirt. With a minute to spare, she was down again, the T-shirt sticking to her wet back.

On the way to the kennels she said, 'I wish you hadn't come today. I wish I wasn't so weak. I wish I could be happy with William.'

They walked the dogs across the downs. Her took her hand in his. The wind was strong, buffeting the long grass. The sun was hot. It felt good on her face and her bare arms. The greyhounds disturbed a hare, and it raced across the rough grass, the hounds coursing it in full pursuit. It broke to the right. They followed. It jinked. They turned.

'Don't let them kill it!' cried Francesca.

'A hare's their natural quarry. You know that. Greyhounds have been coursing hares for centuries in England. The track sport only began in 1919, in the States, when Smith invented the mechanical lure. The dogs chased it because that's their nature. But they won't catch this hare, any more than they catch the lure, if she's clever and runs for the copse. They're gaze hounds not scent hounds. Out of sight and she's out of mind.'

'But I don't want to see death.' Francesca ran up the field, waving her arms to head the hare for the wood. She couldn't bear the chase, and yet she was mesmerised by the turning, twisting hare, its ears flat back in terror, and the two athletic dogs bounding after it. The hare was tiring. It broke more slowly. The dogs were nearly on it as it reached the copse and disappeared into the undergrowth.

Jack whistled. The dogs came trotting back to him. 'It's not the kill that's important in coursing, it's the contest,' he called to Francesca. 'I'm glad she got away.'

'Then why set them on her?'

'There is no hunt without death. No life without danger.'

'Your life!'

'Our life.' He came up the field towards her, striding out through the long grass. 'You can't fight nature.'

'At the weekend I was determined never to see you again.'

He seized her by the shoulders, forcing her to look at him. 'And now?'

She could no longer resist this man who had got under her skin and into her mind as no one ever had. His mouth covered hers. Her lips parted. He kissed her gently, and she clung to him. He kissed her hard. She opened up to him, pressing against him, her body soft against his. He took off his jacket and laid it on top of the long grass. She sank down, holding out her arms to him, welcoming him to her. He lay with her, kissing her neck and her shoulders. He said, 'I want to make love to you more than I've ever wanted any woman. You make me laugh. You make me furious. When we're together, we fight. When you leave, I can't wait to see you again.' He unbuttoned her shirt to reveal her breasts. He unzipped her jeans to kiss the flat of her stomach. The open hillside, the roaming dogs, the buffeting wind brought urgency. There was no time for gentle, slow lovemaking. He crushed her with his weight. She relished it. He took her. She trembled and cried out for more. They made love fiercely, almost angrily, resenting that they would have to part. They made love

91

passionately, completely, because that was the way they felt about each other.

Afterwards, as she lay sprawled in his arms, she caught sight of her watch and gasped, 'I must go.'

'No!' He held her tight.

'Don't you think I'd stay with you if I could?'

'As long as I know that, I can almost bear it.' He kissed her tenderly and sat up, whistling for the dogs as she dressed.

During the drive back to London, he held her hand and talked about his early life, as though it were now essential she understood his side. 'Phoebe used to visit me in borstal to tell me about vacancies for apprentice packers,' he said. 'Fifty hours a week for a tenner! She couldn't understand why I craved excitement, why I wouldn't sign away my life as factory fodder.'

'But you must have been to a good school. You're so articulate.'

'I was taught Scrabble by a fraudulent solicitor. He was such a cheat that he even added Latin words to the dictionary and claimed they were admissible.'

She laughed at his story. 'You joke, but it can't have been easy. When you heard your sentence you must have wished you'd followed Aunt Phoebe's advice and got a job.'

'They say, "If you can't face the time, don't do the crime." Of course, that first morning when I woke in my narrow bed in a crowded, stinking cell, with years stretching ahead of me, I wanted to die. I didn't show it. In prison you're either predator or victim. But whichever you are, all you think about is your ERD – earliest release date. You ask Marius what prison's like. He knows.'

Francesca was shocked. 'You met Marius in prison?'

Jack chuckled. 'My dear lady barrister, didn't they teach you not to prejudge? Marius was my prison visitor. I applied for a visitor because I hoped to influence the parole board. I didn't succeed. There was no parole for Jack Broderick. But I met Marius. He works for a voluntary group. He visits prisoners, every Monday afternoon. He loves to save. Look how he tried to save your father. Marius visited me every month for five years. He was never late, he never cancelled. You have to have been on the inside to understand how important that is. He told me all about the stadium. I knew every inch of the track, without ever having

92

seen it. He told me wonderful stories about his uncle who started Richmond Racing, the one who was killed in the war. Did you know they attended the first British greyhound meeting at Belle Vue, in Manchester, on the day it opened in July 1926. That's what gave them the idea. Within a week, they'd bought the land.'

Francesca shook her head. 'My mother kept me away from the dog-racing as much as she could.'

'Yes. Of course.' He smiled. 'Two years before I was released, Marius asked me to join him at the stadium. Of course I'd hoped he would, but most visitors cut contact once once a prisoner is out. From that day onwards, we talked of nothing else. He gave me a reason to look forward. And a chance to go straight when I came out. I owe that old man my life. Without him, I'd already be back doing crime. What else could I do? Get a job at thirty-six with a fourteen-year reference from Her Majesty's Prison?'

'Do you regret those years?' she asked.

'I can't allow myself to dwell on them. If I did, I'd be doing a never-ending sentence. The past would embitter the present, as it does with many victims of crime. Old Marius taught me that.' He smiled fondly. 'So I think about today and tomorrow. I think of you. Us. Of how I can help Marius. No one understands more about dog-racing than him, but he has no head for business. That's why he had to close. He let people run up huge debts and was too soft to make them pay. They've all paid him now.'

'You made them?'

'I asked them.'

She knew that she shouldn't persist, but the need to know the very worst of him drove her on. 'How did you kill the grass?' she asked.

'I'm not going to tell you. If you want to, you can find out. You're a barrister, you have contacts. But what happened is in the past. At least, it is for me. And if you and I have any future, it must be in the past for you, or each time you hold my hand you will think, this hand has killed.'

Francesca raised his hand to her lips and kissed his hard palm. 'I won't try to find out.'

They had reached Islington. Jack parked at the far end of her street. 'I love you,' he said, very softly, and for the first time. 'I want to go to sleep with you. I want to wake beside you. I don't just want half an hour in the grass.'

She shouted down the devils of her conscience. 'William's going away this weekend. I can stay tomorrow night.'

He kissed her. They didn't speak. Tomorrow hung between them, written in the purple grapiness of that summer evening.

From the window of their bedroom William watched Francesca walk down the street, her pace slowing as she drew near the house. She was dangling her shoulder bag from one finger, swinging it as if neither money nor possessions meant anything to her. She pushed back her hair, gently, as though caressing it. She smiled.

He'd come home, five hours earlier, to find the house empty but the car parked outside. He'd waited an hour, then phoned White Oast. Her mother hadn't heard from her. He'd opened her desk diary. It was blank. He'd flicked through her mail. It gave no clues. He'd glanced down her credit card statement. It was the usual mix of clothes, petrol and groceries. He was about to put it away, when two entries for petrol caught his eye. They were from a garage in Richmond, both during the week when she had come home glowing and defiant. Very precisely, he'd folded the statement back into its envelope.

Francesca was horrified to discover William was already at home. 'I'm in our room,' he called cheerfully over the banisters, setting her mind at rest. 'Come up, I have a nice surprise for you.' He handed her an envelope.

She opened it and her eyes widened.

'Yes,' he said. 'Two tickets for Heraklion. We're joining Simon and Mel tonight. You'd better pack quickly. We leave in two hours.'

'What . . . what about work?'

'You're on holiday. You told me so. I spoke to Nailsworth. You had no appointments in your chambers diary. Aren't you pleased, darling? It's what you wanted.'

'I must phone Mother.' Francesca hurried down to the kitchen to use the telephone.

'The line's out of order,' he called after her. 'But don't worry, I spoke to your mother from the Riddle-Longmans'.'

Francesca went out into the garden and stood looking up into the night. In that bittersweet moment she knew that Jack was thinking of her, and of tomorrow.

Twelve

Simon and Melanie were waiting for them in the stuffy, poorly lit air terminal. They looked suntanned, relaxed and happy. Francesca was desperate. She still hadn't managed to telephone Jack.

At Gatwick airport she'd escaped from William, ostensibly to buy duty-free scent, only to see their flight board before she was even halfway up the telephone queue. On the aeroplane he'd calmly read Kazantzakis's *Zorba*, whilst she clenched and unclenched her fists underneath the plastic table, wondering if she dared to ask a stewardess to call Jack for her. She didn't. She wanted to speak to him herself.

As if to mock her, the villa could not have been more wildly romantic. Part-way up the cliff and built into the rock above a secluded beach, it was designed for lovers. The lap of waves caressed its feet. Jasmine and bougainvillaea cascaded down its walls. Cicadas played into the balmy night.

Melanie had prepared a light snack of cheeses, olives and wine. They ate sitting out on the terrace, enveloped by the night. Melanie and Simon swung together on a hammock, William stretched out on a sunlounger. Francesca perched on the wall looking across the bay at the lights and music of the nearest village. The villa had one telephone. It was in the hall, exposed on all sides. She didn't dare use it.

In the morning, whilst the others were in the kitchen preparing breakfast, she slipped down the narrow rocky path towards the village.

'Darling, where are you going?' William called to her from the terrace.

'To the shops. I need sun lotion, a sun hat, sandals. You didn't give me time to buy anything.'

'I'll take you in the car.'

'I want to walk.' She hurried on down the track.

William turned to Melanie who was making coffee. 'I'm worried

95

about Frankie. I don't want her to get too tired. It isn't good for her, at the moment.'

Melanie lowered the coffee pot. 'You don't mean . . . ?'

'You're not to say anything. Promise! She'd be furious with me. But this time we're hoping she is pregnant. We've had a few problems.' He paused and studied Melanie's smiling, anxious face. 'Didn't she tell you?'

'Not a word.'

'I thought women always told each other everything.'

'Not Frankie.' Melanie grabbed the car keys. 'I'll pick her up in the car. We need bread and milk, that'll be my excuse. And don't worry, I'll say nothing.'

The village was a jumble of narrow whitewashed alleys running between pretty white houses, all with profusions of red geraniums or purple bougainvillaea. The shops were in the main square. The only public telephone was near the entrance of the only bar.

Francesca had just reached the bar when Melanie drove up. She spun round. 'Why are you following me?'

'I'm not. We need bread.'

In the past weeks Francesca had longed to confide in Melanie, but now things with Jack had gone too far. She stood behind her in the bread queue, silent and frowning. As Mel reached the counter, Frankie said, 'I'll be back in a second.'

Halfway across the square, she remembered she had no Greek money. She dashed across to the only bank. It had just opened. There was a queue twenty deep waiting be to served by one man with an old-fashioned, hand-operated adding machine.

She found Melanie in the greengrocer. 'I need some Greek money.'

'Hang on. I'll only be a few minutes.'

'I want to phone Mother.'

'Do it from the villa.'

'I must phone her now!'

'All right! Calm down, you'll make yourself ill. Here's the equivalent of twenty quid.'

Frankie hurried to the bar. Inside, it was smoky and dark and full of old men playing backgammon. 'I want to telephone England,' she told the barman, holding out her drachmas.

He gave her a toothless grin. 'Telephone not working. Come tomorrow.'

Fate was working against her. Frankie returned to the car and sat in the front seat, biting her thumbnail as she waited for Melanie.

The day was glorious. At least, it was for everyone but Francesca. They lay on the beach below the villa, soaking up the sun, chatting idly over ice-cold retsina. William read *Zorba*. Simon listened to Mahler through his Walkman. Mel dozed. Francesca calculated the time in England.

She waited until they were all settled before slipping back, up the steps, to the villa. As she dialled Jack's number, she wondered if she dared whisper, 'I love you.'

There was a scrape on the terrace. She turned. William was walking towards her. Guiltily, she replaced the receiver. 'I wanted to phone Mother, but there's no answer.'

'I spoke to her yesterday. I told you so.'

'I must have forgotten.' She picked up a guide to Crete and walked back down to the beach.

Francesca was being difficult. The others exchanged glances behind her back but she couldn't stop herself. She resented them for taking her away from Jack, and blamed herself for not having had the courage to stay in England.

It was three days before she could reach a telephone. They'd stopped at a garage on the road to the Minoan palace at Knossos. William was studying the guidebook. Simon was filling the car with petrol. Melanie had gone to the loo. Pretending to follow her, Frankie slipped inside the garage office. An old woman sat behind the desk, knitting. Frankie pointed at the telephone. The woman shook her head. Frankie clasped her hands together, pleading. It made no difference. She produced all her drachmas. The crone looked away. Through the window Frankie could see Melanie walking back to the car. She grabbed a pen, drew a heart on a scrap of paper and waved it under the old woman's nose. The wrinkled face broke into a smile. Beaming, the old woman scooped up the money, picked up the phone, tapped a number and held the receiver towards Frankie. 'England,' she said.

By now, William, Simon and Melanie were all in the car, waiting in the blazing heat. With sweat pouring down her face,

Frankie gave Jack's number to the exchange. It seemed to take a decade of clicks before she heard the familiar British double ringing tone, and a further age before Jack answered.

'I'm in Greece,' she hissed down the line. 'I'm sorry. I tried to phone you, but . . .'

'I don't want your excuses.'

'You don't understand.'

'I understand all too well. You had a choice to make and you made it.' There was a click, and the line went dead.

She turned to find William staring at her through the dusty window of the garage office. 'What the hell are you doing?' he shouted.

'Phoning Mother.' She thanked the old lady, and walked out of the office, straight past William to the car. She didn't know if he believed her. At that moment, she didn't care.

But William was particularly solicitous towards Francesca that day. He reached for her hand to help her along the stony path as they explored the ruined site where the minotaur, according to legend, once lived. When they stopped for lunch, he ordered the white wine she liked, not the retsina she found too bitter. That night, in an act of desperation, Francesca let William make love to her. By closing her eyes, she could almost imagine he was Jack. In the morning he brought her tea in bed, and didn't click his tongue when she spilt it in the saucer.

For the rest of that week in Crete, Jack and the stadium seemed remote, as if they were a dream. But back in London, they became reality. Jack drew Frankie like a magnet. She returned to the stadium.

Even during her short absence, work had progressed. The roof was repaired. The broken terrace steps had been replaced. She hurried through the grandstand to the Paddock House. The office door was ajar, and she pushed it open. Inside, a red-haired woman in a purple kaftan was playing patience on Jack's desk.

She was carelessly handsome, with long, uncombed hennaed hair and sleepy, sensuous eyes. Probably in her late forties, though it was hard to tell; her manner was young and sappy, but her face was lined. The remnants of a late breakfast were pushed to one side. 'Can I help you?' she asked, yawning and stretching out a bare foot as if to emphasise that she'd stayed the night.

'No, thank you.' Francesca backed away. 'I've made a mistake.'

Jack drove his beloved black Bentley slowly up the M23 towards London. He'd had too much to drink. He didn't usually drink and drive, but tonight he didn't care.

On the seat beside him lolled a tousled redhead, her pink leather skirt rolled halfway up her thighs, her legs sprawled open and inviting. She was drunk. Her eyes were half closed. Jack could see the white strip of dried glue along her eyelids where her false eyelashes had come unstuck. A cigarette drooped from her sulky mouth. It was smeared with vermilion lipstick.

Jack had picked her up at the Brighton track. Or rather, she'd picked him up, pushing in next to him at the bar, her pink tongue caressing the points of her pearly white teeth as she gave him a good view of the valley between her full breasts. Jack had offered her a drink. She'd accepted. Her name was Rita.

'You're a good-looking bloke,' she said, scuffling in her cheap bag for a cigarette lighter. 'How come you don't have a girlfriend?'

'I don't want one.'

'OK! Don't bite my head off. I'm only making conversation.' She closed her eyes. Jack drove on in silence.

Marius was at the kitchen table. He looked up, smiling, when Jack walked in. Then his face froze.

'This is Rita,' said Jack. 'Come on, Rita, say hello to Marius.'

The girl tottered forward, filling the room with her cheap scent and her stale glamour.

'Frankie was here,' said Marius, not looking at Rita.

'I don't want to know.'

'I'm glad she didn't wait.'

'Oh, so suddenly you approve of her.'

'It was the fact she was married I didn't like.'

'And that Dominique is her mother?' Jack picked up a bottle of champagne and two glasses. 'Come on, Rita. Upstairs! We don't want to waste time talking to an old man who thinks he owns me. No one owns me.' He crashed the bottle on to the table. 'Not you. Not Marius. Not . . .' He couldn't bring himself to say Frankie's name.

Makepeace Buildings hadn't changed. Chambers hadn't changed.

99

Francesca had. She was a different person from the one she had been at the beginning of the summer. For a brief time, she'd loved and been loved. She'd tasted freedom and laughter. She'd been herself, and never felt that there was some other better self Jack would prefer. She'd risked, though not risked quite enough – and lost.

Summer was over. The days were crisp and autumnal. The leaves on the trees which flanked the gravel path near the Embankment were turning to gold. In the mornings the dew hung like diamonds on the grass of the Inner Temple Gardens. In the evenings, when Francesca left chambers, the lamplight glistened on the damp air.

Francesca was subdued and sad. Jack didn't contact her and she didn't return to the stadium. Yet, even weeks later, when the telephone rang she still hoped it would be him. William hadn't tried to make love to her since the night of their visit to Knossos. In fact, he'd barely spoken to her. They existed, she in her loveless prison, he her involuntary gaoler. At times she wished she'd never met Jack Broderick.

She didn't confide in Melanie. There seemed no point now. They still met for lunch. Melanie did most of the talking.

'Frankie, you haven't uttered a word today,' she complained one lunchtime. 'William told me you're having . . . problems. I promised him I wouldn't say anything, but I can't keep silent. You look so unhappy.'

Francesca stared at her incredulously. 'He told you?'

'Don't be angry. We only want to help. I'm sure you'll have a baby soon.'

'Mel, I'm not pregnant and I'm not likely to be.' Francesca stood up. 'I'm sorry, I have to go.' She hurried across the hall and pushed her way through the crowd near the door. Melanie tried not to feel hurt. She wondered if Frankie had had a miscarriage or had simply failed to conceive.

It was Monday before Francesca telephoned her to apologise. 'I owe you an explanation,' she said. 'How about an after-work drink?'

'I'd love to meet.' Melanie's voice bubbled with pleasure.

Francesca was seated as far as possible from everyone else when Melanie arrived at the wine bar. 'I need to talk to you,' she said.

100

'So do I.' Melanie couldn't keep her secret any longer. With a flourish she produced her left hand. On her third finger was a sapphire engagement ring. 'Simon and I are getting married.'

'That's wonderful news!' Francesca jumped up and hugged her. 'Tell me all about it.'

'He asked me on Friday.' Melanie giggled. 'I said yes, even before he'd finished speaking. We bought the ring on Saturday. Rushed down to see Mother on Sunday. Simon insisted on asking her formally! And we'll be married at Christmas. I know it's soon, but what's the point in waiting. We've decided on the Temple Church, just like you and William. Simon's father was Jewish but his mother was Church of England. I'm Welsh Baptist, but it's the Temple which has brought us together.' She touched the ring and turned pink with pleasure. 'We're going to buy a house. Something big, like yours, which we can have decorated to our own taste. But first, we're having an engagement party. Will you help me organise it? You're so good at giving large parties.' She paused. 'What were you going to tell me, Frankie?'

'It's not important.' Francesca forced a smile. How could she spoil Melanie's special day.

Helping Melanie to transform Simon's austere bachelor flat in the Barbican into a romantic bower for the party was fun. They called in a caterer, selected the menu, ordered the flowers, reorganised the lighting and sampled the champagne. At Harvey Nichols they bought new dresses. Melanie's was romantic blue and floaty, Frankie's short, sharp and crimson.

On the evening of the party, she came downstairs in her red dress, her hair folded into a loose French roll from which a long silky strand hung loose in front of each ear. William stared at her in disbelief. 'You're not wearing that,' he spluttered.

'William, this is a very expensive dress.'

'I don't care. It looks cheap. Go and change.'

'No!' She draped her long black cloak about her shoulders and walked out of the house.

Simon was welcoming guests at the door of his flat. He kissed Frankie on both cheeks. 'Being with you two on holiday made me realise what I was missing,' he said, as he ushered them inside.

'Oh, I didn't marry until I was thirty-six.' William put an arm around Francesca's shoulders. 'Of course Frankie was barely out of school. She'd never been anywhere till she met me. Isn't that right, darling?'

'William was my first proper date.' She smiled at Simon. 'He took me to the opera, then out to dinner. I was so nervous he had to choose from the menu for me.'

She sensed that William was pleased with her response. They separated, and talked to different people. All her colleagues from chambers were present. Huge, jowly Geoffrey Culmstock with tiny, exquisite, brittle Virginia, whom Francesca secretly disliked. Sanjiv and Deepa. Dapper Desmond with his doggy wife. Rupert with yet another girlfriend. Hugo and Thomas on their own. James with a pretty, pink-cheeked kindergarten teacher from Suffolk. They drank toasts to Simon and Melanie. For the first time since Jack, Francesca felt happy. She'd been right to stay with William. These people were her friends, this was her life. Jack was a fantasy.

They left the party late. When they reached home, she asked William, 'Do you want a nightcap?'

'No.' He locked the front door.

She started up the stairs, slowly, her hand trailing on the wooden banister, her cloak draped over her shoulder. She had gone only four steps when William said, very quietly, 'Burn that dress and don't you ever defy me again.'

She laughed. 'Don't be silly!'

'I said burn it! You're my wife. I will not be made a fool of.'

'William, I haven't made a fool of you. I wore a dress which everyone said was beautiful.' She walked on, up the stairs. He followed.

'Did you think you'd get away with it?' he hissed, as they reached the landing. 'That I wouldn't realise?'

'I don't know what you're talking about.'

'Jack Broderick!'

She turned, astonished. He seized her wrist. 'It took me time to realise who it was,' he said, 'but I put the picture together, piece by piece. The petrol bought at Richmond on your credit card statement. The phone call from the garage on the way to Knossos. Yes, I went back there one afternoon when you were asleep. The old woman kept your secret but her grandson had no such scruples. He had a friend at the telephone exchange, and for the price of a new tyre for his motorbike, he obtained the number you'd called.'

He was shouting. Francesca was afraid. She tried to pull away but he tightened his grip. 'My final proof was Clarissa Riddle-Longman,' he went on. 'She mentioned that a dark man with a Land Rover and two greyhounds in the back had come to this house. She thought we'd bought a dog. You know how dog-mad she is. But it wasn't that, was it? You were entertaining your criminal lover. In my home!' Without warning, William punched Francesca in the stomach, his fist catching the bottom of her ribs, the force knocking all the breath from her, sending her reeling to the floor. 'A murderer. A criminal. My wife! Sneaking out! Risking my career!' He shouted at her as she lay on the ground, retching and gasping for air. 'Did you think I was stupid? When I came home, you weren't here. If I rang, you were out. You're so useless you can't even manage to deceive me.'

'But I can leave you.' She pulled herself upright. 'You've bullied me for years, whilst I've tried to please you. If our marriage has gone wrong, it's your fault as much as mine. If I've turned to another man, it's because you neglected me.'

'Get out of my house!'

'I'm going.' She started down the stairs.

'To live with your murderer?'

'That was over before it began. If you're so clever you should know.' She picked up her cape, slung it over her shoulders, and walked out into the winter night.

Thirteen

Francesca woke with the sun in her face. She was lying on the floor of her office, wrapped in her black cloak. Her face was sore, her ribs ached. For a moment she couldn't think what she was doing there. Then she remembered.

After leaving the house, she'd driven around for hours, through the night streets of North London, through the City, around St Paul's. On any other occasion, she'd have phoned Melanie. But not on the night of her engagement party. So Francesca had come here, to chambers, the only place available to her.

She rose unsteadily and opened the door.

Sanjiv was helping himself to coffee. He stared at her in astonishment. 'Frankie! What are you doing here?'

'I had a row with William.' She slumped on to a chair. 'I walked out, in the middle of the night.' She opened her cloak to show him her strapless dress. 'Remember? I was wearing it at Melanie's.' Even to Sanjiv, whom she'd known for ten years, she couldn't bring herself to confess that William had hit her.

'Everyone argues. It'll blow over.' He handed her his mug of coffee, adding, 'Have this. Then phone him. He must be worried.'

She drank his coffee gratefully, and shook the remaining pins from her hair. 'It isn't as simple as that, Sanjiv. William and I haven't been . . . er . . . getting on well lately.'

'Oh, you'll make it up. You're the Inn's golden couple.'

She realised that he didn't want to hear of problems in her marriage, not because he was unsympathetic but because he admired William. Everyone did. 'Perhaps we need time apart,' she said, without believing that could help.

Sanjiv nodded. He thought she meant a break of a few hours. 'Then come home to lunch with me and my family. Food will make you feel better. You can rest. Life won't seem so bad then.'

She protested that she didn't want to intrude, but he was insistent. So she went with him, following in her own car, glad of somewhere to go, embarrassed at interrupting his Sunday, embarrassed also that she and William had never invited him to their dinner parties, only to drinks parties when they invited everyone in chambers.

He lived with his mother, sister and new wife, Deepa, in North Finchley. Frankie had never been inside an Indian household before. In spite of her state of mind she found it fascinating, full of bright colours, silky carpets, and pictures of the god Shiva. She had no idea how Sanjiv explained her sudden arrival and her evening dress to his family, but they clucked about her, washing her face and hands and lending her a shawl to cover her bare shoulders.

It was late afternoon before they began to eat. The curry was so hot that it brought tears to Frankie's eyes. They laughed at her, in their gentle way. She planned to leave straight afterwards but Sanjiv's mother insisted she rest, and she fell asleep on the sofa. It was dark when she woke. Someone had tucked a rug around her. She fell asleep again and didn't wake until Deepa shook her arm saying, 'Frankie, it's seven o'clock. Sanjiv has left for chambers. He thinks you're due in court this morning.'

'He's right.' Frankie stood up slowly. She was still sore and stiff. 'I don't know how to thank you.' She kissed Deepa on both cheeks. 'You've all been so kind.'

She drove home at top speed. Lindsey Dault's hearing was that morning, and she needed to change into her working suit. It crossed her mind that William might have altered the locks, but luckily he hadn't. She took a quick shower, then stood in front of the mirror, twisting to examine her bruised ribs. An ugly purple mark stretched right round to her back.

Taking advantage of William's absence, Frankie switched her essential clothing from the main bedroom to the spare room cupboard. As she finished, she heard Mrs MacDougall open the front door and shouted, 'Good morning!' She wrote William a note – *I'll be keeping my things in the spare room until I've found somewhere to live* – and placed it in an envelope, so Mrs MacDougall couldn't read it.

'Any dinner parties this week, Mrs Eastgate?' Mrs MacDougall asked her.

'Definitely not!'

On Francesca's instructions, Lindsay was wearing a respectable blue coat and little make-up, and her limp hair was held in a neat bow. She looked like a scared rabbit with its ears tied behind its head.

Her case wasn't heard until the late morning. Francesca asked for an adjournment, for the social worker's updated report. The judge agreed.

'Another fuckin' three months!' Lindsay moaned as they walked out of the court building. 'I wish you'd let them get on with it.'

'We need the social worker's update. It's your best hope of staying out of prison.'

'I want to get on wi' my life.' Lindsay stared listlessly at the office workers hurrying down the street to sandwich bars or the pub. The scene meant nothing to her. She'd never worked. She'd never been inside an office, except to see David or her social worker.

They walked along the pavement, Francesca and Lindsay side by side, with David following. 'Why don't you learn to type?' Francesca suggested. 'Now the kids are at school in the mornings, you could go to adult education classes. If you got a job, even a part-time one, you'd be less dependent on other people.'

'I'm too stupid.'

'You're not.' Francesca suddenly, desperately wanted to help the girl. 'You're just as good as anyone else.'

Lindsay blushed. 'No one's ever said that to me.'

'It's true.'

'Who'd want me? I have a record, remember.' Lindsay scrabbled in her handbag for a cigarette and a lighter. 'I'm better trying to find meself a nice bloke. One who ain't in trouble all the time. Your 'usband treat you nicely?'

'Yes . . . yes, of course he does.'

Lindsay's face turned sly. 'You don't sound very sure.'

'All marriages have their ups and downs.'

'Yours ain't too happy, is it?' Lindsay took a step closer. 'And you 'ave the cheek to tell me to learn bleedin' typin'. You're no better than I am.'

'I never said I was.'

'But you're meant to be. That's the whole point.' Lindsay yanked the restricting bow from her hair and threw it in the gutter. Then she stormed off towards the underground station.

Too embarrassed to look at David, Francesca bent to pick up the bow, busying herself by smoothing its blue satin wings.

'You didn't ask to be her heroine.' He placed his hand under her arm. 'Come on! You need a drink.'

They went into a nearby pub. He settled her in a quiet corner, away from the crowd at the bar, and went to order a bottle of inexpensive wine and some sandwiches. Francesca felt ashamed at having once been so dismissive of him.

On his return, she said, 'Lindsay has every reason to feel disillusioned with me.'

David poured her a glass of wine. 'If it weren't for Marius Charlwood's recommendation, I'd never have asked you to take her on because I wouldn't have believed the smart Mrs Eastgate could understand the shades of guilt in crime.'

'Do you know Marius well?'

'My sister does. He helped her set up her antique shop. Actually, she's my stepsister. There are twenty years between us. You've met her. She has long red hair and dresses like a hippy.'

'You mean, the woman with no shoes?'

'That's Nicoletta.'

Francesca helped herself to more wine and asked, as casually as she could, 'Have she and Jack Broderick been together long?'

'You've got it wrong! Nicoletta's with Marius. He's been her saviour. When she met him, she was on hard drugs, her marriage was breaking up, and she was losing custody of Jolyon, her adopted son. Marius made her believe in a future.'

'As he did with Jack.' Francesca was overwhelmed with longing to see Jack. It came over her in waves as she listened to David talk of all Marius had done for Nicoletta. She wanted to run out of the pub, hail a taxi, and go straight to him. But fear of his rebuff stopped her.

It would have been sensible to move into the spare room but she couldn't bear to share a roof with William, who might think he could hit her again. And even if he didn't, she would live in fear of it. She returned to the house, packed an overnight bag, and drove round the streets of Camden until she found a hotel. It was small and anonymous. As she closed the door of her room and kicked off her shoes, she felt safe in her rented isolation. She lay on the bed, eating a takeaway and watching television. Outside, the traffic raced north to Hampstead. She wondered if William was worried about her. If anyone was worried about her. She felt as if she'd taken a step into limbo.

In the morning she went down into the unfamiliar street. She had an early conference, with a solicitor and his lay client, a Mrs Blackbird, a smart middle-aged woman who'd discovered that her recently deceased husband had a second family. A girl from Newcastle with two small children had filed a claim against his estate. In Mr Blackbird's papers there was no mention of this girl. But he had regularly withdrawn a thousand pounds in cash, every two months, from the Newcastle branch of his bank, money which the girl claimed he'd given to her. Money which Mrs Blackbird knew nothing about.

Her husband's estate consisted of a large house in Surrey, a London flat, and several businesses spread across the country. Mrs Blackbird had helped set these up. Inheritance from her parents had kept them afloat throughout the 1979–80 recession. She refused to believe her husband had deceived her. Francesca advised DNA fingerprinting to prove if the children were Mr Blackbird's. Mrs Blackbird agreed. She was convinced they weren't.

This story kept Francesca's mind off her own problems. At lunchtime she returned to Islington, read her mail, collected some clothes, left money for Mrs MacDougall, and fed Jaws and Big Ears. In the evening she went straight to the hotel.

William was sitting at her desk when she arrived in chambers next morning. It angered her to see him there, glancing through her diary. 'What are you playing at?' he demanded.

'You punched me. Or have you forgotten?'

'You're my wife. Do you expect me to condone your adultery?'

'William, it wouldn't have happened if you weren't so harsh. I loved you once. But you killed my feelings with your constant criticism.' She took a deep breath. 'If you wish to divorce me, that's your prerogative.'

'The Eastgates do not divorce!' He marched to the door, threw it open, then closed it again. 'I could never forget your infidelity, Francesca.' He spoke in a quiet, sad voice. 'But if I could trust it wouldn't happen again, I might be able to forgive you.'

'And hold it over me for the rest of my life?'

'I wouldn't, I promise. Please come back.'

'I don't know,' she said, gently. 'I can't think straight. Give me time.'

As he left the room, her telephone rang. It was Alexander's solicitor. 'Bad news,' he said. 'the boy's playschool teacher was killed in a boating accident.'

'What about the doctors' reports?'

'The psychologist says the boy's unlikely to develop beyond a mental age of ten. The paediatrician confirms brain damage but can't pinpoint the age at which it occurred. Tests at the time of birth show normal. But, of course, they didn't do a brain scan. There appeared no need.'

Francesca tried to concentrate but she was still reeling from William and his quiet, sad voice. The solicitor was babbling on about 'discovery of documents' – the time when each side in a civil action has to supply the other with a list of, and access to, all documents held.

Francesca interrupted him. 'Without more proof we'll lose the case – and the twenty-thousand-pound offer. Have you checked other operations on that day? I know you can't see third parties' medical records. You just need to know if there was a problem with the oxygen during a previous or subsequent operation. Any logged calls to the manufacturers of equipment? What about the theatre staff? Any reports from the anaesthetist or whoever checks the equipment? Any disagreements?' Suddenly she realised that she was shouting down the telephone. 'I'll let you know if I have further ideas,' she concluded.

For the remainder of that week Francesca thought about what William had said, but she didn't contact him. She was afraid of going back for the wrong reasons: loneliness and fear. No one in chambers was aware anything was wrong. Melanie was on holiday, househunting. They spoke on the telephone, but Francesca confided nothing of her problems. To Sanjiv, she merely said, 'Everything's all right now. Please thank Deepa and your mother for their kindness.'

But she wasn't used to living alone. As the days passed, she was aware of how dependent on William she'd been. At times she felt lonely. At others, merely alone. At the weekend she went to the cinema. She'd never been to the cinema alone before. She felt

109

brave and independent. Afterwards, she went to an Italian restaurant and ordered a pizza. Around her, couples held hands, friends chatted, and families with small children ate out early. It came home to Francesca that, save for Melanie, she had no close friends. She hadn't needed them. Or rather, William hadn't thought she'd needed them. And she had made the mistake of not questioning.

On Sunday she wandered around Camden Market, buying a thick yellow sweater with a big green dragon on the front, not because she needed it but because the man selling them was jolly and chatty. 'Haven't seen you around here before,' he said.

'I haven't been.'

'Just come to London?'

'Something like that.' She longed to stay and talk but other customers needed his attention.

His friendliness brought on a wave of loneliness. She went into a telephone box and called her mother. 'But darling,' her mother gasped on hearing the news, 'you shouldn't move out. He'll change the locks. You'll lose everything.'

'I don't care.' Francesca replaced the receiver.

Back in the hotel she lay on the bed, staring at the dull draped curtains. This was no longer an adventure into limbo. It was for real. Tears pricked her eyes. She tried to fight them, but she couldn't.

She struggled through another week, trying to concentrate on her work. Each morning she woke more exhausted than when she'd gone to sleep. Each mouthful of food made her want to throw up. It was a relief to escape from the hotel and go to chambers, her daytime family. Now her only family. She missed William, although she questioned her reasons. She missed being with someone, talking to someone, even if he ignored her.

Melanie was still househunting. She phoned to discuss the properties she'd seen. They talked of colour and decor. It seemed incredible to Frankie that she could hold this rational conversation whilst her life had so drastically changed.

In the alleyway leading from King's Bench Walk to the Temple Church, Francesca came face to face with Wiliam. When she saw him walking towards her, her heart began to thud. She didn't know if it was from fear or love or nerves.

110

'Have you thought about what I said?' he asked her stiffly.

'Yes. But I need more time, William. I don't want to make a mistake.' She gave him a tentative smile. 'For both of our sakes.'

He took a step towards her. She thought he was going to take her in his arms. But he grabbed her roughly by the shoulder, digging his fingers into her so hard that she could feel his fingernails through the material of her jacket. 'That's where we said our wedding vows,' he hissed, turning her to face the Temple Church. 'Where you promised to forsake all others. Or have you forgotten?'

'And you promised to love and cherish me, not to hit me and bully me!' She twisted away and hurried on. How could she have considered going back to him?

She went to White Oast at the weekend because her mother threatened to come to London if she didn't. 'I won't ask any questions,' her mother promised. 'But I wish you'd let me help you. I'm terrified you'll end up homeless, as I was when I left Ben.'

'Let's talk of something else. Please!' Frankie didn't add that her mother couldn't understand because she had given up passion for security. Love for fondness. Ben for Steven. Frankie was living her life the other way round.

After the comforts of White Oast it was even harder to return to the dreary hotel. She dragged herself through another week. Then another. She heard nothing from William, although she continued to return to the house to collect her mail and clothes and to feed Big Ears and Jaws. Melanie came back. She and Simon had found a house in West Kensington. She chatted excitedly about it. Francesca listened. She didn't confide. Once again, she was too far along.

Slowly, she began to feel better. She got used to eating out alone. She joined the National Film Theatre and saw every film on the programme. By the time David Jarrow telephoned to suggest lunch, she felt she was coming out of the worst. They met again in the pub near the court and talked of this and that. 'How's Jack?' she asked eventually, in her most casual voice.

'I saw him yesterday. He asked the same question about you.' He grinned. 'And in the same I-don't-care voice.'

*

111

Jack was with the architect, inspecting the repairs to the structural frame of the stadium, when Francesca burst through the upper grandstand door and out on to the top step of the terrace. She was wearing the same black suit with cropped jacket and tight skirt she'd worn on her first visit. It was smart and severe. With her hair in its plait, she looked every inch the barrister. 'I have to talk to you,' she shouted down at him.

'I'm busy.'

'I can't wait.'

He took no notice.

'Jack, this is hard for me.'

He said something to the architect, then turned and walked slowly towards her. 'What do you want, Frankie?'

She stood above him, clenching and unclenching her fists. Then she gave her helpless, vulnerable little shrug. 'I wanted to see you.'

He ran up the wide steps, seized her by the hand and ran her along the front of the grandstand to the Paddock House.

'Jack! Wait!' She laughed, her face flushed and her eyes shining in the frosty morning air.

He pulled her up the stairs to the attic, kicked open the door, then kicked it shut behind them. Just as suddenly, he released her. 'I don't want another man's woman,' he said. 'If it's stolen moments you've come to offer, I prefer to do without. I want to wake with you in the morning. I want to talk without counting minutes. Without thinking that if we talk, there'll be no time for love. I want to take you out at night, glittering on my arm, and be proud when other men envy me. I want to see you here, scruffy, hair unbrushed, that funny straight-eyebrowed frown on your face. I want to argue, and not be afraid you won't come back tomorrow. I want to run up these stairs and know you're here. I want to love. To fight. To laugh.'

'I left William a month ago.'

'Why didn't you come then?'

'I had to be sure.'

'That you weren't merely filling the gap?'

'And that I was strong enough to survive if you turned me away.'

He cupped her face in his hands. She reached up to him. His

112

mouth brushed hers, so gently that his lips barely touched her. But that touch was enough to send a current through her. Her lips parted. He kissed the soft corner of her mouth. She melted. He came down hard on her, kissing her deeply, drawing her up and out of herself.

He unplaited her hair and fluffed it about her face. He slipped the jacket from her shoulders and undid the buttons of her cream blouse. He slid the skirt from her hips. It fell to the floor, leaving her in just wisps of cream silk underwear and pale silk stockings clipped by tiny cream suspenders.

'What's that?' He held her at arm's length as he stared at the remnants of the yellowing bruise which still marked the lower part of her ribcage. 'Did that hypocrite, who prosecutes men for assault, batter his own wife?'

'He found out about you.'

'And you still didn't come to me?' He picked her up and laid her tenderly on his bed. Then he bent to kiss the bruise. 'I hate men who beat up women. It's the ultimate cowardice. Rough men do it. The poor. The uneducated. Those who can't express themselves in words. They do it from frustration. That is almost comprehensible. With a man like William Eastgate, it is not.'

She reached up to him and drew him down to her. 'It doesn't matter, Jack. We have each other. Don't think about William. He's in the past. He can't touch me now.'

He undressed quickly and lay down beside her, kissing her bare shoulders and running his mouth down the valley between her breasts. He drew his fingers up her leg, stroking the soft skin on the inside of her thighs. Moving upwards, slowly circling. She whispered in his ear. He caressed her, unhurried. His mouth travelled across the flat of her stomach. She reached for him. They loved in ways that with William she had found embarrassing, even disgusting. With Jack, it was different. She loved to sense his excitement. To know that she gave him great pleasure. He was around her. In her. With her. Above her. It was as if their skins were fused into one. Beyond the attic, nothing existed. He carried her with him, never hurrying, till she cried out, till neither could hold back.

Unlike William, Jack didn't roll away, but lay heavy along her. She relished his weight. 'More comfortable than the grass?' he asked, kissing the tip of her nose.

113

'Oh, I liked that spot on the Downs. I've thought of it often. One day I nearly went back, just to be there again.'

'I did go. But it wasn't the same. You weren't there.'

'Then why didn't you get in touch with me? You knew I wanted to see you. I came here.'

'And told Nicoletta you'd made a mistake.'

'I thought she was your new girlfriend.'

He smiled. 'Were you jealous? I hope you were.'

'Very! You haven't answered my question.'

He rolled on to his back, taking her with him in his arms so that a moment later she lay with her face nestled on his chest. 'When you didn't come on that Saturday, I ran through every emotion. Worry. Fear. Disbelief. Anger. More worry. I telephoned your house. I drove down your street. I saw your car. But not the bigger car – his! I saw your neighbour go into your house. The nosy lady. She had her own key. I deduced you must be away. I was so hurt and angry I wanted to kill you.'

'I had no idea William had bought the tickets till I arrived home. I tried to reach a telephone, in the house, the airport, in the village on our first morning. But I was never alone.'

'And you weren't prepared to tell him you wouldn't go?' said Jack quietly.

'I couldn't bring myself to make him look a fool.'

'Your barrister friends won't stand by you when they find out about us.'

'Mel will.' Francesca smiled. 'She's my closest friend. The others can think what they like. It's none of their business.'

He gripped her arms. 'I don't want to see you hurt.'

'I won't be. And if I am, I'll have you, so I won't feel the cuts so deep.'

They made love again. The morning passed. They drank champagne and ate scrambled eggs, made by Jack. They talked, then slept, and when they awoke it was early evening. Marius was with Nicoletta. Frankie was glad. On that first night she would have felt embarrassed by the old man's presence.

She woke at dawn and lay beside Jack, not moving, listening to his breathing and watching the strange shapes in the unfamiliar room. Eventually she slipped from the bed, took a shower, and dressed in the clothes she'd worn the day before. She had no others. 'I have to go,' she murmured in Jack's ear.

He opened one eye. 'What are you doing in that black suit? It reminds me of prison.'

'I have a conference at nine. A custody case.'

'What time will you be back?'

'As soon as possible.'

He grabbed her round the legs and pulled her down on to the bed.

She squealed, 'No! Jack! I'll be late.'

'No you won't.'

She lay sprawled across the bed, her tight black skirt halfway up her thighs, revealing her pale-cream silky suspenders. He didn't take off her jacket or her skirt or even her shoes. They made love, quickly, urgently, heightened by the lack of time.

William's car was outside Makepeace Buildings. Francesca left hers as far away as she could. Then she dashed across the car park and up the stairs to her office, thankful not to meet any of her colleagues.

The custody case would have been straightforward except that the mother was determined to deny the father any access. Her only reason was that he was living with another woman. Francesca thought of her own situation. She was glad she had no children. William would have fought her all the way.

Throughout the morning, Jack wafted in and out of her thoughts. Her skin still tingled from his touch. Her cheeks burned, her eyes felt polished. Her mouth was swollen from his kisses. When she moved she could smell him, very faintly on her clothes. He had a lovely smell. She could not get enough of it. She raised her arm to touch her face, so as to bring the sleeve of her jacket nearer.

At lunchtime she drove to the hotel in Camden, packed, paid her bill, and closed the door on the soulless room which had been her limbo. From there she raced across to Islington, collected some clothes, fed Jaws and Big Ears, and telephoned her mother. 'Thanks for being so understanding,' she said.

'Are you still in that horrid hotel?'

'No. I'm at the house,' Francesca answered truthfully, but she didn't elaborate.

On her desk was a note from Melanie: *Lunch tomorrow?*

She wrote back: *Sorry, I can't this week. Will explain everything soon. Love Frankie.*

That evening Jack took her to a small, intimate Italian restaurant off Richmond Hill. They sat for four hours, talking. 'I wish you could have met Aunt Phoebe,' he said. 'You'd have liked her. And she'd have liked you.'

'Did she look like your mother?'

'Oh, she wasn't really my aunt. She adopted me. Not officially. People weren't so fussy then. She wouldn't tell me where she met my mother. I often think it must have been in one of those City offices she cleaned. All I know is that my mother was seventeen, unmarried, and her name was Jackie.'

'And your father?'

'He was married and he didn't want to know.'

'Did you never try to find your mother?'

'What for?' He stirred sugar into his black coffee. 'She might be a drunk, and I'd be disgusted. Or respectable, and horrified at a son who'd done time. Phoebe was mother to me.'

He spoke vehemently. Francesca reached out a hand to him across the chequered tablecloth.

Living with Jack was so different to being with William. A night person, he liked to talk till three or four in the morning, either downstairs over a bottle of whisky with Marius and Nicoletta, or in bed with Frankie, cuddled up in a world of their own. During the week they had a pact. She had to go to sleep by midnight in order to be fresh for work. But at the weekend, she became a night person.

Jack hated routine. In that way, he was like her father. Sometimes they ate early. Sometimes late. Sometimes not at all. He liked to play cards with Marius and Eamonn for ten hours at a stretch. In spite of Marius's chiding, Frankie refused to join in. He liked to walk beside the river in the middle of the night, under the bridges and along the towpath below the gardens of the old Richmond Palace. 'For fourteen years I was ruled by walls and a bell,' he explained to Frankie.

Only in the morning did he follow a pattern. As soon as he got up, he threw open all the windows, regardless of the weather. When Francesca protested, he said, 'Each morning as I open the window, I remember I'm free,' and she knew there was no point in arguing.

Because of Big Ears and Jaws, Francesca returned to Islington every day. On one visit she found a note from William propped on the spare-room bed: *We must talk. Please meet me here, Friday, 5.00p.m*

When she told Jack, he wasn't pleased. 'We were going racing at Brighton,' he protested.

She slipped her arms around him. 'I'll be with you by six-thirty, I promise. But I have to see William. The sooner things are sorted out, the better.'

William was waiting for her in the study when she arrived. He sat perfectly still, his long, pale fingers gripping the edge of his desk. 'You look different,' he said, icily. 'But I suppose that's not surprising, since you've been associating with a murderer.'

She didn't sit down. 'If you're going to be offensive, I'll leave.'

'You're my wife!' He pounded the desk with his fist.

'I want a divorce.'

'After one tiny argument?'

'You hit me. You bullied me. I put up with it for years. I tried to make our marriage work. Don't you remember how often I asked you to talk to me? No, I believe you don't. You saw me as a possession, like your books. A robotic hostess to be praised only in front of others. I strived so hard to please you, William, but you were never satisfied.'

'You were unfaithful. You disgraced my name.'

'Our marriage didn't go wrong because of Jack. He's the result, not the reason.' She rose. 'I'll move my stuff out at the weekend.'

'To your murderer?'

Francesca didn't answer. She walked out of the study and up the stairs.

'Where are you going?' he shouted after her.

'To collect some clothes. They are mine!'

When she came down again, a few minutes later, changed into black velvet trousers and an emerald jacket, he called, very softly, 'Francesca!'

She went to the doorway.

He was sitting at the desk, head bowed, his fingers stroking the leatherbound copy of Alexander Pope which she'd given him that summer. 'Had you been unfaithful when you gave me this?' he asked.

She shook her head.

He studied her, pale anguish in his eyes. 'Have you any idea what this house is like without you?'

'I'm sorry. I didn't want us to end this way.'

'Don't go yet. Have a drink. You look so pretty. All glowing, just as you used to look when we first married. We were happy then, weren't we?'

She nodded.

'Please sit down. Just for a few minutes.'

She glanced at the clock. It was after half past five. 'All right. But I must use the phone.'

He pushed the telephone towards her but she didn't want to speak to Jack in front of him. She went into the kitchen, dialled the Paddock House, and asked Marius to tell Jack she'd be a little late.

William had his back to her when she returned. He was staring out at the garden. There was a glass of sherry on the desk. 'Can I ask you not to tell anyone about Broderick?' he said. 'It wouldn't help either of our careers. We all know that the Lord Chancellor's department keeps files on potential judges. The scandal of my wife and an ex-criminal could ruin my chances.'

'Of course I'll be discreet. I don't want to harm your career.'

'In fact,' he went on, 'could we keep up the pretence of our marriage until Christmas? I'm not asking you to sleep here. But we have accepted Simon and Melanie's wedding and the Culmstocks' Christmas party. People will gossip if we arrive separately.'

Francesca couldn't help feeling sorry for him. He was frozen by rules whereas she, thanks to Jack, was free. 'We'll go together,' she said. Jack might not like it but she couldn't bring herself to hurt William more than necessary.

Fourteen

By the time Francesca reached the stadium, Jack had already left for Brighton. She went up to the attic, lay on the bed, watched television, and waited. At midnight she went to sleep. In the morning he still hadn't come home.

Down in the kitchen a boy with the face of a cherub, but with tattoos up both arms, was painting the window frames. Two young, scruffy, very pretty girls were lounging on chairs nearby. They had the sullen wariness of truants. 'Has Jack come back?' Francesca asked the boy.

He grinned insolently. 'Don't worry, luv. He'll be home sometime. Today. Tomorrow. You know Jack.'

When he hadn't returned by midday, Francesca went to see Nicoletta in her small crowded antique shop. Like its owner, the contents were a mixture of beauty and neglect. There was a delicate floral Coalport breakfast service set out on a broken dresser, a Regency card table marred by a cigarette burn, and fresh flowers in a cracked Ming vase.

Francesca had intended to drop in and mention Jack, casually, but within a few minutes she was pacing the narrow aisle between a *Directoire* chair and a Victorian rocking horse, raging, 'I was half an hour late and he went without me, and he still hasn't come home!'

Nicoletta laughed and switched on the kettle. Then she stood in front of the mirror, smoothing long, straight strands of hennaed hair behind her ears. 'How was Jack to know that seeing your husband and your comfortable home wouldn't change your mind?' She spoke in a measured way, which reminded Frankie of the way her mother spoke.

'I'll never go back to William.'

'You can't blame Jack for thinking you might.' Nicoletta moved a pile of ancient sheet music from an old leather chair next to the Calor Gas fire. 'Sit down, Frankie, before you break something.'

'I found two girls at the house.' Francesca tried to sound unconcerned as she bent to admire a Georgian dressing table.

'The girls belong to Angel. He was Jack's gofer on the inside. He was released yesterday.'

'I don't like him.'

Nicoletta handed her a mug of tea. 'You won't like lots of Jack's friends. I don't like some of Marius's. I don't like dog-racing or noise or crowds. I don't drink alcohol. I'm a vegetarian. But I don't expect to change my man.'

'I don't want to change Jack.'

'All women want to reform a wolf. It's in our nature.'

Francesca hesitated, then smiled. 'You're right.'

'But men who've done time bring their own problems,' Nicoletta warned. 'They say you can take the man out of prison, but not prison out of the man.'

'So when he comes home, having stayed out all night, I have to be sweet and understanding and uncomplaining and . . .' She ground her teeth '. . . all those mealy-mouthed virtues that aren't really me.'

'Then be yourself.'

Francesca was about to argue. Then, suddenly, she gave her throaty laugh. 'I've spent years frustrated because I didn't dare be the real me, and just now I was about to fall into the same trap.'

An hour later she returned to the stadium but there was still no sign of Jack. She telephoned her mother, pretending to be at Islington. She left a message on Melanie's answering machine, saying she was sorry she'd been too busy to meet: she could have reached her at Simon's, but that would have entailed answering direct questions.

The Paddock House was freezing because Angel had left the kitchen windows open to dry the paint. She searched for a tin opener to open a can of soup. In a drawer she found some photographs. One was of her father, identical to the picture which Marius had given her. Another was of a gaunt old man. She turned it over. *Ben, Summer 1984.*

She found Marius examining the track. 'Why did you lie to me about my father?' she asked.

'Because I wanted you to see him at his best.'

'For my sake or his?'

'For both of you.' He frowned and scratched his goatee beard. 'Don't hurt my Jack, Frankie.'

'Hurt him! Marius, I love him.'

'That's what I wanted to hear.' Jack was standing on the terrace.

'Where the hell have you been?' she demanded.

'Let's go for a walk. I love the park in winter when there's no one around.'

'Don't change the subject, Jack!'

'I'll tell you when we're alone.'

Richmond Park was deserted except for the deer, who huddled in groups against the cold, their breath heavy on the damp air. The winter grass was dark and subdued, the sky thick and grey. The ancient oak trees were leafless, their bare branches raised in supplication to the invisible sun.

Jack took her hand very tightly. 'I was angry. I was afraid you weren't coming back, so I went to a hotel.'

'I was furious too.' She twisted her fingers through his. 'I went to see Nicoletta and raged at her.'

She told him about William as they walked through the long wet grass, saying, 'He's asked me to keep up the façade of our marriage till Christmas. If he'd shouted, I'd have refused. But he was humble.'

'So you agreed?'

'Don't be angry, Jack. It's only another month.'

'I'll never be angry when you tell me the truth. It's the half-lies I can't take.'

She reached up to kiss him. 'It's the half-lies which William preferred. I'm out of practice with telling the ungarnished truth.'

Francesca continued to return to Islington. She considered moving Big Ears and Jaws to the stadium, but reasons which she couldn't explain, even to herself, prevented her. Jack said she wanted an excuse to go to the house. She suspected he was right. She rarely saw William, and never there. At the most, she caught glimpses of him across the Makepeace car park. One morning they came face to face outside the library. She stopped to speak. He nodded and hurried on. One afternoon she found a note on her desk: *Sir Giles and Lady Henrietta have invited us to dinner. Have said you'll be away.*

She was underemployed at work, which concerned her, but at

the same time suited her. She had time to walk with Jack on the Downs, to make love with him in their attic, to hold him, kiss him, be with him.

Her cases were all in the preparatory period. She hadn't seen Lindsay Dault since that day outside the court, but her hearing was set for January. The social worker's report was good. She emphasised Lindsay's qualities as a mother.

Mrs Blackbird, the wronged wife, was becoming complicated. The DNA test proved Mr Blackbird to be the father of one child, not both. This reduced the Newcastle mother's claim. But another woman living in Florida had produced a letter in which Mr Blackbird promised to look after her for life. This had been sent to a handwriting expert for verification. Meanwhile, the probate solicitor had discovered Mr Blackbird owned several properties in Miami which his wife had never mentioned. The supposedly modest, home-loving Mr Blackbird was turning into a wealthy womaniser.

One lunchtime, as Francesca was leaving for Islington, Alexander's solicitor telephoned. 'Mrs Eastgate. Good news! We followed up your idea of checking on the theatre staff. A nurse, who has now left, has told us that the anaesthetist complained that the oxygen regulator was malfunctioning. An adult deprived of oxygen for three minutes will be brain damaged or brain dead. A child survives longer. This regulator was letting through some oxygen, but not enough. It was replaced early on, during the operation.'

'Why wasn't it in the report?'

'God only knows! But I gather from the nurse that the theatre staff are terrified to stupidity by the surgeon.'

'Will the nurse give evidence?'

'Yes. But other staff may be afraid to speak.'

'Have you told Alexander's father the news?'

'Yes. He particularly asked me to pass his thanks on to you.'

Francesca drove up to Islington in a glow of satisfaction. For the first time she believed she could win for Alexander. She was cleaning Jaws's tank when the doorbell rang. She cursed and ran to answer.

Melanie was standing on the doorstep, jigging nervously from one very high heel to the other. 'I want to know what I've done wrong,' she said. 'You haven't spoken to me for nearly a month. If I've offended you, say so.'

'You haven't.'

'But you have been avoiding me.'

'I'm sorry. You're right. Come in.' Francesca led the way to the kitchen where Jaws was angrily attacking the side of his jam jar. She returned him to his clean tank. 'Have a drink . . . coffee . . . tea.'

'Coffee. Thanks.' Melanie settled herself on one of the bar stools. 'Frankie, why are you cleaning the fish tank in the middle of the day? Why won't you and William have dinner with us any more? What's going on?'

Francesca flicked the kettle on. 'I meant to talk to you earlier. But things have moved so quickly. Now I can't talk, I've promised William.'

'So it's not to do with a baby?'

'Mel, there never was a baby. If I was pregnant, wouldn't I have shared my news with you, my closest friend?'

'I always thought so. But in Crete, William told me you'd had problems but hoped at last to be pregnant. He said you didn't want to talk about it. He even asked us not to tire you. Then, last month, he told Nailbag to reduce your caseload.'

'So that's why I've been given so few decent cases lately. God, that makes me mad. How dare William interfere?' Francesca thumped the coffee into the cafetiere and poured boiling water on to it.

'So what is wrong?' asked Melanie.

Francesca hesitated. She was torn between her promise to William and her anger at his interference. Anger won. 'Will you swear not to tell anyone, not even Simon?'

'Of course.'

'I'm in love. I can't tell you who he is, I shouldn't even tell you this much. I promised William I wouldn't.'

Melanie tapped six saccharins into her coffee without realising. 'You're having an affair!'

'If it were just an affair, things wouldn't be so complicated.' Frankie paced the kitchen, clenching and unclenching her fists. 'But I've met a wonderful man. I'm passionately in love with him. For the first time in years, I feel good about myself. I can be me,

123

not some other me I think he would prefer. I realise now just how suppressed I was by William. I should never have let myself be bullied. But I was in a trap. To get out, I had to admit my marriage had failed. My lover is the catalyst, not the cause, for me to free myself. Mel, I'm so happy. I feel sixteen! No, better than I did at sixteen. We talk, we love, we argue, we laugh. He's difficult – I seem to go for difficult men! But unlike William, he can admit he's wrong. If I'm upset, he senses and he comes back. Each time we grow stronger. I can't believe that this man, whom a year ago I had not even met, is now the pivot of my existence.'

Melanie was staring at her, open-mouthed, a teaspoon poised in her right hand. 'Are you going to leave William?'

'I can't tell you any more. I must keep part of my promise.'

'Does your mother know?'

'She knew before I did that I was unhappy. Or rather, before I'd admit it. She always said William was too old for me. Not just in years, in attitude. She knew I'd met another man though I'm not sure if she realises how far it's gone.'

'Is the man . . . another barrister?'

Francesca laughed. 'No. You'd be horrified. Everyone would. But I love him. He's everything I shouldn't want in a man – but I do!'

Melanie didn't intend to betray Francesca's confidence, but she was so shocked that she found herself blurting it all out to Simon. He was appalled. 'Poor William. No wonder he's been so abrupt lately.'

'If he'd been kinder to Frankie, I'm sure this wouldn't have happened.'

'Mel, he's the most devoted husband. You saw him in Crete, fussing over her.'

'That was in public. He's cold in private, she told me so, months ago. Simon, you must keep this to yourself. Promise! I've only told you because I'm upset. I hope it blows over.'

He put his arms around her. 'That is never going to happen to us.'

She snuggled against him. 'I won't let it.'

Afterwards Melanie wished she hadn't confided in Simon. From that day onwards, whenever she mentioned Frankie's name, he stiffened. She realised he would have condemned Frankie whoever she'd been married to. He condemned her twofold because it was William.

Francesca also felt guilty for having talked. To make up for it, she was particularly nice to William over the Culmstocks' party, offering to drive both ways. During the journey out to Windsor, she even enquired after his mother.

The Culmstocks' house glowed welcoming into the wintry night. 'Ah, there you are, you two. Happy Christmas.' Geoffrey put an arm around each of them and drew them into the warmth and the chatter.

Francesca accepted a glass of champagne, smiled and made small talk. She thanked Virginia Culmstock, spoke to Rupert who had yet another girlfriend, to Charlotte who was unusually pleasant, to Sanjiv and Deepa, asking after Sanjiv's mother, to Thomas who was drunk, and to Hugo and James who made her laugh with the latest tale of Old Nailbag's grumpiness. The party was exactly the same as the previous year, and the one before that, even down to the decorations and the conversation. It occurred to Francesca, as she bent, smiling, to Geoffrey's elderly mother, that she was saying the same things to the same people. She wondered what they would say next year, when they knew abut Jack.

On the far side of the room, Simon and Melanie were standing by the Christmas tree. Francesca smiled. Melanie waved, but Simon stared straight through her.

Francesca had to wait until after dinner before she could corner Melanie alone. 'Blabbermouth!' she hissed.

Melanie flushed. 'I'm sorry, Frankie. But I was so worried. Simon's very discreet. Surely you used to confide in William!'

'Not your secrets!'

They were interrupted by William. 'We have to leave,' he told Francesca abruptly. 'I've said goodbye. Your coat's in the hall.'

She hardly had time to thank Virginia and Geoffrey before he hustled her out of the party and into the car. He was silent until they were well away from the house, then he said, 'You told Melanie about Broderick. Don't deny it! Simon was looking at me with pity. Pity! For me!'

'I didn't tell her Jack's name.'

'You promised to say nothing at all.'

'I know. I'm sorry.' She felt guilty. 'But I was angry. Mel told me you'd instructed Nailbag to scale down my work.'

'Oh, so it's my fault. I'm ruining your career. But you were nothing when I met you. Just a tongue-tied eighteen-year-old who was too shy to speak.'

'Which is how you preferred me!' She put her foot down flat and roared along the fast lane of the M4.

'Will you take up murder or robbery to earn your living?' he shouted at her above the noise of the engine.

'I'm not giving up the law.'

'Your chambers won't want Jack Broderick's mistress.'

'They won't know about Jack till they've had a chance to see he makes no difference to my input.'

He put his hand on her thigh and pinched her hard. 'I should have hit you more often. It's what you deserve. But I expect you secretly enjoy it. Women like you do.'

'Take your hand off me!' she shouted.

He pinched her even harder. She took a swipe at him but he pulled back. She hit out again. This time her hand slipped on the steering wheel and the car careered into the centre lane, just missing a lorry.

'Watch out!' he screamed, white with fear.

'Then stop hurting me.' She kept on going, right across the inside lane and up the slipway to the Heston service station. She stopped in front of the restaurant. 'Get out!' she said.

He didn't move.

She raised the hem of her dress to reveal the angry mark on her thigh. 'Do you want me to call the police and tell them you assaulted me?'

'You wouldn't dare.'

'Try me!'

He hesitated, then undid his safety belt and opened the car door. 'You'll regret this, Francesca. I shall make sure of that.'

She drove off quickly. Her last view of William was as he walked towards the pay phones to summon a taxi.

She was still shaking with emotion when she reached the stadium, and Jack. He took her in his arms and made love to her gently, tenderly, sensing that the evening had made her very vulnerable. He reassured her. He held her tight, caressing

126

her, saying, 'I love you. We have each other. No one can hurt us.'

She stayed away from chambers and worked in the attic, whilst Jack worked downstairs in the old card room. He was both quick and meticulous, making long lists of everything which needed to be done at the stadium, graded according to urgency. The project absorbed him. No job was too much trouble if it meant getting the stadium right. In this way he was completely different from her father, who'd never done a day's work in his life. Each afternoon Frankie accompanied Jack on his tour of the stadium. Muffled against the cold in one of his oversize sweaters, she listened as he talked to the architect, the builder, the carpenters, the electricians. She was impressed by his ability to see both the overall picture and the detail. He was enthusiastic. It was contagious; the workmen came early, stayed late. He paid well. He was fair. Frankie saw how they respected him. He was a big man in every sense of the word, and she loved him for it.

Two days after the Culmstocks' party, Melanie and Simon moved into their new home, a large, dilapidated Victorian house in West Kensington. There was no central heating and little hot water, the kitchen was just usable and only two of the five bedrooms were habitable, but Melanie was thrilled with it.

When Francesca telephoned her from the stadium, Melanie said, 'I was afraid you might never speak to me again. You were right to be cross.'

'I was at fault. I shouldn't have told you in the first place.' Francesca paused. 'How's the new house? Are you going to invite me over?'

'Come today! Now! Mother's here, scrubbing the place from top to bottom. She's convinced the last owner had AIDS. As if we could catch it from the house, even if he had.'

Francesca arrived to find the place reeking of disinfectant. It hit her as she stepped inside the front door.

'Come up before you're asphyxiated!' Melanie shouted from the landing. 'I have to try on my wedding dress. I think it bags. I've lost so much weight, pure nerves!' She lowered her voice. 'Mother's driving me mad. I told her the reception's in Hall and the food's being done by caterers, but she insists on making plates of sandwiches.'

127

The dress was of ivory silk, with a scooped neckline, long, tight-fitted sleeves and a wide, billowing, luxuriant skirt. It made Melanie look feminine and fragile and very pretty.

Francesca watched her pirouette in front of the mirror. 'It's beautiful. Perfect. Tighter it would look vulgar.'

'Will you lend me my "something borrowed"?'

'Am I the right person?'

Melanie stopped still. 'Oh, Frankie, I wish you'd give William another chance. He does love you, even if he's no good at saying so.'

'He's an emotional icicle. His mother's partly to blame. She's the least affectionate of women. But I put up with his reserve whilst I loved him, because his mother isn't his fault any more than my father was mine. Now I don't love him. He killed my love with his bullying and criticism.' Frankie paused before adding, 'He beat me up after your party.'

Melanie was so shocked she could only splutter, 'You're joking!'

'Oh, not in the face. Then everyone would have commented. He punched me in the stomach, where no one could see.'

'Frankie, you should have told me earlier. That's terrible. William Eastgate a wife-beater! He's tipped to become a judge.'

'It's wrong, isn't it?'

'And you still can't tell me who the other man is?'

'I mustn't. I feel bad enough about last time.'

Melanie slipped out of her wedding gown and hung it carefully on a silken padded hanger. Then she wrapped herself in a pink fluffy dressing gown, tying it tightly against the chill of the poorly heated house. 'Frankie,' she said in a worried voice, 'William's already told Simon that your marriage is under strain. He's also told Rupert and Sanjiv. Even Charlotte knows. Oh, not that you have another man, but that you keep getting into debt. He told Simon you've lost thousands by gambling and that he'd had to pay your debts.'

'I never gamble and William knows it. I saw what it did to my father.'

'I told Simon it wasn't true, but you often leave chambers at lunchtime.'

'I work from home – my other home.'

Melanie anxiously twisted her dressing-gown cord in and out of her fingers. 'I'm only telling you this, Frankie, because people in chambers are becoming concerned.'

'I should have realised William would try to destroy my career. First he influences chambers! Next he'll want me out of the Inn. Out of the law. You want to know who my lover is?' Francesca clenched her fists. 'His name's Jack Broderick.'

Melanie's face changed from expectation to utter disbelief. 'Not the gold bullion robber? The one who reported you? But he's a thief and a murderer. Frankie, you have to give him up. He'll ruin you.'

'I love him. When you meet him, you'll understand why.'

'I don't want to meet Jack Broderick. He nobbled a juror and killed a witness.'

'An informer. In prison. But he's changed, Mel. He's reformed.'

'For God's sake, Frankie! He still killed a man.'

Francesca picked up her bag and walked towards the door. 'I'm leaving William at Christmas,' she said. 'I'm going to live with Jack.'

As she opened the door, Melanie jumped in front of her. 'Are you going to throw everything away for a criminal? Not just William. Your friends, me. The law, chambers, your colleagues, your career. Frankie, don't do it!'

'I'm not giving up the law. Especially when I've broken into an area which really interests me. I told you about the brain-damaged boy.'

'But you can't practise without a chambers, and the others will vote you out.'

'You won't vote against me?'

'Of course I won't. We're friends, whatever happens.' Melanie hesitated. 'You will still come to my wedding, won't you? Even though I can't invite Jack Broderick?'

Francesca hugged her. 'I wouldn't stay away for any man.'

Fifteen

Francesca stood in front of the ornate mirror in the drawing room at Islington, adjusting her black pillbox hat. It had a small spidery veil flecked with scarlet, which matched her smart tailored suit bought especially for Melanie's wedding. She picked up her lip brush, dipped it in the end of her lipstick, and began to paint her lips scarlet. Once, she wouldn't have dared to wear red lipstick.

The telephone rang. Upstairs William moved to answer it. A moment later he shouted, 'Francesca! It's for you.' It was the first time he'd spoken to her since she'd arrived that morning.

She put down her lip brush and reached for the receiver.

'I know I shouldn't ring you at 'ome but I 'ad to. I tried David Jarrow's office but there's no answer.'

It took Francesca a moment to recognise Lindsay Dault's voice. 'How did you find my number?' she asked. 'We're ex-directory.'

'I took a notepad from David's office, for my kids to draw on. Your number was on the top.'

Frankie felt like screaming, 'Lindsay, you idiot! That's how you get into trouble, taking things which aren't yours,' but instead she asked, 'Well? What's the problem?'

'Derek's taken the kids. He came whilst I was out. I'd only gone to the pub, to buy cigarettes. I was away five minutes. Maybe ten. He must 'ave been watching the place.' Lindsay began to cry in big, dry, hollow sobs. 'He told my neighbour he'd got a job in Australia and that he'd give the kids a better 'ome than I ever could. He said if I tried to get 'em back, he'd tell the court I'd left 'em alone at night.'

With one hand Francesca removed her hat, while with the other she reached for a pen. 'When did this happen?'

'Last night, before the pub closed.'

Francesca glanced at her watch. 'It's nearly ten. We'll have to act quickly. They must be made wards of court.'

'No!'

130

'It's the only way to prevent Derek taking them out of the country.'

'The judge'll say it's my fault for leaving them alone.' Lindsay's voice wavered. 'I know you think I'm not much good, but I 'ave tried.'

'I know you have,' said Frankie, more gently. 'Wait at home. I'll find David or your social worker.'

'Will you come too, Mrs Eastgate? You're so capable.' Lindsay's voice was barely audible. 'I'm sorry I was rude to you the other day.'

Francesca thought of Melanie's wedding. It was still five hours away. 'I'll come,' she said.

Through Nicoletta, she tracked down David Jarrow. He was asleep, but soon woke as she explained the situation. 'I'll go myself,' he said. There was a rustle as he pushed aside his duvet. 'I would be without my car this weekend.'

'I'll pick you up at the Elephant & Castle. In the mean time, I'll get the name of this weekend's duty judge from the High Court.'

They finalised details. Francesca phoned the High Court. As she finished speaking, William came downstairs, elegant in morning dress. His lips narrowed in disapproval at the brightness of her lipstick.

'A client's children have been abducted,' she told him. 'I have to make them wards of court.'

'We're due at the Culmstocks' for lunch.'

'Explain to Geoffrey, he'll understand. It's work. If I miss lunch, I'll meet you at the church.'

'You're going to Broderick. I knew you'd let me down.'

'I'm going to Lindsay Dault, one of the few clients you failed to influence Nailsworth against allocating to me.' She picked up her bag and hat, and slammed out of the house.

David was at their meeting-place, hovering on the edge of the pavement, searching for her among the lorries and buses which belched filth and exhaust at the Elephant & Castle. He leaped into Frankie's car. 'Good God!' He gaped at her elegant red suit. 'Where are you going?'

'My best friend's wedding.'

'You should have told me.'

'It's not till three. I'm only missing the lunch – and I'm not sorry.'

They drove east along the Old Kent Road, through neighbourhoods which suffered from the same tired poverty as Lindsay, until they came to a vast and soulless tower-block estate: a defeated sprawl of cracked tarmac, broken windows and graffiti-covered municipal garages. There was a sense of despair, anger and brooding violence. Francesca thought of Jack. He'd grown up in a place like this.

Lindsay lived on the seventh floor. The lift stank of urine. Francesca gagged. Once outside, they followed an open concrete walkway past front doors, each with frosted glass reinforced by security bars. They heard voices raised in anger, a baby crying, someone laughing, rock music, folk music, a television turned up loud, more rock music.

David knocked on a yellow front door.

There was no answer.

He opened the letter box. 'Lindsay! It's me, David Jarrow.'

They heard shuffling footsteps, then a chain and the scrape of a heavy bolt. Lindsay stood in the doorway, wearing a faded pink track suit. Her face was blotched from crying. A damp cigarette dangled from her fingers. She was too crushed to say she was pleased to see them.

'We've come to help.' David ushered her back inside. From the inner pocket of his coat he took a pint of milk and a small box of tea bags. 'We'll have a cup of tea whilst you tell us exactly what happened.'

The flat had little furniture, just a sofa, two chairs and a table, but it didn't seem so bare because of the rag dolls sitting on every surface; on the chairs, the table, the television. They were crudely made from cheap fabric but there was something very attractive about them. Every face was different. Every face was smiling.

'Did you make them?' asked Francesca.

Lindsay brightened. 'Yes. I love to do it. I use my kids' old clothes.'

Francesca made the tea whilst David tried to reassure Lindsay that she wouldn't lose her children. As he carried the mugs into the sitting room, her watch said midday. 'I've spoken to the duty judge.' She removed two dolls from a chair and sat down. 'I've explained the situation, without giving any names. He's at his house in Pimlico, and could issue the order as soon as we get there.'

Lindsay looked doubtful. 'Are you sure they won't take the kids into care?'

'We'll do our best.' David smiled encouragingly. 'Now we need the names and addresses of everyone Derek might have taken them to.'

'But you can't promise I won't lose the kids?'

'No,' said Francesca. 'But if he gets them to Australia, Lindsay, you've certainly lost them.'

Half an hour later they arrived at the judge's house. He received them in his study, whose French windows overlooked a formal garden. Whilst he issued the order, David alerted the police, who in turn alerted the airports and the docks. Francesca tried not to clockwatch.

A Filipino maid brought in a tray of coffee and biscuits. Lindsay was so nervous she ate nothing. Francesca thought of the depressing walkway and the lift which stank of urine. She wanted to reach out and calm the childish, calloused hands which shook too much to help themselves to the expensive biscuits.

As they left the judge's house, David turned to Francesca. 'Go to the wedding. I can manage the rest. All we can do is wait by my phone.'

'I'll drive you to your office. The wedding doesn't start till three. I've missed the lunch already.'

His office was on the ground floor of a three-storey house just off the Brixton Road. He was in partnership with three other young solicitors. Their accomodation was cramped. David's room was tiny, with space only for a desk and three upright chairs.

Francesca made coffee. Lindsay chain-smoked. The minutes ticked slowly by. At two-fifteen, Francesca stood up. 'I'll have to go,' she said apologetically. 'I can't miss Melanie's wedding.' She went into the minuscule loo to retouch her make-up in a tiny mirror.

The telephone rang. They all jumped. David reached for it. 'Yes? Yes!' His face broke into a broad grin. 'They've found the children at Derek's sister's house,' he told Lindsay. 'The police are taking them to Bethnal Green.'

133

Lindsay laid her small head on the desk and cried with relief.

Francesca's own eyes brimmed with tears. They smudged her newly applied mascara, but she didn't care. 'Come on!' she said, picking up her car keys. 'I'll drive you there. But we must be quick.'

In spite of David's protest that they could easily catch a cab, Francesca took them to Bethnal Green. As they reached the police station, Lindsay jumped out of the car and dashed inside to where the children were being looked after by a policewoman.

'You wouldn't let me take a taxi because you've seen how impoverished I am.' David kissed Francesca on both cheeks. 'Now, go to your wedding! The police will take us home.'

Simon and Melanie were already signing the register by the time Francesca reached the Temple Church. She slipped into a back row pew near the Round Church, the oldest part, where the effigies of thirteenth-century knights slept on the stone floor. The pews were aisle-facing. William was in the front row, near the altar. He was next to the Culmstocks. There was an empty space – hers – beside him. She hoped Melanie wouldn't notice.

The organist struck up Widor's 'Toccata'. Arm in arm, Simon and Melanie started down the aisle. Melanie was smiling, her face flushed with excitement and happiness. As she walked, the flounces of her ivory silk skirt swished the stone floor. As she saw each friend, she smiled. But when she reached William, her eyes fell on the empty seat. She faltered, then she carried on.

People didn't linger in the cold square once the official photographs had been taken. They hurried across to the reception and the warmth of the Hall. Francesca touched Virginia Culmstock on the shoulder. 'I'm sorry about lunch. I hope William explained.'

'I'm sorry for William.' Virginia moved away.

Francesca bit back a sharp retort and moved on to congratulate Mrs Llanellen. 'Melanie looks wonderful. The dress is gorgeous.'

'Thank you, dear.' Mrs Llanellen gave her a startled look, like a rabbit fixed by a fox.

Simon and Melanie were surrounded by well-wishers. Francesca slipped through the crowd. 'I'm so sorry I was late.' She kissed Melanie on both cheeks. 'I hope William explained.'

Melanie stepped back. Her voice high and quavering. 'If you didn't want to come to my wedding without that man, Frankie, you should have been honest enough to tell me so.' She spun round and, with a swish of her bridal gown, disappeared into the crowd.

Francesca was aware of people whispering. Across the room she could see William. He stood alone, staring at her, expressionless. With what dignity she could muster, she walked out of the Hall.

The square outside was deserted. She crossed to the church. The door was unlocked. She walked up the long aisle to the altar. On either side were stained-glass windows. Now bereft of external light, they produced the minimum of colour. On the day she had married William, the sun had thrown a pool of red, like a bloodstain, across the front of her white dress.

The church door opened behind her and William stepped inside. 'I don't know how you dare to appear in this church,' he said.

'Why did you lie to Melanie? Why didn't you tell her about the custody case?'

'Don't talk to me about truth and lies. Have you forgotten the promises you made in this very church?' He drew closer. 'Do you know whose tablet you're standing beneath?'

On the wall above Francesca was a marble tablet commemorating the death of Lady Anne Morton.

'Read it! William grabbed her by the shoulders.

'Let me go!'

He forced her to face the words, as he read out, in a hoarse voice, '*A Lady orthodox and exemplary for piety, charity, humility, chastity, constancy and patient sufferings*. That's what I expected from my wife. Chastity. Constancy. And what did I get? An adulteress!'

Francesca twisted away from him and ran down the aisle. As she went out of the church, the door crashed shut behind her.

William stood in the gloom, listening to her footsteps cross the square. He knew where she was going. He sank on to the stone ledge, and bowed his head.

Sixteen

Jack came home from racing to find Francesca asleep in his bed. She lay on her back, her head slightly to one side, her hands palm upwards and defenceless, her hair spread over the pillow. On the chair was her red suit. On the dressing table her veiled hat and her bag. He stood at the end of the bed, watching her. She stirred and opened her eyes.

'You've left William for good,' he said.

'How did you know?'

'I've seen an enormous goldfish in the kitchen and a very anxious rabbit in a hutch in the hall.'

'Poor Big Ears. He can smell the dogs. He's terrified that he's about to be eaten.'

'I'll make him a dog-proof run in the walled garden tomorrow.' He scooped her up into his arms, burying his face in the sleepiness of her hair, kissing her neck and her breasts. He tasted of brandy, cigarettes and cigars, as William never had. There was a feel in him of the night. For a moment she was afraid: of his world, which would now have to become hers. Then he covered her mouth with his and kissed her deeply, drawing her up to him and into him, so that she forgot everything.

In the morning she felt that the weight of indecision had been lifted. They lay in bed, making love, dozing, talking. He drew her on top of him, his fingers twisted into her tousled hair. 'I hate you being attached to another man. I hate you bearing his name. Tell him you want a divorce. I want to marry you, I want you to bear my name, my children.'

She kissed the tip of his nose. 'Jack, I can't be divorced in less than two years, unless William accuses me of adultery. He won't do that, because he doesn't want the scandal. And we don't want people gossiping and sniggering about us.' She hesitated before continuing. 'In any case, I don't want to marry again. Not immediately. In two years, I'll feel differently. Even in one year. But now, I've only just left William. I was married for ten years.

136

I need to put space between that me and this me.'

He smoothed her hair. 'I understand. But do me one favour. Use your maiden name.'

'I can here, but not at work. It would confuse everyone. I was called to the Bar as Eastgate.'

He cupped her face in his hands. 'When you're with me, you're Frankie Tiernay.'

They took hours to get up and shower. When they went downstairs, they found Marius feeding carrots through the bars of Big Ears's hutch. 'Don't tell me this is the same rabbit that Ben gave you for your birthday?' he said.

She smiled at the memory. 'Oh, no. That Big Ears died long ago. This one escaped from a rabbit farm.'

Jack picked up the hutch with the rabbit inside and carried it out into the small walled garden at the back of the Paddock House. 'We'll fence in a strip down the side.' He paced it out. 'This'll give him a good run, though I hate to see him behind bars.'

Frankie laid her hand on his shoulder. 'I know. But Big Ears isn't like you, Jack. He can't survive on the outside.'

That afternoon they went for a long walk, down through old Richmond and along by the river. With her hand tucked inside his, in his jacket pocket, they talked of everything and nothing. On their way, they passed a pet shop. There was a large white rabbit sitting in the window.

'Big Ears needs a wife,' said Jack, entering the shop.

Laughing, Frankie grabbed his arm. 'No! We'll be swamped by baby rabbits.'

'All right. We'll buy one for Jaws.'

They went home with a pretty black and gold fish whom they christened Mathilda.

Francesca told no one that she'd left William, not even her mother. She advised Nailbag that she was on holiday until after the New Year. He made no comment. Nor did she return to Islington. She had some clothes at the stadium. She borrowed thick sweaters from Jack. She needed them. Living at the Paddock House was cold. Jack left all the doors open. As with the window, he liked to know he was free.

On Christmas morning Jack refused to allow Frankie to open her eyes. 'If you do, you won't have your present,' he said.

She lay in bed, listening as he scuffled on the stairs and across the attic floor. Finally he told her, 'You can open them now.'

Standing in the alcove, near the window, was the exquisite Georgian dressing-table which she had admired in Nicoletta's shop.

'Jack, it's beautiful.' She jumped out of bed and, wrapping the duvet around herself to keep warm, hurried to it. She opened all the drawers, one by one. She ran her hand across the smooth surface. Its delicate lines and the warm glow of the mahogany seemed incongruous in the bright white modern attic. And yet it looked perfect. She hugged him. 'I've already given you your present. I put it in your side of the bed last night and you slept on top of it.'

He smiled at her enthusiasm. 'Who do you think I am? The Prince and the Pea? I've slept in too many lumpy prison beds in my life.' He ran his hand under the sheet and extracted a small, beautifully wrapped box. Very slowly he undid the red ribbon. Then, painstakingly, he unwrapped the paper.

Frankie watched him with amusement 'It won't bite, Jack.'

'I haven't unwrapped an unchecked Christmas present for fourteen years. I want to enjoy it.' He placed the paper on one side, smoothed it as if to save it, and opened the box. Inside was a pair of gold cufflinks, each engraved with the head of a greyhound. He stared at them, expressionless.

'Don't you like them?' she asked, anxiously.

The hint of tears came into his very blue eyes. Carefully, he laid the cufflinks in their box. Then he took her in his arms, duvet and all. 'I love them. And I love you.'

There were more presents, downstairs with Marius and Nicoletta, and laughter as they all helped to prepare dinner. Frankie was reminded of her last Christmas in the Paddock House, over twenty years ago. Her father had dressed up as Father Christmas and she'd pretended that she still believed, because she didn't want to spoil his fun. She slipped away to the card room to telephone her mother and Steven. 'Happy Christmas,' she said brightly.

'Thank you, darling,' replied her mother. 'How's everyone at Kingly Grange?'

'Er . . . fine. Just fine.'

138

'Are you and William coming over for lunch tomorrow? We have your presents under the tree.'

'Well . . . no. Actually, we're going away for a few days, until after the New Year. We've only just decided.'

'I understand. You need a break. Have a lovely time.'

She heard the disappointment in her mother's voice, and ached with guilt. Later, she said to Jack. 'I hate to lie to my mother but I didn't want to worry her on Christmas Day.'

At the end of that week, Francesca telephoned William. When he heard her voice, he shouted, 'Had enough of living with a murderer?'

Her tongue felt thick. It stuck to the roof of her mouth. 'I want to collect some clothes,' she stuttered.

He was silent. Then he said, 'I don't want to see you, Francesca. It would be too painful. You must come when I'm out. Tomorrow. But don't bring Broderick to my house!'

'I wouldn't do that to you, William.'

It was only a week since she'd left Islington, but it could have been a decade. As she turned into the street, she half expected a rush of confused anguish. But there was only a vague nostalgia, as if she'd lived here long ago, as a child.

As she parked Jack's Land Rover, the front door opened and her mother-in-law stepped out. 'Well, Francesca! With a father like yours I suppose your behaviour was to be expected. My poor William!' She spoke loudly so that Clarissa Riddle-Longman, who was walking her dog, could hear.

'My father has nothing to do with it.' Francesca pushed past her into the house.

In the hall, her set of five smart suitcases was lined up against the wall. Beyond them was a packing case containing her shoes and bags, several boxes of books, her cassettes, two large plastic sacks of sweaters, a pile of jackets and coats, and the grey felt elephant she'd had since she was three.

'Everything of yours is here,' said Audrey crisply. 'William and I spent all night packing.'

'Thank you.' Francesca started up the stairs.

'You've no need to go up there.'

'But I want to.' She carried on. Audrey followed. She checked the spare room. The shelves were bare. The hangers swung free.

She went into the main bedroom, now William's room, once their room. Suddenly a sense of failure rolled over her. How could she have shared this bed, this room, this bathroom, every intimacy, with someone whom she would seldom see or speak to? 'Tell William that I'll collect my pictures and furniture at a later date,' she said.

'I knew you'd try to strip the place.'

'I only want what's mine.'

'If you try for alimony, he'll fight you. I'll make sure of that.'

'I don't want William's money. I'll earn my own.' Francesca hurried down the stairs, away from the memories, and started to load her suitcases.

For New Year's Eve, Jack took Frankie greyhound-racing at Brighton. She wore a black stretch-velvet tube dress which a year earlier had cost her a small fortune. The neckline was scooped to reveal a cleavage she didn't know she possessed. The hem ended high above the knee. The material clung to her body like a second skin. William had hated it. 'I can't even eat a peanut without it showing,' she told Jack as she slid into the car.

'Then you'll be the least expensive lady I've taken to dinner.'

They'd never talked about past women in his life, because in their brief, stolen moments they had been too obssessed with her escape from William. Now Frankie was avidly curious. 'Have you taken many ladies to dinner?' she asked.

He reached for her hand. 'None who gave up what you have.'

She leaned against him in the dark intimacy of the car. 'Were you in love with any of them?'

'Not love. Lust. Don't forget, I was fourteen years inside. There were no women. Some men turned to each other. I didn't. I used to lie in my cell and fantasise about the hundreds of women I'd have once I was free. For a while I had them, a different one every night. Then I realised that wasn't what I wanted from life.'

'How old were you when you had your first lover?'

He laughed. 'You are curious!'

'I like to know these things.'

'I was thirteen. It was with our neighbour's daughter, in the back of a Rover I'd stolen.' He patted the seats of the Bentley. 'I've liked leather seats ever since.'

The car park was full, but Jack was waved to a space at the front. The crowds streamed past, into the main grandstand. Those aiming for the ground floor and the open terraces were muffled against the cold in leather jackets and thick scarves. Those, like Jack and Francesca, who were to dine in the grandstand restaurant were dressed for the evening. Most of the men wore suits, but the women came in every conceivable outfit, from elegant, under-stated designer dresses to rhinestone-encrusted boob tubes with gold lamé ski pants and white patent stilettos.

They found Eamonn in the crowded cocktail bar, discussing the racecard with two other trainers. 'So you've moved in with this outlaw!' He winked at Francesca.

They laughed, and left the trainer with his friends. As they walked towards the dining-room, she was aware that people were watching them. She heard low murmurs of 'Jack Broderick'. Again, she felt apprehensive of his world.

The restaurant was terraced, so that every diner could see the arena. Jack had reserved a table beside the huge plate-glass window. A bottle of champagne was waiting. From their position, they overlooked the finishing straight, with a perfect view around the track. On the far side was the low-priced popular enclosure, with its cheap fast-food stalls and open, packed terraces. On the near side, below the dining room, were more open terraces, with access to interior bars. Those people who preferred to stand outside milled around the bookies, stamping their feet against the cold.

The betting flashed up on a huge television screen.

'Jet's the favourite in the first race,' said Jack. 'He's a widerunner, drawn trap five though he prefers trap six, The W next to his name in the racecard means he's a widerunner.' He showed her. 'If he breaks quickly and doesn't get bumped, he should win. The railers, the dogs that hug the inside rail, are all drawn traps one to three. And maybe four. Dogs don't have riders to steer them. A railer in trap six would cut straight across the field and crash into all the other dogs.' He went on to explain the totalisator. 'It offers six different pools. You can bet to win. Or on a place. Or to forecast which dogs come first and second. Or various other combinations, up to the most difficult, the super jackpot, where you name the first three dogs in three races.' He stopped and laughed. 'What am I telling you this for? You must remember it from your father.'

'I'd forgotten. Or chosen to forget.' She gave him a rueful smile. It was strange to be with the man she loved in a world on which she'd turned her back.

'Your father was a gambler,' said Jack gently. 'He couldn't stop. He was the same with drink. Clever betters stay sober. I decide how much I can afford to lose, then stop. For me, it's the thrill of pitting my mental-arithmetic ability against that of the bookies. Not the tote! With the tote you divide the pool. If you're the only one to place a large bet, you're splitting your own money.' He ran his finger down the list of dogs in the first race. 'Some people follow a system. They always back the dog in, say, trap two. I select a dog on good form, correctly graded, and at reasonable odds. A dog's grade, as you must remember, depends on its trialling speed.'

'You have to back Jet.'

'I'll put a hundred pounds each way on him for you.'

She shook her head. 'I never gamble. I saw what it did to my father.'

Jack linked his fingers through hers. 'Frankie, greyhound-racing exists as a medium for betting. You may not like it, but that's the truth. The stadium pays the dog-owner an appearance fee. I'll get a tenner tonight for Jet, even if he comes last. When we open Richmond, our earnings will come from the gate, the bar and restaurant, and our seventeen per cent cut on the tote. Our success will depend on people wanting to gamble.'

'I accept that, but I don't have to be one of them.' She leaned across the table and kissed him. 'Now we've got the serious conversation over, Mr Broderick, would you take me down to the track for the first race. I've always loved the raw excitement beside the rails.'

The terraces were packed, the ground littered with cigarette butts. The crowd was a strange mixture. Rich men in gangster camel coats with gold-ringed fingers dug deep into their pockets. Their wives and girlfriends, tanned and blonde, fur coats clutched around their tummy tucks. Young stockbrokers talking loudly to girls in velvet headbands. Rough men with Seventies' hairstyles and heavy leather jackets. Old men, thin like rich whippets, studying the racecard through Doctor Crippen bifocals. Solitary men, heavy betters, speaking to no one.

They clasped their betting slips and stared out across the oval to where the paraders walked the greyhounds in single file beneath the yellowing light on the edge of the track. The dogs were muzzled and jacketed. They turned their heads at the sounds from the grandstand.

Jack pointed to number five in an orange jacket. 'There's Jet.'

From the tannoy came, 'Greyhounds approaching the traps. Two minutes to the off.'

Some dogs went in easily. Some balked. One tried to turn. Finally, they were all facing forward.

'The hare is moving,' announced the tannoy.

There was a rattling sound from the far side of the stadium. It echoed along the trolley. The dogs began to yelp with excitement. Francesca could see Jet's long black nose through the bars of number five. The rattling grew louder. The dogs dropped to the ground, whimpering. As the hare passed the traps, it triggered the gate, which flew upwards.

The dogs shot out, with Dale Hill Olga, a small black railer, in the lead. Jet was in fourth place. At the first bend they jostled. One dog tripped and fell. On the curve, Olga tired. On the far straight, in front of the popular stands, they spread out. Twineham Digby pushed to the front. Jet was third. At the final bend, they bunched again. Another dog fell back. Now it was between the three leaders, Twineham Digby, Roman Lisa and Jet. With the crowd cheering, they raced up the final stretch, flat out, teeth bared, their long bodies horizontal to the sand.

'Come on, Jet!' Francesca clutched Jack's hand.

He laughed at her excitement. 'It was a photo finish. They always take a photo. Roman Lisa won. Jet came second.'

'His feet were in front.'

'It's the first dog's nose which counts. Let's see him come off the track. I've bought him some chocolate drops, he loves them.'

The paraders had caught the dogs and were leading them in. 'Well done, old boy.' Jack leaned over the gate to pat Jet's heaving flanks.

'Poor Jet.' Francesca stroked his head. 'He should have accelerated earlier.'

143

Eamonn caught Jack's eye, but before either man could speak Frankie said, 'I know greyhounds don't pace themselves. They run flat out till they tire. They don't care about the finishing post – or how much money you've put on them.'

Jack put his arms around her. 'Come on, my expert. Our dinner is waiting.' As they walked back upstairs he stopped to kiss her. 'Happy New Year,' he said. 'This is the first of always.'

Seventeen

Frankie put off returning to chambers because she didn't want her happiness sullied by other people's outrage. Gossip travelled fast at the Inn. Those standing near her at the wedding would have heard Mel's comment about 'that man'. She reasoned that within a week or so, other scandals would supplant her. In the mean time, a messenger collected papers for her from chambers. She worked on them at the stadium.

She heard nothing from William. Although she wouldn't have admitted so to Jack, she thought of him often. He'd been in her life for too long to forget.

One morning, when she was working on the Alexander Swaffield case, her mother walked into the Paddock House. 'You should have told me you were living here,' she told Frankie angrily. 'You shouldn't have left me to hear it from Audrey Eastgate. I'm your mother, I deserve better than that.'

'I know. I'm sorry.'

'You lied to me on the telephone on Christmas Day.'

'I was going to tell you the truth, but . . .'

Jack appeared in the doorway. 'It's my fault, Dominique.'

Marius fiddled with his pipe. 'No, it's mine.'

'It isn't either of your faults. You are not my daughter. Francesca, I'm taking you to lunch. I want to talk to you.'

Frankie grabbed a jacket and slunk out after her mother. In silence, they drove to the nearby Italian restaurant. Her mother ordered lasagne. Frankie chose the same. They waited, still without speaking, until the waitress had brought their order. Then Frankie said, 'I'm sorry I didn't tell you the truth, but I didn't want to spoil your Christmas.'

'You lied, just as your father used to.'

'That's not fair. You knew about Jack.'

'I never realised you meant to move in with him. You forget I know what these people are like. Oh, they're fun. Charming. But they gamble. Drink. Womanise.'

145

'I love Jack. He's not like that!'

'He's dangerous.'

'I don't understand you.' Francesca broke a piece of bread in half. 'It was you who told me everyone should know great love.'

'I never suggested you should leave your husband to live at a dogtrack with an ex-criminal.'

'You mean, I should see him in secret, as you saw my father?'

'Francesca!'

They sat, frozen in angry silence. Eventually her mother spoke. 'I always said William was too old for you, but he was a good provider. That's important.'

'He was a despot.' Francesca stabbed her pasta with her fork. 'I led a double life for two months up till Christmas. I'd rather be destitute than do that again.'

'That's because you've never been destitute.'

They finished the meal without talking, without looking at each other. Frankie was miserable. Being so happy with Jack, she wanted her mother to be pleased for her. She felt both resentful and very guilty. At the same time she was aware, in a way that she hadn't been before, that just as her father's irresponsibility had driven her to seek security with William, so his lying had made her mother crave honesty. But because she was angry, she didn't say so.

They parted stiffly outside the restaurant. Her mother drove home to White Oast. Frankie walked back up Queen's Road to the stadium in the drizzle. She was still indignant when she recounted the conversation to Jack.

To her surprise, he wasn't offended. He merely smiled and said, 'When we have a daughter, I'll feel exactly the same if she gets involved with a man like me.'

Melanie leaned her elbows on the stone ramparts of the old fortress and gazed down the sheer rock drop from the hill town of Orvieto at the Paglia Valley and the wide grey ribbon of the *autostrada* heading south to Rome. It was the last day of their honeymoon. She should have been so happy. 'I'm sorry to keep on about Frankie, but I'm so hurt,' she said. 'She knew I couldn't ask Jack Broderick to our wedding. She promised nothing would keep her away.'

Simon was just adjusting the zoom lens of the Leica camera Melanie had bought him as a wedding present. 'Darling, Broderick has changed her. She's no longer the Frankie we knew. Of course William shouldn't have hit her – if he did, which I find hard to believe – but you can't blame him for being angry if his wife runs off with a criminal.'

Melanie sighed. 'I always admired Frankie. That's partly why I feel let down. Oh, I'm sorry to be such a bore.'

Simon kissed the curly blonde top of her head. 'You're not a bore. And even if you are, I still love you.'

They left the fortress and walked down through the narrow medieval streets to their hotel. Simon held Melanie tight. She didn't deserve to be hurt.

On the night before Francesca was due back in chambers, she couldn't sleep for nerves, but as soon as she arrived at the Inn, her courage returned. She parked her car outside Makepeace, where it could be seen by everyone. She took the time to look around to see if William's or Melanie's car was present. Neither was. She walked calmly up the stairs, stuck her head into the reception and called out cheerfully, 'Happy New Year!' to Rupert, Charlotte and Nailsworth.

'Oh, Mrs Eastgate,' said Nailsworth, frowning. 'Mr Culmstock wishes to see you.'

'I have a conference in fifteen minutes.'

'He said it was urgent.'

'I'll be free straight after lunch.' She walked into her office. She wasn't going to be bullied by Geoffrey or Nailsworth or anyone.

The air in her room was stale and closed. She opened the window. Wintry sun and fresh air rushed in. She sat down at her desk and prepared her papers for Mrs Blackbird.

The telephone rang. It was Jack. 'Have they torn you limb from limb?' he asked.

'I think they've forgotten.'

'You were awake all night. You were so worried. You didn't say so, but I could tell. I could feel you biting your fingersnails in the dark.'

She chuckled. 'I've stopped now. Everything's fine. I love you. I'll see you later.'

Mrs Blackbird was becoming increasingly belligerent. She arrived, arguing with her solicitor. 'My husband intended those properties abroad to pay for my old age,' she complained to Francesca. 'It's unfair to include them in a valuation to give that little . . . tart's baby more of my money.'

'But your husband did own them, and the child is his.' Francesca tried to reason with her. 'Also, you did originally say you weren't aware of properties abroad.'

The woman was spoiling for a fight. 'You're meant to be on my side, dear.'

'I am. And in view of your conflicting evidence, my advice is that we try for an out-of-court settlement.'

'You mean, we give in.' Mrs Blackbird picked up her handbag and marched to the door. 'I wish I'd never begun this case.' She looked accusingly at Francesca. 'I suppose I have to pay you even though you haven't had to go to court.'

'You certainly do – for my time.'

Francesca was relieved to see the back of them. She settled down to study the theatre nurse's report in Alexander Swaffield's case. At lunchtime she ate sandwiches in her room, then, at two o'clock sharp, made her way to Geoffrey's office. He was sitting behind his huge leather-topped desk, his big hands holding a small gold pen with which he was making notes in the margin of a brief.

'Happy New Year, Geoffrey,' she said, gaily.

He looked at her without expression. 'Francesca, I'm giving you a chance to resign from chambers before you're voted out.'

Her smile disappeared. 'On what grounds?'

'We don't need grounds. It's sufficient that your colleagues want you to leave. But if there were grounds, they would be that you're bringing our chambers into disrepute.' He paused, then added quietly, 'I'm trying to make this easy for you, Francesca.'

'I'm not resigning.'

'Then you're a fool. If you leave of your own accord, you stand a chance of finding another chambers – not that many will welcome Jack Broderick's mistress.'

She flushed. 'That is meant to be confidential between William and me.'

'He spent New Year's Eve with us. He became very upset and told us the whole story. Rupert was there. So was Desmond. And

Hugo and Thomas. They were all very shocked and very sorry for William.'

'Geoffrey, I will not go. My personal life is my own affair. It will not intrude on my work.'

'Personal life becomes a chamber's affair if you're living with Broderick. Every law student studies his trial. He nobbled half the jury! His retrial cost the taxpayer a fortune. He killed an informer. I prosecuted him. For God's sake, Francesca, how can you expect your colleagues to turn a blind eye when chambers' reputation is at stake. Leave, or you'll be kicked out at the next chambers' meeting.'

'Not by Mel and Sanjiv. They'll stand up for me. They're loyal.' She stalked out of the room, allowing his door to crash behind her.

It was impossible for Frankie to return to her room and work. She was too upset and agitated. She paced up and down, clenching and unclenching her fists. Finally, she gave up and went home to Jack. 'My head of chambers tried to get me to resign,' she told him through a mixture of rage and misery. 'He says I'm going to be voted out at the next meeting.'

'Because of me?'

'You, and the fact that they all hero-worship William.'

'What about your friend, Melanie?'

'Mel will be on my side. She was upset because I was late for her wedding but she'll forgive me once she knows the truth. Mel warned me about chambers, so I shouldn't have been shocked. But I was!' She pulled a face. 'They won't get me out. It just annoys me that they dare to try, the backstabbers!'

Several days later, Melanie returned to chambers. Francesca saw her car outside Makepeace and dashed upstairs, two at a time, into Mel's room. 'I'm so glad you're back.' She hugged her. 'Did you have a wonderful time? You looked fabulous. Oh, Mel, I've wanted to explain about the wedding, but I expect you've heard the truth by now.'

Melanie said nothing.

'I mean, about the child custody case,' Frankie went on. 'The reason I was late.'

'Frankie, I know why you were late. I don't want to talk about it. Please leave my room.'

'But you're not giving me a chance to explain.'

149

'I've given you every chance. I even telephoned William to ask why you'd been late. He told me you had a phone call that morning, as you were about to leave for the Culmstocks'.'

'From my lay client!'

'From Broderick!'

'That's a lie. It was from Lindsay Dault.' Francesca backed away. 'But you'd clearly prefer to believe William than me. I expect Simon's told you to. Well, if that's the case, you're going to be just as downtrodden and miserable in your marriage as I was in mine. And you'll bloody well deserve it!' She turned round. Only then did she realise that James was at his desk. He was staring at her, appalled.

She stormed out of the room. Ten minutes later, she returned. James had disappeared. Melanie was alone, sitting at her desk, with tears sliding down her cheeks. 'I'm sorry, Mel,' said Frankie. 'I shouldn't have said that. It was cruel and untrue. But I'm upset because you're taking William's side.'

'Simon's right. Broderick has changed you.' Melanie spoke in a small, flat voice. 'Please leave me alone.'

Frankie didn't immediately tell Jack about Melanie, but he came up to the attic to find her crying. 'William's turned Melanie against me,' she sobbed. 'They all want me out. I knew he'd try to ruin my career. But I was so sure I could fight him.'

'When is the chambers' meeting?'

'Tomorrow evening.'

'Shall I burst in and shoot them all, or pick them off one by one as they leave?'

She laughed through her tears.

His kissed the tip of her nose. 'I want you to win because you want to. But if you don't succeed, I love you just the same. Remember that!'

She linked her arms around him and drew him closer. He kissed her hard, his mouth pressing down on hers, drawing her fears out of her. They made love through that early evening. Then they lay and watched television, eating pâté and crispy French bread, laughing as they flicked the crumbs from their bed. She went to sleep in his arms. In the morning, she felt strong.

She passed Melanie on the stairs. 'Good morning,' she called out cheerfully.

150

Melanie looked startled.

By the coffee machine, she met Sanjiv. 'I hope you're not against me too,' she told him in a bouncy voice.

'I'm against divorce.'

'Half the Inn is divorced. Personal life has nothing to do with work.' She poured herself some coffee.

'I like you, Frankie.' He gave her a sad smile, then disappeared into his room.

Francesca spent that day working on her cases. She discussed Lindsay's hearing with David Jarrow, and wrote a long letter to Alexander's solicitor on their strategy at the hearing. But it was hard to concentrate whilst all around she smelled betrayal.

At five minutes to six, Jack telephoned. 'Good luck,' he said.

'Thanks.' Her voice was choked. 'I'm going to need it.'

She walked through the reception to Geoffrey's office. Everyone was already seated: Geoffrey behind his desk; Rupert and Charlotte near the window; Melanie next to Sanjiv; Desmond, Hugo, Thomas and James in a line against the wall. There was just one spare chair, next to the door.

Frankie didn't take it. She remained standing. They all stared at her, except for Melanie who studied the carpet. 'As I'm the reason for this meeting, I shall speak first,' said Frankie in a loud, clear voice. 'You want to vote me out of chambers. Or rather, you hoped I'd slip away so you didn't have to face me. But I have the right to be heard.' She took a deep breath. 'My private life is not your business. But I don't deny I've left William, to whom I was unhappily married. I am now living with another man. I don't deny that that man is Jack Broderick. But I do object to the suggestion that this affects my contribution to chambers. So I can only presume that you are succumbing to pressure from William to end my tenancy. In which case, you are weak and cowardly, and I don't wish to be a member of this chambers.' She walked away before anyone else had a chance to speak. She knew they'd have voted her out. At least she went down fighting.

It was strange to have no workplace to go to. Of course, she could have sat out her lease in chambers, but to return there, even for a day, was unthinkable. Until her lease expired, she belonged there officially and could still practise, not that Nailsworth passed her

151

any new briefs. For the first few weeks, she was kept busy finishing off paperwork. Then a sense of deep mourning came over her. She didn't approach another chambers: she knew instinctively that she'd be rejected. This meant she had to return those cases whose hearings were scheduled after her lease expired.

She telephoned David Jarrow. He listened quietly as she explained. 'I have no new chambers, so I can't represent Lindsay. Ask for Melanie Llanellen. She's very good and she specialises in family work. And tell Lindsay I'm very sorry to let her down.'

She wrote a letter to Alexander's solicitor and another to Mr Swaffield. 'I feel so guilty about letting them down,' she told Jack. 'Especially this little boy. His father believed in me and our case was going well.

'You're out of that chambers but not out of the law. Set up on your own.'

'What solicitor would instruct me? Not one! William would blacken my name before I had a chance to prove myself.' She gritted her teeth and tried to look brighter for Jack's sake. 'You'll just have to involve me in the stadium to stop me brooding.'

'I'll speak to Marius.'

'Why? What's the problem?'

'We'll have to tread gently. I don't want the old boy to feel squeezed out. It's his stadium. Remember, he gave me a chance.'

She linked her arms around him. 'You mean that without Marius you'd be back sewing mailbags?'

'We don't sew mailbags any more. They're made by machines.' He kissed the tip of her nose. 'Thank you for understanding.

Goldie had her puppies during the night. When Jack and Francesca arrived the following afternoon, she was resting in her raised bed of shredded paper, with eight fat little puppies pushing their tiny, chubby faces into her teats. Two were black. Three were brindle. Three were fawn, like their mother. They had a fusty smell of warm sleep and milk.

Francesca picked up the two black ones. They squeaked and wriggled. She kissed one velvet face, then the other. They reminded her of moles: the velvet-coated gentlemen of her childhood stories.

On the other side of the yard a dog threw itself against the wire fencing, yelping and howling.

'Shut up, Blue!' shouted Eamonn. 'That dog's a damned nuisance. I can't think why I didn't let them put him down.'

Jack smiled. 'Because you never do. You keep them all.'

The dog in question was more an overgrown puppy. Big, clumsy and the colour of blue taupe, he had huge feet and a pair of tawny eyes. He sank to the concrete floor and stared dolefully across at the attention being shown to the newborn pups.

'What's wrong with him?' asked Francesca.

'He's a blue,' said Jack. 'They're considered unlucky. They're said to be difficult. They don't chase.'

'It ain't that dog's fault.' Eamonn lifted his cap to scratch his head. 'His owner tried to handslip him but he wouldn't chase, which ain't surprising when he's only eight months. You handslip at a year. Now they've scared 'im useless, so they don't want 'im.'

'Then he isn't to blame at all.' Francesca settled the little black puppies into the bed with Goldie. She crossed the yard to the blue dog. Unlike all the other greyhounds at the kennels, he didn't jump joyfully to greet a visitor. Instead, he cowered on the ground on his stomach, with his jawbone parallel to the floor, and his eyes turned away as if to say he didn't care if she didn't want to speak to him.

She opened the door to his run. 'Hello, Blue.'

He trembled.

Francesca stepped inside. 'Come here!' She held out her hand.

The dog rose uncertainly and walked slowly towards her, as if trying not to let her see how clumsy and ungainly he was. But then, a yard away, he forgot. He threw himself at her, slobbering with excitement, his great big white paws on her waist, his big, tawny teddy-bear eyes pleading, 'Take me!'

Francesca looked at Jack, who shook his head in mock despair. 'You don't want that dog,' he said. 'He'll never race. Have one of Goldie's puppies, properly trained by Eamonn.'

'I don't want one of Goldie's puppies.' Francesca smiled at the big adolescent greyhound. 'Blue's just had a bad start – like someone else I know!'

Frankie didn't forget about her own involvement with Richmond

Racing: she merely decided to give Jack time to accustom Marius to the idea. With Blue to look after, to walk, to play with and to train, she had less time to brood on her ruined career. Her main problem with Blue was to keep him away from Big Ears. Once when she left the garden door open, she raced outside to find Blue jumping up and down beside the run, and the poor rabbit cowering in his hutch, nearly dead of fright. That afternoon, Jack installed a second security door.

The stadium was progressing fast. Frankie loved to see the place come alive. Often when she walked Blue around the track she felt her father's presence beside her, laughing, joking, an unrepentant rogue. She was no longer ashamed of him. She was only sorry for the missed years.

Once the structural work was complete, the decorators moved in and the whole place reeked of paint. To escape the gagging fumes, Jack and Frankie went to Rome for a short holiday. She'd flown all over the world with William, but never had any flight been so intimate or such fun as the two hours she spent on the aeroplane with Jack. Even the delay in the airport was funny. Even the wait to collect their luggage, which was last off the conveyor belt. An inconvenience for which William would have blamed her.

They stayed at the Villa Medici. From their bedroom window, they looked across the rooftops to the dome of St Peter's. Jack had never been to Italy. He spoke no Italian. Nor did Francesca. But because they were dark, other tourists mistook them for Italians and stopped them in the street to ask the way. If Jack didn't like the look of them, he waved his arms, gabbled in some unknown tongue, and pointed them in the wrong direction, whilst Francesca stood by, helpless with laughter.

Unlike William, he hated museums. They reminded him of prison. He even sat outside whilst Francesca visited the Sistine Chapel. What appealed to Jack was the life in the streets. To sit in pavement cafés watching the parade of people, or to wander through alleyways to small cobbled squares, listening to voices call to each other from behind shuttered windows. He loved to walk beside the Tiber, or to stand on the ancient and narrow Ponte Sisto, looking down into the dark waters of the river and wondering about all the people who had stood on that spot before them.

He had a charm which transcended language. He joked with grandmothers in family trattorias. He was one of the men at the bar, talking football in English whilst they replied in Italian. He bought a dozen red roses for Francesca and kissed the hand of the old lady selling flowers. He told taxi drivers they were on their honeymoon. They laughed and winked and wished them luck. They understood Jack. Everyone did.

On their first day back at the stadium, Francesca was in the attic, unpacking, when Angel buzzed her on the intercom. 'You have a visitor,' he said.

She ran down, hoping it was Melanie.

Standing in the hall was Mr Swaffield. He held her letter in his hand. 'You shouldn't get away with this, Mrs Eastgate,' he bellowed. 'You gave my family hope. I trusted you, my wife believed in you. We thought you truly wanted to help our son.'

Francesca flushed. 'I did. I was very sorry at having to return the case. That's why I wrote to you personally.'

'You shouldn't have resigned, whatever your problems, until after Alexander's hearing. But you just abandoned us to someone else. You didn't give a damn. It'll serve you right if *you* have a disabled child.' He turned on his heel and left.

Frankie stood in the middle of the hall, She could see Marius watching her from the card room, but she was too mortified to speak. With Blue following, she slunk outside and along the terraces, away from the grandstand, to the deserted side of the arena. She climbed up to the top step. There she sat, her jumper pulled over her knees against the cold, Blue cuddled in her arms.

It was an hour before Jack found her. 'Marius told me what happened,' he said. 'You should have called me. I'd have thrown him out.'

'Mr Swaffield was right.'

He walked up the steps to stand in front of her. 'You're losing everything because of me, aren't you? Your mother. Melanie. Your career. Do you regret . . . us?'

She shook her head, 'Never. Before, I was dead. Now, I'm alive.'

Eighteen

Jack was determined that Richmond Racing would open at Easter. He spent many days away from the stadium, negotiating with advertisers and with race sponsors. Francesca accompanied him for the pure pleasure of being near him. She waited in the car, reading a book or listening to the radio.

Marius remained at the Paddock House in mounting chaos. He stamped, cursed and shuffled papers, interviewing a constant stream of office staff, track staff, restaurant staff – though since he took no notes, he couldn't remember who was who.

'We'll never be ready on time,' Jack complained to Frankie, as they walked home from one of their favourite restaurants, through the narrow paved streets in the old part of the town.

'Let me help, Jack. I need an occupation.'

'There's a thousand pounds in the top drawer of my desk if you need money.'

'I don't want a hand-out. I want to be involved. You took on that rogue Angel. Why not me?'

'Is Angel being a nuisance to you?'

'He cheeks me. I don't trust him.' She paused. 'Stop trying to change the subject.'

He put his arm around her. 'I'll talk to Marius again.'

'You mean, he's already said no?'

'He's an old man. The stadium's his baby.'

'Sometimes I think he doesn't like me,' said Frankie. 'I don't think he liked my mother either.'

'You're wrong. He was in love with her and she only had eyes for Ben. But that didn't stop her twisting Marius around her finger when she needed him. It was he who used to drive her round the bars looking for your father when he hadn't come home.'

'I had no idea Marius loved her.' Frankie shook her head in surprise. 'I'm more and more aware that I know my mother so little. I suppose that's as much my fault as hers.'

'We're all alone. It's better that way.'

156

'Except for you and me.' She smiled and leaned against him.

But Jack didn't kiss her as she expected. He pulled away and walked on without a word.

Frankie followed slowly. She was near to tears. He was so flawed, by life, by prison, by himself.

Halfway up Richmond Hill, she stopped. He was well ahead, almost out of sight. 'Jack!' she shouted. 'I spent ten years with a man whose favourite weapon was the silence of disapproval. I love you, but I will not fight silence again.'

He walked back down the hill and took both her hands in his.

The chaos continued. When Jack complained, Frankie laughed and sang, 'Didn't I tell you so?' to the tune of 'Happy Birthday'.

Sometimes, instead of accompanying Jack, she helped Nicoletta in the antique shop. She updated the stock book, something Nicoletta disliked doing, checking through invoices and ticking off items sold. Her training at the Bar had taught her to work quickly and methodically. It was interesting, and Frankie enjoyed the comings and goings of the little shop.

One afternoon Frankie was minding the shop for Nicoletta who'd gone to a house clearance sale in the country. It was quiet. She hadn't had a customer all day. The spring sunshine streamed in through the lead-paned windows, capturing particles of dust in its rays. The shop grew warmer. Settling into an old leather armchair, Frankie dozed, her head on the arm, Blue stretched out at her feet.

She was brought back to earth by the tinkle of the brass bell above the door. But before she had time to uncurl, David Jarrow appeared. He looked from her to the dog, then laughed. 'I'm sorry to interrupt your siesta, but I thought you'd like to know that Lindsay hasn't gone back to prison.'

'Oh, I'm so glad.' Frankie pulled herself upright. 'I felt very guilty about letting her down.'

'She often asks after you. She told Melanie that you were her heroine.'

'I expect she got short shrift.'

'Not at all. Melanie was very complimentary about you.'

'Are you sure?'

'Why would I lie?'

157

'I'm sorry. It's just that Mel was my best friend but she took my husband's side. At least, it seemed that way.'

'Maybe you were mistaken. People often misread situations when they're under strain.'

Frankie brightened. As soon as David left, she wrote to Melanie. She meant to keep the letter short but it ran to eight pages of explanations and apologies. She posted it straightaway, before she could change her mind.

That evening she told Jack, 'Mel was my best friend. I can't lose her without a fight.'

He nodded. 'Of course you can't. I couldn't lose Marius.'

Each morning when the post arrived, Frankie anticipated Melanie's reply. A fortnight passed, and she heard nothing. She wished she hadn't bothered to write.

As Blue developed, Francesca followed Eamonn's advice and took him for long walks through the park or across the downs, encouraging him to run free and fast. He was growing bigger. Taller. Stronger. One day on the Downs, a hare got up from under his nose. He coursed it across the hillside, jinking and turning, his mouth open and teeth bared. With her hands covering her mouth, she stifled her cries for him to stop. He caught it and ripped it apart. She screamed as the hare screamed. Bending over, she was sick on the grass.

Eamonn was waiting for her when she returned to the kennels to collect her car. 'That dog's killed,' he said. 'I can see it in his eyes.'

'I should have tried to stop him. It was horrible. But I didn't.'

'Maybe there's hope for you both yet.'

She drove back to Richmond, still thinking about the hare. In the hall of the Paddock House she found an irate representative from the National Greyhound Racing Club. 'Where's Mr Charlwood?' he demanded. 'He invited me to inspect your paddock kennels. I've been waiting for over an hour.'

Through the open door Francesca saw Marius approaching. She raised her voice. 'I'm so sorry. Do let me make you some coffee. Ah, here's Mr Charlwood. I know he'll be most apologetic.'

After the inspector had left, Francesca went into the card room. She sat down at the long table, picked up a sheaf of papers relating to the track, and started to read through them.

'What are you doing?' demanded Marius.

'Helping you organise this muddle.'

'You know nothing about greyhounds – apart from picking blue dogs which won't chase.'

'You know nothing about business.'

'It's my stadium.'

'Sit down, you old bear.' Francesca patted his chair. 'We're going to work together.'

'And if I refuse?'

She smiled sweetly. 'I'll tell Jack that you forgot about the NGRC inspector's visit.'

When Jack arrived home, Francesca was on the telephone placing an advertisement for an experienced personnel manager whilst Marius listed magazines and newspapers they should approach for editorials. Jack looked from one to the other and raised an eyebrow, but said nothing. Later he asked Francesca, 'How did you persuade him?'

'Blackmail!'

She employed a manager called Bernard, an accountant with casino experience. He was very tall and very thin with a calm, soft voice. Even Marius couldn't fault him. He produced a short list of catering managers, track managers and tote managers. They interviewed them all, selecting Signor Umberto to act as catering manager, an old friend of Marius's called Godfrey to be track manager, and another accountant to oversee the tote.

'What about typists, kennel-maids, waitresses, chefs, bar staff?' Marius asked Jack when Frankie and Bernard had left the room. 'These high-faluting managers won't type a letter, clean a kennel or serve the punters their dinners.'

'Each manager, together with Bernard, will hire his own staff. It's called delegation.' Jack handed Marius a glass of whisky. 'All you need to worry about are the greyhounds.'

Organising the gala evening was hard work, but Frankie enjoyed it. With Marius, she drew up a guest list of NGRC officials, local dignitaries, journalists, and greyhound aficionados. With Jack, she'd visited nightclubs and jazz clubs to select a jazz quartet. They called in a graphic artist to redesign the stadium's logo. It was to appear on the invitations and the menus. They chose the flowers to decorate the stairs to the grandstand

159

restaurant, arguing the merits of white roses versus pale-peach orchids. They settled for orchids. They were more exotic.

'We have Eamonn and four other trainers to supply the track full time,' Jack told Marius, late one night when Frankie had gone to bed. 'Are you sure that's enough? Twelve races require seventy-two dogs per evening, three times a week.'

The old man thumped his whisky glass down on the desk. 'Frankie may think I'm an incompetent bungler, but I raced dogs before she was born.'

'I know the way you felt about Dominique, but that's not Frankie's fault,' said Jack evenly. 'Why are you so against her? She's very fond of you.'

Marius sucked on his pipe. 'I'm worried for her. She's the nearest I have to a daughter. She's my little Frankie. I can see her now, sitting on Ben's knee, cards clutched in her tiny fingers, trying to win her pocket money. Even when she did win it, half the time he'd go to her money box and take it back because he needed a drink. She never told her mother that. She didn't want to get Ben into more trouble. She was so loyal. But what scares me, Jack, is that she's got under your skin, as Dominique got under mine. I loved Ben, except when I wished him dead so I could have his wife. If you go to prison again, it'll be over Frankie.'

'Why do you say that?'

'Because if she goes back to her husband. I am afraid you'll kill him. And her! And I love you both.'

Jack took Marius by the shoulders and looked into his eyes. 'Frankie's not going back to her husband and I'm never going back to prison.'

Dominique's birthday approached. Frankie bought a card, then angrily decided not to send it. But on the morning, she was choked with guilt. She telephoned. 'Am I still welcome at your birthday lunch?'

'Come for breakfast, darling! Come all day!'

Steven took them to his favourite restaurant. He ordered for all of them, mushrooms in garlic followed by steak au poivre, the exact menu he and her mother had eaten on their first visit to that restaurant, over twenty years earlier.

They kept off the subject of Jack, although it hovered between

160

them. Frankie wasn't sure how much Steven knew. Once, she would have sworn her mother told him everything. Now, she was uncertain.

In the afternoon they played Scrabble, Steven's favourite game, whilst Blue lay sprawled on the rug in front of the fire. They had tea with home-made scones with lashings of butter and jam and cream. When Frankie carried the tea tray through to the kitchen before leaving, she found her mother leaning against the wall near the window, her face pale, perspiration beading her forehead.

'Mummy! What's the matter?' Frankie nearly dropped the tray.

'I get such indigestion nowadays.'

'Why didn't you order less rich dishes?'

'Steven would be disappointed. To eat the same is part of his ritual.' Dominique forced herself to walk upright as she followed Francesca out to her car. 'I was hurt because you didn't confide in me,' she said.

'I know, Mum. I was wrong.'

'Have you collected your furniture and pictures?'

'I can't bear to go back.'

'You must be sensible and ask William for your share of the house. If things don't work out with Jack, you'll need a roof.'

'I'm not fighting with you on your birthday.' Frankie waved Blue into the back of the car.

'When you have children, you'll understand. You won't want your daughter getting involved with a man like Jack Broderick.'

'That's exactly what he says!'

For the gala dinner Francesca wore a dress of magenta crêpe de Chine. It had a clinging tulip skirt, calf-length at the back but curved seductively at the front, so high that it nearly revealed the tops of her sheer, shining black silk stockings. On one bare arm she wore twelve gold slave bangles, on the other a small, neat gold watch. When she walked, the skirt undulated over her taut buttocks. It hinted rather than revealed. It did not expose, it suggested.

Jack was in the hall checking final details with Bernard when Frankie appeared at the top of the stairs. He glanced up and raised one eyebrow. She gave him her mock-haughty look. He winked. She blew him a little kiss. In evening dress, he looked wonderfully

161

debonair and handsome. His black dinner jacket fitted beautifully. His bow tie was perfectly tied. His gold cufflinks, those she had given him, were clearly expensive but in no way obvious. Yet there was something of his violent past which never left him.

She watched the crowd below. Guests were arriving in droves. Cloakroom ladies took their coats; waitresses, smart in black and white, offered pink champagne. The flowers were perfect. Peach and cream orchids burst with tropical profusion over the banisters. As Francesca came down the stairs, the band struck up 'The Entertainer', Jack's favourite tune.

He turned and smiled. He was proud of her, she knew, and she walked tall. Her eyes danced, her lips glistened. She threw back her mane of brown curls and gave a throaty chuckle.

As she reached the bottom step, she had a clear view over the heads of the guests to the front door, where a pasty-faced, thickset thug was showing his invitation to the security guards. Francesca knew she'd seen him before but she couldn't place him. Jack's eyes followed hers. He frowned, signalled to Angel. In an instant, the guards were grouped around the thug. He disappeared.

Francesca slipped through the crowds to join Jack. 'Who was that man?'

He looked surprised by her question. 'A troublemaker.'

'I've seen him before but I can't remember where.'

'He won't come again.' Jack reached for her hand. 'Well, Bernard, do you think I'll have to fight a duel over Frankie tonight?'

'If she belonged to anyone else but you, Jack.'

He'd headed her off, and she knew it. That made her more curious. But it was useless to question him. So she linked her arm through his and said to Bernard, 'With all these glamorous women round, I'll have to watch Jack.'

Jack squeezed her wrist. She smiled. He nudged her, she nudged him back, and forgot about the thug. She thought only that she wanted to make love to Jack. That she would like to pull him into the office, close the door, and feel him around her, with her, inside her. She shivered and leaned against him. He looked into her eyes, and read her mind. She ran the tip of her tongue along her teeth. He rolled the tip of her little finger between his thumb and forefinger as if it were her nipple.

162

'Stop it, Jack!' she murmured when no one was listening.

'Why?'

'I enjoy it too much.'

'Tonight I'm going to make love to you till you beg me to stop.'

She lifted her chin and looked him in the eyes. 'Is that a promise or a challenge?'

The jazz band was playing *Rhapsody in Blue*, more of the speakeasy-era music Jack so loved. The musicians were almost drowned by the laughter and voices of the crowd who thronged the grand staircase. The women wore cocktail dresses. Some were elegant, some were pretty. Others fluttered in short, frothy feathers or frou-frou skirts of spangled muslin, whilst their men wore Sixties' ruffled shirts under velvet dinner jackets, and chain bracelets with their names engraved in loopy italic lettering. Frankie giggled helplessly as she pictured William's face.

She was still giggling when Jack escorted her up the stairs to the dining room. 'When I tire of you I shall sell you to Fat Dudley.' He pointed to a table of some twenty people, dominated by a huge fat man with a smooth pink face and a delicate, girlish rosebud mouth. He was bald, except for a little white baby fluff on the top of his domed head. Francesca watched with fascination as he pulled a stack of brand-new notes from his pocket and counted a thousand pounds into the hand of the waitress taking bets. It wasn't the size of the bet which held her, she'd seen greater sums than that placed by her father. It was the way he caressed the notes with his beautifully manicured fingers, each one bearing a thick gold ring like a knuckleduster.

She leaned close to Jack. 'He looks a real villain.'

'He is. The best kind. He's never been caught.'

'You're teasing me again!'

Their table was in the centre, on the top tier so that Jack could slip away if needed. Nicoletta was already seated, resplendent in a purple antique gypsy dress with a headband of gold coins which tinkled each time she moved. She was deep in conversation with a journalist from the *Racing Post*. Opposite her were two National Greyhound Racing Club officials and their wives. Francesca sat down opposite Eamonn.

I'd like to ask you a secret favour,' she said, when everyone was distracted. 'I want to handslip Blue. I want to see if he'll chase.'

He gave her his bland, contented, tortoise smile. 'Monday morning. Early!'

The evening sky began to darken. The central grass bowl of the arena turned to deep emerald. Bright lights reflected up from the trackside and the huge scoreboard. Outside, on the terraces, people climbed higher to get a better view. By the track rail, the bookies shouted their prices above the babble. In the grandstand dining room, the tickertape whirring of the totalisator by the cash desks made an incessant background noise.

The tannoy crackled into life and Marius's voice boomed out. 'Good evening, ladies and gentlemen. This is a great day for Richmond Racing. I'm glad you can share it with us. Some of you must have wondered if you'd ever see the old track reopen. It has. And it's thanks to my friend, Jack Broderick.'

People clapped or raised their glasses.

Jack looked humble. Under the tablecloth Francesca reached for his thigh and ran the crimson tips of her fingernails up the inside of his leg. 'You deserve it,' she said.

'You helped.' He clamped his hand about her wrist, and stroked the softness of her palm, adding in a low voice, 'Behave yourself!' But he didn't try to stop her.

The first race was graded A1. All the dogs were very fast. The screens flicked with the pool forecast. The announcer came over the tannoy. 'Five minutes to the off. First race: trap one, Suzie's Alice; trap two, Irish Alfie; trap three, Patch Millie; trap four, The Gloucester Piper; trap five, Battersea Ben; trap six, Jet Landing.'

The dogs were being paraded. The starter bent to check each jacket and muzzle.

'One minute to the off.'

The starter placed the dogs inside their traps.

'The hare is moving.'

From the far side of the arena came the rattling of the trolley. The dogs yelped. As it drew nearer, they dropped to the ground, whimpering with excitement. The hare passed the traps. The doors flew upwards and the greyhounds streaked out. Jet was running fourth, with the railers, Suzie's Alice, Patch Millie and Irish Alfie in the lead. On the first bend, Jet was crowded. He ran out wide, to be overtaken by Battersea Ben. On the far straight he caught up, but was crowded again on the bend. Suzie's Alice tired.

164

So did Patch Millie. Now it was between Jet, Irish Alfie and Battersea Ben, with The Gloucester Piper steady in fourth. On the final turn, Ben tripped. He brought down Irish Alfie. Jet, the widerunner, missed the fray. He was in the lead. The crowd cheered. A nose ahead of The Gloucester Piper, Jet flew past the winning post.

It was well after midnight by the time the stadium was clear of guests and staff. Jack and Frankie walked through the deserted bars strewn with betting slips and cigarette ends, where the air was heavy with nicotine and beer. They went out on to the terrace. The arena was silent, lit only by the pale light from a half-moon. The air was fresh. It smelt of early summer and the approach of morning dew. The only trace of the huge crowd was the litter. The only sign of life was the yellow light from the night guard's office near the entrance.

'When I was in prison, I used to plan every detail of this day,' said Jack. 'But the one detail I didn't allow for was you.' He linked his arms around Frankie and drew her close. 'Oh, I knew I'd have a girlfriend. I didn't think I'd be without. I imagined her sexy, adoring, willing and probably stupid. I saw myself as master, she as slave. I never thought that I would love. That when I came home, I would run up to our room. I don't walk up, I have to run. I can't waste a minute of our time. But not just because I want to make love to you, because I want to talk. I want to hear of your day and tell you of mine. I want to share. To hear you laugh.'

They picked their way across the terrace to the Paddock House. It was deserted. Marius had gone home with Nicoletta. In the doorway, Jack took Frankie in his arms and kissed her deeply. He led her up the stairs, stopping every so often to kiss her in the gloom of the stairwell. The attic shone above them, lit by the ghostly fingers of moonlight. Jack didn't turn on the light or lower the blinds. He stood Francesca in the brightest ray of moonlight as he slipped the magenta silk from her shoulders and her hips, tracing a path down her neck to the soft mounds of her breasts. He unclipped her black muslin brassiere. He slid the muslin panties from her hips and kissed the flat of her stomach. Then he gently laid her on the bed.

She sprawled amongst the pillows and watched him throw his clothes in a pile. When he turned towards her, she held out her

165

arms. 'For the first time I feel we have forever,' she whispered against his mouth.

'We do.' He ran his fingers through her thick mahogany hair. 'Always!' He kissed her neck and her breasts, and rolled each nipple between his thumb and his forefinger, as he had rolled her little finger in the restaurant. She nibbled the lobes of his ears, her tongue searching. He rolled her over on her stomach and kissed each vertebra. She relished his weight on her back and on her buttocks. They rolled over again, their legs and arms entwined, the moonlight bathing their naked bodies. She reached for him, her face in the warmth of his stomach. He teased and probed, so gently that she cried out for more. The moonlight pervaded the room, the night, and their bodies. It gave them its romance. They made love as if this were the first time, and the last.

In the dawn Francesca woke and remembered the name of the pale-faced thug. She woke Jack. 'It was Lex Gunter.'

He didn't even bother to open his eyes. 'I know.'

Nineteen

Eamonn was testing the traps on the schooling track when Frankie arrived with Blue. It was a damp, overcast morning. Dew lay on the sand. From the kennels came the yelping of the other dogs. On the hillside, she could see five of them being walked by kennel-maids.

'You remember 'ow to handslip, don't you?' said Eamonn. He whistled Blue on to the track and demonstrated, bending his short, stocky body over the dog, lifting him up on his hind legs, right hand supporting the barrel of the body, left firm on the dog's chest. 'When the hare starts moving, you make Blue watch it. Like this!' Eamonn steadied the dog's jaw with his left hand. 'As the hare turns, you turn the dog's head. He must watch the quarry all the way. Only when it's past, you let 'im chase. Ease 'im after it. Encourage 'im.'

'I'll love him just the same, even if he won't chase.'

'Stop talking nonsense! You're making me nervous. God knows what you're doing to the dog.' Eamonn lumbered away towards the control tower.

Frankie held Blue up on his hind legs. At least, she attempted to. But he wriggled and tried to lick her face.

'Grip 'im firm,' Eamonn shouted down at her. 'Let 'im lean into the curve of your body.'

He set the hare in motion. At the rattling of the trolley, Blue pricked his ears.

'Up on 'is back legs!' shouted Eamonn.

The hare rattled round the top bend. Blue yelped.

'Make 'im watch it!'

The hare approached. Blue squealed. He wriggled in Frankie's arms.

'Don't let 'im go till it's past you!'

'I'm trying!' She grabbed at Blue, but he slipped from her grasp and bounded up the track to meet the hare head-on. As Blue sank his teeth into its furry face, Eamonn halted the trolley.

167

I'm sorry!' Frankie pulled Blue away. 'It was my fault. Can he try again? Please!'

Grumbling, the old trainer returned to the control tower.

Frankie called after him, 'Eamonn, why don't you handslip him? You're an expert.'

'And have you blame me if 'e doesn't chase? Not bloody likely!'

This time Frankie held Blue correctly. Her right hand was firmly under his stomach, her left crossed his chest to steady his jaw. She took his weight against her, bending slightly so that his long body was supported by hers. When the hare approached, he yelped and wriggled but she held him. As the hare passed, she let him slip, sending him after it with a cry of encouragement.

Blue needed no pushing. He raced after his quarry, bounding along the iron trolley track. At the bend, he came off the iron and cut across the sand to head off the hare. But Eamonn increased its speed, keeping it the standard eleven yards ahead. On the far side Blue ran so wide that again he hit the trolley tracks. On the final straight, he managed to keep steady, chasing flat out, his long body horizontal to the sandy track and his long legs reaching out and back.

Frankie didn't tell Jack or Marius about Blue. As far as they were concerned, he was just a pet, a big, ungainly shadow who followed her every footstep. A month later she and Eamonn tried him in the starting traps. The first time, he banged his head as the door went up. The second, he hesitated. The third, he came out like a bullet to chase his quarry, as if there had never been any other purpose to his existence.

With the stadium open, life at Richmond settled into a routine. The offices bustled with quiet efficiency. Telephones rang and were answered promptly. Telexes chattered to other telexes. Vans delivered food and drink. Lorries brought the dogs from their out-of-town kennels. Only the Paddock House was strictly private. Freed from the details of organisation, Jack and Frankie occasionally snatched an afternoon in bed. Like him, she was becoming a night person.

One morning she cleared out the storeroom next to the kitchen. Whilst Angel decorated it, she and Nicoletta went shopping for furniture. They bought a squashly sofa, a couple of armchairs and

168

some pot plants. By the end of the week, the storeroom was a cosy sitting-room. On the next sunny day, Frankie turned her attention to the walled garden, adding pot plants and garden furniture so that it became a patio where they could sit out. From his run, Big Ears watched with apprehension. He liked the company but he was still nervous of the dogs.

On racing nights, Jack and Frankie always dined in the grandstand restaurant. Jack liked to be on call in case of trouble. Usually they ate with Marius. Occasionally, Nicoletta joined them, though she didn't drink alcohol, gamble, or enjoy the crowds. She never came on Saturdays, when there were ten or twenty people at their table. Friends of Marius. Business acquaintances of Jack. People who needed to be entertained.

This was the only aspect of Frankie's new life which was similar to her marriage. As for the rest, it could hardly have been more different. By being so, it enabled her, for the most part, to forget about her wasted career, although she could not forget about Melanie – or William. Nor could she break through the barrier of her mother's disapproval. She longed to take Jack to White Oast, but her mother made it clear he wasn't welcome. So Frankie restricted her own visits to the occasional lunch.

On her way home after one visit, she took Blue to Eamonn's kennels. The old trainer was waiting for her. She handed her dog to him in silence, then drove on to Richmond.

That evening over dinner in the restaurant, Marius asked, What's happened to that blue monster? He's not at the house.'

'He's at Eamonn's.'

'Eammon only takes dogs in training.'

'Exactly.' Frankie smiled smugly and picked up her racecard.

Jack was standing behind her chair. He cupped his hands under her chin. 'Now I know where you've been slinking off to. You're lucky I'm not a jealous man.'

Nicoletta laughed loudly. 'You've been racked by suspicion. And don't glare at me, Jack! Others may be scared of you. I'm not.'

Frankie smiled at him. 'Don't you trust me?'

'I trust no one.' He walked away.

She turned white, as if he'd slapped her, which in a way he had. He was walking away from her, pushing through the crowds

169

toward the exit. She jumped up and followed, catching up with him at the swing doors. 'You hurt me,' she said. 'You've hurt me before. If you do it again, Jack, I'm going to leave you – however much I love you.'

'Why should I trust your love?'

'I've walked out on my whole life for you.'

'Not everything. Divorce William!'

It took her a week of drafting before she finally posted a letter to William. He didn't reply. She wrote again. This time he returned her letter with *If you want to talk, come to the house* written across the top in red ink.

'I'll have to see him,' she told Jack.

'No, you don't. Instruct a solicitor.'

'Why antagonise William if he's prepared to be civil? It's within his power to make me wait two years. He could even contest, and make me wait five!'

Jack walked away, shouting, 'You're dancing to his tune again.'

Frankie drove down to Eamonn's and took Blue out on the Downs, relishing the wind and the sun on her face and in her hair. She wondered what flaw existed in herself that drew her to difficult men. Or them to her. She made allowances for Jack because he'd been in prison, but she was not going to let him ride roughshod over her.

He was waiting for her on her return to the stadium. 'You have a visitor in the office,' he said, in a manner which made her think it must be William.

Running her fingers through her windswept hair, she hurried to the grandstand. She wished she was wearing something smarter than an old shirt and a pair of jeans, because William would see and judge, as he'd judged throughout their marriage.

Melanie was standing near the window, jigging from foot to foot. She turned as Frankie came into the room.

'Mel!' Frankie felt the tension drain away. 'I was afraid you were William. Oh, I'm so pleased to see you.'

Melanie had a plastic bag in her hand. She held it out. 'Lindsay Dault asked me to give you this.'

Frankie took it. Inside was a rag doll, just like those in Lindsay's flat. It's face was made out of white muslin. Its eyes were brown coat buttons, with thick dark eyebrows carefully stitched above them. Its hair was brown wool, plaited neatly, and it wore a red suit, like the one Frankie had worn on the day she'd helped to find the children.

'She made it especially for you,' Melanie went on. 'I should have given it to you long ago. I meant to post it but . . .' Her voice trailed away.

'I'm glad you didn't. I'm glad you came.'

'I've had it since the trial.'

'Mel, it doesn't matter. I have her address, I'll write and explain. I'm just pleased to see you. Come upstairs, let's have a drink. Let's talk. I've missed you. Why didn't you answer my letter?

'I can't stay.'

'Because Simon doesn't know you're here?' Frankie couldn't keep the bitterness out of her voice.

'He does, but he doesn't like it,' Melanie replied, defensively.

'Can't we forget about the men in our lives? We were friends. Best friends.'

'That's why I came today, Frankie. But Simon was right. You've changed. You're so combative.'

'You try being kicked out of chambers by people you thought were your friends.'

Melanie flushed. 'I was your friend. I defended you, even after you left. But the Frankie I knew wouldn't have dropped a brain-damaged boy halfway through his case. His hearing was last week. He only got the twenty thousand. To last a lifetime! He should have won twenty times that. But you don't care. Not any more.'

Frankie opened the door. 'Get out!'

She was crying when Jack returned to the office. Forgetting their quarrel, he went straight to her and put his arms around her. 'What's wrong?'

'Melanie accused me of not caring about that little boy.'

'But you did. I saw you.'

'She believes I didn't. Oh, I knew she was angry about her wedding, and we might never have spoken again, but I still thought of her as my best friend.'

'She was Mrs Eastgate's friend, not Frankie Tiernay's.'

*

171

Any intentions Francesca had about being gracious to William ended with Melanie's visit. She wanted to cut the past. She instructed David Jarrow to ask William for a quick divorce. Her decision brought a new closeness with Jack.

'I didn't realise it meant so much to you,' she told him in the intimate darkness of their bedroom.

He drew her close. 'A side of me will always be the borstal boy from the wrong side of the tracks, whilst you're the unattainable uptown lady.'

When Marius heard she was getting a divorce, he came into the kitchen where she was making sandwiches for lunch, placed his arms on her shoulders and looked her in her eyes. 'I was wrong about you,' he said.

She kissed his grizzled cheek. 'You were protecting Jack.'

He went through into the card room and said loudly, so she could hear, 'As Frankie's here to stay, I suppose we'd better put her on the payroll, eh, Jack?'

'I'm happy with a percentage,' she called after him. 'Of the gross, not the net!'

Marius spluttered. 'That's the trouble with women. You give them an inch and they want a mile.'

Frankie smiled as she spread a thick layer of pickle inside Marius's cheese sandwich, the way he liked it. 'I'm worth it, you old chauvinist! Why, I'm even polite to Fat Dudley in the interests of the track.'

Fat Dudley was one of their most regular punters. He made Frankie's flesh creep. He was like a huge middle-aged baby. His fluffed, balding head gleamed pink. His rosebud mouth twitched. When he took her hand in his, his flesh was clammy and cold.

'You always did fancy a bit of class,' he told Jack one evening, as he pressed his soft, wet lips on to the back of Frankie's hand. 'I like the type myself.'

Jack put a protective arm around Frankie's shoulders. 'You're talking to my future wife.'

'My congratulations! I meant no offence.' Fat Dudley lowered his bulk into an extra-large chair provided for him. He waited until Jack and Frankie had moved away before sending one of his gofers to fetch Marius. 'I'm interested in buying the track,' he told the old man.

'It's not for sale, Dudley.'

'It will be. You may own the land and the buildings but Jack's financed the refurbishment. He can force a sale. And he will. His classy new wife won't want him involved with people like me.' Dudley chuckled. 'Or you!'

'Jack won't drop me for anyone.'

'Ben Tiernay's daughter will. She never even visited her poor father when he was dying.'

David Jarrow arrived at the Paddock House whilst Jack and Frankie were dawdling over a late breakfast. 'Your husband wants to meet you alone,' he told Frankie, handing her the letter he'd received from William.

'So he can beat her up again?' said Jack. 'It's out of the question.'

David looked to Frankie. 'Is that your answer?'

She hesitated. 'Say I disagree, but don't back him into a corner.' She laid a hand on Jack's arm. 'Listen! Please! I know William, I'll have to appear to give on something. He cannot bear to lose on every count.'

They heard nothing for a fortnight. When David made enquiries, he was advised that William had left for America and wouldn't be back for some weeks.

Jack was philosophical. Now that Frankie had instigated the divorce, he saw an end to her link with William. She was furious. 'William's left me dangling on purpose,' she confided to Nicoletta, one afternoon in the shop. 'I recognise his tactics.'

'My husband did the same. His pride refused to accept that I had left him. Gaining custody of Jolyon was his revenge. And now, suddenly, he has a new girlfriend and he wants me to have Jolyon for part of the holidays.'

'But that's wonderful! You must be thrilled.'

A big tear slid down Nicoletta's pale, lined cheek. 'Of course I am! But I'm also scared. I haven't seen him for two years. He may not like me any more.'

'He will.' Frankie put her arm around Nicoletta. 'And we'll all help to entertain him.'

August was the stadium's first slack month. Punters were on holiday. Bernard took a fortnight off. Signor Umberto went to

Italy. Jack and Frankie escaped to Sète, the old French sea town to the west of Montpellier. By day, they windsurfed or lay on wide sandy beaches. In the evenings, they ate delicious food in tiny port-side restaurants, or drove inland to explore villages in whose windswept cemeteries were the graves of young men who'd died fighting for the Resistance: the maquisards who took their nickname from the golden broom which covered the hills in springtime.

Jolyon arrived on the day they returned to Richmond. Nicoletta brought him to the Paddock House for lunch. He was an attractive little boy with black hair cut in a pudding-basin hairstyle, and huge, dark Oriental eyes.

'Hello Jolyon,' said Frankie, smiling at him.

He stared straight through her.

Jack held out a bag of crisps. 'I expect you're hungry.'

Jolyon turned away. He looked at Marius. 'Will you show me where the hare is kept?'

'Of course,' the old man smiled and held out his hand. 'Come on!' They went out, on to the track.

'He's just shy.' Nicoletta tried not to appear anxious. 'He'll be better when he knows you.'

At lunch, Jolyon refused to sit down. He hid behind Marius's chair. The only time he spoke to Frankie was to ask if he could feed Jaws and Mathilda. Later, she took him outside to see Big Ears. Side by side, they poked baby carrots through the wire around the run whilst she explained how to care for a rabbit. It was several days before the boy would speak to Jack. He wasn't as reserved with Frankie, so long as they talked about her pets.

'I hope I'm better than this when we have children,' she confided in Jack.

He kissed the tip of her nose. 'I hope I'm better, too.'

By early September all the staff had returned from their holidays. The punters came back, the restaurant bookings picked up, the terraces were full. The dogs ran in the nip of autumn.

Frankie was so wrapped up in her life with Jack that she was barely aware of the world beyond the stadium. When she turned on the television to find the City celebrating Big Bang, it was Jack who explained to her what it was all about. Once, she would have known. Once, she would have cared.

174

On a blustery Monday morning Blue trialled at Richmond. In order to race on a National Greyhound Racing Club track, he had to grade in three times a minimum of five hundred and fifteen metres in thirty-two seconds. This would make him A12, the lowest grade. If he failed to grade in, he could try again. If he failed indefinitely, he would never race on a top-class track.

Frankie was hovering in the car park when Eamonn's kennel van arrived. 'I know you're going to do well,' she told Blue.

'He might, if you don't upset him.'

'I'm only telling him I love him.'

'If Jack has a rival, it's that blue dog. He gets more cuddling in a day than most of us get in a lifetime.'

He trialled the experienced dogs first, those who'd been off sick or injured. There was an ugly brindle called The Mugger. He graded in at A9.

'Blue's next,' Eamonn called to her.

She led Blue to the traps. His ears were pricked. He looked around the stadium, distracted and excited. With difficulty she eased him into trap 4. He tried to turn. She dashed round to the front, calling his name. The hare rattled on its trolley. Blue yelped. The hare drew closer. Blue's head was still up. 'Down! Down!' Frankie slapped the ground.

His jaws were open, he squealed. The hare drew nearer. Frankie screamed at him to drop. She was terrified he would come flying out and hit his head on the trap door. He sank as the hare triggered the release. The door flew up. Blue shot out, running so wide he was almost on top of the iron trolley. On the bend, he lost speed. On the straight he caught up, stretching out, reaching his big paws right out in front of him.

Frankie gathered him at the pick-up. He was still searching for the hare which had disappeared into its box.

Eamonn checked the stopwatch. 'He just made it. Thirty-two seconds. Grade A12.'

'I don't believe it. That hideous brindle was A9. Blue ran much faster.

'The Mugger stayed on the track. Your dog ran 'alfway round the country. He ain't a bad dog but 'e's still backward.'

'Then I don't want him to race. I don't want Blue in the bottom

175

class. It's humiliating for him.' Leading Blue, she set off towards the grandstand.

Eamonn caught up with her. 'I ain't spent weeks training a pup for nothing. This dog'll race because I'm his trainer and I say so.' He picked up Blue as though he were a baby and carried him to the kennel van.

Blue trialled twice more. On the third attempt he graded in at A9. There was less than a second between each grade, but smaller, lighter pups continued to run faster and were graded higher.

William stood at the window of his office in Makepeace Buildings. In one hand he held David Jarrow's letter. He'd had a trying weekend at Kingly. His mother had continually criticised Francesca, saying that a girl whose father was a drunk and whose mother was a divorcee was bound to have no morals. William had snapped. His mother had been shocked. As always, she'd claimed to speak for his own good. He'd walked around the garden, past the spot where Francesca had found Big Ears fleeing from the rabbit farm. No one else but her could have calmed the terrified rabbit. He remembered how she'd held it close, her arms around its trembling body. It was the same, protective way that Dominique hugged everyone who visited White Oast. He tried to recall the last time his mother had hugged him. He thought it was when he was seven, on the day he started boarding school.

Now, back in London, he reached for the telephone and tapped out a series of numbers. His call was answered on the sixth ring. 'Dominique? Oh, hello Steven. How silly of me. I forgot she is always out on Tuesday mornings. Yes, Steven, I am William. Look, I realise I shouldn't involve you, but I am very concerned about Francesca. I'm still fond of her, in spite of the fact she has hurt me. I would hate to see her ruin her life, and this request for me to divorce her for adultery seems most unwise. You didn't know she's living with another man? I'm astonished. Yes, Dominique certainly does. Well, I don't like being the one to tell you, but Francesca's living at Richmond Racing with an ex-criminal. That's correct, where her father used to live.'

Frankie and Jack came home from a meeting with a new race

sponsor to find her mother pacing up and down in the office. 'Why did you have to upset poor Steven?' she demanded.

'I haven't done anything to him.' Frankie dropped her bags on to a chair.

'William phoned White Oast this morning when I was out. He told Steven that you'd asked for a divorce and that you were living here.'

Jack stepped towards her. 'And you hadn't told him?'

Dominique raised her chin. 'Don't threaten me, Jack. I lived here once. I had eight years of people like you.'

'I wouldn't hurt you,' he said softly. 'You're the mother of the woman I love.'

'Then let her go before you ruin her life.'

Frankie reached for Jack's hand. 'I won't leave him. Not for anyone or anything.'

Her mother looked from one to the other, then left without another word. They stood in silence, listening to the neat click of her high heels as she crossed the grandstand terrace. Then Frankie dropped Jack's hand and raced after her. 'Mummy! Wait! I'm sorry if Steven was upset. But Jack's my life. Please try to understand.'

Her mother stopped. 'You think you can change him, don't you? But no woman ever reforms a man like that. She merely thinks she has, until it's too late.'

'Jack is not like my father.'

'No. He's far worse. At least Ben never killed anyone – except himself!'

Twenty

Eamonn didn't tell Frankie he was entering Blue for a race. It was only at dinner, when she picked up her race card, that she saw his name, drawn trap 6, in the first puppy race. 'But he isn't ready!' she protested.

'I ain't scratching 'im.'

'Blue is my dog, Eamonn.'

'If you ain't satisfied with me, madam, you may remove your animal from my kennels.'

'Of course I'm satisfied.' Frankie sat back into her chair. 'I just don't want him to come last. I don't care about me, it's him. I don't want people to laugh at him.'

The trainer softened. He patted her hand. 'He's a good dog. You and I know that.'

The dogs were paraded along the track. Blue was at the rear, wearing trap 6's black and white striped jacket. He looked young and clumsy and vulnerable. In front of him were four lightweight railers and The Mugger.

The tannoy announced, 'Two minutes to the off.'

The paraders turned towards the traps. Frankie twisted her hands into each other. She longed for Jack, but he was in the office with Bernard and she hesitated to send for him when he was busy. Blue was eased into trap 6. Frankie prayed he wouldn't panic. The tannoy announced, 'The hare is running.' She heard the rattle of the trolley. The greyhounds began to yelp. The hare came round the turn. One by one the dogs sank to the ground. Except for Blue. He stood, legs straight, head up, ears pricked. Frankie wanted to cry.

Suddenly a hand fell on her shoulder. She turned. Jack and Marius were standing behind her. 'Did you think we'd leave you to watch alone?' asked Jack.

She couldn't answer.

'You did, didn't you?' He shook his head. 'How little you trust me.'

The hare triggered the trap release. The dogs shot out. The small, light railers tore along the inside rail, all bunched together, a black and white bitch called Miss Scallywag in the lead from Digger Brown and a big yellow dog named Elsing Hermes. Blue was miles behind. He'd hit his head on the trap door.

At the first bend Miss Scallywag fell. She tripped Digger Brown and put Elsing Hermes off his stride. Another dog crashed into them. When the group recovered and ran on, that dog was limping.

'Broken wrist,' said Jack.

Frankie tried not to think of Blue being injured.

On the far straight, Blue was moving up. He overtook Miss Scallywag and pushed past Elsing Hermes, knocking him off his stride. As the dogs approached the final bend, the crowds cheered. Blue was in third place, bunched behind Digger Brown. At the turn he swung out, falling back but free. He came up the final straight, overtaking Digger Brown, lolloping past as though he wasn't even trying. But he didn't beat the winning dog, the ugly brindle called The Mugger.

Frankie was on her feet as soon as the race was over. She hugged Jack, hugged Eamonn, and squeezed Marius's gnarled hand. 'That'll teach you all to mock my beautiful dog,' she crowed.

Jack laughed at her exuberance. 'I was wrong,' he conceded. 'He's a good dog. He has stamina. He should try a marathon.'

Frankie bent to kiss the corner of his mouth. She knew how difficult it was for him to admit he was wrong.

In the middle of the night, she was woken by Jack slipping from their bed. 'What's wrong?' she asked.

He held up his hand to silence her and moved stealthily towards the window, the pale light of a half-moon touching his naked body. Against the wall he stopped, totally immobile, listening. Then he whispered, 'I heard a noise. Someone's on the kennel roof.'

'Call Angel. He's the night guard.'

'I've tried. He didn't answer.'

The stadium was lit by sporadic moonlight, with large dark clouds casting their chasing shadows over one section after another, like the intermittent probe of a searchlight. Jack watched. Frankie sat in the middle of their bed, the duvet pulled tight around her.

'Why the kennel roof?' she whispered. 'Why not the office? That's where the safe is.'

'Dope.'

'But all the dogs have gone home.'

He shrugged and tried the internal phone again. Angel answered breathlessly, 'Guard here.'

'There's someone on the kennel roof. Check it!'

'Right away, Jack.'

Frankie joined Jack at the window. They watched the light from Angel's torch move along the terraces to the paddock. They heard his boots scrape on the concrete and the click of the paddock door as he opened it. They watched him take a ladder and climb up, waving his torch over the kennel roof. 'Nothing here, Jack,' he reported.

'Where were you when I called the first time?'

'I was taking a leak.'

'You have a mobile phone to carry at all times.'

'I forgot, Jack. I'm sorry.'

'Who was with you in the guards' room?'

There was a short, sharp silence. 'No one.' ·

'Don't lie to me, Angel!'

'OK! She was a girl I met in a pub. I know I shouldn't have let her into the stadium but she came up here, looking for me. I didn't ask her to, I swear. But she was hot for it, Jack. She couldn't get enough of me.'

'Like the girl you had here last night? The one I found trying to enter my office this morning?'

Angel didn't answer.

Jack replaced the phone and climbed into bed.

'You didn't tell me about the girl,' said Frankie.

'Angel's my problem.'

Jack was up at first light. Frankie knew better than to follow. By the time he returned, she was at her desk. 'I found a broken tile on the roof,' he told her.

'What does Angel say?'

'I've fired him.'

'I'm not sorry. I never liked him. But isn't that a bit hasty?'

180

'Angel despises weakness. I couldn't let him stay after he'd disobeyed me.'

Frankie reached for Jack's hand. 'I'm sorry he let you down.'

Jack linked his fingers through hers. 'Angel wasn't a bad kid, not when he first went inside. He ran errands, did what he was told. I wanted to help him.'

'As Marius helped you?'

He nodded.

'Maybe Angel thought you were growing weak because of me?'

'They all do. Angel. Fat Dudley.' He smiled. 'But they're wrong. I'm stronger because I have you. Marius gave me the chance to go straight. You've given me the reason to stay that way.' He crossed to the office window and stared out at the drizzle which was softening the sandy track. 'A big doping scandal would finish us. With my past, no one would believe we were clean. We have to catch the intruder. I've ordered the closed-circuit television to be extended to all rooftops and exteriors, with monitors in every office and in our attic. It could be a punter who's heavily in debt and needs a killing. Or someone who wants to break us, like Fat Dudley. He's always dreamed of owning a track.'

'Or Lex Gunter. I shouldn't tell you this, but you do already suspect something. Marmintoll Construction, the big City company, were behind Gunter when he attacked Marius. They want the land for houses. They could be after it again.'

'Perhaps.' Jack's eyes narrowed. 'Don't tell Marius. He'll only worry.'

'I won't tell him so long as you don't take risks,' she said. 'I don't want to be a prison widow.'

He gave her a smile of fierce vulnerability. 'That's the first time you've talked of when we're married. I want to hear you saying it again.'

The monitors were installed that afternoon. When Jack gave an order, it was instantly executed. That night, he and Frankie sat up, fully dressed, watching the flickering screen and listening for footsteps. Only when dawn broke did they allow themselves to sink into bed.

'It was probably kids,' said Frankie, thankfully closing her eyes against the daylight.

'You don't have to sit up with me.'

'No.' She yawned. 'But I want to.'

By the end of the week they were both exhausted. Saturday nights drew the largest crowds, with open races, ungraded races, and dogs from other tracks. The prize money was higher. The betting was heavier. The stadium's rake-off from the tote was twice that of any other night. Men, who on other nights came alone, brought wives or girlfriends. They drank more, ate more. The restaurant was always fully booked. It was a late night for Jack and Frankie. Neither had the strength to watch the monitor.

Jack woke at four in the morning and was out of bed, pulling on his jeans, before Frankie had even opened her eyes. 'Footsteps,' he whispered. 'Stay here.'

'Call the guard.'

'He's in Fat Dudley's pay.'

'You took him on knowing that?'

'I prefer to know my enemy.' Silently, and without turning on the light, Jack removed a mirror from the wall. He tapped the corner of what Frankie had thought to be an obsolete light switch.

On the far side of the room, one of ten blanched oak panels, no different from the other nine, slid down to reveal a narrow safe. Jack reached inside and took out a vicious, black Colt .45 pistol.

'No!' Frankie leaped out of bed. 'Not this way.'

'Be quiet!'

She seized his arm. 'Jack! Call the police!'

He shook her off. 'Don't be a fool.' He loaded seven bullets into the magazine.

She stood with her back against the door, arms outstretched, naked, vulnerable but determined. 'I won't let you go back to gaol. You'll have to shoot me first.'

He walked towards her, the gun in his right hand, and she gripped the door handle to steady herself. He seized her by the wrist and twisted her arm. She gave a cry and let go of the door. It flew open.

There was a noise on the landing below. 'What the hell's going on?' asked Marius.

'Jack's going to shoot a man on the roof. And don't try to shut me up, Jack! I don't care who I tell or what noise I make if I save you from going back to prison.'

'Out of my way!' He pushed her out of the way, not hard, more in sorrow, and ran downstairs, the pistol in his hand.

'She's right, Jack,' Marius begged. 'Only this time, I won't visit you.'

Jack didn't answer. He went out into the night.

Marius and Frankie stared at each other in the gloom of the stairwell. Suddenly she was aware of being naked. She turned back into the bedroom. But before she had time to close the door, Marius came up the stairs. He walked straight into the bedroom, brushing her bare arm with the sleeve of his striped pyjamas. She jumped away, unable to believe this was happening, hating Marius for taking advantage and hating Jack for leaving her alone.

Marius picked up her kimono dressing gown and held open the arms. 'Come on,' he said gently. 'We deserve some of my special coffee laced with brandy.'

Unable to speak, she slipped her arms through the folds of material and wrapped the kimono around herself. For a moment, Marius rested his hands on her shoulders. Protective. Fatherly. She was deeply ashamed.

Jacked climbed on to the kennel roof. From the kitchen Frankie and Marius could hear his footsteps. Through the window they caught glimpses of his shadow moving along the side of the parapet. He didn't walk on top, where his silhouette would have stood out darker than the night sky. He crept along the slope, as only someone accustomed to entering other people's houses would know to do.

When he returned, Frankie and Marius were still at the kitchen table. 'Six tiles have been loosened,' he told them. 'Underneath each, a hole has been drilled down into the kennels. The holes are large enough to take a morsel of doped meat. The dogs are kennelled two deep. Twelve dogs could be affected. If you hadn't interfered, I'd have caught him.'

'What use is the stadium if you're in prison?' said Frankie. 'Marius and I can't fight Fat Dudley or Marmintoll.'

'With a doping scandal there'll be no stadium. We'll be bankrupt.' He marched upstairs.

She ran after him, shouting, 'Jack, you're playing straight into their hands. They expect you to answer with violence. They want you to carry a gun. With your record, they know you'd never be allowed a firearms certificate. Can't you see, they want you to break the law. They want you back in prison.'

He had his back to her as he replaced the gun in the wall safe. 'Violence is my language.'

'It needn't be. Call the police. Show them that you're clean.'

'Do you think the police would treat me deferentially? Do you think they'd offer me tea and comfort, and assure me that urban crime is not as high as *Daily Telegraph* readers fear? No, they'd laugh. They'd love to see Jack Broderick screwed by his own kind.'

'Better their laughter than prison.'

'So you think the police would nail Fat Dudley or Gunter or whoever? Grow up, Frankie. This is the real world. They're probably in his pay.'

'Why do you say that?'

'Because they're not in mine.'

'Not all police are dishonest.'

'Everyone's dishonest. Even you. Look how you betrayed your husband.'

She paled, but didn't answer. Slipping off her kimono, she drew on a pair of trousers and a sweater. Then she pulled her suitcase out of the cupboard, opened the drawers of her dressing table and tipped the contents inside, not bothering to smooth them, merely tossing them in as if they were rubbish which she didn't want to take but couldn't leave behind.

'What are you doing?' he demanded.

'I'm not going to sit by and watch you be arrested.'

'So much for love!'

'It's because I love you.' She scooped her dresses from their rail and dropped them into another case. They fell in a tangle of hangers and material, the hangers catching and twisting in the fabric.

'I shouldn't have said that about William,' he said. 'I'm sorry. I do trust you.'

'That isn't the reason I'm leaving. It's the gun.'

'But why should my battle with Fat Dudley make you walk out? What has it to do with us?'

'I'm terrified of violence. I saw my father beaten up when I was little. It happened here, beside the track. I can still see his blood.' Frankie picked up her cases. 'Goodbye, Jack.'

She expected him to run after her. As she went down the stairs she anticipated his footsteps. But he didn't follow.

The guard stared at her in amazement as she opened the main gate and walked over to her car. Switching on the engine, she sat with her foot on the accelerator, telling herself the motor needed to warm up. Finally, she slipped the car into gear and turned for the exit. The guard watched. She wondered how soon Fat Dudley would know she'd left Jack.

As she approached the outer barrier, she pressed her automatic opener. The bar rose. She accelerated. But just as she reached the bar it came straight down, missing the bonnet of the car by less than an inch.

'Did you think I'd let you go without a fight?' asked Jack's voice over the tannoy.

She remained at the wheel, trembling, her head in her hands. He came down to collect her, reaching inside to lift her out, tenderly, as if she were a child. 'You could have killed me,' she murmured, burying her face in the warmth of his jacket.

'I was watching on the monitor.' He carried her through the stadium to the Paddock House, back up to their room which still bore the traces of her angry departure in the twisted sheets, the swinging coat hangers and the open drawers of her dressing table.

He laid her down on the bed and smoothed back her hair from her face, studying her as if he wanted to learn so much about her that they would never fight again. 'I'm sorry about your father,' he said. 'Why didn't you tell me before?'

'It's something I try to forget.'

'Would you really have left me tonight?'

'Rather than watch you go back to prison, yes.'

He kissed her hard and fiercely. She opened to him, wanting him to envelop her. He pulled the sweater over her head and the trousers from her hips. She wore no bra or panties. She'd not had time to put them on in her flight from him. Or, more truthfully, if she'd waited one more minute she might never have left. He kissed her neck and her shoulder, gently, barely touching. He ran his mouth down the length of her body, kissing her stomach and the soft inside of her thighs. She responded, reaching for him, wanting him with all the acuteness of nearly having lost him. She wanted to give him pleasure because to do so gave her pleasure, so

185

much so that she did not know where her feelings ended and his began. It had never been that way with William. There had always been a line between what he did to her and she did to him. Mostly, she'd pleased him.

With Jack it was different. She wanted to do things for him she would not do, and had not done, for any other man. Things which outside this relationship and without his love would disgust her. But nothing she did with Jack disgusted her. All the prudery she had felt with William disappeared. She wanted Jack to make love to her in every way and all ways. She craved him deep inside her, reaching for her womb, her muscles contracting to hold him longer and tighter. She wanted him to make love to her eyes, her ears, her feet, every part of her. She relished his mouth, his tongue, his fingers, his sex. She enjoyed it when he hurt her. Not each time they made love, or even every other time, and sometimes not for weeks. Just occasionally, when she craved the eroticism of brutality. When she wanted to be dominated. But this act, like so many others, could only be with Jack.

On other occasions, and this was one of them, she desired tenderness, and he gave it to her. He was gentle and loving. They touched so subtly that their skin barely met. They made love slowly, languorously, gently exploring, waiting one for the other. He held back till she was ready. He kissed her as he entered her. The grey fingers of dawn caressing their rhythmic bodies. They looked into each other's eyes, and the world of violence did not exist.

Twenty-One

Frankie didn't mention the intruder or the police to Jack, although the subject hung between them. She'd stood her ground. If necessary, she'd stand it again. In the mean time, she gave him time to think.

He came into the bathroom when she was lying in the bath. 'All right,' he said. 'We'll do it your way. If we hear someone, we'll call the cops. But if they don't catch him, I go back to my way.'

She held out a slippery, soapy hand to him. 'Jack, my way is that we call the police now.'

'And have them crawling over the place for no reason!'

'They'll react to you better if you confide in them from the start.'

She thought he would refuse, but he didn't. He laughed and threw the sponge at her. 'Yes, Madame Manipulator!'

Two plain-clothes detectives arrived within an hour of Frankie's telephone call. The younger was small, dark and curly-haired, the older was large and fair and square-faced. In jeans and scruffy leather jackets, T-shirts and trainers, they could have been two mature students at an inner-city poly-technic. They settled into chairs, and produced notepads and cheap biros. Jack watched them from his leather armchair, as a fox watches the huntsmen.

Frankie did the talking. Jack listened. 'Well, I think that's all,' she said at the end, nervously bright and wishing he would speak.

'You must suspect someone, Miss Tiernay,' said the small, dark detective.

'Oh, there are a couple of people,' she began. Then she stopped as she sensed Jack's outrage.

'Their names?'

'Umm . . . no one in particular.'

'But you just said there were a couple of people.'

'No she didn't!' cut in Jack.

The detectives exchanged glances. They stood up. 'We'll be back tonight, and every night till we catch him,' said the large fair

187

one. He held out his hand to Jack. 'We're glad you called us, sir. It's not your usual habit.'

Frankie thought Jack would explode. His knuckles were white. His jaw was set. Then, suddenly, he gave them his boyish grin. 'I was outmanœuvred by the woman I love.' He shook hands with the detectives. 'It happens to the best of us.'

That night they sat up watching the card-room monitor, Jack and Frankie, Marius and Nicoletta, and the two detectives whom Jack nicknamed Starsky and Hutch after the detectives in the television series.

'Of course, no cop really leads the glamorous life depicted on the screen,' said Jack, his eyes drifting over the scuffed, cheap clothes of the two detectives. 'It's the criminals who do that. But television can't show that crime pays. The censor wouldn't like it.'

'Jack,' Frankie laid a hand on his arm, 'Don't bait them.'

'Why not? Baiting the police used to be my favourite hobby.'

'I bet they've been warned not to rise to it.'

'Have you?' He turned to the detectives.

They wouldn't answer. But the possibility intrigued Jack. He offered them whisky. They refused, but accepted coffee. As dawn broke, he stood up and stretched. 'They won't come now.' He started up the stairs. Then he stopped. 'Hey, Starsky, I'll tell you something. Criminals have more fun. They don't have to hang around like you do. They know what time the job's to be done.' He went on up the stairs, singing *Jailhouse Rock*.

For a week the detectives staked out the stadium. Jack sat up with them, at first to make sure they didn't snoop: his past made him mistrust all policemen. But as the days passed, he grew to like the detectives, although he refused to admit it to Frankie. But she would hear muffled laughter as she drifted into sleep. One evening she came downstairs to find him happily setting out the Scrabble board in anticipation of the detectives' arrival, and she pondered the similarity between the huntsmen and the fox.

'Of course, it would help if we could give them a few names,' she told him when he sank into bed at dawn, grumbling of exhaustion.

'I'm no grass.'

'I thought you liked the detectives.'

'That has nothing to do with it.'

'But Jack, we know it's either Fat Dudley or Gunter.'

'Do we?' He propped himself up on his elbow and looked into her sleepy face. 'It could be your husband.'

'William wouldn't go climbing around on the roof. He's far too conscious of his position. In any case, why would he want to?'

'To ruin me. To ruin us.'

Blue's first win was in a marathon. He beat The Mugger into second place by a short head. Frankie was so excited she could hardly watch the final moments. Afterwards, she ran down to the paddock to hug her dog. When she returned to the table, Jack had ordered champagne and strawberries. He had more strawberries delivered to the Paddock House, saying they were for his breakfast. Frankie smiled but said nothing. It was no good Jack denying that he liked the detectives.

They did their best to keep secret the police surveillance of the stadium, but word got out.

'I smell a copper, Jack,' said Fat Dudley one evening as he settled his crumpled bulk into the specially upholstered chair. 'Is it you or me they're watching?'

Jack leaned casually against the totalisator desk. He looked elegant and relaxed, the perfect host in his black dinner jacket and his polite smile. 'You tell me, Fatman.'

'My dear boy, if I stood up on your roof there'd be nothing left of it.'

'What makes you think they're watching the roof?'

'Like you, I know most things.' Dudley pursed his small rosebud mouth to take a sip of champagne. Then he dabbed his pink lips with the corner of the damask tablecloth. 'You clean up well, Jack,' he said. 'No one would guess your past. Most men carry the odour of prison. It's in their eyes, their walk, the way they talk. But not you. You're clever. I always thought so, even when you were a kid stealing radios from parked cars. But it was silly to kill that man in prison. You should have got someone else to do it. I would have. Never dirty your own hands, Jack. Never involve emotion. It doesn't pay.' Dudley raised his champagne glass again and took another small sip. 'You and I would make a brilliant partnership. I have money. You have charm. People tell us things, through fear, for money, for future favours, for protection. We're two of a kind, Jack. We are both clever, ruthless and dishonest.'

189

'Ruthless, maybe. But not dishonest. Not any more. Those days are finished for me, Dudley.'

'Because of a woman?' Fat Dudley giggled. 'Really, Jack, I'd never have expected you to go soft.'

'Love hasn't made me soft. It's given me a reason to go straight. I have someone else's ideals to live up to.'

'You really care for her, don't you?'

'I'd kill the man who harmed her. Or Marius. They're the most important people in my world.' As Jack walked away, he wished he hadn't voiced his feelings. By doing so, he'd made Frankie and Marius very vulnerable.

Dominique lay on her bed at White Oast, a dressing gown wrapped defensively around her body. The light from the bedside lamp swathed her in pale gold. It enhanced the pale pink of her satin dressing gown. It caressed her pale gold hair. She heard the shuffle of Steven's footsteps on the stairs. He tapped on her door. 'A cup of tea, dear?'

'Thank you.' She forced herself to sit up, gritting her teeth against the pain in her side.

He came in, smiling with gentle anxiety, and settled the cup on her bedside table. 'Feeling better?'

'A little.'

'I've called the doctor. He'll be here in an hour. Don't argue with me! You have to see him, you're ill.' He started back towards the door.

She called after him. 'Steven, I'm sorry if you were upset by William. I planned to tell you that Frankie was living at Richmond, but I didn't know how to. I understand how you feel about the stadium.'

He shuffled back. 'My dear, I always knew you never loved me as you loved Ben.' He raised his hand to silence any denial. 'But knowing he's dead helps me. You see, I was always afraid you might return to him.'

'Oh no! You shouldn't have worried. I never once considered it. If only you'd asked me, I'd have reassured you.' Dominique clasped one of his gnarled hands in both of hers. 'I'm far happier with you. I love the gentle order of our life. I love the peace and safety. That's why I fear for Frankie. Not just because she's in love with a man like Jack Broderick, but because she's so like Ben.'

In spite of Frankie having answered William through her solicitor, he wrote to her directly, again asking to meet her alone. She handed the letter to Jack, saying, 'I'll have to go or he'll never give me the divorce.'

'Not unless I come too.'

She reached for his hand. 'Jack, I should face William on my own. I need to confront the minotaur.'

He linked his fingers through hers. 'If that bastard hurts you, I'll kill him. I don't care what the penalty is.'

Neither Islington nor the street affected Frankie, but the house did, more than on her previous visit. She was afraid, although she tried to pretend she wasn't. Her mouth felt dry. Her hands were clammy. She pressed the front door bell. Instantly, she heard William's footsteps in the hall. The key turned, the bolts scraped back. They stared at each other in silence. He looked paler and older. His fair hair appeared greyer. He was very thin. Compared to Jack, he seemed fragile. She couldn't believe he'd had the strength to hit her. She wondered how she could have let herself be suppressed by such a man.

'Good evening, Francesca,' he said quietly.

She tried to say 'Hello', but the word came out strangled.

He stepped back. 'Do come in.'

She walked into the hall, her hall. Only it wasn't hers any more. He ushered her into his study. She sat in one of the armchairs near the fire, which was neither laid nor lit. The black grate was empty and dusty. It made the room look sad.

William handed her a dry sherry without asking if she wanted something different, then he took his place behind the desk, tipping slightly backwards in his heavy leather chair. 'How are you?' he asked.

'Fine . . . thank you.'

'And your mother and Steven?'

'You know that for yourself, William. You telephoned Steven. He was very upset.'

'My parents have also been upset.' He frowned. 'Are you pregnant.'

191

She flushed. 'No.'

'Then why the quick divorce?'

'We'd prefer not to wait two years.'

'I'm amazed such niceties as marriage matter at a dogtrack.'

She took a deep breath. Now she remembered all too well how he'd crushed her with his mockery and his criticism. 'William,' she said, 'I haven't come here to argue. If you don't agree to an early divorce, say so and I'll leave.'

He drew the tips of his fingers together in an arch and rested his chin on them. 'You've learned to fight. I imagine you've had to, living with a criminal. Tell me, does he slap you around?'

'No, he doesn't. Unlike you!' Frankie stood up. 'Don't bother to show me out.'

As she walked towards the door, he called after her, 'Have you any idea what it's been like for me, living in this house without you? Sleeping in the bed we once shared. Coming home to silence. Sitting at the table and looking up, and seeing no one.'

Her anger receded. 'I'm sorry. I wish it hadn't happened this way.'

'You could come back.'

She was stunned to silence.

When she didn't reply, he went on, 'Give me until May, then I'll start proceedings.'

She spoke as gently as she could. 'It won't make any difference, William. I'm in love with Jack and I'm going to marry him, even if I have to wait five years!'

'It'll make a difference to me,' he answered crisply. 'I am due to be sworn in as a High Court judge in April. The scandal of my wife consorting with an ex-criminal like Broderick could jeopardise my future.'

By the time Frankie reached the stadium, her head was throbbing and her throat was raw and dry. Racing was well underway, so she had no chance to talk to Jack alone. She joined Marius and Nicoletta at their table, watched Blue again beat The Mugger by a head, and discussed with Eamonn the possibility of entering the dog for an open race at another track, such as Walthamstow or Wimbledon. Halfway through the evening, she slipped away to the attic.

Jack came up around midnight to find her tossing and turning with a high fever. 'I'll call a doctor,' he said.

'No. It's just flu.' She pulled a face. 'The strain of seeing William brought it on.'

Jack sat down on the side of the bed and smoothed back her hair from her hot forehead. 'What did he say about the divorce?'

'He wants to wait till May. He's to become a High Court judge in April and he doesn't want any scandal beforehand.'

'That's another five months.'

What's the point of destroying his career? We can wait. We have each other.'

'That's not the point. He still has a hold on you.'

'Don't shout at me, Jack! I can't force a quick divorce. It's up to William.'

'I expect he told you he'd forgive you if you came back to him.'

She was saved from having to answer by a buzz from the bedside telephone. 'Yes,' shouted Jack.

'Intruder behind grandstand proceeding towards kennel block. Short, male, balaclava over face,' said one of the detectives.

Jack switched on the monitor. It revealed a small, dark figure moving along the base of the grandstand wall, slipping from one patch of shadows to another.

'He seems to know his way around,' said Jack, quickly exchanging his jacket for a dark sweater, one with a high neck to cover the collar of his white shirt.

Frankie pushed back the duvet.

'Stay here,' said Jack. 'You're ill.'

'I want to come.' She was out of bed, pulling on a tracksuit and trying to forget her thumping headache.

Without turning on the lights, they felt their way down the stairs to the office where the detectives sat in the gloom, away from the window. Marius joined them. Then Nicoletta, appearing like a ghost in a grey kaftan. They crowded around the monitor, switching the focus from one camera to another, homing in on him, so close that they could see his eyes darting from side to side in the slits of the balaclava.

'It's an inside job,' said Jack. 'He knows where the cameras are. Look at the way he turns his face away.'

193

At the far corner of the kennel block, the intruder took a length of rope from his pocket and tied a small anchor to one end. With a backward flick of his arm, he hurled the anchor upwards. The first time, it bounced off the side of the wall. The second, it caught in the roof. He stood still, listening. They sensed the tautness of his nerves. He gave a few tugs on the rope, as if fearing it had merely caught in the gutter. Then, satisfied he started to pull himself up the wall, his arms straining from their sockets as, step by step, he walked his feet up the brickwork.

'That is a young, fit man,' said Hutch with grudging admiration.

Once on the roof, the intruder pulled up his rope and coiled it neatly, available but out of sight. He crouched and listened, waiting a full minute before he began to pick his way across the tiles, like a cat in unknown territory.

When he was directly over the back row of kennels, he took out a screwdriver and eased a tile from its place. With a long, sharp hand-drill, he bored a hole right down into the ceiling of the kennels. He checked his work with a pinprick torch, poked something into the hole with a stick, and replaced the tile. Then he measured one yard to the right, exactly over the adjacent kennel, and removed another tile.

'I knew it was dope.' Jack lit a cigarette, turning the glowing end inwards, into the cup of his hand, so that no light warned the intruder. 'He's dropping drugged meat into the holes.'

'He must be in league with a parader, who's releasing the cube to a certain dog as he places it in that kennel,' said big blond Hutch.

'You're right.'

'But surely it would show in their urine test,' whispered Starsky, who didn't like his nickname.

'Not if the dogs eat the meat between the test and the race,' said Marius. 'We had a man do that before the war. Those that bet on the losing dog broke the cheat's right leg to teach him a lesson.'

Frankie thought of her father. Nothing had taught him a lesson.

As they whispered, the intruder began to work faster. He kept looking over his shoulder.

'You have to pull him,' Jack told Hutch.

'Arrest him now and we scare off the parader.'

'He's suspicious. I can tell by the way he moves. That man has smelled a cop. The only reason he hasn't run before he's finished the job is that he's more scared of whoever sent him. But that's the last kennel.' Before the detectives could intervene, Jack leaned across the monitor and switched on the stadium lights. Instantly the roof was bathed in bright white light. 'You on the roof.' His voice echoed through the tannoy system. 'Stand up and show your face.'

The figure froze.

'Ten seconds or I shoot.'

Cautiously, the figure started to uncurl.

'Take off that balaclava!'

The hands came up. The fingers gripped the bottom of the knitted cover and rolled it up slowly, till suddenly, with a strange bravado, the black woollen camouflage was flung away and the head came up, the face looking straight into the camera, the white light showing every feature in dark and shade, like the flat shadows of an old black and white photograph. It was Angel.

'You little bastard!' shouted Jack. He was out of the room before anyone could stop him.

Angel scuttled across the roof. The police shouted at him to freeze, but he took no notice. He reached the corner, threw down the rope, and turned to abseil down it. He came down fast, jumping out, both feet together. But before he was even halfway down, Jack arrived. He seized the rope and jerked it up and down, so that Angel was swung about like a rag doll, his body smashing against the wall until he let go and fell to the ground.

Jack pulled the boy to his feet and gripped him by the throat. He squeezed slowly. 'Why?'

It was the police who saved Angel's life. They dragged Jack off him, saying with considerable understanding, 'Come on, sir, he isn't worth another gaol sentence.'

They cautioned Angel and slipped on the handcuffs. Then they searched his pockets and found the rope, the drill, and a small freezer bag with half a dozen cubes of dried meat. 'Drugged, I suppose?' Hutch sniffed the bag.

Angel didn't reply.

Jack watched in silence, expressionless. Only when the detectives were about to usher Angel away did he take a menacing step forward. For a moment, Frankie was afraid Jack would hit him. But all he said was, 'Why did you betray me?'

195

The curly head came up. The eyes were mutinous. 'They say you're going soft, Jack. I want to be on the winning side.'

'Who says I'm going soft?'

'Him. You know. I can't say 'is name. He said you were planning to sell the track and if I helped 'im, there'd be a job for me.'

'And you believed him? You're a fool, Angel. He wanted a scandal at Richmond Racing so we'd lose our licence. Or for me to kill you, so that I'd go back inside. Either way, you'd be dead or in prison.'

'You would say that, wouldn't you?'

'Have I ever lied to you?'

'No.' Angel sagged dejectedly. 'You've been straight, Jack. You 'elped me on the inside. You gave me a chance when I came out.'

The detectives led him to the waiting police car. 'If you make a full confession it may help your sentence,' said Hutch.

Angel's chin came up. He straightened his shoulders. 'I won't talk. I may be many things but I ain't a grass. I 'ave my pride.' He turned around for Jack's approval, and got it.

Twenty-Two

The meat cubes in Angel's pocket contained acelylpromazine, a form of tranquilliser. The dose was sufficient to make a greyhound run off form, but not strong enough to warrant suspicion. Angel was charged and remanded in custody. Jack never spoke his name again.

Frankie heard most of this second-hand from Nicoletta or Marius as she lay in bed suffering from flu. She could not remember ever feeling so ill. Her throat was raw. Her temperature rose. Her limbs ached. Her eyes streamed. She shivered and sweated, alternately pulling all the bedclothes up under her chin or kicking them off as if she were in the tropics. To leave her free to toss and turn, Jack moved into the spare room. But he slept with his door open, ready to come if she called.

Each morning, he carried up her breakfast tray, although she was usually too ill to eat. At lunchtime, he brought her soup and a fresh roll of wholemeal bread, all beautifully arranged on a tray, with a crisp white napkin and a red rose. On racing nights he returned to the house several times during the evening to make sure she was all right.

'You'd make a good doctor,' she said one evening, as he plumped up her pillows, straightened her covers, and brushed back her hair from her forehead.

'I enjoy looking after you.' He lowered the blinds to cut out the bright lights of the track. 'I love you when you're fit and healthy and laughing. But I also love you when you're ill, with your runny nose, your sticky face, and your period pain which hollows out your eyes. I love you then, because you need me. You're my little girl. I shall enjoy looking after our children.'

'What a strange combination you are, Jack.' She snuggled down into the pillows, closed her eyes, and fell asleep.

Her mother came to see her, bringing a bouquet of delicately perfumed freesias and a huge bag of grapes.

'How did you know I was ill?' asked Frankie, struggling to sit up.

197

'Jack telephoned.' Her mother sank on to the edge of the bed. It was a few moments before she recovered her breath from the climb up to the attic.

Frankie watched her with concern. 'You look tired, you've lost weight. Is something . . . wrong? Is it that pain again?'

'That's what I want to talk to you about. You remember that day you found me in the kitchen? I thought it was indigestion. The pain got worse. In the end, I told Steven. Of course, he made me see our doctor.' Her mother forced a smile. 'I have to go into hospital next week.'

'Is it . . . serious?'

'Oh, you know what doctors are like.'

'Mother!'

'I have a lump in my womb. Just a small one. But they've decided I should have a hysterectomy.'

'Is it . . . malignant?'

'I won't know till afterwards. Frankie, will you keep Steven company at White Oast while I'm in hospital? He does hate to be alone. I'll be away about a week.'

'Of course I'll stay with Steven. What about when you come out? You must let me help.'

'Dear old Mrs Broom will come in every day. She'll cook and shop as well as clean.' Dominique paused and picked at the duvet cover. 'Frankie, you mustn't bring Jack to White Oast. It would upset Steven.'

'If you insist. But I am going to marry him, so it would be easier if you and Steven tried to like him.'

Her mother sighed. 'We'll discuss it when I'm better.'

'When you're better,' Frankie repeated. Suddenly, she was gripped by a terrible sense of foreboding.

Jack went racing at Brighton. Although Frankie was better she wasn't strong enough to accompany him. Instead, she lounged on the bed, watching *Out of Africa* on video, and imagining herself on safari with Jack.

He returned at midnight, saying,' I have a visitor for you.'

She sat up. 'At this hour?'

He opened the door and Blue bounded in. He jumped up on to

198

the bed, trampling Frankie into the mattress, trying to lick her face as she fought him off, laughing.

'Off the bed!' hissed Jack. 'And don't make a noise, you ungrateful brute, or you'll wake Marius.'

Blue took no notice. He stretched out on top of the duvet, his nose up near Frankie's face, his lips drawn back from his teeth in a big smile, his thin, curved tail beating against the bed.

'Off!' Jack slapped him, but not hard. 'I'm not having you in my place. You're my rival in love. I'm lucky that Jaws has Mathilda or he'd be up here too, fighting for your affection. So would Big Ears, if he were house-trained.' He laid a thick rug in the warmest corner of the room, folding it several times so that it was comfortable. 'Come here, Blue,' he said with mock severity. 'And don't let me catch you trying to get into bed with us.'

In the early hours of the morning, Jack carried Blue down the stairs so that Marius wouldn't be woken by the dog's nails scratching on the floorboards. Frankie leaned over the banister and took a photograph. She caught them at the point where Jack was turning in the stairwell, with Blue in his arms, the dog's long legs dangling with abandon, long nose nestling affectionately under Jack's chin.

The first time Frankie left the Paddock House after her illness was on the day of her mother's operation. Jack drove her down to White Oast because, as she explained to Steven, she was too weak to drive herself.

Her mother had been admitted to hospital the previous evening, so it was her stepfather who came unsteadily out of the front door, looking more than ever like an elderly hamster. He kissed Frankie on the cheek, his whiskers tickling her face. Then he held out his hand to Jack. 'Thank you for bringing Frankie. I won't say I welcome you to my house, because that would be a lie. But I'm grateful.'

'I wouldn't want you to pretend, sir,' said Jack, with a politeness Frankie could have hugged him for.

They sat in front of the drawing-room fire, waiting for the hospital to telephone. Frankie tried not to think of her mother lying on the operating table. She told herself that this sense of foreboding was imaginary, a product of her own illness. Of course she knew her mother would die one day, just as teenagers know, without believing, that one day they will reach thirty. But one day was not now.

The telephone rang. They all jumped. 'Answer it, dear,' said Steven nervously, clutching the arms of his chair.

It was the hospital to say that an emergency had caused her mother's operation to be delayed until the afternoon.

They ate a cold lunch of ham, salad and baked potatoes. Only the potatoes weren't cooked properly. They were warm but raw, because Steven had confused the oven dial with the plate-warmer. Not that Frankie minded. She felt too sick to eat.

The afternoon drew on. The clouds thickened and blocked out the light. Frankie felt sure it did not usually get dark so early. Again she was gripped by premonition.

'You look terrible,' said Jack, gently shaking her arm. 'Go to bed.'

Steven nodded. 'Do what he says. We'll let you know if there's any news.'

After Frankie had gone, the two men continued to watch the fire in silence, until Steven said, 'Do you like Scrabble?'

'I used to play every day.'

'Good heavens! You must be good.' Steven hurried to his desk to fetch the board and letters. 'I love a game myself. Frankie always plays with me.'

Some hours later, Jack woke Frankie to say her mother's operation had been a success.

'Are you sure?' she asked anxiously, still enveloped by foreboding.

'Don't worry, she's going to be fine. They're doing the tests. She'll have the results in a few days. But the surgeon is pleased.'

Frankie lay against the pillows. 'I thought my mother was going to die. I don't know why, but I was convinced.' She smiled up at him. 'Thanks for being so patient with Steven.'

'I like him. He's a nice old man. We've been playing Scrabble. I won!' Jack winked. 'I didn't tell him that I was taught to play in prison by a fraudulent solicitor.'

Frankie giggled. 'Don't! He'd be mortified.'

He kissed her tenderly. 'Sleep well. I'll phone you tomorrow.'

He left, and a few minutes later she heard the front door open and voices outside. 'Good night,' came Steven's voice. 'We must play again on Friday, when you collect Frankie. No one has beaten me for years.'

Frankie smiled into the darkness. Once again she was surrounded by her childhood, her books and toys, her father's walkie-talkie doll on the top shelf, the smell of fresh-washed cotton from the bedspread and the muffled sounds of the garden coming in through the window. She tried to work out why she'd been so afraid for her mother. Was her foreboding more acute because Jack had uncaged her emotions? With him she loved and hated, laughed and cried. He had unleashed her feelings. She was free, like the child she had been before she became afraid to be different.

Jack sat at his desk in his office on the ground floor of the grandstand, checking the takings from that evening. It was late, well after midnight. It should have been an ideal time to work. No Frankie. No distractions. But the figures on the tote sheet swam before his eyes. He kept thinking of her. He missed her. He'd missed her from the moment he'd left White Oast.

He pictured her in her little bedroom, and felt a rush of warmth and love which was both a part of, and separate from, his physical desire for her. He imagined her stepfather shuffling quietly through the old house, trying not to wake her, and he wondered what he himself would have been like had he grown up in the rural safety of Rockhurst, from where a bus went once a day to Tunbridge Wells and twice on Saturdays.

More than ever he was aware how stark his life had been before Frankie. He'd known little but grinding poverty, borstal, a period of wild, brash luxury, then prison. The lack of privacy was what got to him most about prison. Going to the lavatory in front of three other men. Sleeping in the stench of someone else's faeces. It was dehumanising, degrading. He could never escape from the smell. He could never get away from the noise. The banging of doors, the shouting. The acute loneliness of never being alone. It had destroyed many men, but not him. Nothing had touched him. He'd witnessed grown men become zombies, and boys, like Angel, turn into monsters. He'd seen men cry. He'd made men cry.

His office door opened and Fat Dudley stepped inside. 'I thought I'd find you here,' he said amiably.

'The stadium's closed, Dudley. I'm about to go to bed.'

Fat Dudley took no notice. He lowered his bulk on to a chair, 'How unwise of you to be alone. Not like you, Jack, to take a risk.'

'I have plenty of guards.'

'As reliable as Angel?' Dudley giggled. 'You've caused me a lot of trouble. I was surprised by that boy's loyalty. It cost time and money to turn him against you.'

Jack's right hand moved slowly towards the open drawer of his desk. 'Angel will expect you to look after him when he comes out,' he said. 'Of course, you hoped I'd shoot him. Then we'd both be out of your way.'

The chair creaked as Fat Dudley leaned backwards. 'Let's stop pussyfooting. I'll make you a good offer.'

'The track's not for sale.'

'I want this place. Nothing's going to stop me. Marius will do as you say. So let's be reasonable men.'

'You're wasting your time, Fatman.'

'If you don't sell to me, Jack, you'll be sorry. You and your classy lady.'

In an instant, Jack had the pistol out of the drawer and pointing straight at Dudley's heart. 'Touch Frankie and you're dead.'

Fat Dudley didn't flinch. 'Oh, dear me! I thought you were trying to go straight so Frankie could be proud of you. What would your pals from Scotland Yard say if they could see you now? Is it three years for unlawful possession of firearms? Or have they bent the rules to give a firearms certificate to a man who did fourteen years for armed robbery? I doubt it.'

Jack's finger curled around the trigger. 'Don't blackmail me, Fatty!'

'Shoot me, Jack, and you'll do life. I can't see Ben Tiernay's daughter as a faithful prison widow, can you?'

Jack deflected the barrel as he squeezed the trigger. The bullet skimmed the fat man's cheek and embedded itself in the wall beside him. He gave a squeal of fear. 'You nearly killed me.'

'If I'd aimed to kill, Dudley, you'd be dead. Now get out of my office before I change my mind.'

'As Fat Dudley lumbered from the room, Jack felt a warm glow of satisfaction. Frankie would have been proud of him. He wished he could tell her how he'd purposely not harmed Dudley, but he couldn't without frightening her with the dark side of his life.

Twenty-Three

Her mother's tumour proved to be malignant. Steven and Frankie were told the news by the doctor as they were leaving the hospital after their daily visit. It came as a complete shock to Frankie. Because her mother looked so much better, she'd believed the worst was over. Now it seemed that she'd woken from a nightmare only to find it was reality.

'To be on the safe side, we're recommending a course of chemotherapy,' the doctor explained gently. 'We'll start her in January, when she's recovered from the operation. She'll have four sessions, one every month. Chemotherapy is a drip of cytotoxic drugs. The unpleasant side-effects have been greatly reduced in recent years, but she may feel nauseous.'

'But she won't die?' said Steven in anguish.

'We're optimistic of her recovery.'

'And her beautiful hair. Will it fall out? My wife would hate that.'

'It'll grow back.'

As she listened to Steven's anxious questions, Frankie crunched her lower lip between her teeth to prevent herself from crying, and turned away so as not to upset him further with her own distress. Two nurses, deep in conversation, were walking towards her along the harshly lit corridor. Behind them came an elderly couple, supporting each other, grief etched into their faces. Frankie wondered if they'd lost a daughter, a son, a grandchild.

She thought of her father. Had she not turned her back on him, she would have lived through this already: hospital corridors, the smell of antiseptic, doctors trying to be kind. She felt her father's loss more acutely in that moment than ever before, as though he had died yesterday and not two years earlier. She remembered when Melanie's father had died, five years ago, very suddenly of a heart attack. Mel had been devastated. Frankie had offered sympathy, but at the time she hadn't understood what it meant to lose a parent.

Driving Steven back to White Oast, she said, in as bright a voice as she could muster, 'She'll be all right, you know. I'm sure she will.'

He reached across and patted her shoulder. 'We mustn't frighten her by showing how worried we are. But I think we should phone Robert and Priscilla. Perhaps you could explain to them.'

'Of course I will.'

Frankie offered to remain at White Oast for a further fortnight to give her mother a chance to convalesce. Dear old Mrs Broom tried her best to run the house , but she became flustered if she had to shop and cook as well as clean. And her mother was such a perfectionist that if the house wasn't immaculate or the meals weren't as Steven liked them, she would drag herself out of bed to take charge. So Frankie stayed.

She missed Jack. And he missed her. 'Couldn't he visit, just for a couple of days?' she asked as she helped her mother into bed one evening.

'I'm sorry, darling. I don't approve.' Her mother sank back against the pillows. 'And I'm not well enough to think about it now.'

Frankie took a deep breath and tried not to show her irritation. She loved her mother. They were closer now than ever. But the more she knew her, as a friend rather than a parent, the more she recognised her as one of the most subtly manipulative of women. She remembered Jack saying how her mother had twisted Marius around her little finger.

At the end of the fortnight, Frankie raced back to Richmond. Jack was up in the attic. She went up the stairs two at a time and flung her arms around him. He picked her up and swung her round, kissing her and laughing. There was no racing that evening. They had all the hours of the night to make love, slowly, languorously, the light from the bedside lamps playing on their naked bodies.

'I didn't think it was possible to miss anyone so much,' he said. 'I had no one to talk to as I fell asleep. No one to wake up to. Don't leave me again for so long.'

'I won't,' she promised. 'Not for anyone.'

As Christmas approached, her mother fussed endlessly about who would cook the dinner at White Oast. 'I'm not up to it,' she said pointedly, for the third time in one day. 'Steven will be so disappointed if we have to go to a hotel.' She was lying on the sofa in the drawing room, watching Frankie arrange a bowl of chrysanthemums. 'What are you doing for Christmas?' she asked.

'I'll be with Jack. I can't leave him alone at Christmas.'

Silence followed. Frankie carried on adding flowers, her back turned. She could imagine her mother's face and she nearly laughed. At any other time she would have given in.

It was five hours before her mother capitulated. 'I suppose you could ask him here,' she said. 'Just for the day.'

Frankie hugged her.

Jack went out of his way to charm her mother. He presented her with a huge bouquet of freesias. He walked slowly, and admiringly, around the freezing wintry garden. He accompanied Frankie and her mother to mass. He let Steven win at Scrabble. Whilst Frankie stuffed the turkey, he chopped enough wood for a fortnight. When she waved at him from the kitchen window, he shook his head as if to say, 'The things I do for love!'

At dinner, Jack continued to charm. Frankie watched him proudly through the flickering light of the candles. He caught her eye. She smiled. He smiled back. She loved him more than ever.

Her mother went to bed early. When Frankie went up to say goodbye, she found her sitting up in bed, a soft peach shawl around her shoulders. 'I never thought I'd say this, but I like Jack,' said her mother. 'He's generous. I heard you laughing, just as you used to when you were a child. Always full of life and laughter. Never secretive. Oh, I don't blame William. I was at fault, for telling you not to talk of the track after we moved here. I made you feel you had something to be ashamed of.'

Frankie kissed her mother on the forehead. 'It was just as much my fault. I used to tell people my father was dead. I blocked out the past. And sometimes even the present, during that last year with William. I'm never going to live like that again. Pretending I don't care when I do.'

Her mother smiled. 'Good night, darling. It's been a lovely Christmas.'

Frankie turned out the bedside light and crossed to the door. As

206

she opened it, her mother called through the darkness, 'Say thank you to Jack for me.'

In early January, her mother started chemotherapy. Frankie and Steven took her to the hospital for her first session. To fill the time, they drove on to Tunbridge Wells to stock up on groceries at the supermarket. Frankie would have been quicker without Steven pushing the trolley slowly up and down the aisles, his stiff leg playing up although he refused to admit it, but she sensed he needed company. They had just reached the bakery counter and were trying to decide between muffins and crumpets when they were interrupted by a strident voice. 'Francesca! What on earth are you doing here?'

Frankie turned to find William's mother glaring at her. She was in one of the Tory-blue woollen dresses she ordered two at a time from the Army & Navy.

'Frankie's looking after us,' said Steven, protectively. 'My wife's not well.'

'Nothing serious?'

'She's at the hospital, having chemotherapy.'

'A waste of time! All illness is psychosomatic. Well, I must hurry. No time to stand around gossiping.' Audrey Eastgate picked up the cheapest loaf, one which had reached its sell-by-date, and marched off towards the recycled lavatory paper.

Steven and Frankie turned to each other and giggled. 'She always was a ghastly woman,' he said. 'But I liked poor old Mortimer. Now, Frankie dear, after that we deserve both crumpets and muffins.'

'And jam. And lashings of cream.'

They selected their purchases and crept down the aisles like naughty schoolchildren, hiding each time they saw Audrey Eastgate's wool-encased bulk. At the checkout desk, they were well ahead of her. When she joined the back of their queue, they pretended not to notice. They were still laughing when they collected Dominique.

During the following weeks, Frankie lived between White Oast and Richmond. Jack was sympathetic. Although he had little experience of family life, he accepted the umbilical cord of love and obligation that existed between Frankie and her mother and

207

Steven, recognising in himself a variation of those feelings for Marius.

The treatment made her mother feel listless and nauseous. Her golden hair was limp. It fell out in tufts. For someone so conscious of beauty, it was heartbreaking.

Frankie tried to reassure her. 'The doctor told you it would grow back.'

'Supposing it doesn't?'

'It will. Everything's going to be all right.' Frankie was aware that their roles were reversing. She was reminded of the times, years ago, after they had left her father, when she would ask, over and over again, 'What's going to happen to us?' and her mother would reply, 'Everything's going to be all right.'

'I wish I didn't feel so tired, for Steven's sake,' her mother went on. 'Do you have to go back to Richmond tonight? He's so lonely sitting downstairs when I've gone to bed.'

'I'll stay down,' said Frankie. 'Don't worry.'

She telephoned Jack, explaining, 'If I don't stay, I'm afraid Mother will sit up to keep him company.'

'Frankie, I understand. I'll come down tomorrow and let Steven win at Scrabble. That'll make him feel better.'

She smiled into the telephone. 'Have I told you recently how much I love you?'

'Yes, but you can tell me again.'

On the following morning, Frankie was in the kitchen washing up the breakfast dishes when she heard a car draw up and the front doorbell ring. She dried her hands on a tea towel and hurried through the old house, surprised that Jack had arrived so early when she knew the late hours he kept.

'I'll get it,' she called up to Steven, who was helping her mother down the stairs. Smiling, she opened the front door. Then she froze. It was a moment before she could speak. 'William!'

He was standing on the doorstep, wearing a dark work suit. The pale wintry sunshine reflected on his pale hair, as it had the first time they'd met, when he'd interviewed her in his chambers. He looked thinner and taller. But not threatening. In fact, he was quite nervous. In his right hand was a bunch of pale pink roses, still in bud and wrapped in dark green tissue paper. He kept picking at the paper. 'I'm sorry to hear your mother's unwell,' he

208

said. 'Mother told me last night.' He handed the roses to Frankie. 'Pink roses were your mother's favourites, if I remember rightly.'

He was wrong. She liked freesias. But Frankie didn't correct him. 'Thank you.' She could hardly get the words out.

Suddenly, she remembered her mother and Steven. They had reached the bottom step and were staring at William, astonished.

'Good morning,' he said with dignity. 'I'm sorry you've been ill, Dominique.'

'Oh, William. How kind of you to come,' said her mother, in her perfect hostess voice. 'Pink roses! My favourites!'

There was an awkward silence whilst William hovered on the doorstep. Frankie wanted him to leave so that Jack didn't see him. At the same time, he had driven fifty miles and it seemed churlish not to invite him inside.

'We're about to have a cup of coffee,' her mother went on. 'Do join us before you go back,

William looked directly at Frankie. 'Only if you want me to.'

What could she do but say yes yes and hurry through to the kitchen to make the coffee as fast as she could, to get him out of the house as soon as possible. But before the water had boiled, she heard car wheels crunching in the gravel. Again she dashed through the house, and flung open the front door, crying, 'Jack! Listen . . .'

'Is something wrong?' He put his arms around her in a comforting embrace. 'Is it . . . your mother?'

'No, it's . . .'

At that moment Jack glanced through the open door of the drawing room where Steven, her mother and William were sitting around the fire. He released Frankie. 'What the hell's going on?' he demanded.

'Jack! Please! Don't make a scene. William only came to ask after Mother.'

'When? Last night? Is that why you wanted to stay down?'

'He came this morning.'

'All the way from London? Oh, come on, Frankie, what do you think I am? An idiot? He was here last night, wasn't he?'

'No.' Aware that the occupants of the drawing room had stopped talking, she grabbed Jack's arm to keep him in the hall, saying, 'Don't spoil everything, Jack. Not after you've worked so hard to make them accept you.'

In the drawing room, William was standing up. 'I think I should leave,' he was saying to her mother. 'I don't want to cause trouble, especially not when you're unwell. Perhaps I'd better use the garden door.'

'What's the matter?' asked Jack, pushing Frankie to one side. 'Afraid to face me?' His voice sounder rougher, or was that merely in comparison to William?

'I was only thinking of Dominique,' replied William. Ramrod-stiff and very pale, he walked towards Jack, who blocked the doorway with his powerful form.

For a moment they stared at each other, less than a yard apart. Frankie could see the pulse in William's neck beating furiously and she realised he was afraid. She felt sudden sympathy for him. Beyond William, she could see her mother's startled expression and her stepfather rising bravely to his feet, though he was too small and elderly to protect anyone.

Once, Jack would have pulverised William. Now, for Frankie's sake, he gritted his teeth and stepped aside. As William passed, he said, 'Don't come near Frankie again.'

With relief, William reached the safety of the front door. Only then did he reply, in his most well-bred voice, 'My dear chap, Francesca is still my wife.'

Before William could escape, Jack was across the hall. He didn't punch him hard, but enough to send him staggering back, down the steps and into the side of his car.

Frankie gave a cry of fright. 'Jack! No!' She dashed outside and placed herself between the two men. William stood up slowly. His nose was only slightly bloodied but he was deathly pale and looked as though he were about to be sick. Ignoring Jack, Frankie took William's arm. She could feel him trembling against her. 'Come inside,' she urged. 'I'll help you clean up.'

'No, thank you.' He took a snowy-white handkerchief from his breast pocket and dabbed at the blood. There was very little. He didn't look at Jack, who was standing to one side of the top step, but at Steven and Dominique, who were anxiously crowded on the other side. 'I apologise for the disturbance,' he said. 'I shan't press charges.' He opened his car door, stepped inside, and drove slowly down the drive, revving hard in the way Frankie recalled so well.

Jack turned to Steven. 'I shouldn't have hit him in your house, but I was provoked.'

Steven was trembling with anger. 'You've upset my wife. Please leave.'

'But you heard what he said.'

'That is no excuse, Jack. We're not used to your kind of violence. We don't want it. You're not welcome at White Oast.'

For a moment Frankie was afraid Jack would hit her stepfather. He clenched his fists, then unclenched them: it was a strange time to realise they shared this habit.

'Come inside, Francesca,' said Steven. 'You mother needs you.' He put an arm around her mother's shoulders and ushered her gently inside.

Frankie turned on Jack. She was almost crying with vexation. 'Couldn't you control yourself for my sake?' she shouted. 'Just once.'

'He asked for it.'

'Just as you're asking to go back to prison.'

His jaw tightened. 'I'll wait for you in the car.'

She felt as if they were speaking a different language. 'Jack, I can't leave them now. They're upset.' She went into the house and closed the door. A few minutes later, she heard Jack drive away.

Her mother and Steven made no mention of Jack all day, although the subject was in each of their minds, most of all in Frankie's. She was furious with him. It was late afternoon before she felt able to leave for Richmond. When Steven accompanied her out to her car, he said, 'You'd be wise to think carefully about a person who loses his temper so quickly.'

She didn't answer. What could she say in Jack's defence?

Jack was in the card room when she arrived at the Paddock House. He studied her as she leaned against the doorpost, her leather jacket zipped tight against the night air, her hair unbrushed, her face pale and drawn. He was reminded of the first afternoon when he'd found her at the track and she'd told him with haughty bravado that criminals deserved gaol.

Frankie looked at him, and saw a stranger instead of the man she loved. She remembered Gunter saying, 'I'd never have gone near the fuckin' track if I'd known Jack Broderick was out of prison.'

211

'I love you,' he said.

'Maybe you do, Jack, but I'm not sure that I can stand your way of showing it.' She turned away from him and walked sadly upstairs. She'd risked, and lost. And she'd hurt so many people.

But before she reached the attic, Jack was with her, his arms around her, pulling her to him, ignoring her barriers of doubt. 'I acted out of anger.' He spoke into her hair. 'I saw William sitting with your mother and Steven, whilst I am barely allowed in the house. I wanted to destroy him, but all I destroyed was us. If I could put back the clock, believe me I would.'

She felt weak. Her emotion for Jack rolled over her and out of her and into him. Love hadn't died, it was wounded. It was cut. The incisions were deep, they hurt. But how could she not love Jack when he was big enough to admit when he was wrong?

Twenty-Four

Without telling Frankie, Jack wrote a letter of apology to Steven. She only discovered this on her next visit to White Oast. 'His letter makes no difference,' Steven told her, quietly but firmly. 'Jack Broderick is not welcome in my home.'

'Couldn't you give him another chance? Please! I thought you liked him.'

'I did, but I can't have your mother upset. I'm worried for you too, dear. That man will finish back in prison.'

When Frankie returned to the stadium, she told Jack what Steven had said. She was too disappointed to camouflage her feelings.

'I'm sure William's welcome,' he said sarcastically, stabbing his desktop with his biro. 'But of course he's about to become a judge.'

Frankie didn't reply. She went into the kitchen, where Marius was helping Jolyon with his homework. 'How's Dominique?' he asked her.

'Trying to be brave.'

Jolyon insisted on showing Frankie how well he had kept Jaws and Mathilda's tank. Then he led her outside to visit Big Ears. When Frankie was away, he liked to feed the rabbit. A groundsman cleaned the cage.

On her return, alone, to the kitchen, Marius said, 'Jack told me what happened. It's a shame. But at least he apologised. That's more than he'd have done before he met you.'

Frankie sighed. 'I love Jack, but sometimes I wonder if I can cope. He scares me when he lashes out. I feel as though I'm facing not the Jack Broderick I know but another Jack Broderick. A stranger.'

The old man handed her a mug of tea. 'You're the best influence Jack has. Look how you made him call the police to catch Angel. He loves and respects you. He'd be devastated to lose you.' He paused, shaking his head in disbelief. 'You know, I once said these

213

same words to your mother, in this very kitchen, when she was on about Ben's drinking.'

'Did you tell her my father would be devastated if she left?'

'Yes. And I was right. But there's a big difference between Jack and Ben. Jack wants to give up his old ways. Ben was happy as he was. Give him a chance, Frankie. He's a good man, or I wouldn't have trusted him with my stadium.'

She kissed the old man on the cheek, picked up her tea and went up to the attic. When Jack came up she was fast asleep, her hair ruffled about her face, her arm thrown across his pillow. Very gently he laid a blanket over her.

When her mother had first become ill, Frankie had been physically divided between Richmond and White Oast. Now she was emotionally torn. Steven and her mother never mentioned Jack. He asked only after her mother's health. He wasn't barred from telephoning her at White Oast, but pride prevented him. If they telephoned her at the stadium, they left a message with the switchboard instead of using Jack's private number, the one which rang in the attic bedroom. For Frankie, this friction was an added strain. She lived in two worlds which had little communication, as though she were straddling the East-West divide at the height of the Cold War.

Often, if it were still light enough, she stopped off at the kennels to see Blue on the way back to London. Walking with him on the Downs gave her time to adjust between one world and the other.

She didn't hear from William, although she thought about him more than she cared to admit. It had been considerate of him to bring roses to her mother. She recalled other instances, early in their marriage, when he had been kind, such as her early attempts at entertaining. When her first summer pudding had fallen flat, he'd put his arms around her and said, in front of everyone, 'Aren't I lucky?' It was only later, when she spent less time trying to please and more time questioning, that he began to belittle her.

Seeing William had revived her memories of her other life: of the Inn, the law, and especially of Melanie. During her drives up and down to Rockhurst, Frankie thought a great deal about Mel. She held imaginary conversations whereby within three sentences they were the best of friends again.

One evening she didn't stop at Richmond, but drove on to West

214

Kensington. Only when she reached Simon and Melanie's street did she lose her nerve, parking well beyond their house. She sat in the car, watching the front doorstep through her rearview mirror, nervous of facing Melanie but knowing that if she drove away she'd regret it. Eventually she took a deep breath and stepped out of the car.

The last time Frankie had visited this house was a few days before their wedding. It had been barely habitable. Now, the front façade was gleaming white. The porch had been restored, the black wrought-iron railings replaced. She pressed the front door-bell. It resounded through the house. She heard the click of high heels on a polished floor and steeled herself as the door opened.

'Frankie!' Melanie had just arrived home from court and was still wearing her black suit. She was expecting a courier from chambers. When she saw Frankie hovering on her doorstep, she could hardly believe her eyes.

After all the speeches Frankie had prepared, she could only say, 'Forgive me!'

Melanie's face crumpled. 'Oh, Frankie. It was my fault too. I should have believed you about our wedding day. And I shouldn't have berated you over that little boy when I came to the stadium. But I was hurt, so I wanted to hurt you.'

'I shouldn't have told you to get out. After you'd gone, I was sorry. I nearly ran after you.'

They hugged on the doorstep.

'Come in,' said Melanie. 'Let's have a drink. Let's celebrate. We've so much to catch up on.'

'Won't Simon object?'

'Frankie, it was you who said we mustn't be ruled by the men in our lives.'

'Only because I let myself be ruled by William for so long,' said Frankie, stepping into the cream-painted hall.

'But you were right, I was in danger of becoming a doormat to Simon. I was so anxious to get married, I was afraid to argue in case he left me. Now, if I don't agree, I say so. He complains I'm even bossier than his mother!' She giggled with happiness and affection. 'Come and see the house. I think you'll be surprised.' She opened the drawing-room door.

Frankie was stunned. Melanie's drawing room was an exact

replica of Islington. The walls, curtains, loose covers and cushions were the same shades of lemon and pale turquoise.

'I hope you don't mind us copying you,' said Melanie shyly. 'We always admired your taste.'

'I'm flattered.' It wasn't the moment to remind Mel that Islington had been mainly Virginia Culmstock's taste.

They went through into the kitchen. Like Islington, it was white and bright, but far more cluttered. On the table, standing brazenly upright, was a carrier bag from Dining & Wining. Frankie wondered if William had found those she'd hidden under the Welsh dresser.

'William told Simon about your mother,' said Melanie, taking a bottle of chilled white wine from the fridge. 'I was going to write to you. Is she going to be all right?'

'The doctor is pleased. Thank God! When they told us the tumour had been malignant, I was sure she was going to die. I thought of you often then. I remember when your father died. I wish now that I'd been more sympathetic.'

'Frankie, you couldn't have been kinder. You and William took me to Paris for a weekend.' Melanie handed Frankie a glass of wine. 'I've missed you.'

'I've missed you too. It's easy to make acquaintances, but not real friends.'

They smiled and clinked glasses.

'Chambers isn't the same now you've gone,' said Melanie. 'There's no one for me to have a laugh with. No one I can say things to and be sure that they go no further.'

Frankie longed for news of the Inn. She was surprised by the strength of her craving. 'How's everyone? How's Old Nailbag?' she asked, settling herself on to a kitchen stool.

'Suffering from piles and grumpy as ever.'

'And Sanjiv?'

'Over the moon. Deepa is expecting a baby in the spring.'

'And Rupert? Has Charlotte seduced him yet?'

'Once! After a drunken evening. Now he's in hot pursuit of our new pupil. Nothing changes. Hugo is as fat and pompous as ever. James got married and they're expecting a baby. Thomas has lost his licence for drunken driving.' Melanie cut a slice of rich, ripe Brie and spread it on thick, chunky wholemeal bread. She handed

216

a slice to Frankie. The bread reminded Frankie of Jack. It was the kind he liked.

As they talked, their estrangement rolled away, but not without trace. It was as if a large stone had been lifted. Its mark would remain for some time, perhaps for ever, and their friendship would resume with the vulnerability of new grass growing where the stone once lay.

Melanie refilled their glasses. 'Lindsay Dault's in trouble again. That freckle-faced solicitor of hers rang as I was leaving today. She allowed her new boyfriend to store ten stolen VCRs under her bed. I'm afraid she'll go to prison this time.'

'Poor Lindsay. Life dealt her a bad hand.'

'She's a bad picker of men.'

'She's not the only one.'

'Are things . . . all right?' Melanie enquired tentatively.

'Did William tell Simon what happened at White Oast?'

Melanie nodded. 'Frankie, if you need to get away you can always stay here.'

'I'm fine. Really. We have the odd row. So does everyone. Jack can't stand the sight of William. That's to be expected. And William did provoke him.' Frankie forced a smile. She longed to confide her fears about Jack but she was afraid Melanie would think that was the only reason for her visit. She rose. 'I'd better go. It's late. Jack will be worried. I've come straight from White Oast.' As Frankie walked towards the front door, it opened and Simon came in.

'Don't worry, Simon,' she said airily. 'I'm just leaving. Melanie's not abandoning you for a life of vice and crime.'

Frankie's only joking,' Melanie cut in. 'She came to talk. And I'm glad. Very glad.'

On the front doorstep, they hugged each other with the sadness of women whose men belong to opposing sides.

Racing had started by the time Frankie reached the stadium. She could hear Marius's voice on the tannoy. She could see Jack inside the entrance. There had been a moment in Melanie's kitchen when she'd forgotten about him in her desire for news of chambers and a world which had once been hers.

She hurried up to the attic, showered, and slipped on her

magenta crêpe dress, the one she'd worn at the gala opening, the dress Jack liked so much. It clung to her body in soft folds. It brightened her eyes. It made her skin glow. Her desire to re-establish herself with him made her hurry. She glossed her lips and outlined them with a darker brush, filling in the soft centre of her lower lip until it looked full and pouting.

Jack was at their table, talking to Marius. As Frankie approached, he lowered his racecard and looked her up and down.

'Aren't you going to kiss me?' she asked, smiling.

'Steven rang. Nothing important. Except that I thought you were still at White Oast. He said you left straight after lunch. I presumed you were with Eamonn. But he hadn't seen you all day.'

'I went to see Melanie.'

'Are you sure you don't mean William?'

'Quite sure.' She pulled out a chair for herself, as Jack was clearly not intending to do so.

He kicked it away. It fell over backwards. People turned to look, then quickly turned away. 'Don't lie to me!' he hissed.

'I gave up a lot to be with you, Jack, and I deserve your trust.' Frankie pulled up another chair and sat down at the table, beckoning to a stupefied waiter to bring her a glass of champagne.

The restaurant fell silent. People were frozen in anticipation. The only sound was the whirring of the totalisator and the muffle of waitresses' shoes as they crept across the carpeted restaurant floor.

Jack clenched his fist and moved towards her. She raised her chin and met his eyes with hers. For a moment she thought he would hit her, as he had punched William. But he laughed softly and stroked her cheek with his knuckles, murmuring, 'I've given up boxing, you'll be glad to know.'

She took his hand in both of hers, unfolded his fingers and kissed his palm.

That night they made love with desperation, as if it were for the last time.

218

Twenty-Five

Frankie's confrontation with Jack cleared the air, and their relationship became as loving and sharing as before. She concluded that her fears about him had been exacerbated by worry over her mother.

Melanie was defending a teenage mother accused of murdering her baby. It was a sad case, and one that took up a lot of Mel's energy. Although she and Frankie spoke frequently on the telephone, they didn't meet. Not that this mattered. What counted was that they were friends again.

With her final chemotherapy session over, her mother's spirits rose. The doctor's prognosis was good, although she would need regular check-ups. When Frankie visited White Oast she found her mother sitting outside in the spring sunshine, surrounded by nodding yellow daffodils, smiling as she planned what new shrubs she would plant that year.

'Come and sit down, darling!' her mother called out gaily. 'You don't need to fuss around me any more. You've been a wonderful help to us.' She reached for Frankie's hand. 'It hasn't been easy, I realise, but everything's going to be fine now. Steven's taking me to France in September. We'll buy a new car. An automatic, so it should be less tiring for me to drive. Of course, if his legs weren't so stiff he could drive, but he doesn't want to risk it. So we'll take the boat to Dieppe and travel a little each day. Oh, it'll be lovely to see France again. I just hope my hair grows back in time. I haven't met my cousins for ten years.' She gave her old tinkling laugh. 'I can't let them see me bald.'

Frankie smiled. 'You won't be. You'll look beautiful. You look better already.'

They sat side by side in the sunshine. Frankie hoped her mother would mention Jack, but she didn't, and Frankie decided it was too soon to press for a second chance.

Blue had been on a winning streak. It came to an end when he was third in a race. A week later he finished last. At Eamonn's

219

suggestion, Frankie gave him a break from training. One spring day, she and Jack took the dogs for a long walk, right over the Downs. They stayed out until late in the afternoon, with Blue and Jet bounding through the grass, Blue running the faster but Jet trying his rugby tackles at every opportunity. Goldie was more sedate. She was in pup again to Jet, and feeling the extra weight. Small and feminine, she walked by Jack's side like a pretty girl ignoring her rumbustious brothers.

For the first time, Frankie and Jack talked seriously about buying their own home, away from the track.

'There's only one problem,' he said. 'Nicoletta wouldn't live at the Paddock House and I couldn't leave Marius there on his own. He'd be so lonely. After everything he'd done for me, I couldn't see him miserable.'

'Of course we can't abandon him.' Frankie linked her arm through Jack's. 'He can have a room in our house, then he can come to us whenever he wants.'

Jack drew her closer. 'You wouldn't mind that?'

'He's part of my childhood. I didn't help my own father when he was dying. Perhaps I can make it up by being kind to his dear friend.'

They turned back towards the kennels. The air was cold. The sun was palest gold. It gave the landscape that curious painted quality which Frankie had loved about the Inner Temple Gardens. She wondered if the magnolias were flowering opposite Makepeace Buildings.

Frankie continued to visit White Oast, although not as frequently as before. There was no mention of Jack. She decided not to press the issue until her mother was stronger.

On the evening before Frankie was due to take her mother for her first check-up, she and Jack dined alone in the grandstand restaurant. When he left the table to deal with a customer query, Fat Dudley approached. He laid a hand on Frankie's shoulder. 'I'm glad to hear your mummy's better.'

'Thank you, Dudley.' She tried not to cringe from his flabby fingers.

'Pretty village, Rockhurst. I nearly bought a house there once.' He waddled away towards his own table.

Later that night, Frankie told Jack. 'Can you imagine what

220

Mother and Steven would have said if Fat Dudley had moved in next door?' she wailed with a mixture of horror and laughter.

But Jack didn't laugh.

On the following morning, Frankie arrived at White Oast to find her mother's Ford Fiesta missing, and a smart dark red Peugeot in its place. Steven came out of the house beaming. 'I was going to buy it nearer the holiday,' he said, 'but I thought the sight of it would encourage your mother.' He patted the shiny red bonnet. 'It's a French car. I usually buy British but I've made an exception, for her sake.'

'You'll have a wonderful holiday,' said Frankie, going into the house to find her mother. As she crossed the hall, her foot caught in the rug and she fell headlong, twisting her ankle.

'Are you hurt?' her mother cried from the drawing room.

'I'll be all right.' Frankie clutched her ankle. The pain was excruciating.

With Steven's help, she pulled herself upright. Gingerly, she placed her foot on the ground. It was agony. She hopped into the drawing room and collapsed into an armchair.

'You won't be able to drive me to the hospital,' said her mother anxiously. 'I'd better book a taxi. You must come too and have that foot examined.' Whilst she was searching for the number of the mini-cab service, the telephone rang. She answered, then turned to look at Frankie, saying, 'Can she ring you later, William? She's twisted her ankle and I need to call a cab to take me to hospital.' From the sofa, Frankie could hear the squeak of William's voice. Then her mother covered the mouthpiece. 'He's offered to drive us.'

'I'd rather not.'

'I know, darling, but supposing we can't get a cab. I can't miss my appointment.'

Frankie thought of Jack. He'd be furious. But she had no option. Reluctantly, she agreed.

William arrived promptly. He drove them to the hospital, where he escorted her mother to her check-up whilst Frankie hopped into Casualty. Her ankle was sprained, not broken. A nurse bandaged it. Afterwards, she returned to the reception. From the window she could see William and Steven walking slowly around the grounds, William bent patiently to the elderly lameness of her stepfather. She was reminded of that Saturday at White Oast when she had gone upstairs to make her first, secret telephone call to Jack.

'It was good of you to drive us,' Steven said to William on their return to White Oast. 'Do stay to tea.'

William looked at Frankie. 'I don't want to cause trouble.'

'Stay,' she said, hobbling through the house to the old pantry where Blue was wailing to be let out.

William followed her. 'I didn't know you had a dog.'

'His name's Blue.' She waited for William to say, 'Dogs are dirty creatures', but he didn't.

She opened the garden door and Blue shot outside. At the far end of the garden, a squirrel raced to a tree. Blue roared after it. But by the time he reached the tree, the squirrel was up in the branches, skipping from one to another as though to tease him.

'Did Broderick give you the dog?' asked William, his mouth puckering.

'No. He was going to give me one when his bitch Goldie had pups. But when I went to choose one, I saw Blue. His owners didn't want him. You see, blue dogs are meant to be unlucky.'

'Why did you never tell me you wanted a dog?'

She turned to face him. 'William, you always called them dirty. Anyhow, we were both out all day. We'd have had to find a dogwalker.'

'But you wanted one, didn't you?' There was an urgency in his voice which went beyond the issue.

Frankie nodded.

He sighed. 'I wish you'd said so. I wish you'd told me many things. If you had, perhaps none of this would have happened.'

She was so surprised by the humility in his voice that she didn't know what to reply. To fill the awkwardness, she busied herself with the tea tray.

William paced up and down, his hands dug deep in his pockets, talking as much to himself as to her. 'My first reaction when I discovered about Broderick was disbelief. My wife! The woman who bore my name with another man! And yet, the signs had been there. I suppose I was too arrogant to read them. My second reaction was rage. That you should leave me for a man like that. I'm sorry if it hurts you, but that's the way I feel. My anger lasted

222

until after you moved out. In fact, in the first few weeks I was glad you'd gone. I assured myself I was well shot of you. Then you came to the house. You looked so pretty, so happy. I was reminded of when we were first married. You used to look like that all the time. I knew then how much I missed you.' He'd stopped pacing and was standing in the centre of the kitchen, watching her. 'As you know, it isn't easy for me to admit to being at fault. But I realise now that I was hard on you. I should have been more sympathetic when you were reported to the Bar Council. I was brought up not to show affection. My parents aren't demonstrative. You know all that. I should have understood you were different. But I turned my back when you needed me.' He paused, his arms hanging helplessly by his sides. 'If you and I had still been happy, would you have gone off with Broderick?'

Frankie shook her head.

They smiled tentatively at each other, in sorrow, resignation, but also relief that they had not been deluded. There had been something good between them once.

William left straight after tea. Frankie was glad. Stretching out on the sofa, her sore ankle propped on a cushion, she closed her eyes and relived the conversation in the kitchen. She telephoned Jack, as she did most evenings they were separated. As soon as she heard his voice, her warmth towards William fell into perspective. It was merely relief at the end to hostility. 'I sprained my ankle as we were about to leave,' she told Jack.

'How did you get to the hospital?'

'We had a lift.' She took a deep breath. 'Jack, I refuse to have secrets. William took us.'

'What!'

'He rang just after I'd hurt my ankle. It was obvious I couldn't drive.'

'And you couldn't call a mini-cab?'

'We had to be at the hospital in an hour. Mother was afraid we might not get a cab at short notice. This is Rockhurst, not London. She couldn't miss her appointment. I had to let William take us.' Frankie cradled the telephone under her chin and spoke softly. 'Jack, don't snarl at me. It's you I love. If I had anything to hide, I wouldn't have told you William had been here, would I?'

'Is he staying the night?'

'Of course not! He left after tea.'

'But he's welcome at White Oast whereas I am not?'

'That's your own fault!'

She didn't know if he or she hung up first, but when she looked up she found Steven watching her from the doorway. 'Don't tell your mother you're having problems,' he said. 'She'd only worry. People say stress contributes to . . .' Even now he couldn't bring himself to say the word 'cancer'.

That night, Frankie took a long time to fall asleep. Images of Jack and William chased through her mind. She woke to find Steven shaking her arm. 'Get up!' he whispered. 'Come on!'

'Is it . . . Mummy?'

'No! Come down! Don't make a noise.' He disappeared down the stairs.

Sleepily, she pulled on her dressing gown and limped after him, wondering what could be so urgent. The front door was wide open. Blue was snuffling around in the undergrowth. Steven stood rigidly beside her mother's new car.

She crunched across the gravel in her slippers. 'What's wrong?'

His eyes filled with tears. 'That!' All the tyres had been let down. 'It's Broderick,' he spluttered. 'Oh, I knew something like this would happen. We must call the police.'

'Jack wouldn't do that,' said Frankie. 'It's vandals or kids playing a joke. It's a nuisance, but we'll soon get them pumped up. Don't worry!'

'It's Broderick. Didn't you argue with him last night? Isn't he angry about William?'

'Yes, but . . .'

Steven was in no mood to be deflected. 'He came down last night, found this car, and thought it was William's. This is what happens when you get involved with a man like that. Oh, how can I tell your mother? An upset like this could make her ill again.'

In her life, Frankie had had few arguments with Steven. Now, as he muttered obstinately, blaming Jack, she felt like screaming, but instead she said, very calmly, 'I'll ask the garage to collect the car. They'll deal with it. You tell Mother they're replacing a tyre. But don't keep telling me Jack did it. He may have his faults but he isn't petty. If he'd wanted to damage the car, he'd have blown it

224

up.' Tightening the belt of her dressing gown around her waist, she hobbled into the house.

Later that morning, after she'd sorted out the car, she telephoned Jack. When he heard her voice, he said, 'I couldn't sleep last night. I wanted to phone you back but I was afraid of waking your mother. I'm sorry I shouted. You didn't deserve it. You need love and sympathy. I'm only angry because I'm excluded.'

Immediately, she forgave him. After years with William who'd never admitted to any faults, it was so refreshing to be with someone who did. 'I've had a morning that would try a saint,' she told him, lowering her voice so as not to be overheard. 'Someone let the tyres down on my mother's new car. Steven hasn't stopped fussing. Anyone would think he'd found a body in the boot.'

Jack's voice took on a different tone, more of an interrogator. 'Did anyone come near the house last night, after William left?'

'No one. I'd have heard them.'

'Are you sure?'

'Definitely. Like you, I was awake for hours. I hate it when we argue and I'm not with you to make up.'

He spoke softly. 'I won't snarl again. I'll change. I say that every time, don't I? It's my stupid jealousy. You're my uptown lady and I'm the borstal boy. Sometimes I can't believe you'll stay with me. I shout at you, almost as if I want you to leave me so I can say I knew you would all along.'

'I don't want you to change, Jack,' she said with a throaty chuckle. 'I like you as my tiger. I just wish you'd draw in your claws before you take a swipe.'

Twenty-Six

It was several days before Frankie could return to Richmond. Because of her foot, she travelled by train, leaving her car and Blue at White Oast. Jack was waiting eagerly for her on the platform at Victoria station. He hurried to her, swinging her up into his arms and kissing her. Then, to the amusement of other travellers, he started to carry her through the station.

She blushed and laughed, saying, 'Put me down, Jack. I can walk.'

He kissed the tip of her nose. 'I like to look after you.'

During the drive out to Richmond, he asked, 'No more trouble with vandals?'

'None. You asked me that last night. And the night before.'

'I worry about you.'

Smiling, she slid her hand under his arm and rested it on his thigh, her fingers gently circling. 'I promise you, Jack,' she said, 'there's no mafia in Rockhurst.'

It was wonderful to be home at the Paddock House, where Marius and Nicoletta greeted her warmly and Jolyon even managed a small smile. He'd been caring for Jaws and Mathilda.

'They look very happy,' she assured him. 'Their tank positively sparkles.'

Up in the attic she didn't unpack, but stood by the window watching the familiar bustle of the stadium. On the balcony beside the grandstand restaurant, Bernard, the manager, was talking to Signor Umberto. On the ground, the water sprinkler was moving slowly over the sandy track. By the traps, the mechanic was testing the triggered doors.

Frankie ran a long, hot bath, dosed it liberally with scented oil, then soaked away the journey, her injured foot propped on the side. There was no racing that night. She was glad. She wanted Jack to herself.

As she stepped from the bath, a thick towel wrapped around her, he came up with a bottle of champagne and two glasses.

226

'So there was no more trouble with vandals?' he said.

'No, Jack. You keep asking me that.' Guilty again of her suspicions, she linked her arms around his neck and drew him close, balancing on her one good foot. He ran his mouth down her bare neck and shoulders, kissing her warm, naked skin.

It was over a week since they had made love. It seemed a decade. They kissed, gently, tenderly, aware that they had all evening. He slipped the towel from her body desiring her because he knew every inch of her, and yet as excited by her as if she were a brand-new lover. He picked her up and carried her to the bed, laying her down carefully so as not to touch her injured foot. He undressed and lay beside her, taking her in his arms. He kissed her breasts and her stomach. He kissed her neck and arms. He ran his fingers down her back, touching each vertebra. She responded with her mouth, stroking him with the tip of her tongue, pointed and searching, sending shivers of delight through his body. Reaching into the bedside drawer, she took out a small bottle of exquisite-smelling oil and anointed her breasts and stomach, her thighs and her upper arms. Then, deftly, and without putting weight on her foot, she massaged him with her naked body, right up the length of him until the hair on his chest glistened with warm oil. She slid down to his feet, kissing his toes and licking in between them. She came up a little higher, to the soft skin on the inside of his knees. And higher still. She slid up him, massaging his body with hers, rolling the oil between them. As she moved, she titillated, pulling away, teasing. She made love to him, not for her own physical pleasure but for the pleasure of submission and the need to reassure him of her love. Of her trust.

To Frankie's surprise, Jack rose early next morning. 'I have to be out of town all day,' he said. 'I won't be back till midnight.'

'On my first day home?'

'I can't help it.'

'Jack, you never mentioned it yesterday.'

'I'm sure I did.'

'You didn't.' She paused, hurt and surprised. 'Where are you going?'

'Oh . . . all over the place,' he answered with irritation, and disappeared into the bathroom.

She lay in bed, listening as he showered and shaved. She was puzzled and disappointed, and once again uncertain. When he returned to the bedroom, she asked, 'Can I come with you?'

'You'd be bored. I'll be in meetings all day.'

'Jack, is something wrong?'

'I want to open another stadium. Keep that to yourself. It's just an idea.'

'That's wonderful. Of course I'll keep it secret.' She felt flattered, and relieved. That relief made her gabble. 'I'll help you. I hate hanging around not working. Talking to Mel has reminded me how much satisfaction I used to get out of my work. It gave me a sense of purpose.'

He slipped on his jacket. 'I've never stopped you going back to the law.'

'I know. It's me. The idea of approaching other chambers only to be rejected is too daunting. And to set up on my own. Well . . . That would be hard. To make it alone, a barrister needs a terrific reputation and a stable of loyal clients.'

'If you'd wanted to do it, I'd have supported you.' Jack unlocked the safe, took out a roll of money and secreted it in various pockets. Then he turned towards the attic door. 'I'll see you tonight.'

'Aren't you going to kiss me goodbye?' she asked in disbelief.

He returned to the bed, kissed her quickly, then hurried out.

She listened to his footsteps as they went downstairs. She heard him pause to speak to Marius. Then the front door slammed, and he was gone. Frankie lay in bed, biting the corner of the duvet. Something was wrong. There was no denying it. For the first time she faced the possibility that he might have another woman. The idea made her feel sick. Was he hurrying to her? Was he kissing her? Was he making love to her? Was he with her, beside her, in her?

It was an effort for Frankie to get up and face the world but she forced herself to do so. In the card room she found Marius and Nicoletta. Their heads were close together and they were laughing. She felt envy.

'Jack seems worried,' she remarked, as casually as she could.

Marius glanced at Nicoletta, or so it seemed to Frankie, then he answered airily, 'It's this new stadium. I can't think why he wants to expand but he's dead set on it.'

'I'm sure that's it.' Frankie poured herself a mug of coffee and retreated to the attic. The glow of being Jack's sole confidante evaporated. She wondered how long Marius and Nicoletta had known about the new stadium and why Jack hadn't told her before.

She telephoned Melanie, not intending to talk about Jack, but she found herself confiding, 'Something's wrong and I don't know what it is.'

Melanie was instantly sympathetic. 'Come over this evening. Simon's up in Birmingham on a case. It'll be just us. Bring a toothbrush and stay the night.'

At eight o'clock sharp Frankie was on Melanie's doorstep, her mini-cab drawing away behind her. When Melanie opened the door, Frankie thrust a bottle of champagne into her hands. 'Please don't think I've only come here to burden you with my problems,' she said.

'But I'm flattered you've turned to me.' Melanie helped her into the drawing room, arranging the cushions on the sofa so that Frankie could prop up her foot. 'In the ten years we worked together, I battered your ear about Simon, Rupert, and I hate to think how many others. You never talked of your problems. We were the best of friends, yet I was too busy banging on about myself to realise you were unhappy. I saw your life only as a dream to be envied. You were my role model, Frankie. That day when we were walking back from lunch, I was astonished when you said you were miserable. It taught me not to take things at face value.'

'So long as I kept my misery to myself, I could pretend nothing was wrong with my marriage,' said Frankie. 'One lesson I've learned from Jack is that if something's wrong, I say so.'

'So what is the matter?'

'I don't know. But he's up to something. I have no concrete evidence, only intuition.'

'Another woman?'

'This morning I thought so. Now I'm not sure. But something is wrong. Today is my first day home. He's gone out and won't be back till midnight. When I asked if I could go with him, he said I'd be bored. He didn't want me, Mel. That's the truth.' Frankie clenched her fists. 'There's another thing. I was convinced Jack wanted to go straight. I couldn't stay with him if I didn't believe that. But recently I've felt a violence in him, one which he isn't trying to control. That business of him punching William was just the surface.'

'When you're with him is he violent?'

'Oh, no! He's kind and loving and . . .' Frankie blushed. 'The sex is great. Which in its own way worries me. Because it's so good, I'm scared that's all we have. That I'm being blinded.'

Frankie had intended to stay the night but as the evening drew on she changed her mind. 'Don't be offended, Mel,' she said. 'But I want to go home. I can't stand this hanging over me. I have to confront Jack.'

By the time a mini-cab had arrived and driven Frankie to Richmond, it was well after midnight. The lights from the Paddock House shone out into the darkness, although the ground floor was deserted. So was Marius's room: his door was wide open. She presumed he was with Nicoletta. She hobbled up the stairs. Jack would be worried by her absence.

The door to the attic was closed. She opened it, expecting him to call out her name. He didn't. The interior was dark but she didn't put the light on because she didn't want to wake him. Instead, she opened the door wider. But as the light from the stairwell fell across the room, she saw that the bed was empty. She switched on the light. From the way she'd left their room, she could tell Jack hadn't been home.

She told herself it wasn't late, not by Jack's standards. He could have been delayed. His meeting had run on, his car had broken down. There were a thousand reasons, all perfectly legitimate, but they didn't prevent her from feeling uneasy. Without bothering to undress, she lay down on the bed, the duvet covering her legs. From somewhere out in the night came the howl of a police siren. She shivered.

At three o'clock she could stand it no longer. If Jack was lying injured by the roadside, he needed help. If he'd been arrested, she preferred to know. She tapped out the special police number they'd been given at the time of Angel's break-in.

To her relief, Starsky answered. He checked the computer, and said, 'No accient reported.'

'Would you know if Jack had been arrested?'

Starsky's voice became gently probing. 'Is there any reason why he should be?'

230

'No! Of course not.' She wished she hadn't mentioned it. 'I'm just worried because he hasn't come home. But I'm sure he will. Thank you.' She was left with the other possibility: Jack had another woman. Was she younger? Prettier? More fun? Where did she live? How had they met? What qualities did she possess which Frankie didn't have? Was he making love to her now, or lying beside her, sated? Was she better in bed? As the night ticked on, her feelings alternated between worry and jealousy.

Jack drove hard and fast, clipping the outer edge of Brighton before picking up the A23, north to London. He couldn't have brought Frankie. She'd have interrogated him. He'd tried to play life by her rules and it irked him to fail, even this once. But violence was the only language Fat Dudley understood. Others he interpreted as weakness. One day, Jack was determined, he'd put all this behind him. In the mean time, he couldn't afford to let Fat Dudley better him. Not for his own safety, for Frankie's.

Blackmail was a dirty trick. He wished it hadn't come to that. But with dirt, he'd had to play dirty. He'd had to grip the Fatman in a pincer from which he didn't dare move. If Fat Dudley approached Frankie or her family, Jack would send the disgusting photographs to the police.

He glanced at the brown envelope on the passenger seat. Its contents sickened him. He hadn't expected to be so shocked. He'd seen enough vice in prison and out of it to deaden surprise at any deviation in human sexuality. But the memory of those childish faces staring terrified into the camera made him want to kill both the abusers and the procurers. He kept thinking that they could be his children. His and Frankie's.

Fat Dudley paced the marble floor of his spacious flat. A mirror was smashed. A vase of lilies lay on its side, the porcelain broken, the blooms trampled. His favourite onyx statue of a naked little girl was in many pieces. He cursed himself for opening the door. Foolishly, he'd believed Jack had come to offer him Richmond Racing. It had seemed so plausible; the late-night meeting away from Marius's suspicions.

He cursed himself for being compromised. To keep the photographs had been silly. To be photographed with that young girl had been an error of judgement. But he liked to look at the pictures. He hadn't hurt the girl. Not really. And who cared if a few street urchins in some far-off South American town bared their pubescent bodies for him. He paid well. Within a couple of years they'd be on the game anyhow. It was just that he liked them young, he had to be the first. That's what he paid for. He liked to pay, because then they couldn't laugh at him.

It was none of Jack Broderick's business what other men did in private. But since that woman had come into his life, Jack had acted differently. Fancy threatening to turn in another man. Dudley couldn't believe it. He kicked the onyx statue to one side with his small, pointed foot. In his youth, women like Frankie had called him fat and laughed at his little penis. That was why he paid these little girls. He pursed his small rosebud mouth. It wasn't his fault. It was the fault of those women like Frankie who'd mocked him.

Frankie woke at six to find Jack standing by the end of the bed. He looked tired and dishevelled. 'Do you have another woman?' she asked. 'I have to know the truth.'

'Of course not!'

'Then where have you been?'

'Where were you at midnight, when I called?'

'With Melanie. Jack, you haven't answered my question.' Now that her eyes focused she saw that the pocket of his jacket was torn and he was missing a shirt button. 'What's happened? Jack, are you hurt?'

'It's nothing. I got into an argument. That's all. Don't worry, it's over now.'

'I called Starsky,' she said. 'I thought you'd had an accident.'

'That was a damned stupid thing to do.'

'Only if you have something to hide.'

'That's rubbish, and you know it. No one who's done time wants the police around.' He crossed to the safe, slipped his pistol out of his pocket and locked it away. It was only then that Frankie realised he'd taken it with him. 'There are some things I can't tell you,' he said. 'One day they'll be in the past. I promise. Trust me!'

'How can I trust you when you won't confide in me? Where did you go last night, till six in the morning? Why did you need a gun? I can't bear it, Jack. I refuse to be sucked into a web of violence. It frightens me, you frighten me. I can't live with you if all the time I'm afraid that the police may knock on the door and take you away for years on end.'

'If I've broken the law, it's to protect you.'

'For me!' She stared at him in disbelief. 'What have you done?'

'If you trusted me, you wouldn't need to ask.'

'If you loved me, you'd tell me,' she shouted in frustration.

He walked to the door, then turned back to look at her. She was kneeling in the middle of the bed, her fists clenched in anger. He would have explained about Fat Dudley but he didn't want to frighten her. He'd questioned Marius about the day the men beat up her father: Ben's blood had spattered not only on her dungarees, but in her face and eyes. She'd been so terrified that she hadn't spoken for a week.

As Jack walked out of the room, Frankie sank back against the pillows. This wasn't the sharing love she thought they possessed. Or maybe that had never existed. She'd given up her career, her marriage, her position, for an illusion. She remembered Jack telling her that all those who'd owed Marius money had now paid. He's made them. How? With violence, like the men who'd come for her father?

The telephone rang. She answered.

'Your mother's back in hospital,' cried Steven. 'I'm speaking from there now. She was in pain last night. I called the doctor and he sent for an ambulance. I've just seen the doctor, Frankie. The . . . disease has spread through the lymph system. It's gone everywhere.' He began to sob. 'There's nothing they can do for her. She's going to die.'

'I'll be with you as soon as I can but I still can't drive. In any case, my car is at White Oast.'

'Take a taxi. Go via the house. She wants her peach dressing down and her matching hairbrushes.'

Frankie hobbled to the door and screamed down the stairs, 'Jack!'

Marius replied from the hall. 'He's gone out.'

'Mother's in hospital. 'The . . . cancer has spread. I have to get back to White Oast.'

Marius looked up at her through the gloom of the stairwell. She saw tears in his eyes. 'I'll find someone to drive you down,' he said gently. 'I'd take you myself but I don't think your stepfather would like that. I wish I could see Dominique. She's always been very special to me, but then you know that.' He straightened up. 'How long before you're ready?'

'Two minutes.' She tucked her sponge bag into her suitcase and closed it. She hadn't unpacked. It was as if subconsciously she'd known this would be a fleeting visit.

When she reached the ground floor, she remembered she'd left no message for Jack. She went into the card room and reached for his pen and notepad. Then she pushed them away. She didn't know what to say to him. He'd become a stranger.

Twenty-Seven

By the time Frankie reached White Oast, she was sorry to have parted from Jack in anger. As she stepped from the car, Blue raced around the corner of the house, yelping with excitement. He was followed by William. 'What are you doing here?' she demanded, thrown by his presence.

'Steven asked me to let the dog out and to take you over to the hospital.'

'Oh . . . I see.' She turned to her driver, the groundsman who helped Jolyon look after Big Ears. 'Thank you for bringing me.' She wanted to add a message for Jack, but with William hovering beside her she decided to save it for later.

At the hospital, they found Steven in the waiting room, clutching a plastic cup of sweet black coffee. 'She's going to be all right,' he told them, his voice shaking. 'At least for a few months. Maybe as long as a year. No one knows. She has to stay here for a day or two. Then she can come home. She's still talking about going to France but I don't think she'll be well enough to drive there.'

Frankie kissed his whiskery cheek. 'We'll get her there, even if I have to take you.'

'Thank you, dear.' He squeezed her hand. 'Oh, you remember the tyres. The police caught some lads doing the same to the vicar's car. They had a dare to see if they could do every car in the village. Young rascals! I'm sorry if I suspected . . . you know who.'

'Don't worry,' said Frankie, remembering how fiercely she'd defended Jack. It seemed inconceivable that things could have gone wrong so quickly.

They saw her mother briefly before they left the hospital. She looked pale and tired. Back at White Oast, it was natural that William should stay for lunch. As Frankie watched him settle her stepfather into his chair beside the fire, she was grateful for his presence.

Jack returned to the stadium within an hour of Frankie's departure. After driving three times round Richmond Park, he'd realised that by walking out on Frankie he was making matters worse. When Marius told him about Dominique, he instantly forgot their argument and dialled White Oast. There was no reply.

At lunchtime he sought out the groundsman who'd given her a lift. 'Did you take her on to the hospital?' he asked.

'I would 'ave, Jack, but there was a gentleman waiting for 'er.'

'A small, elderly gentleman?'

'Oh, no! Tall. Fair. A real toff.'

Jack walked back to the Paddock House, marched upstairs, and slammed the door. He crossed to the dressing table he had given Frankie for Christmas and chopped the side of his hand down on the mirror. It shattered into several pieces.

When Frankie telephoned the Paddock House, Marius answered. 'How's Dominique?' he asked.

'Still in hospital but more comfortable. She's becoming very forgetful. That worries her. Today she couldn't remember Blue's name. She kept calling him Grey.' Frankie paused. 'Is Jack around?'

'He's out.'

'Did you tell him about Mother?'

'Of course.'

'I'm surprised he hasn't phoned me.' She was hurt and it showed. Marius said nothing.

Frankie remained at White Oast because Steven was too distressed to be left alone. She telephoned Jack a dozen times over the next few days. He was never in and he never returned her calls. Eventually she said to Nicoletta, 'I'm not chasing him any more. Please tell him that.' She was angry and upset. Her mother was ill. She needed Jack's support. She wouldn't forget this.

Her mother came home from hospital greatly weakened, and Frankie felt unable to leave White Oast. Once her foot had healed and she could drive again, she took over all the shopping and cooking from Mrs Broom. She missed Jack and longed to talk about him but she didn't dare worry her mother. Instead, she berated him silently in the bathroom mirror, argued with him as

236

she shopped for food in Tunbridge Wells, and conceded the odd point as she cooked lunch.

At the weekend, William came to lunch. Frankie didn't object. She saw how much Steven and her mother needed the distraction. And, if the truth were known, she was pleased to see him. He was dependable, he said the right things. His world was safe: it wasn't inhabited by men who carried snub-nosed pistols in their belts.

Melanie telephoned frequently. She became Frankie's lifeline to the world outside White Oast. 'Have you seen any more of William?' she asked.

'He was here at the weekend.'

'Really! Do you think you'll go back to him?'

'Heavens, no! I haven't forgotten how he bullied me. Or hit me. To return to William would be like putting on an old, very tight shoe. I loved Jack too much to settle for anything less.'

Only later did Frankie realise that she'd talked of Jack in the past.

It was a fortnight since she'd spoken to him. The longer she didn't hear from him, the more his dark side dominated her memories, until she saw him not as her friend, her lover, the man who made her laugh, but as a vicious, gun-toting criminal. A man who didn't phone her when her mother was ill. A man who had killed.

Nevertheless, he was a drug. She craved him and craved news of him. She telephoned Marius. He enquired after her mother and she told him the latest news. They talked of Nicoletta, Jolyon, Jaws and Mathilda, Big Ears, Blue. Of which dogs had won last night and which had run badly. He didn't mention Jack. Finally, Frankie was forced to ask, 'Is Jack all right?'

'He's alive, if that's what you mean.'

'That isn't what I mean and you know it.'

'Frankie,' said the old man, 'I love the pair of you but I ain't playing marriage counsellor. All I ask is that if you go back to your husband, you tell Jack to his face. Don't leave my boy dangling.'

'I'm not going back to William, but I don't want to live with a fugitive either. Or be a prison widow. Or maybe a widow.'

'Life isn't easy for a man with Jack's past.'

'I know. But the slightest problem and he reaches for his gun.'

'The smallest argument and you mistrust him.'

237

'With good reason!' she shouted.

Frankie had to confront Jack. She decided to return to Richmond on the following day. But that evening, her mother lost her balance in the bathroom and cut her forehead on the edge of the basin. Afterwards she admitted it wasn't the first time she'd fallen.

Steven was distraught. 'You said she'd have a year,' he told the doctor, tears in his eyes. 'We're going to France in September. Her heart's set on it.'

There was nothing the doctor could say to comfort him. Dominique wasn't hospitalised. She remained at White Oast, in bed. Frankie shelved her plans to return to Richmond. She couldn't leave her mother, not now.

Towards the end of the week, William telephoned. He was very sympathetic. 'You need a break from that house, Francesca,' he said. 'Let me take you out to dinner on Saturday.'

'I couldn't leave them alone. Not after this.'

'We'd go somewhere local.'

She hesitated.

'I promise I won't bully you. I had no right to do so before. I certainly have none now.'

'All right,' she said. 'Thank you. I'd like to go out.'

Afterwards, she wished she'd said no. She wanted to stay at home with her mother, to make up for all the evenings in the future which they wouldn't have together. When William phoned to tell her she must wear a cocktail dress and be ready early, she said, 'Perhaps we should leave it.'

'If you insist.' He sounded devastated.

'Oh, very well. But not a late night. Please!'

Her mother and Steven made no comment about William. She sensed they'd decided together on this tactic. That in itself put her under pressure. She purposely selected the kind of dress of which William disapproved: a slinky, black crêpe sheath which moulded to her body.

He arrived punctually, very correct in a dinner jacket. 'Will you tell me now why I have to be ready so early?' she asked briskly, trying to hide her nervousness.

'Look!' He held out two tickets.

She stared. '*La Bohème*!'

'The opera we saw on our first evening together. Glyndebourne are putting on a pre-season performance.' He smiled. 'You look very pretty.'

During their marriage, they had been to Glyndebourne many times, but never alone. They'd always taken a party, with judges or eminent QCs as their guests. Frankie loved Glyndebourne, the great country house dedicated to opera which nestled amongst the green folds of the South Downs. She found the park and the lake wildly romantic. But her previous visits had been marred by fear that her picnic would not meet with William's approval. It was traditional for the audience to take exotic feasts of smoked salmon, quails' eggs, champagne and strawberries to eat beside the lake during the interval. He'd expected her picnic to be the best.

Driving up to the house, it seemed incredible that she should have been so suppressed by the man sitting beside her. They parked the car and walked down to the auditorium. Curious to see his reaction, she said, as they took their seats, 'We don't have a picnic.'

William handed her a programme. 'I could hardly have asked you to provide one.'

'You know, I used to order food from Dining & Wining.'

'I found thirty of their carrier bags under the dresser.'

They looked at each other and smiled in that moment of darkness before the curtain rose and the stage was flooded with light.

The performance was exquisite. As always, Frankie was entranced by the music. It took her out of her life and transported her to a world of make-believe.

In the interval, they dined in the restaurant. William talked of chambers. Frankie talked of her mother. He spoke of Kingly Grange. She said she'd seen Mel. To Frankie's relief, they skirted around the subject of themselves.

Only as they were finishing their coffee, with the performance due to start in fifteen minutes, did William say, 'I wish you'd give us another chance. I promise you things would be different. I'd really try to make you happy.'

His suggestion shouldn't have come as a shock after what he'd said in the kitchen at White Oast, but she was still surprised by his intensity. 'I'm not the same person who lived with you,' she said. 'I've grown up. I've changed.'

'I could accept that.'

'We can't go back,' she said, as gently as she could. 'Too much has happened. It wouldn't work.'

'If you mean that I couldn't forgive you, I've thought about it a great deal and I know I could. I wouldn't forget, but I could put it behind me.'

'I couldn't forget,' she said. 'You were a tyrant to me. I shouldn't have allowed you to be, but you were.'

William's jaw tightened. They both thought of the night when he'd punched her. 'Are you still in love with Broderick?' he asked stiffly.

'Things aren't easy at the moment, I admit that. Perhaps I should be brave and strike out on my own, but with my mother so ill I find it hard to be dynamic.'

'We should have had children,' he said. 'We both wanted them but never at the same time. We became too involved in our careers. We didn't make time for each other.'

She sighed. 'Life's full of if onlys.'

'I wouldn't neglect you again,' he went on, taking encouragement from her reflective expression. 'At the end of April I become a judge. I'll be the referee, instead of a team captain. The pressure will lessen.' He paused. 'Do you remember when we first bought the house in Islington? We invited our parents to dinner and you spent two whole days making a pudding which looked like the aftermath of a road accident.'

She laughed. 'It was meant to be a summer pudding.'

The bell rang. They stood up.

'All I ask is that you don't come back to me only to leave again,' he said.

'I wouldn't do that to you,' she replied. 'I promise.'

The second half of the performance couldn't hold Frankie. She was thinking about what William had said. She'd loved Jack. Obsessively, wildly, deeply. She'd desired him as she had not imagined herself capable. But had the intensity of their sex blinded her to Jack as a person? William was safe. He wouldn't dare ill-treat her again. He offered the security of marriage. He was responsible. She'd enjoyed being married, in the early days.

240

She liked sharing. He offered respectability. Not that she cared what other people thought, not since being with Jack. Her mother and William were different. They craved a position. Without it, they felt lost. When William became a High Court judge and received a knighthood, he would relish being introduced as Sir William Eastgate. For Frankie, such things were merely window-dressing: amusing but unimportant. Jack hadn't changed her attitude, she'd reverted. This was how her father had viewed life. And what good had that carefree attitude done him? He'd died a penniless drunk. And Jack? How long before he went back to prison?

On stage, Mimi was dying. Rodolfo cried her name, distraught at the passing of his great love. Frankie thought of the love she'd known with Jack. She needed that wild rush of passion. How could she consider anything less? It was only because her mother was dying that she felt so vulnerable.

William drove her straight back home. He didn't talk. He sensed that she had retreated from him. When they reached White Oast, he said, 'I'll just see you safely inside.'

She stepped from the car. 'Thank you. It's been a lovely evening.' She didn't invite him in.

He took her key and unlocked the front door. Blue shot out, raced around the drive, then rushed back inside. 'Well . . .' Frankie whispered so as not to wake Steven and her mother. 'Thank you again.'

He didn't look her in the eyes. 'Good night, Francesca,' he said, and walked despondently back to his car.

Frankie closed the door. More than ever she felt the end of their marriage. She reached down to stroke Blue. 'It'll be just you and me, boy,' she said, and turned to go upstairs. Only then did she notice a note on the table.

Your mother taken ill again. Gone to hospital. Phone me there. Love, Steven.

She rushed to the door, threw it open, and shouted, 'William! Wait!'

He heard her as he reached the gates, and reversed sharply. 'What's wrong?'

'It's Mother. She's gone back to hospital. Please come in, just for a few minutes.'

He came inside and stood beside her whilst she telephoned Steven. 'She had that pain again,' said Steven, 'but they've given her something to make her sleep. You go to bed, Frankie dear. Come and fetch me in the morning. And don't worry!'

She replaced the receiver and began to cry very softly into her hands. The reality of her mother's approaching death hit her. Within a few weeks she'd never see her again. Never pick up the phone and hear that over-perfect English voice. Suddenly, Frankie was aware of William's arms comforting her, drawing her to him. Of her face buried in his shoulder and his long fingers stroking her hair.

'Get into bed,' he said. 'I'll make you some hot milk with brandy. You always find it makes you sleep.'

He spoke to her as though she were a child. But she didn't mind. She wanted to be a child. Upstairs, she pulled off her slinky dress and her glitzy jewellery, throwing them on the floor. Then she slipped into an old cotton nightdress, one she'd had before she was married. In the bathroom she scrubbed away her make-up and cleaned her teeth with Steven's toothpaste because she couldn't find her own. She was already in bed when William came up.

'I've shut Blue in the pantry,' he said.

'Thanks.' She took the mug from him. 'Thank you for staying.' Tears filled her eyes and, quickly, she put the milk down before she spilt it.

William sat down beside her. 'Don't cry, darling.'

'I can't help it.'

He took her hands in his. She leaned towards him, again burying her face in the comfort of his shoulder. At first, he held her tentatively, afraid she might rebuff him. But Frankie was too numb with misery. He kissed her forehead and the soft skin of her cheeks. Still she didn't draw away. She knew that William's arms were around her. Part of her said, this is wrong. This isn't fair. But the other side cried out, hold me. Comfort me! Make me safe. He brushed her mouth with his, tenderly. She felt a rush of warmth towards him, fondness which was not passion but an affection born of familiarity, of shared memories. He was her husband, he offered her a sanctuary from all the things which frightened her, like death and violence.

William undressed quickly and slipped in beside her, into her

242

narrow childhood bed. He took her in his arms and kissed her neck and shoulders. 'This is right, darling,' he murmured. 'I know it is.'

She covered his mouth with hers. She didn't want to talk. He drew her on to him, as he'd always liked to do, and looked up into her eyes. She moved slowly, massaging his body with hers, her breasts on his chest, her legs caressing his thighs. She made love to him as she had done so often in the past. She gave him pleasure, and tried to take some for herself. He gasped and dug his fingers into her flesh, crying, 'Don't move.' She didn't, even though she longed to. In that moment she remembered Jack, and the ecstacy they'd shared.

For once William didn't fall asleep. He held her close, stroking her hair, kissing her small ears. 'Let's have children straightaway,' he said. 'That's what we both want, isn't it, darling? You don't need to work.' He kissed her. 'I'll look after you. You need looking after.'

By making love with William, Frankie faced that her love affair with Jack was finished. She'd promised William she wouldn't walk out a second time. As for Jack, he wouldn't have her back. He'd read it in her eyes and know instantly what had happened. She thought of the passion they'd shared. The laughter. But he wasn't for her. William was her husband. Everyone would be pleased they were together again. They'd say she'd come to her senses and that he was a saint to forgive her. She'd do her best to make him a good wife. He'd be strict but fair with their children, kind to Steven when her mother had gone. She saw herself, in years to come, hosting Christmas at Kingly Grange.

It seemed very natural to wake up with William and to watch his precise movements as he walked between the bedroom and the bathroom. She felt content and sleepy. Not sated, as she had been with Jack. But she mustn't think of Jack any more. This was ordered contentment. This was for life.

Over breakfast they divided *The Sunday Times*. She read the colour supplement, he read the business section. Only when she let Blue into the garden did he look up. 'What will you do with the dog?' he asked.

'He can either live with us or I can put him back into training.'

'Big dogs shouldn't live in London. Training would be better.'

She watched Blue race around the lawn. 'You're right.'

At midday, they left the house to drive to the hospital. William automatically handed Frankie the car keys, saying, 'You drive, darling.' He turned on Radio 3. They listened to Bach. Only when they reached the hospital did he ask her shyly, 'Can we tell them about us?'

She smiled. 'I think they'll guess.'

Her mother was sitting up in bed, looking pale but smiling. Her eyes danced from Frankie to William. 'At least you don't need to get married,' she said, with her old laugh, and she reached up to squeeze Frankie's hand.

But later, when Steven and William went for a stroll around the grounds, she said, 'Frankie, are you sure you're doing the right thing? William's not a man to forgive an errant wife. I'd hate you to go back because of me.'

'I'm not. It's right for both of us.' Frankie didn't want to listen to her mother's doubts.

It was some days before Frankie could leave White Oast, by which time her mother was home and Mrs Broom's daughter-in-law had been employed to shop and cook.

'I wish you'd drop in and see Mother,' William said to Frankie as he helped her settle Blue in the back of her car. 'You'll have to meet her at the Lord Chancellor's Office, when I'm sworn in.'

She closed the boot. 'I have to go to the stadium. I owe it to Jack to tell him personally.'

'You're my wife, Francesca! You don't owe anything to that criminal.'

'Don't start shouting at me already, William.'

She thought he was going to blow up. Then he took a deep breath. 'You're right. I'm sorry, darling. But you do understand why I'm worried. I'm not very sure of you yet.'

Warmed by his confession, she put her arms around him. 'You've nothing to fear. I've made my decision. I won't let you down again.'

It was raining hard by the time she reached the kennels. April winds buffeted the long grass on the Downs and blew gusts of wet across the lane and into her windscreen. Eamonn was out, much to Frankie's relief. All the way on, up to Richmond, she rehearsed her speech to Jack. She was reasonably calm until she touched the park. Then nerves attacked her. She had to stop in one of the gravel car parks and take deep breaths. On the slope in front of her a herd of deer drifted through the soaking grass. Frankie envied them. They never had to worry about tomorrow.

The stadium looked spruce. The white demarcation lines in the car park had been repainted. She walked through the grandstand, which was alive with the familiar mid-morning bustle of cleaners, secretaries, caterers and kennel staff, all hurrying to prepare the track for the evening meeting. Bernard called down the stairs to ask about her mother. So did Signor Umberto. She answered as normally as she could, but all the time she was on edge for Jack's footsteps.

The Paddock House was its usual endearing muddle of Edwardian home and hi-tech office. She could hear the telex chattering in the card room and the honky-tonk of 'The Entertainer' coming from behind the closed door. She realised how much she was going to miss life at the track. Nothing would ever be quite like it. She clenched her fists, and unclenched them. Then she opened the card-room door.

Marius and Nicoletta were sitting on the sofa by the window. 'Is Jack around?' she asked, her words coming out squeaky.

Marius frowned. 'He's out. And if I were you, I'd get clear before he comes back.'

'I want to tell him to his face.'

'Why? To rub it in? To see his hurt?'

'Of course not! Look, I know he'll never forgive me. You won't either. But if Jack had kept away from crime, I wouldn't have left him. I loved him.' She choked on the words, turned, and hurried out of the card room.

Nicoletta followed. She laid a sympathetic hand on Frankie's arm. 'Do you need help? Shall I fetch a groundsman to load your cases? What about Big Ears?'

'Could you ask someone to bring my car round and load him? But not Jaws and Mathilda. I'd like to give them to Jolyon. He looks after them so well.'

'He'll be thrilled.'

Frankie hesitated. 'Do you blame me for leaving Jack?'

'You should leave both men and strike out alone.'

'Maybe you're right. But I'm not very brave at the moment, with my mother so ill. I need something stable in my life. I may not be in love with William, but I care for him. I want to have children, a family. I know I can be happy with William – if I can forget about Jack.'

'And if you can't forget?'

'I will, I'm determined.' She hurried up the stairs. On the landing, she stopped and leaned over the banisters. 'I'd be sorry not to see you again, Nicoletta.'

'Call me at the shop. If things don't work out, Frankie, you can always help me with my stocktaking. No one does it as well as you do.'

Frankie laughed and went on up.

The attic was in chaos. The bed was unmade, the pillows thrown on the floor. A tap was dripping in the bathroom. Suddenly, she didn't want to face Jack. She wanted to get away. In a frenzy, she pulled her suitcases out of the cupboard and threw in her dresses and jackets, all tangled up with their hangers. She scooped up her shoes and threw them into a box. She crossed to her dressing table. Only then did she see the smashed mirror and her scent bottles thrown on to the floor, as if Jack had tried to wipe away all visible evidence of her. She brushed the bottles up into another case, emptying the contents of her drawers on top. When she had everything ready, she placed the cases on the landing and called down to the groundsman to put them in her car.

Back inside the room, Frankie closed the door and sat down on the end of the bed, quiet for that one last moment, remembering. The first time she'd come here, when they'd held the tape to stick the drawings. The night she'd left William, when Jack had come home to find her in his bed. The time when she was ill and he'd telephoned her mother. The evening when he'd carried Blue up to visit her.

She heard footsteps on the stairs. 'That's all the luggage,' she called out.

Jack flung open the door. They stared at each other, he from the threshold, she, hands clenched nervously, sitting on the end of the bed where they had shared such love and laughter.

'Get out!' he shouted.

'Jack,' she began, 'please let me explain.'

He took a step towards her. 'Get out before I kill you!'

She fled from the room, down the stairs, and out to her car. All her fears about Jack had been proved correct. He was uncontrollably violent. She drove home to Islington, to safety.

Twenty-Eight

William was waiting on the doorstep when Frankie drew up. He looked so relieved to see her. This lack of confidence made her realise how he'd changed and brought out her motherly feelings. She wanted to reassure him. He carried her cases inside, groaning at the reappearance of Big Ears. 'Surely you could have left that wretched rabbit behind?' he said.

'Not at Richmond. He was terrified that the dogs would eat him. But I have given Jaws away, you'll be glad to know.'

'I suppose that's something!'

Once, his criticism would have upset her. Now, she took a deep breath and shrugged it off. She too had changed.

From the study came the strains of Mozart. She wandered through the familiar rooms. She could hardly believe she'd been away. It was as though Jack had never existed.

'I threw out all those pot plants,' William said sheepishly, finding her in the bare kitchen. 'I couldn't stand to see them once you'd gone.'

She slipped her arms around his waist. 'I'll soon have more. And before you complain, remember, I won't be working. At least, not for a year or two.'

'What about the baby?'

She gave him a small butterfly kiss. 'William, babies take nine months – and I'm not pregnant yet.'

He smoothed back her hair. 'We'll have to do something about that.'

She didn't remind him that first she must have her coil removed, because he was squeamish about such things.

William had business in chambers that afternoon. He had to complete his last case before he became a judge. As soon as he left the house, Frankie telephoned Melanie, saying, 'Guess where I am?'

'Back in Islington?'

'How did you know?'

'Frankie, you may not tell me all your secrets, but I'm not completely stupid. You were so adamant, I knew something was up. And I'm thrilled. Are you coming back to work?'

'Not yet. I want to have a baby. And we don't want to fall into the old trap of working so hard that we never have time for each other. But let's gossip later. Come to dinner tonight.'

'Oh, no. We couldn't. Not on your first evening.'

'William would love it.'

'So would we. I'm so happy. Everything's going to be just as it was.'

'No. It's going to be better. I'm determined.'

Frankie replaced the receiver and wrote out her shopping list. After the bustle of the stadium, the house seemed very silent. She turned on the radio and twiddled the knob until she found an LBC traffic update. Anything to break the silence. She wondered what Jack was thinking. What he was doing. She stared at the telephone, and was seized by a longing to hear his voice. Quickly, she picked up her car keys and hurried out of the house, away from temptation.

William returned punctually, with a dozen red roses. 'You don't know what it means to come home and find you here,' he said as he watched her arrange them in a silver bowl.

'I've invited Simon and Mel.'

'Oh good! Everything's going to be just as it used to be.'

She smiled. 'That's what Mel said. But I said it's going to be better.' She kissed him on the chin and returned to smoothing her home-made pâté into an oval dish. 'I'll need a project if I'm going to stay at home. I think we should redecorate the house.'

'Virginia Culmstock would love to help again.'

'And have her clicking her tongue at me? No, William. This time we'll choose. I want lovely warm colours for our new beginning.'

'Whatever you say, darling.' He went down into the cellar to choose the wine for dinner. From the kitchen, Frankie could hear him humming out of tune.

In the following days, Frankie thought of Jack frequently. But she kept herself busy. She visited her gynaecologist. She unpacked, and reorganised the house. She stocked up on groceries, and meat for the freezer. In chambers, she'd always been efficient.

At home, she'd tended to be forgetful. At least, William had said she was. Now she kept lists in an effort to be more organised. When William came home, she had dinner in preparation. If he wanted to go to the theatre, she remembered to book the seats. If they went out, she booked the restaurant.

Frankie's only contact with the stadium was through Eamonn. Blue was on a winning streak. She wished she could see him. Often, on her way home from Rockhurst, she was tempted to call at the kennels, but fear of meeting Jack prevented her.

Every couple of days she drove down to White Oast. Her mother was weak and very thin. There was no mention of France. Instead they talked of the past, of Frankie's childhood. They relived a wonderful holiday in Cornwall with her father, their only holiday with him. He'd arrived home one day to announce that he'd rented an isolated farm cottage on the North Cornwall coast: years later they'd discovered he was hiding from a gambling debt. The cottage was above a beach where the Atlantic waves battered the sand until it was hard and dark. Frankie had almost forgotten the holiday. Together with everything else to do with her father, she'd spent a long time with the memory battened down. Now she recalled hours of peering into the rock pools left behind by the tide, watching as her father caught tiny crabs and shrimps in her green fishing net. She remembered the day he'd caught a lobster, the excitement, the triumphant march back to the cottage to cook it.

'You boiled your petticoats in sugar,' she said to her mother.

'Ben took me dancing one night. Rock and roll! We left you with the farmer's wife. You were furious.' Her mother laughed, and in a quavering voice she sang the first few lines of *Rock Around the Clock*. Then she stopped, tears in her eyes.

A week before Williiam was due to be sworn in, Frankie met Mel in Harvey Nichols to choose an outfit. 'Smart and chic,' she said, as they waded through the whole of the designer floor. 'And I need a hat for the Lord Chancellor's swearing-in.'

'At least you won't be upstaged by William's mother,' said Mel with a cackle. 'She'll probably wear her gumboots.'

'The old hag! She doesn't even phone the house in case I answer. The swearing-in will be the first time I've met her since I've been back with William.' Frankie slipped on an extremely smart black crêpe dress with taupe insets.

'You'll see everyone from our chambers as well,' said Melanie, helping Frankie with the zip. 'They're all invited to William's chambers for the party.' She stepped back. 'That dress is terrific.'

'I can imagine what they've said about me.' Frankie settled a high-brimmed, black hussar hat on to her head. ' "Oh, poor William! Such a saint! How could he have her back!" '

Melanie giggled. 'Don't worry! Virginia Culmstock will grovel once you're Lady Eastgate.'

'I can't start calling myself Lady Eastgate to people who've known me for years.'

'You're the only woman I know who wouldn't.'

'I'd feel a fraud. I haven't earned a title. William has. And I can't claim to have given him my continuous support. We were separated.' Frankie took off the hat. She gave Melanie a wink. 'Shame it's not a royal title. Then my mother-in-law would be obliged to curtsey to me!'

On a sunny afternoon in late April, Frankie sat beside William in the back of their rented limousine as it swept them through Parliament Square to the House of Lords. She was in her black crêpe dress and black hussar hat. He wore full judge's regalia: a red robe, white collar, and shoulder-length curling wig. He was tense. She reached for his hand. 'You're going to be a brilliant judge,' she said. 'I'm proud of you.'

They passed through the Chancellor's Gate and into a Gothic courtyard, now used as a car park. William's parents were waiting with his clerk from chambers, a member of the Lord Chancellor's Office, and the official photographer. Mortimer was making polite conversation. Audrey was fierce in Tory-blue wool and a cloche hat which made her look like Goebbels.

'Good morning, Francesca,' she said loudly and pointedly. 'I hope you're very proud of your husband.'

'I am. I've just told him so in the car.' Smiling, Frankie shook hands with the Lord Chancellor's staff, kissed her father-in-law, and greeted Wiliam's clerk. She chatted pleasantly to everyone, refusing to be upset by Audrey on William's great day.

They bunched together for the family photograph, but stood back whilst William had his official head-and-shoulder picture taken. Then they were ushered upstairs, up a wide, ornate staircase creaking with history, to the office of the Lord Chancellor's Permanent Secretary, who ran through the ceremony with them. Even Audrey was silenced by the solemnity of the occasion. Finally, they were ready. William turned to Frankie. He looked very pale. She gave him a big smile. Then, with the Bible in his right hand, and the oath in his left, he led the way into the Lord Chancellor's Office.

It was a large, partially panelled room with gilt-framed portraits of past Lord Chancellors hanging on the walls and highly polished antique furniture reflecting the warmth of a deep red carpet. From the windows Frankie caught sight of a stupendous view of the river. The Lord Chancellor was standing in front of his desk. As instructed, William turned immediately to the left and stood beside an octagonal library table. Frankie, his parents and his clerk lined up in front of the window. Because she knew William was nervous, she was nervous. She clenched her fists behind her back to prevent herself from fiddling and distracting him.

The Lord Chancellor nodded to William, who read the first oath, the allegiance to the Crown: 'I William Alexander Eastgate do swear by Almighty God that I will be faithful and bear true allegiance to her Majesty Queen Elizabeth the Second, her heirs and successors, according to the Law.' He went straight into the second oath, the Judicial Oath. As Frankie listened, she was even more convinced that she had done right by coming back to William. He was going to be a great judge. She felt honoured to be at his side.

After William had signed the book of oaths, the Lord Chancellor gave him his letter patent, the handwritten open letter whereby the Queen appointed him judge. It was stamped with the great seal, rolled, tied with red ribbon, and nestling in a long red leather box.

'Congratulations!' The Lord Chancellor shook William warmly by the hand. 'Would you like to introduce me to your family?'

Very firmly, Audrey stepped forward. As William's wife, Frankie should have taken precedence, but she didn't mind. She listened as the Lord Chancellor told her parents-in-law, 'You must be very proud of your son.'

Then William said, 'May I introduce my wife, Francesca.'

Frankie held out her hand. She met the Lord Chancellor's smile

251

with her own. But his eyes were shrewd. She was sure he knew that she hadn't always been at William's side.

The ceremony took barely half an hour, after which they went straight to William's chambers, he still in his judge's regalia. Everyone was there to congratulate him. Apart from his own chambers, there was Sir Giles and Lady Henrietta, Geoffrey and Virgina Culmstock, Simon and Melanie, small, dapper Desmond and his doggy wife, Rupert Barbour with his eye on one of William's pupils, Sanjiv and Deepa, expecting their second child, James and his heavily pregnant teacher wife, Hugo and Thomas, both already the worse for champagne. And Old Nailbag, gazing morosely around the cheerful room.

Most people knew that Frankie was back with William but they still exchanged glances at her appearance.

'This is a surprise, Francesca,' said Virginia in her metallic voice.

'Yes.' Melanie linked a supportive arm through Frankie's. 'Isn't it wonderful?'

'I agree.' Sanjiv joined in. 'Frankie, I wish you were back with us in chambers. I miss your bright smile.'

'So do I,' said James. 'When I joined chambers, it was you and Melanie who made me feel welcome.'

Frankie was pink with surprise and pleasure. 'I'm grateful, but I'm not planning to work at the moment. Maybe in a year or two.' She turned to place her drink on a side table and found Geoffrey Culmstock standing behind her.

'William's a good man to have you back. I wouldn't,' he growled in his gruff Yorkshire voice. 'But don't think you can waltz back into chambers. A few might be in favour, but the majority are against it. They've already told me so.'

Frankie turned crimson and Geoffrey walked away. She wanted to yell after him that she had no intention of sharing a chambers with hypocrites, but she held back the words. It wouldn't be fair on William to make a scene. This was his day.

A fortnight later, William received a letter announcing his knighthood: unlike most titles, a High Court judge's knighthood did not necessarily appear in the honours list. They could now call themselves Sir William and Lady Eastgate, although his visit to Buckingham Palace to be dubbed with the sword wouldn't take place until September, after the Queen returned from her summer holiday at Balmoral.

William was thrilled with his title. Immediately, he ordered new notepaper. His mother was ecstatic. She peppered her conversation with, 'My son, Sir William.' Even Mrs MacDougall was impressed. She informed Frankie that a titled household needed a better class of Hoover. Only Frankie was slightly embarrassed. She couldn't bring herself to say Lady Eastgate at the dry cleaners who'd always known her as Mrs Eastgate.

Their life settled into a pleasant routine. They entertained most Thursdays, and accepted a maximum of three other invitations a week. At her insistence they invited Sanjiv and Deepa to one of their smarter dinner parties: she hadn't forgotten their kindness. At the weekends they went to Kingly on Saturdays and White Oast on Sundays. Frankie visited her mother at least one other time during the week. She preferred these weekday visits because they could reminisce uninterrupted.

In London, Frankie concentrated on the house. She enjoyed working out colour schemes, drawing up plans of each room and stapling samples to the paper. 'Which do you like best?' she asked William one evening. 'This rust and blue chintz or that burned orange.'

'Not the orange. It's too bright.' He pointed at a squiggle. 'What's that?'

'The smaller spare room.'

He linked his arms around her. 'You mean the nursery?'

'Sssh. We mustn't tempt fate. I might never get pregnant.'

He kissed the top of her head. 'Of course you will.'

That night, as they were going to bed, she said, 'William, I only have a hundred pounds to my name. Now I'm not working, I'm afraid you're going to have to keep me.'

'I'll leave you twenty pounds tomorrow.'

'That won't go anywhere. Not if you want to eat smoked salmon and quails' eggs.'

'Fifty, then.'

She didn't argue. It was too late. But she wondered how other women extracted money from their husbands. William had always paid the mortgage and the bills. She'd paid for the food, Mrs MacDougall and her own clothes. She'd had a bank account, credit cards, charge cards, shop cards. Now she was totally dependent.

On her next visit to White Oast, she asked her mother's advice. 'You must make him give you an allowance,' her mother replied, deeply concerned. 'You can't live on hand-outs. And why should you? For someone so bright, darling, you're very naïve. And do remember to open a separate account for yourself and pay in a little each month. For emergencies.'

'I'm not intending to leave William again.'

'He might leave you. Is the house still in his name?'

'Mother! Don't worry!' Frankie reached across and clasped her mother's hand, and changed the subject.

Nevertheless, she presented William with a carefully worked-out budget.

'Twelve hundred a month!' he gasped.

'Shall I cancel your caviare?'

'No darling, but . . .' His eyes ran down her list of expenses. 'What's this? Kennel fees, a hundred and fifty pounds? I'm not paying that kind of money to keep your dog in training.'

'All right. But let's not argue.'

He opened his mouth to say something, but she covered it with her hand. 'William, we're not fighting over Blue.'

It was two days before Frankie had time to collect Blue. She didn't tell William the reason for the delay: that she had an appointment with her gynaecologist. On the way down to the kennels, she felt perfectly calm. But when she turned into the lane, her heart began to thud.

Eamonn appeared immediately. He was leading Blue. 'You shouldn't take him out of training,' he grumbled. 'It's a waste of a good dog.'

'My husband doesn't want him here.'

'Because of Jack?'

'Partly.' Frankie wasn't going to tell Eamonn that William was mean.

The old trainer glanced at the lane behind her. 'Then you'd best get goin' quick.'

She turned around. Jack's Land Rover was coming up the lane, dust and stones shooting out from beneath its tyres. He was alone, driving fast. She stood next to the car, the front door open, knowing she could drive away but unable to move. He stared at her through the dirty windscreen. Chin up, she met his eyes. He opened the Land Rover door and stepped down. He was everything she remembered and more. So much more. The muscles around her heart and lungs contracted. Her mouth went dry and she swallowed hard. Jack walked towards her. She waited for him to speak, but he kept on walking until he disappeared into the kennels.

She knew then that she still loved him. Or maybe hated him. But never indifferent. Keeping Blue at the kennels had been a link. She recognised that now. William was right to make her take the dog away. As she drove back to London, she wondered if she'd tell the child she was carrying that everyone should know great love once, just as her mother had told her.

Twenty-Nine

By the time Frankie reached home, she was berating herself for being disloyal to William. He was her husband, the father of her unborn child. Jack was her madness, as her father had been her mother's madness.

She planned the perfect setting to tell William about the baby, fetching up a bottle of his favourite Krug from the cellar and spreading Beluga caviare on tiny triangles of brown bread. Then she ran a bath, adding liberal doses of scent, but careful not to have the water too hot in case it harmed the baby. As she lay in the warm water, she carefuly soaped her tummy, wondering if the baby could feel her stroking movement. When she dried herself she was careful again not to rub too hard with the towel.

William came home to find her sitting in the garden, wearing a pretty cream silk dress and a string of pearls. The champagne was on the table, perfectly chilled in a silver ice bucket. Beside it stood two of their best Waterford champagne glasses and a plate of caviare. He stared at the champagne. Frankie smiled. But before she had time to speak, Blue came bounding through from the kitchen.

'What's that dog doing here?' William demanded.

'You told me to take him out of training.'

'I never said bring him to the house.'

'Where else am I going to take him? He's my dog.'

William pursed his lips. 'And what's this champagne? For God's sake, Francesca! My Krug is for special occasions.'

Tears filled her eyes. 'This is a special occasion,' she whispered. 'I'm going to have a baby.'

'Oh, darling!' In an instant, he was by her side. 'I'm sorry I snapped. You should have told me straightaway. Oh, I'm so happy.' He kissed her very tenderly. 'When?'

'January.'

'I can't wait that long.'

She laughed. 'You'll have to.'

He smiled proudly. 'We must have a family celebration this weekend at Kingly. Have you told your mother yet?'

'No. I wanted to tell you first.'

'We must decide on a name. We'll study the Eastgate family tree. I've always liked Alexander. And it is my second name.'

'William, it might be a girl.'

He ran his hand over her stomach. 'No, this is definitely a boy.'

They sat outside until dusk crept over the garden, talking excitedly about the baby, their voices carrying on the warmth of the May evening. William telephoned his parents. She telephoned White Oast: her mother cried with happiness. They telephoned Simon and Melanie. It was late when they went to bed. They kissed and held each other close.

'Will it hurt the baby if we make love?' William whispered in her ear.

She smiled. 'Of course not.'

He was especially gentle. Afterwards, he didn't turn his back but held her close. As Frankie listened to his deep breathing, she felt safe. The baby would fill her life. If it was a girl, they would call her Dominique. A daughter wouldn't take her mother's place, but she would be a link. God, if he existed, was pleased that she'd gone back to William.

The excitement of the baby drove Jack from her mind. Only once did she allow herself to think that this could have been his child. Then she reminded herself that Jack's child would have grown up in a world of guns.

Everyone was pleased about the baby. Her mother-in-law kissed her. Virginia Culmstock sent her flowers. In the days that followed, William was most considerate. When the decorators arrived and the house was in chaos, he drove Frankie down to White Oast to escape the upheaval and the reek of paint. She was relieved. She'd begun to feel nauseous.

It was lovely to sit in the garden with her mother, talking about the baby whilst Blue chased the never-ending supply of squirrels. The fresh air and warm weather brought colour to Frankie's pale cheeks. Occasionally, she was bothered by a slight pain in her abdomen. She decided to consult her mother's doctor, but by the time she saw him it had disappeared.

One morning her mother spoke of what was paramount in both

257

their thoughts. 'I only wish I could live long enough to see the baby,' she said. 'Just to hold her in my arms. Even once.'

'I'll tell her all about you.' Frankie smiled through her tears. 'But William's convinced it's a boy.'

'Oh, no! It's a girl! When I was expecting you, I knew you were a girl. I used to sing to you. French lullabies. Ben was convinced you were a boy. He used to sing you rugger songs. Awful rude ones. I was young and innocent, and so shocked!' Her mother shook her head. 'After all these years I still can't believe that someone as practical as me could have married a man like Ben. And within ten days of meeting him! It was winter. We had no money. I never had any money until I met Steven. We spent our honeymoon in a cheap hotel in Brighton. It was the kind of place where they only put the heating on in the evening, so we passed the afternoons in the cinema, in the cheap seats, or wandering in and out of antique shops in the Lanes. Sometimes we pretended we wanted to buy something, just to come in out of the cold. I didn't contact my English cousins until after I was married. Poor creatures! They'd been frantic with worry when I failed to arrive as planned. When they met Ben, they were appalled. They called him "that Irishman". But I was in love. I didn't care. Later, after I was divorced, I met them by accident in Selfridges. I pretended I was still married. I couldn't bear to give them the satisfaction of having been right.'

Frankie laughed out loud at her mother's story.

Back in London, she was delighted to find the house in order, the new blue and rust curtains already hanging in the freshly decorated drawing room, the dining room transformed by warm, burgundy-red velvet and the bright white space-age kitchen softened by light oak and pretty Spanish tiles. Upstairs, their bedroom was no longer pale blue but shades of biscuit and buttermilk: William's choice.

She went down to fetch her case but as she reached the hall, a wave of nausea washed over her. Thinking it was the smell of paint, she hurried out into the garden. Even there she felt unwell. It wasn't just sickness, but also the nagging pain in her side.

When William came home, she was lying on their bed, clutching her stomach. 'You look terrible,' he exclaimed. 'Have you called the doctor?'

258

'I have an appointment tomorrow.'

'Darling, you need him now.' He reached for the phone.

By the time the doctor arrived, Frankie was feeling slightly better. He examined her thoroughly, then said, 'Everything seems to be in order, Lady Eastgate. Of course, not all problems can be picked up by a clinical examination or even by an ultrasound scan, but I don't want to maul you around more than necessary. If you're not losing blood and the pain has subsided, I think we should monitor the situation. Stay in bed. Have a good rest. If the pain returns, telephone me. Otherwise, let me know how you feel in the morning.'

William plumped up her pillows whilst she undressed. As she was slipping on her nightgown, the telephone rang. William answered. She heard him say, 'Of course I'll tell her, Steven. We'll be there at midday.' He replaced the receiver and reached for Frankie's hand. 'Darling, your mother's gone into hospital. Well, not a hospital. A hospice.'

'Oh, no!'

He put his arms around her. 'She isn't dead yet. She has a few weeks, maybe more. And she'll be more comfortable in a hospice. They'll be able to give her the right drugs.'

'I must go to her now.'

'I'll take you tomorrow.'

'She might die in the night. I want to be with her.' She began to cry.

'Darling, you must think of our son. You haven't been well. You can't go driving around in the middle of the night. That's irresponsible. Your mother wouldn't want you to harm our baby. Get into bed. The doctor told you to rest.'

Frankie allowed herself to be persuaded. William was right. She must think of the baby. He went downstairs and she listened to him move around the kitchen as he prepared his supper. She thought of her mother lying in another bed, and tears slid down her nose and on to the pillow.

William had to go into court next morning, but he promised to be home by ten o'clock. To fill time, Frankie took Blue for a short walk. It was a sunny morning, the kind of morning her mother loved. That thought choked her. She felt sick and faint, although she wasn't sure if it was the baby or worry. She'd barely reached the end of her street before the nagging pain in her abdomen returned. She started back towards the house. The sun beat on her head. Sweat trickled down the side of her face and the pain grew worse. She stopped to see if it would pass. It didn't. She took a few steps forwards. It became excruciating. She felt as though her stomach was being ripped apart. She staggered and grabbed at a lamppost. Blue looked at her, puzzled. She tried to cry out, but no sound came. The street and the houses began to spin. She slid to the ground. As she fell, she cracked her head on the edge of the pavement.

She came round to find herself lying on a bed in a small bare room, with a nurse sitting on a chair beside her. The pain in her stomach was still bad and her head was throbbing. Gingerly she raised her hand and met a bandage.

The door opened and William came in. He saw her eyes flicker. 'How are you, darling?' he asked.

'Is the baby all right?'

'Oh, the . . . er . . . doctor will tell you.'

'What about Mother?'

'She's fine. Oh . . . er . . . here's the doctor, darling.'

'I'm afraid it's what I feared,' said her doctor, patting her hand. 'An ectopic pregnancy. The fertilised egg is developing in the Fallopian tube. That's what's causing you the pain.'

'Can you save my baby?' she asked weakly.

'I'm sorry.'

'How soon will she be able to get pregnant again?' asked William.

'Let's get this over with first, shall we, Sir William?' The doctor gave Frankie a sympathetic smile. 'You had a nasty crack on the head. Nevertheless, we have to operate later today. We suspect the foetus has ruptured the Fallopian tube and we want to remove it whilst the tube is still repairable. No food between now and the op. Try to rest, and don't worry! I'm sure there'll be other babies.'

'But I wanted this one.'

'I understand.'

'No, you don't. My mother's dying. This baby was a part of her.' She turned her face away and began to cry softly into her pillow.

Wiliam returned that evening, just before the operation. He looked stiff and awkward. 'How are you feeling?' he asked.

'Miserable but resigned. How's Mother?'

He reached for her hand and played with her pale fingers, not looking her in the eye.

'Something's wrong, isn't it?' Her voice rose. 'Is it my mother?'

He looked even more awkward. 'Darling, I'm not meant to tell you till after your operation.'

'Is she . . . dead?'

'This afternoon. She just slipped away. Steven was with her.'

'Did she know I'd lost the baby?'

'Yes. But she was dying anyway, Frankie. That had nothing to do with it.' He carried on talking, asking her what flowers he should send for the funeral, wanting to know if he should tell Melanie. But Frankie couldn't answer him. She was stunned by grief. She didn't even feel the prick on her arm as the doctor gave her a sedative. All she knew was that she was sinking into an oblivion from which she never wished to emerge.

Thirty

Frankie wasn't well enough to go to her mother's funeral. Instead, she lay in her hospital bed, tears sliding down her cheeks, as she pictured the little stone church and the sloping graveyard where her mother was to be buried beneath an ancient yew tree.

She cried endlessly. The doctor said this was natural, a mixture of grief and hormones. William was sympathetic. He tried to cheer her up by saying, 'We'll have another baby soon,' but that made her cry all the more. Nothing could fill the emptiness. The deep mourning for her mother, to whom she hadn't been able to say goodbye. Her hollow of despair about the baby. She blamed herself for losing it, which was illogical, but logic had nothing to do with misery.

To make matters worse, Melanie was pregnant. 'I nearly didn't tell you,' she said, visiting Francesca on her first day home from hospital. 'Then I decided that was demeaning to you.'

'I'm happy for you.' Frankie tried to sound pleased but it was impossible not to be envious. Melanie had a baby, alive and growing inside her, whilst she, Frankie, had failed.

Robert and Priscilla had come over for the funeral. They were staying with Steven. They called on Frankie in hospital, and again at home. 'You and William are visiting us as soon as you're well,' Robert told her in his most organising voice. 'You were set to come two years ago. We want no excuses. We relocate back to San Francisco in September, but we expect you in Dallas before then.'

She nodded weakly. Robert was exhausting but kind. Everyone was kind. In a way, that made it worse.

'I lost a baby too,' said Priscilla, seeing the desolation come into Frankie's face. 'At three months. I thought I'd never get over it. But I did.'

'I never knew.' Frankie looked at Priscilla through new eyes. They'd branded her stupid because she wasn't clever, but she had other qualities, such as patience and warmth. Frankie would have

262

liked to talk more, but Robert was in a hurry to reach Harrods before it closed for the night.

That first weekend, William drove her down to White Oast. She was shocked by Steven's appearance. He'd shrivelled and aged. Always lame, now he could barely walk without help. William left her there with Blue, and went on to Kingly. She was glad to be alone with Steven, in the house which had so much of her mother in it but which no longer echoed to her light step.

'She made me very happy,' said Steven, as they walked slowly up the lane to the graveyard.

'She was very happy with you.' Frankie squeezed his skeletal hand. 'Much happier than with my father. It's taken me years to admit that.'

'Were you upset when she married me?'

'Oh, Steven, you were always so kind. But like most children of separated parents, I hoped mine would get back together and we'd live happily ever after. Her remarriage ended that. What was unfair is that although I rejected my father for the same reasons my mother left him, I still blamed her for leaving him. If I have children, I hope they won't be as hard on me as I was on my mother.'

Steven patted her hand. 'You were very good to her in later years. You were good to both of us.'

They'd reached the little church where her mother had worshipped. It was old and built of grey stone, with a sloping graveyard running down to a wood. They followed a path between old weatherbeaten gravestones, many lying on their sides, to the yew trees. Even from a distance, Frankie recognised her mother's grave. It was covered with freesias.

'Did you come this morning?' she asked Steven.

He nodded. 'I give her freesias every day. They were her favourites.'

For some time they stood in silence, looking at the grave, each lost in their own thoughts. Then they walked slowly back to White Oast, to tea in the garden which was already showing signs of neglect. It cried out for her mother's touch.

In London, Frankie did her best to pick up the threads of her life. The routine of their existence carried her along. William was kind but busy. She felt empty, even when they made love.

She'd received a number of letters of condolence. Answering them kept her busy. There was even one from Marius. She would have liked to meet him and talk of her mother, but she felt too vulnerable. She thanked him briefly, just two lines on her Lady Eastgate notepaper.

She'd inherited her mother's jewellery and personal possessions. The clothes she left at White Oast. They were too short for her in any case, and she sensed that Steven dreaded an empty cupboard. The jewellery case she took back to London. Cataloguing it occupied half a day. Her favourite item was her mother's delicate Piaget watch.

For William's sake Frankie tried to be cheerful, but frequently when he had left for work, she returned to bed to lie under the duvet, crying. Except in recent months, when she'd had the house and the baby to think about, she'd always worked. Now she had nothing. Mrs MacDougall came twice a week. On the other days, often Frankie saw no one from the moment William left for court until his return.

Because of Blue, she was obliged to go out every day. Sometimes she drove to Hampstead Heath and walked him through the long grass. That was his favourite walk. Other days, she took him around the streets in her neighbourhood, trying to smile when other women passed her, hoping they'd stop to chat. They didn't. They hurried away, thinking her odd.

The weather was glorious. People sunbathed in their gardens and held barbecues, their laughter and the smell of burned sausages drifting over the walls. Through the open windows, Frankie heard women's voices in the street, mothers gossiping as they took their children to school, or arranging to meet for coffee in each other's houses. There was a clique of five, of whom Clarissa Riddle-Longman was the bossiest and the oldest. The others Frankie only knew by sight, because she'd never been at home during the day and she had no children to go to their children's parties. Sometimes she stood by the window, watching them enviously through the curtains. But if she went outside, they stopped talking. Or so it seemed.

Once, when she was sunbathing in the garden, she heard them arrive at the Riddle-Longmans'. She lay still, listening as they talked of children and schools. Then one mother said, 'I say, Clarissa, has your neighbour's wife bolted again?'

'No. She came back to become Lady Eastgate.'

There was laughter. Frankie slunk inside and closed the door. Standing in the shadows of the kitchen, she was suddenly reminded of the hot weekend she'd spent here, on her own, before she and Jack became lovers, and she was seized with a fierce longing for the wonderful lovemaking they had shared. It came over her in waves, so strong that she closed her eyes and whimpered. She reached for the telephone. Then she jumped back, rushed upstairs, threw on some clothes, and took Blue out for a walk, marching briskly along the warm pavements.

Melanie came to lunch. She was glowing and busy. Frankie longed to cry, 'Help me! I'm so lonely!' but she bottled it up inside her, as she'd done for all those years.

To be positive, she joined a health club, signing on for an aerobics class three mornings a week. In the health club shop she bought a bright-pink leotard. Of the twenty other women in her class, not one wore anything but black. Being a new girl, Frankie was placed in the front row. The routine was fast and furious and she had no idea what she was meant to be doing. Whilst the other girls stretched and kicked in time to the music, she floundered like a hot pink shrimp, skipping to the right when meant to go to the left, and crashing into her neighbour, a supercilious friend of Clarissa Riddle-Longman with a face like a constipated giraffe. At the end of the class, every one rushed off in a gaggle to the fruit juice bar. Frankie was left alone to pull on her track suit and slink home.

'I can't even skip in time to the music,' she told William when recounting her morning.

Laughing, he put his arms around her. 'You need another baby.'

'We have to wait a few months.'

'You must do something. Mother's worried about you. So's Steven. I think we should start entertaining again. It'll keep you busy. I want to invite the Lord Chancellor to dinner. Phone his office wtih some possible dates.'

'William, not yet. Please! I couldn't cope.'

'Don't be silly, Francesca. Of course you can.' William kissed her lightly on the cheek and walked through to the study to read his newspaper.

Frankie felt as though a trap were closing in around her. It wasn't William's fault, it was her own. She began to study the legal vacancies in *The Times*. She didn't tell anyone, not even William, because she felt so worthless that she couldn't believe she'd even get an interview. But a fortnight later, she saw an advertisment: *International medical company requires experienced barrister for legal department.*

It took her all morning to prepare her letter and curriculum vitae. In the afternoon, she walked Blue to the letter box. Even if she didn't get this job, the fact of trying made her feel less crushed. Next morning, she returned to aerobics, and almost managed to keep in step. She no longer smiled meekly at other women in the street. So what if they didn't want to speak to her!

The medical company telephoned to invite her for an interview on the following morning. When William came home, she was in the bedroom trying on her work suits, all several years out of date. 'I have good news,' she called out.

'You're pregnant again?'

'Not yet!' She smiled as he came up the stairs. 'I applied for a job and I have an interview tomorrow.'

He stared at her. 'What job?'

'In the legal department of Health & Medicine. They advertised in *The Times*. It's not a terrific salary but it sounds interesting. And it won't be too demanding.'

'So you wrote behind my back?'

She was astonished by his venom. 'William, I didn't tell you in case they didn't want to see me. I've felt so useless lately.'

'What about the baby? Or have you decided against that, too, without informing me?'

'Of course not! But I'm not pregnant yet. And I can't hang around the house for months. I'm not used to it. You know how miserable I've been. I like to earn my own money, I like to contribute. I thought you'd be pleased about the job. You said yourself I must do something.'

'I meant be a wife,' he shouted. 'Entertain. Run my house. Have my children. Not go out to work to meet other men.'

She stood her ground, answering calmly where once she would

266

have backed down. 'I'm not trying to meet other men. I've purposely chosen a job to fit in with our marriage. But I am not going to stay at home all day, on my own.' She slipped out of her black suit and hung it up whilst he watched her, pale with anger. Then she pulled on a T-shirt and shorts, and went downstairs to feed Big Ears and Blue.

They didn't speak again that evening.

In the morning, Frankie had to leave before William. 'Good-bye!' she called up to him.

He didn't answer.

Health & Medicine had their headquarters in Knightsbridge. She parked behind Harrods, and arrived at the smartly renovated Georgian building with five minutes to spare.

'Eastgate? Oh, yes.' The receptionist gave her a brisk smile. 'Mr Brewer is expecting you. First floor.'

Until that moment Frankie had felt confident. Now, she wished she'd stayed at home.

Roland Brewer, head of personnel, was waiting for her at the top of the stairs. He was rotund, with pebble glasses and an engaging schoolboy grin. Frankie liked him. 'We have a team of three in-house lawyers,' he explained, ushering her into a comfortable office and calling for coffee. 'As a medical company we receive a number of negligence claims. Some justified. Most not. Your task would be to assess them.'

'And not go to trial more than necessary?'

'Exactly. It's so expensive. Far better to settle out of court.'

They discussed her experience. He told her about the company. At the end he shook her firmly by the hand. 'Is your husband Sir William Eastgate, our new High Court judge?' he asked.

'Yes. But at work I'd like to be Mrs Eastgate.'

'We'd prefer that too.' He smiled. 'You'll be hearing from us.'

She went out, feeling happy. If William hadn't been so unpleasant about the job, she'd have telephoned him to share her news. Instead, she returned to Islington.

By the time she reached the house, Blue had been shut in for five hours. As she stepped into the hall, he nearly knocked her over in excitement. 'All right! I'll take you out,' she said, reminding herself that she'd have to find a dogwalker if she took a job.

As she tossed her jacket on to the kitchen chair, she saw, to her surprise, that the garden door was open. She stepped outside, and felt herself grow cold. Her plant pots were smashed. Her plants were broken. Around the perimeter fence, the earth was flattened. Then she gave a small scream. The door to Big Ears's hutch was open. Odd bits of bloody fur were scattered in one corner of the garden. 'Blue!' she shouted. 'You've killed Big Ears!' She lashed out at the dog, who slunk away.

William found her standing beside a small mound of earth in the garden. 'Big Ears is dead,' she said, tears filling her eyes. 'Blue killed him. Poor rabbit! He must have run round and round, terrorised, till he was exhausted. And it's my fault. I must have forgotten to lock the hutch when I fed him this morning.'

'That's what comes of having too much to do,' said William, putting a comforting arm around her shoulders. 'You don't have time to finish any one thing properly. That's always been your problem, darling.'

He didn't ask her about the interview, and she didn't tell him. They talked of Robert and Priscilla and whether Dallas would be too hot for their summer holiday.

When Frankie heard she'd been short-listed for the job, she was very excited. She phoned Melanie and explained the situation. 'I need your support,' she said. 'Can you come to supper tomorrow night? My second interview's the next day. I need William to see reason.'

'Oh, he'll come round to it. We'll both support you. The last thing you need, after your mother and the baby, is to hang around the house all day.'

All through supper, no one mentioned her interview. But as Frankie brought in the cheese and coffee, Melanie raised her glass. 'Congratulations, Frankie,' she said, loudly and clearly. 'You deserve to get the job.'

William turned pale. 'What job?'

'The one I told you about,' Frankie replied, as lightly as she could. 'I've been short-listed.'

There was an awkward silence, then William said, 'I've already told you, Francesca, that you're not going back to work.' He stood up. 'Simon, I apologise. My wife is so stupid she can't understand plain English. But what can one expect from a woman who walks

268

out on her marriage to live at a dogtrack? A woman so useless she can't even hold on to her baby.'

Frankie was too wounded to speak. She felt as if he'd punched her in the stomach.

Melanie and Simon were staring at her, shocked. 'Come on, Mel.' Simon stood up. 'We'd better go home.'

'No,' said Melanie. 'I'm not leaving Frankie. William, you're a bully. I never really understood why Frankie left you. Even when she told me that you'd hit her, I could almost excuse you on the grounds of jealousy. Not now! What you just said is the cruellest thing a man could say to his wife. If she leaves you again, you bloody well deserve it!'

'Melanie!' Simon took her by the arm. 'This is not our argument. Come on!'

'It's all right, Mel.' Frankie forced a smile. 'Thanks for supporting me. I'll speak to you tomorrow.' She raised her chin defiantly. 'After my interview!'

Whilst William accompanied them to the front door, Frankie went upstairs into the spare bedroom and closed the door. Her mother had been right. William could not forgive.

The door flew open. He stood on the threshold. 'You're not going to that interview,' he said.

'Our marriage is over.' She spoke quietly. 'Let's be civilised about it, for both our sakes.'

He raised his hand and slapped her, hard, across her face, knocking her backwards on to the bed. 'You're not going anywhere. You're my wife. I will not be made a fool of twice.'

She started to get up. 'Hit me again and I'll call the police.'

He pushed her back. 'I should have whipped you long ago. It's the only language you understand.' Suddenly, he drew a belt from his pocket, flicked it back, and brought the buckle end down on her legs. The metal ripped her stockings and cut her skin. She screamed and kicked out at him. He lashed her again. She rolled across the bed and made a dash for the door. He seized her and threw her back on the bed. 'You're my wife! Mine!' Pinning her legs under his, he ripped off her silk skirt and panties. Then he unzipped his trousers. 'You no longer have Mummy to run to. You have no one but me. You have no money, in spite of your efforts to fleece me. You're mine!' He forced himself into her. 'Mine!'

Frankie stopped fighting. He would only hurt her more. She lay perfectly still, staring at the ceiling.

When he had finished, he stood up. 'Don't tell me you didn't enjoy that,' he said.

She didn't answer.

He went downstairs. She continued to lie on the bed, her torn skirt around her waist. Jack had been in prison. She was in prison too. She'd escaped once, but allowed herself to be recaptured. She must get away again. But it would be harder this time. There was no Jack. No Mother at White Oast. No career.

She went into the bathroom. Her mascara had run down her cheeks. Her left eye showed the beginnings of a bruise. Her lip was bleeding where it had been forced on to her teeth. She undressed and stepped under the shower, letting the water wash Wiliam from her body. But it couldn't wash away her anger.

When she went downstairs, he was in his study, rearranging the leatherbound books on their shelves. She ignored him and called to Blue. He didn't come. She went into the garden. He wasn't there. Then she noticed the front door was slightly open. She rushed out into the street, shouting, 'Blue! Blue!' But there was no sign of him.

Still in her dressing gown, she took her car and drove up and down the streets, stopping to ask everyone if they'd seen a greyhound. She went home to telephone the police. Blue hadn't been reported. Without speaking to William, who was still in the study, she left the house and drove across to the Essex Road, zigzagging up and down all the streets. Blue was nowhere. In her mind she saw his body, broken and bleeding, hit by a car.

Hours later, she returned despondently to the house. William was in bed. She lay down on the sofa, waking only when she heard him leave for work. Exhausted, she dragged herself up. In the hall mirror, she examined her face. The bruise on her cheek was turning purple. Her upper lip was cut and swollen. There was no way she could attend an interview. William had won.

Melanie telephoned. 'Are you all right?' she asked. 'I was so worried about you. What happened at the interview?'

'I couldn't go. He beat me up. He raped me.' Frankie began to cry.

'I'm coming to collect you,' said Melanie. 'Pack a bag. You must stay with us.'

'I can't leave. Blue's missing. William let him out of the house to stop me going to the interview. Mel, I'd better get off the line in case someone rings to say they've found him. I'm so afraid he's been run over. Thanks for caring. I'll speak to you later.'

It was lunchtime when the police phoned to say they were holding Blue. Frankie nearly cried with relief. Before rushing from the house, she dabbed some powder on her lip and put on her largest dark glasses to hide her bruise.

At the police station, Blue was jumping up and down in a kennel. He'd been found wandering along Upper Street. 'I'm so grateful,' Frankie told the policeman. She bent down to hug Blue. As she did so, her glasses slipped forward. Quickly, she adjusted them. But not before the policeman had seen her face.

'You've a right shiner there, madam,' he said gently

She swallowed hard, unable to reply.

'That was no cupboard door, if you don't mind me saying.'

'I know.' She took a deep breath. 'But who'd believe me? My husband's a judge.' She picked up Blue's lead and hurried out of the police station. Behind her the policeman told her story to his shocked colleague.

Frankie didn't go home. Instead, she drove straight down to Eamonn's. The old trainer was loading the dogs into the van for the evening meeting when she arrived. 'Didn't expect to see you 'ere again,' he said.

She led Blue over to him. 'Will you look after him, Eamonn?'

'Jack wouldn't like it.'

She removed her dark glasses. 'Please!'

He stared at her battered face. 'Don't tell me your grand, titled 'usband did that.'

'I can look after myself, but I'm afraid for Blue.'

He held out his hand for the dog's lead. 'I'll put him back in training.'

'Thank you.' She bent to take Blue's face in her hands. 'Goodbye,' she whispered, kissing his sleek head. She longed to ask Eamonn about Jack, but sensed he'd be embarrassed. It was enough that he was taking Blue.

She returned to Islington with every intention of packing her bags. To her surprise, William was back from court. He was sitting in the armchair in his study, the telephone on his lap. 'I spoke to

271

Robert today,' he said amiably. 'I said we'd love to visit them. I'm waiting for him to confirm dates.'

Frankie listened in disbelief. He talked as though the previous night had never happened. Unsure what to do, unable to pack with him present, she went out into the garden. It seemed horribly empty without Blue and poor old Big Ears. She felt the loss of her mother very acutely. Of the baby. Of everything. She wished she could escape to White Oast, but it wasn't fair to let Steven see her bruised face.

She turned to find William watching her. 'Did you find the dog?' he asked.

'Yes.'

'Where is he?'

'Somewhere safe, where you can't get at him. You let Big Ears out too, didn't you?'

He took a step towards her. 'Have you been with Broderick?'

'No. But even if I had been, what are you going to do? Beat me up in the garden in full view of our neighbours? A High Court judge punching his wife! Or do you only want to rape me today?'

He caught her by the wrist and dragged her towards the house. She fought back. but he was too strong for her. Slowly, he pulled her into the kitchen. 'You're going to be sorry now!' he hissed.

The telephone rang. Frankie grabbed it. 'Yes!' she cried.

'Frankie? It's Robert. Are you OK? You sound terrible.'

'Robert! Please! Help me!'

As William twisted the receiver from her hand, she sank to the floor. 'Hello, Robert,' he said. 'Yes, I'm afraid Frankie is upset. She's been through a very sad time, what with her mother and the baby. She tries to be brave. Yes, we're all very worried about her.' There was a silence. William looked at Frankie. His mouth tightened. 'I don't think she's well enough to fly out alone, Robert. I do know what I'm talking about, I am her husband.' He frowned, then handed the receiver to Frankie, hissing, 'Be careful what you say!'

Robert tried to be jolly. 'I'm worried about my little sister. I want you out here, having a good rest. William says you're not up to flying on your own.'

'I am!' she shouted. 'I'll come tomorrow.'

'If you're sure.'

'I am! I am!'

Robert made arrangements with William whilst Frankie remained seated on the floor. She didn't care if William hit her. Tomorrow she'd be free.

He came off the line. She steeled herself for the blow. But all he said was, 'You may have won that round, Francesca, but don't imagine it will make any difference. You're still my wife. When we return from America, you're going to learn to behave.' He walked through to his study, and closed the door.

Thirty-One

It wasn't until Frankie was over the Atlantic that she truly believed William wouldn't try to stop her from leaving. In the departure lounge, she expected the tannoy to call her back to the check-in desk. When she telephoned Melanie from a public phone, she whispered from fear. As she handed in her boarding card, she anticipated being told her ticket had been cancelled. As they took off, she braced herself for the captain's announcement: *Ladies and gentlemen, we are obliged to make an unscheduled return to the United Kingdom.* But there was no announcement. Just the bliss of deliverance as she stretched out in her seat, closed her eyes, and slept.

Eight hours later they approached Dallas/Fort Worth. From her window Frankie could see the shadow of the 747 skimming over the sunbaked earth whose grass had been burned away by the long, hot summer. Scrubby mesquite trees offered no shade, tumbleweed rolled in a light breeze. Tiny specks of brown and white Hereford cattle drifted through the shimmering heat, their heads down as they snatched at the meagre grass. Then the red earth gave way to a choking urban sprawl of one-storey houses, gas stations and fast-food joints. The plane banked. To the south, Frankie saw the shining skyscrapers of downtown Dallas rising into the hazy blue sky. She was free.

Robert and Priscilla were waiting anxiously when she appeared in the arrivals hall. They embraced her. 'You're the last. We thought you'd missed the flight.'

'There was a queue at immigration.' It was a lie. She'd been in the ladies' loo, camouflaging her bruises with pancake. Sooner or later she'd have to tell Robert about William, but she couldn't face doing so today.

Robert appeared even shorter than in England, or maybe it was in comparison to the huge Texans milling around in check shirts and cowboy boots. Priscilla was deeply suntanned. Her flicked-up blonde hair was nearly as white as her teeth, and she was a picture of health. Frankie felt like a corpse beside them.

274

They ushered her out of the terminal, across the suffocating heat of the car park, to their car with its welcome air conditioning. They chattered excitedly, not giving her time to reply. She was glad. 'We want you to rest up, to sleep, and to do exactly as you please,' said Priscilla, settling Frankie into the front seat of the car. 'Hey, what's that bruise on your cheek? A cupboard door? You must be more careful.' Her genuine concern brought tears to Frankie's eyes. It seemed a long time since anyone had spoken to her kindly.

'We've nothing planned till William arrives, then we're having a giant barbecue,' Robert told her as they left the airport. 'All our friends are dying to meet you. People here love titles.' He listed the guests, endless names of people Frankie had never met. She smiled and nodded. Then he listed the people they'd decided not to ask. Again, she nodded and smiled. She still couldn't believe she'd escaped from William

Robert and Priscilla lived in North Dallas. 'Just north of Highland Park,' Robert explained as he turned south off the freeway. 'That's one of the more expensive areas.' He launched into a detailed comparison of house prices in Dallas and San Francisco, from which Frankie gathered the latter was considerably more expensive.

They turned into a grid of wide residential streets. The houses were reasonably large, mainly white or pale grey, and in a potpourri of architectural styles. Some were one-storey ranch style, others were Dutch gabled, a few were columned colonial. There was even a mock-Tudor, complete with lead-paned windows. But whatever the style, each had a double garage on one side, a couple of evergreen oaks to fend off the sun on the other, and a perfectly manicured lawn out front. Frankie was reminded of the Culmstocks' house near Windsor.

Only one house was different. It was a jungle. The Dutch gables above the wooden porch were draped in creepers, and long grass ran down to the gutter and flopped into the road. In the driveway was a battered '69 Chevy with a pair of stag's antlers fixed to the bonnet.

'That old woman's a disgrace to the neighbourhood!' spluttered Robert. 'We've had to drop ten thou' to sell our house.'

'Oh, Robert, she's too far away to affect our property and she ain't so bad. She was kind when Susan fell off her bike.' Priscilla patted Robert's arm as though he were a child, then she smiled at Frankie. 'Miss Tomasina's lived here longer than anyone. They all grumble about her property but no one dares tell her, not since she threatened to shoot a real-estate agent who complained about the grass.'

One street further on, they turned into the driveway of a ranch house, sprawling and white-painted like many of the others. Priscilla led Frankie inside, into the welcome cool. The house was open plan and decorated in ice blue, which in England would have been gloomy but here was wonderfully refreshing.

'We've put you in the guest house. We thought you and William would prefer to be private,' said Priscilla, taking Frankie through a large kitchen and out again, into the oven heat of a spacious garden where a Mexican odd-job man was skimming leaves off a kidney-shaped swimming pool. 'I'm sorry the kids are away, but Susan promised my mom she'd visit her this week, and Dwight is camping in Montana with friends from college. He's left you his car. Its the Volkswagen. The keys are in the kitchen. I hope you won't be bored, Frankie. I have a summer job. I'm helping out at a friend's real-estate agency.'

Frankie looked across at the guest house, a charming cottage with its own small wooden deck. As the odd-job man skimmed the pool and the water rippled, the reflecting light danced up and down the white exterior of the cottage. 'I love it here already. I won't ever want to leave,' she said in a choked voice. 'Thank you for letting me come.'

Priscilla gave her a smile of great sympathy. 'You're welcome at any time. I told you, I lost a baby too. I've been through that empty hollow.'

'It isn't just . . . the baby.'

'I know. You lost your mom as well. You've had a tough time. But at least you're back with William.'

Frankie wanted to scream, 'He raped me!' But she didn't. Even now she could hardly bring herself to admit her marriage had failed again.

After Priscilla had left for work, Frankie stripped off her travel clothes, put on her bikini and stepped outside. The odd-job man had gone. The only life was a pair of mockingbirds who skipped up and down in the branches of an ancient dogwood. She crossed to the pool, dived in, and swam up and down through the clear blue water, washing the journey, the past days, even the past months from her hair and her body. She felt clean and pure. She thought of her mother, the baby. She thought of Jack. She thought of William, and no longer felt so crushed. He was too far away to touch her, too far removed to be a part of her. She'd escaped.

Exhausted but exhilarated, she climbed out of the pool and returned to her new home. It consisted of a bedroom, a bathroom with a jacuzzi, and a small sitting room, all done out in ice-cold igloo green. Stretching diagonally across the double bed, she luxuriated in the peace, and slept as she had not done since her mother became ill.

For three days, Frankie didn't leave the house. She slept and swam and slept again. She didn't read. She didn't watch television. She didn't take up the offer of Dwight's car. She was happy to go nowhere. Her lip healed. The bruise on her face died down. Only a faint dirty-yellow mark remained below her eye. Even that was masked by the beginnings of a suntan. In the evenings when Robert and Priscilla came home, Frankie went through into the main house for dinner. By ten o'clock, she was back in her ice-green igloo, fast asleep.

Each evening, Robert asked her, 'Would you like to call William?' and she lied, 'We've already spoken.'

On the fourth day she woke feeling stronger. She watched the television news. She read Robert's newspaper. She swam fifty lengths with ease. The sun was fierce, but she was growing accustomed to it. Her skin was no longer pallid, but glowing and golden. She stretched out in the shade of a live oak, and thought about the future. Although she knew what she didn't want, it was hard to know what she did.

In the late afternoon she went for a walk. She set off along the road. There were no pavements: no one else seemed to walk. It was hot. The heat from the tarmac bounced up at her. In spite of her dark glasses, she still had to screw up her eyes against the glare of the sun. After a mile of sleepy residential streets, she came to a main road leading up to an enormous glass-arched shopping mall surrounded by acres of car park. Near one entrance to the car park there was an advertisement for an airline. It read: *Visit Dallas –*

Shopping Capital of the US. Underneath it someone had scrawled: *Shop Till Ya Drop*.

With relief, she reached the air-conditioned boulevards of the shopping mall. She wandered up and down, delaying the moment when she would have to return to the oven outside. Now she regretted not having borrowed Dwight's car. In a souvenir shop, she bought postcards for Steven, Melanie and Eamonn. At a fruit juice bar, she stopped to write them: just a few lines to say she'd be in touch again soon. On the way out, she posted them.

The heat seemed even fiercer as she started back to the house. After a while, she realised she'd taken a wrong turn. She went back to a cross-street and followed another road, getting hotter and thirstier. Eventually, she found herself outside the jungle house, the one about which Robert had complained. She stopped to catch her bearings.

'If you're from the real-estate agency I'll shoot you,' shouted a woman's voice.

Frankie stared at the house. A tiny old lady, dressed in grey lace, was glaring at her from the wooden veranda. In her hand she held a rifle, almost bigger than herself. 'I'm not,' said Frankie. 'I was lost. I'm staying wtih my stepbrother and his wife and I couldn't find their house. All the streets look the same, except for yours.'

'Are you insulting my house?'

'No. I like it.'

There was silence. Then the old lady let out a cackle and lowered the rifle. 'Come inside. My name's Miss Tomasina.'

Frankie walked up the overgrown driveway. By the time she reached the deck, Miss Tomasina had disappeared.

'Come on in!' the old lady called from inside the house. 'I won't hurt you.'

Frankie opened the door. Opposite her, in a rocking chair, was the smallest and most exquisite old lady she'd ever seen. She had bright black eyes and a delicate face from which pure white hair was smoothed into a loose bun. Well into her eighties, the skin around her neck was crêped and she had deep laughter lines fanning out from the corners of her eyes, but none of this detracted from her beauty.

The house was as dilapidated inside as out, and yet it was

278

beautiful. It had a fascinating chaos which took Frankie back to Nicoletta's shop. There were antique pioneer trunks spilling with lace and silk cushions, heavy dark furniture draped in antique patchwork quilts, and an old paint tin full of handmade silk flowers.

Miss Tomasina watched as Frankie examined the room. She adjusted the lace shawl about her tiny shoulders and smoothed a half-finished crocheted blanket over her knees. 'I have some English tea,' she said with a twinkle, as though admitting to a secret vice. 'Earl Grey from Fortnum & Mason. Make us a pot, girl. I want it done right, with the pot heated first, just as you do in England. The kitchen's through there.' She waved her hand towards the back of the house as though dismissing a servant.

Frankie was amused. The old lady wasn't dangerous, just eccentric. She made her way down a dark corridor. It was hot in this house. There was no air conditioning, just big overhead fans constantly whirring. The walls, once white, were now dark cream. They were covered in old photographs: stiff couples about to set sail for the New World; a sepia-printed young woman on her wedding day; a tall man with Indian features. In the kitchen, Frankie found a wooden draining board above an old stone sink, and a wobbling cooker, one of whose legs was propped up by bricks. But the porcelain teacups were exquisite. They were by Minton, hand-painted, with dainty floral bouquets on a turquoise ground.

When Frankie returned to Miss Tomasina with the tea tray, she asked by way of making coversation, 'Have you been to England?'

'I've never been out of Texas and I don't wanna go either. I'm of the same mind as Oliver Loving. Guess you don't know who he was. The Goodnight-Loving cattle trail up to South Platte River was named after him and Charles Goodnight. When Loving was dying, wounded by a Comanche arrow, he said, "Don't leave me in foreign soil. Take me back to Texas." That's just how I feel. Now I'm old I don't wanna risk being out of Texas when I die.'

'They could always ship you home,' said Frankie, trying not to giggle.

'I wouldn't risk it. Folks are so damned dishonest nowadays. They'd take my money and bury me where I fell. What are you sniggering about?'

'I'm sorry.' Frankie burst out laughing. 'You're very amusing.'

'Folks round here say I'm crazy. They're trying to push me out.' Miss Tomasina's black eyes glittered. 'But I ain't leavin'. My pa built this house when all around here was open country. He owned land down near San Antonio. Land that's been in the family since we settled it. It's mine now. Zeb manages it for me. You prob'ly saw his old Chevy outside. In Grandpa's day, they drove the cattle up the Chisholm Trail to the railroad stockyards in Kansas to be shipped east. In Pa's day, they used Fort Worth. He built this house so Ma could join him, without living too near the stockyards. She was a delicate woman. He died in this room. So did Ma.' Miss Tomasina crashed her cup down on to her saucer, sending pieces of porcelain flying across the room. 'I ain't movin'.'

'I don't blame you,' said Frankie, retrieving the broken saucer. 'I like your house. It has character.'

Miss Tomasina smiled. 'I like you. But I don't think you're happy.'

'I had a miscarriage recently and . . . and my mother died.'

'You loved her?'

'At the end, yes. Very much.'

'And your husband?'

Frankie didn't want to talk about William. She still had three precious days of freedom. She stood up. 'I'd better hurry. Robert and Priscilla will be home soon.'

'You turn right at the next cross-street.' The old lady leaned back in her rocking chair. 'I never married. I loved one man all my life. But my folks said he was too wild for me. I should have eloped, but I was only eighteen. He died twenty years ago yesterday. We could have had forty years together if only I'd been braver.' She closed her eyes. 'Let yourself out, girl. Come and see me again. Come tomorrow.'

The old lady's words evoked Jack. The memory of desperate love. Frankie wondered if Eamonn had told him about her bruised cheek.

She didn't tell Robert and Priscilla about Miss Tomasina. On the following afternoon she returned to the jungle house to drink tea with the old lady, not leaving until dusk had fallen. Priscilla was in the kitchen, half watching television as she prepared a salad

280

for dinner. 'Where have you been?' she asked. 'I was worried. It's nearly dark and you didn't take the car.'

'I went for a walk.' Frankie settled herself on to one of the tall stools along the breakfast bar.

'William called. He's going to call back.' The phone rang. 'Oh, that'll be him.' Priscilla answered. 'Yes, she's just come home.' She passed the telephone to Frankie.

Frankie felt faint. She held the receiver to her ear. 'Hello,' she whispered.

'Where the hell have you been all afternoon? And yesterday? I rang every hour. Then I phoned Robert at work, and he seemed to think we'd spoken every day. What is going on, Francesca?'

'I went for a walk.'

'You must be feeling better.'

'I am.'

'Good. Because I arrive tomorrow.'

'But . . . but you're not meant to be here till Saturday.'

'I've changed my flight.' He paused. 'You don't sound very pleased. I hope I'm not going to have more trouble with you, Francesca. I'm too busy. Now, write this down! My flight arrives at two o'clock. Don't keep me waiting.'

The line went dead. Frankie replaced the receiver. She looked across at Priscilla who was drowning the salad in French dressing, and said, 'I hate him.'

Priscilla switched off the television and adopted the voice she used whenever the kids had a teenage rebellion. 'Frankie, you must try not to blame William for the baby and your mother.'

'I'm not. You don't know what he's like. He's a bully.'

The door opened. Robert walked in. He looked from Priscilla to Frankie. 'Is something wrong?'

'William's arriving tomorrow,' said Frankie, in a strangely detached voice. 'I should have warned you that things were bad between us, but when I arrived I was too battered and tired to think straight. Now I've made up my mind. I shall divorce William for cruelty.'

Robert exploded, mainly because he thought he should. 'For God's sake! You've only just gone back to him. Marriage is for life, Francesca. Have you no sense of responsibility?'

She meant to say that William had abused her, but she still

found it hard to admit. 'He's cruel,' she said. 'He let my rabbit out and my dog killed him.'

'That's no reason to divorce.'

'He doesn't want me to work, so he let my dog into the street to stop me going for an interview.'

'You told us yourself, when we were over for your mother's funeral, that you didn't want a career to spoil your marriage. It's time you grew up. All couples hit bad times.'

'Do all husbands beat up their wives and rape them? Last week, when I answered the phone and you asked what was wrong, William had raped and beaten me. That bruise on my cheek. That was William.' Now it was out, she felt calmer. Stronger.

Robert was shocked. 'I don't believe it! He's a judge. A man knighted by the Queen.'

'He's a sadist.'

There was silence in the kitchen. Priscilla carried on making the dinner. 'Maybe you're exaggerating,' said Robert after a few minutes. 'You've been through a tough time. It's bound to make you oversensitive. You're under stress. After all, you told me that William had telephoned you every day. Today I found out it isn't true. That isn't rational.'

'I couldn't bear to speak to him.' Frankie pushed back her stool and stood up. 'I couldn't stand his voice to ruin my paradise. I've been so happy here. In spite of what you think, I tried to make my marriage work, I really tried!' She picked up the keys to the guest house, and walked out into the garden.

Some time later, Priscilla brought her a supper tray. 'Robert and I have decided that I'll take tomorrow off and come with you to the airport,' she said, setting the tray down on the bedside cabinet. 'William won't hurt you if I'm there. You must give him another chance, Frankie. He's your husband. We're sure by the time you go home everything will be OK. If it isn't, you can stay on here with us.'

Frankie wanted to scream, 'You haven't listened to me!' But instead she reached over and squeezed Priscilla's hand. 'You're very kind. I don't deserve it. I wasn't always nice to you in England, was I? That makes me ashamed.'

'You all seemed so clever.'

Frankie laughed out loud. 'Not really. Look what a mess I've made of things.'

After Priscilla left, she lay on her bed staring up at the ceiling of the ice-green igloo. It had been her safe house, her haven. Tomorrow it would be invaded by her enemy.

She couldn't sleep. Before dawn, she went out to the pool. The whole garden was bathed in pale moonlight. Stripping off her clothes, she slipped into the pool and swam up and down, the ripples of water passing over her shoulders, stroking her naked body. Tomorrow, it would be William. Touching her. Forcing her. Hitting her. Mocking her.

She climbed out of the pool, hurried into the guest house and rubbed herself dry. Not stopping to dry her hair, she dressed quickly in jeans, a T-shirt and trainers. Then she dragged her suitcase out from under the bed and tossed her clothes inside, packing frantically as though William were due any minute. In her flight bag, she hid fifty dollars. The remaining fifty she folded into her jeans pocket. On the bed she left two notes, scribbled quickly.

Robert and Priscilla. Sorry to walk out. But I won't spend the rest of my life being abused. I'll be in touch. Thanks for everything. Keys in letter box. Love, F.

William, I'm not coming back. We make each other unhappy. Perhaps that's why you're so cruel.' Francesca.

She crept out of the guest house, down the path beside the garage, and out through the security gate. As she went down the drive, she dropped her keys into the mailbox. Then, with her suitcase in one hand and her flight bag over her shoulder, she hurried along the road towards Miss Tomasina's house. The old Chevy with the antlers on the bonnet was in the driveway. As she eased past it, a tall figure stepped from the shadows. She gave a stifled scream.

'Don't be scared,' said the figure. 'I'm Zeb. Didn't Miss Tomasina tell you about me?'

'Oh, yes. Of course. I'm sorry.'

He took another step forward, into the grey dawn light. He was a big man with an eagle face and shoulder-length black hair, streaked with grey and kept in place by a brightly beaded headband worn low on his forehead. 'What are you doing here?' he asked.

'Escaping.'

'Who from?'

'My husband.'

'Then we'd better hide you.' He opened the front door, saying 'Miss Tomasina. It's that English girl.'

The old lady was already up and dressed, and sitting in her rocking chair, her crochet on her lap. 'I know the British are crazy,' she drawled, 'but I didn't know they went calling on folk at four in the morning.'

'I'm sorry but I have nowhere else to go.' Frankie let her suitcase drop to the floor as she sank into a chair and buried her face in her hands, rocking slowly backwards and forwards. 'My husband arrives today. He's a bully. He beats me, he raped me, but because he's a judge and has a knighthood, no one believes me. Or if they do, they think I deserve it. I left him once, for another man. A man I loved deeply. A man everyone said was no good. He'd been in prison. When my mother was dying, I became afraid of my lover's world. My husband was kind to me then. I let myself be swayed. I wanted safety, I wanted children. So I returned to my husband. I tried so hard to make it work. We were happy at first. I became pregnant. But I lost the baby and my mother died. Even then, he was kind. It was when I wanted to return to work that he began to bully me again. Just as he used to, only worse. I realise now that he sees me as a possession. Like the rare books he collects. Except I think he prefers the books. They don't question. They don't answer back.' She looked up. Zeb was crouched down on his haunches, listening. Miss Tomasina was twisting the crochet hook in and out of the blanket. 'I shouldn't have disturbed you,' said Frankie. 'I'm sorry. I'll leave now.'

The old lady lowered her hook. 'Just because I keep working don't mean I ain't hearing you. Where ya goin'?'

'Anywhere. I need time to decide what I'm going to do with the rest of my life. I have my return ticket to England but I don't want to go back yet. I want to get right away. Somewhere completely different. Somewhere no one knows me.'

'I can take you as far as San Antonio,' said Zeb, standing up. 'I leave in an hour.'

Miss Tomasina reached across and patted Frankie's knee. 'I'd like to keep you here with me but you're right. You should get away. That husband of yours is a snake. He ain't gonna change. Zeb can put you on a bus in San Antonio. I have a cousin near Flagstaff, Arizona. Haven't seen her in twenty years but she's always inviting me out there. She has a small hotel. She won't charge you much. You could head there. Got any money?'

'A hundred dollars.'

'You won't get far on that.' Miss Tomasina pointed to a tin high up on a shelf. 'I'll loan you five hundred.'

'Oh, no! I can't borrow your money. You don't even know me. You've been too kind already.'

'Gimme the can and quit arguing!'

Frankie hesitated. She didn't like to take the old lady's money but she saw no alternative. She passed the tin. 'I'm very grateful. I'll send it back as soon as I can.'

Miss Tomasina folded Frankie's fingers around a roll of notes. 'Don't send it, girl! Bring it! I like you, I want to see you again. Now, fetch me my morning bourbon, Zeb. Hell, I need it!'

Thirty-Two

Francesca bought a ticket to Phoenix, Arizona. It cost her a hundred dollars. One bus didn't go all the way; she had to make several changes. It was two o'clock when she boarded the first leg. She pictured William stalking through Dallas/Fort Worth airport, searching for her amongst the huge Texans, and she felt very guilty at leaving Priscilla and Robert to face him. But she had no such feelings for William.

The first bus took her to Laredo, on the Mexican border. From there she picked up a night ride to El Paso. She didn't pay much attention to the other passengers. They were a motley crowd of students on cheap holidays, old men going somewhere, Mexicans visiting home, and tired women married to men who didn't earn enough to provide them with the airfare.

As they were leaving Laredo, a chubby blonde with tousled hair jumped on to the bus, gasping and laughing from the exertion of running. She came down the aisle, assessing the empty seats, then plonked herself down next to Francesca, who until that moment had had the luxury of two seats.

Frankie slept fitfully, dreaming that she was being pursued by Jack, but when she stopped to let him catch her, he turned into William. From time to time her head bumped against the window and she woke up, startled, and looked out at the dark, eerie countryside. Then she drifted off again. Eventually, she woke to find that dawn was breaking. They were travelling through a landscape of desolate beauty: high, craggy mountains and wide, dry riverbeds scattered with the occasional giant cactus. Behind them the sun was rising, red and fierce. Ahead, the night still clung to the peaks.

'Did you see *Paris Texas*?' asked the blonde girl beside her.

Francesca shook her head.

'It was filmed here, in the Trans Pecos. I'll never forget seeing it, because my mother died next morning.'

'Oh, no! How awful.' Francesca could now see that the girl

looked a little like Melanie. She had similar cornflower-blue eyes, blonde curls and an open, friendly face.

The girl glanced down at Francesca's wedding ring. 'You're English. You're married. Where's your husband?'

'I was married.' Francesca hesitated. 'I mean, I was until recently.' She found herself telling her story, ending with, 'On the night he raped me, I knew I had to leave. The problem was to escape without another beating. Now I want to go somewhere different, somewhere new. When I go back, I'll divorce him for cruelty. I refuse to let him get away with it. For that, I'll need to be so strong that nothing he says can hurt me. I'm not that strong now. Not by a long way.'

The girl had listened intently, her face turning from quiet sympathy to disbelief. 'We must be twins,' she exclaimed. 'I went back to my husband too, after my mother died. I left him again yesterday, I waited till he went to work. If he'd known I was going, he'd have killed me. Only people like you and me, who've been through it, can understand what it's like.' The girl held out her hand. 'Friends call me Tucson because I was born there.'

'Frankie.' Francesca shook Tucson's hand. 'Frankie Tiernay.' She slipped her wedding ring from her left hand, put it in the zip pocket of her shoulder bag, and added, 'Goodbye Francesca! Goodbye Eastgate!'

They swapped lives all the way across the Trans Pecos. Or rather, Frankie did. Tucson was so easy to confide in. The more they talked, the more similarities they discovered. Both had lost their fathers. Both were children of divorce. In each case their mothers, not their fathers, had remarried.

'I bet you used to wish you had brothers and sisters,' said Tucson. 'It's tough being an only child.'

'I have a stepbrother in Dallas. The one I was visiting.'

'Oh, I'd forgotten.' For a moment, Tucson looked upset. Then she smiled and asked, 'What did your dad do?'

'He was a gambler.'

'I don't believe it! So was mine! He died in Las Vegas, at the card tables.' She opened a packet of chewing gum and offered Frankie a piece, adding, 'I'm headed there now. It's easy to pick up work in the casinos. Cocktail waitress. Valet parking. I can't go

287

home to Tucson broke, with my marriage failed and my tail between my legs.'

'I feel the same about going back to England.'

In El Paso, they climbed stiffly off the bus and into the nearest bar, where Frankie treated Tucson to an ice-cold beer and a hot dog. They moved on to another bar, and more beer. Frankie bought a baseball hat to protect her face from the sun. Tucson bought nothing. They mooched around the hot streets, drifting in and out of bars. El Paso was a chaos of cheap goods, people, and cars pouring exhaust into the stifling air. Tucson seemed to know the town pretty well, although she said she'd only been there once.

They missed their night bus to Phoenix: the next one left at dawn. 'No point in wasting money on a hotel just for a few hours,' said Tucson, an experienced economy traveller. 'We can sleep in the bus station. With two of us, we'll be safe. We can watch each other, make sure no one creeps up on us.'

'No one'll come near me. I haven't had a shower since yesterday.' Frankie sank on to a hard wooden bench.

'Hey! I've had an idea.' Tucson nudged her awake. 'We'll stop in Phoenix. My brother's with the military there. He'll show us around, give us a good time.'

'I thought you were an only child.'

'He's a stepbrother. I don't see him much. So I tend to forget about him.' Tucson paused. 'What do you say?'

'It sounds fun.' Frankie closed her eyes again.

The journey to Phoenix was exhausting. The road seemed rougher. The miles seemed longer. When they stopped for a break, she could barely climb off the bus. Her bones ached, her head pounded. She longed for a shower and sleep.

Back on the bus, she drifted off, to wake inside the bus depot in Phoenix with Tucson shaking her arm. 'Come on! We're here. I've called my brother. He may have to leave on manœuvres. I said we'd check into a hotel and try him later.' She dragged Frankie to her feet. 'He's dying to meet you.'

They stumbled out into the burning daylight of the desert city. The sun was overpowering. The glare blinded. Heat jumped up from the tarmac. Cars roared past, throwing up dust into their faces. Frankie followed Tucson, her heavy suitcase in one hand,

288

her flight bag over the other shoulder. Tucson only had two small canvas bags. She walked briskly. Frankie trailed.

After a mile or so, Tucson cut down a side street. It led to a drab concrete sprawl of gas stations, fast-food joints, and cheap motels, all bunched around a slipway up to the main highway north. Most of the buildings were one storey. They were spread out as if flattened by the sun. Beside one motel was a huge saguaro cactus, like three giant fingers pointing up to the sky. It was coated in dust.

Tucson was inside, negotiating with a spotty youth at the desk, when Frankie fell, gasping, into the air-conditioned reception. 'Twenty bucks a night,' Tucson called over her shoulder.

'Each?'

'For the room. We could find cheaper if we walk on.'

'I couldn't walk another step.' Frankie produced a fifty-dollar bill from her pocket. 'So I insist on paying.'

The room was basic. Twin beds, two chairs, a TV and a shower. Frankie dropped her case on to the floor and flopped on to one of the beds. Within a minute she was fast asleep.

She woke to find Tucson standing at the bottom of her bed. Clean, and changed into a floral sun dress, she looked demure and fluffy, and even more like Melanie. 'My brother's gone to Tampa,' she said. 'He's real sorry not to meet you.' She walked to the window and peered out through the blinds. 'Nearly dark. Shall we go eat?'

Frankie had a quick shower, relishing the cool water which beat down on her back and breasts, shampooing two days of dust from her hair. She would have liked to have taken longer but Tucson was pacing up and down with uncharacteristic impatience.

Phoenix wasn't a town to be in without a car. The night was hot. There was no proper pavement. Above them the traffic roared north along the flyover. Tucson walked briskly. Frankie had to run to keep up. They crossed under the flyover to the fast-food joints on the other side, but none of the places met with Tucson's approval. So they bought a pizza and a couple of beers, and returned to the motel. Switching on the television, they flopped on to their beds and devoured the pizza in gooey strips, drinking the beers straight from the can.

Tucson was still agitated. She took a small pouch from her shoulder bag. It contained tobacco.

'I didn't know you smoked,' said Frankie, wanting to recapture their previous friendliness.

'Sometimes. And this is one of those times.' Tucson smoothed out two cigarette papers, licked them together, and tapped some tobacco into the fold. Opening up a twist of silver foil, she took a small knife and chopped a lump of black hashish into the tobacco. Then she rolled up the cigarette, making it firm and fat. Finally, she lit it.

Francesca watched with growing concern. She'd never tried marijuana, or any drugs, although she'd often seen them produced in court as evidence. Now she eyed her companion nervously, deciding she'd been unwise to share a room with a stranger and wondering how she could extricate herself without being rude.

'My brother gave me the dope,' said Tucson, reading Frankie's anxiety. 'He came here whilst you were asleep. It's to help me relax. I was OK on the bus, but as soon as we reached Phoenix, I wanted to cry. You see, I lived in Phoenix when I was first married. That's why I've been so uptight today.'

Instantly, Frankie was full of sympathy. 'You should have told me.'

'At least I'm not alone. You're here.' Tucson held out the joint. 'Try some.'

'No, thanks.'

'Don't tell me you've never smoked dope?'

'I haven't, though I know of people who have.' She thought of a party which Melanie had once described. 'I was a law student when I met William. He'd have had a fit.'

Tucson grinned. 'All the more reason for trying some now.' She waved the joint in Frankie's direction. 'It won't harm you. It'll help you relax. Come on! Please don't leave me to smoke alone. I need a friend tonight.'

Frankie hesitated. She was both curious and afraid. 'I don't even smoke ordinary cigarettes.'

'Just one puff to say bye-bye to old William.'

'All right. One puff.' Frankie took the roll-up and put it to her lips. She inhaled deeply, drawing the smoke right down into her lungs. For a moment nothing happened. She stared at Tucson. Then, suddenly, she felt as if her lungs were on fire. She began to cough. Tears came to her eyes. Choking furiously, she hung over the side of the bed, her mouth bitter with the taste of tobacco and hashish.

Tucson handed her a glass of water. 'Want to try again?' she asked when Frankie had recovered. 'But you have to do it gently. Just a little.'

This time Frankie was more careful. She inhaled a little. Nothing happened. She took another puff. 'It doesn't affect me,' she said airily. But as she leaned towards Tucson to hand back the joint, her limbs began to float away. She could hardly focus on Tucson's hand. She shook her head. It felt detached from her body. She started to giggle. Tucson giggled. Suddenly, everything was incredibly funny. The journey, the motel, the baseball on the television. They laughed till tears rolled down their cheeks. Even the wail of a police siren from the highway seemed funny.

Hours later, Frankie woke with a thumping headache and the sun streaming in through the cracks in the blinds. Tucson's bed was ruffled but empty. Her smallest canvas bag lay on top and the shower door was firmly closed. On the bedside table was the coagulating remains of last night's pizza picnic. The sight of it made Frankie feel sick. She closed her eyes and drifted off.

A sharp knock on the door brought her back. 'If you keep the room after noon, you have to pay a second night,' shouted the spotty youth from the reception.

'We're leaving.' Frankie looked at her watch. It was nearly twelve. She rose and walked unsteadily to the bathroom door. 'Tucson!'

There was no reply.

'Hey. We have to leave soon.'

There was still no answer.

She tried the door. It opened easily. The bathroom was empty. She stood on the threshold, frowning, puzzled. Then she turned. Her suitcase had gone. Her clothes had gone. Her in-flight bag lay on the floor, its contents emptied in a pile: a map, her hairbrush, some paper hankies, her washbag and toiletries, her passport and her purse. Feverishly, Frankie opened the purse. In the coins side was a quarter. In the wallet side, where there had been two hundred dollars, there was nothing.

Panicking, she unzipped the pocket in her shoulder bag where

291

she'd hidden a further two hundred dollars. That too was missing. Even her wedding ring had been extracted. All that remained were her dirty clothes: the denim jacket, T-shirt and underwear she'd worn on the bus, the shorts and T-shirt she'd worn the previous evening, and her trainers, baseball cap and sunglasses which had been under her bed. Frankie slumped to the floor. She wanted to cry. She wanted to kill. She thought of Jack. Was this how he had felt when he came face to face with the informer?

There was a knock on the door. The boy shouted, 'I'm gonna have to charge you.'

'No! Wait!' Frankie pulled on her shorts and T-shirt. She opened the door. 'I've been robbed. That girl who was with me . . .'

'Your friend? She left hours ago.'

'She wasn't my friend. I didn't even know her. I met her on the bus. She's robbed me. She's taken everything.'

'I'll still have to charge you for the room.'

'I can't pay! I don't have any money. Don't you understand? She's stolen everything. Call the police. I want her caught.'

He hesitated.

'If you don't, I will.'

He disappeared, grumbling about stupid tourists. She collected up her possessions, rolling her dirty clothes inside a plastic bag. They fitted easily into her shoulder bag. She took Tucson's canvas sack to give the police as evidence.

At the reception, the youth was talking to the police on the telephone. When he'd finished, he told Frankie, 'They'll be here in an hour.'

'She'll be miles away by then.'

'They ain't gonna catch her.' He picked up a comic and read it studiously, ignoring Francesca, who sat on a plastic-covered sofa next to a plastic pot plant.

The policeman arrived on a motorbike, chewing gum and wearing dark glasses. Recalling her barrister training, Francesca told her story coherently and chronologically. He took notes.

'So you shared a room with a stranger?' he said, shaking his head in disbelief.

'I told you. We got talking. She'd been through exactly the same bad times as me. Surely that makes her easy to find. I know everything about her.'

The policeman called to the spotty youth, 'Did a guy come here yesterday for that girl?'

'Nope.'

'I know he did,' protested Frankie. 'He gave her . . .' She stopped. 'I mean, he was going to give us a night out in Phoenix. He wanted to meet me.'

The policeman closed his notebook. 'Do you have any friends in the US who could wire you some money?'

Frankie thought of Robert and Priscilla. William was with them. She thought of Miss Tomasina. She couldn't borrow more. And Miss Tomasina's cousin in Flagstaff? How could she turn up, penniless. 'No one,' she replied.

'The British Consul will advance you your fare home,' he said.

'Aren't you even going to try to arrest Tucson?'

'Lady, this is one big, tough country. We have cocaine coming in from Colombia, illegal aliens from Mexico, a shoot-out three blocks down, and a serial killer on the loose.'

'But I know where she is. She's on her way to Las Vegas.'

'I know where she is too. Or rather, I know what she's doing. She's on a bus or a plane, or in a restaurant, listening to a stranger talk. And you know what? Just like that stranger, she's an only child of a dying mother. She's mirroring. Easiest way in the world to gain a stranger's confidence.'

He scribbled down the British Consul's address. Then he produced a dollar bill from his hip pocket. 'Come on! I'll show you where you take the bus.'

They went out. She put on her sunglasses, hoisted her bag over her shoulder and followed. The spotty youth didn't so much as raise his head from his comic.

The bright white heat of midday hit Frankie with its full force as she left the air-conditioned motel. She staggered in its fierceness.

'The bus stops there!' The policeman pointed to the far side of the highway. He kick-started his motorbike. It sprang into life. As he swung his leg over, he shouted, 'Lady, do me a favour.'

Frankie turned. 'Yes?'

'Don't talk to strangers on the bus!' He roared off in a cloud of dust and heat.

She had never felt such a failure as she did now, standing by the side of the road, clutching the policeman's dollar. She'd lost Jack. She'd lost the baby. Her marriage had failed. She was so stupid that she couldn't even tell the difference between a friend and a thief. London loomed. She could already smell the rain on the tarmac at Heathrow as her aeroplane skidded to its inevitable halt. She pictured herself queuing for a payphone to make a collect call to Melanie, taking a taxi which Mel would have to pay for, asking for a loan.

Suddenly, she remembered the thirty dollars change from the hotel bill. She dropped her bag to the ground, unzipped it, and pulled out her washbag, her brush, her map. At the bottom was the plastic sack containing her dirty clothes. Hardly daring to breathe, she slipped her hand into the front pocket of her jeans. Her fingers touched paper.

She laughed with exhilaration as she smoothed the three ten-dollar bills on her thigh. She recalled the money she'd spent in London: ten times this in a day, without a flicker. But this money was like no other. It proved she wasn't a complete sucker.

Adjusting her baseball cap to protect her face, she repacked her bag, swung it over her shoulder, and headed for the bus stop. She felt stronger, almost carefree. In the distance she could see the bus. She started to run. Then she stopped. She was overwhelmed by rage, mainly against herself. No one was forcing her to slink home, tail between her legs, to become a satisfying caveat in the eyes of her old chambers, William, and his bloody mother that those who buck the system finish in the gutter, one foot permanently trapped in the sewer of life. It was her choice: she could take her thirty dollars and have another bid for freedom.

Bag over her shoulder, she strode to the mouth of the slipway which led up to the interstate. The sun burned her legs, from the hem of her shorts to the tongue of her hot, rubbery trainers. It burned her arms. It made her back sweat and her neck drip beneath her hair. But she didn't care. She felt strong. She had thirty bucks. Tucson hadn't won yet. She checked her map, slipped a pair of nail scissors into her shorts pocket, then took a deep breath. As the first car came up the slope, she stuck out her thumb.

The driver was young. He was gangling and puny, like a

chemistry student who never left his laboratory. 'Where you going?' he asked.

'Las Vegas!' she replied, in a new, punchy voice.

Thirty-Three

That first ride took Frankie only twenty miles, and directly north instead of north-west. 'If you'd warned me, I wouldn't have got in,' she berated the embarrassed driver when he dropped her at an intersection in the middle of deserted scrubland, saying she should take the left turn, heading west.

As she stepped from the air-conditioned car, the heat consumed her. It beat down. It bounced up. It enveloped and suffocated. She was on a small crossroad, not even dual carriageway. There wasn't a vehicle in sight. In each direction the arid landscape stretched away to scrubby, rocky hills, broken only by the tall saguaro cacti, their giant fingers pointing upwards into a cloudless sky.

Frankie walked off the intersection to where the kerb widened into a parking area. There was no shade, nowhere to sit, just a road sign to lean against. It was too late now to realise she should not have set off without water and food. Especially water.

A car passed. It didn't stop. Two lorries passed. They didn't even slow. Another car came. The driver hooted. More cars passed. Not one hesitated. If anything, they accelerated. She circled the road sign, wondering at what stage she should start walking back to Phoenix. Then she stopped dead. On the reverse of the road sign was written: *Federal Penitentiary. Do Not Stop For Hitchhikers*.

She didn't know whether to laugh or cry or curse, so she started walking, following the road due west. Her throat was parched. At times she thought she saw a lake, but it was just a mirage on the tarmac. She began to feel faint. She longed to lie down. But she forced herself to keep walking, along the never-ending road towards the always distant hills.

It was two hours before a lorry stopped. The driver was a big, garrulous Texan. 'Ain't you scared, hitching on your own, a pretty girl like you?' he asked her as she climbed up beside him.

'Not at all. I was the British Junior Judo Champion.'

'That's very interesting.' Hurriedly, he began to talk about his children.

He dropped her at Wickenburg, a dry, dusty two-horse town where both horses were asleep. She went into a fast-food joint and spent the policeman's dollar on a glass of cold milk. She drank it slowly, savouring each mouthful. In the ladies' room, she ran a basin full of cold water and, oblivious of disapproving looks, soaked her arms and face in it. If she'd been alone, she'd have stripped off and washed her whole body.

In a drugstore, she bought a bottle of water and a sandwich. Then she sat down by the side of the road to eat her sandwich and wait for her next ride.

An open-back truck stopped, with a woman driving. She had a leathery face under a stetson, and eyes screwed up from looking into too much sun.

Frankie smiled hopefully. 'Las Vegas?'

'Kingman. It's on your route. Climb in the back!' She drove off with Frankie still clinging to the tailgate.

There was nothing to sit on, and no shade from the sun. But at least it was a lift, and one which took her over halfway to Las Vegas. That was how Frankie consoled herself, as she bounced around in the back, banging her elbows and her head. The road was straight and the land flat. Every time she looked out, she seemed to see the same dry rock and the same saguaro cactus. She lay back, uncomfortable but exhausted, closed her eyes and dozed. Next time she looked out, they were twisting and turning through mountains. The saguaros had disappeared and been replaced by yucca plants. The landscape had a strange and desolate lunar beauty.

The light changed quickly. One moment she was in the white glare of day. The next she was suffused by the mellow glow of early evening in which the leaves of the yucca plants cast pointed shadows over the burnt terrain. The only sign of human habitation was a distant ranch, nestling in the folds of the hills, white walls turning pink in the evening sun, and a lonely gas station, its billboard flapping in the breeze.

Outside Kingman, the woman stopped the truck. She knocked on the dividing glass and Francesca jumped out. The truck was gone before she had time to shout her thanks.

Kingman sprawled ahead of her, a small, isolated town clutching on to the kerb of Interstate 40. Frankie had read somewhere that Clark Gable and Carole Lombard had married here. She found that hard to believe. She stood by the road, uncertain in the fading light. There was a brief purple grapiness before darkness fell, so quickly, so black, so final. On the far side of town she could see the pinprick headlights of cars curling up the mountains. For the first time since leaving Pheonix, she was unsure what to do. She had no money for a hotel, so she had to keep moving. But she couldn't stop cars at night with no idea of who – or how many – was inside.

She walked on, to a gas station where a little old man was filling up his car. In the back window was a sticker saying: *Las Vegas – The City That Never Sleeps.*

'I'm looking for a lift to Las Vegas,' she told him politely.

'I don't give rides. It isn't safe.'

'Please!'

He hesitated. 'Are you alone?'

'Yes. I'm meeting a friend in Las Vegas. But I've run out of money for the bus fare.'

He left her standing by the car, not knowing his answer, whilst he went inside to pay. When he returned, he said, 'Get in. But any trouble and I'll call the police.'

He talked nonstop, his little pouchy face twitching. His name was Horace and he'd been born in California but had retired to Las Vegas. He had a wife, two children and three grandchildren. They'd been to England twice. To France once. But they preferred Switzerland. It was cleaner. Frankie nodded and smiled, and looked out at the hot desert night.

Bright lights and billboards heralded the approach to Las Vegas long before they reached the city. Flashing neon signs screeched: *Win $50,000.* They illuminated the palm trees and the bare red earth beside the road. Huge boards edged with moving dice shouted: *Bake and Shake, Hotel with Pool, $30 a Night, Breakfast $2.99.* Smaller signs offered rooms right there, on the edge of town, for as little as twelve dollars.

'Cheapest place in the world to visit, so long as you don't play the casinos,' warned Horace, as the outer sprawl gave way to the first of the big hotels, a vast light-pulsing spacecraft surrounded by an ocean of parked cars. 'Vegas used to be a small desert town,' he went on. 'Now it's spreading out, like LA. Too many people come here.'

'Surely you need tourists to keep Las Vegas alive?'

'I meant the retirees who settle here. Mind you, I'm one of them. Tourists stay on The Strip. They like the glamour. They go to Caesar's Palace, and The Desert Inn, and Dunes, and all the others. You should try to take in a show, you and your friend. But don't forget downtown.' His eyes sparkled 'It's older and shabbier and gaudy, but it has character. Take Binion's Horseshoe. Old Benny Binion left Dallas in a hurry – or so folks say. He came to Vegas, bought up the Eldorado Hotel on Fremont, named it Binion's Horseshoe, and started the World Series of Poker. That's the old Las Vegas, the kind I like. If you want to see high-stakes poker, go to Binion's during the championships. As they say, "You've gotta hava lotta heart to play high-stakes poker".'

The passion in his voice when he spoke of poker reminded Frankie of her father. 'You must play to talk the way you do,' she said.

He looked appalled. 'Oh, no!'

They rode in silence. She'd upset him. She tried to apologise, but he retreated into his small, elderly world.

Boulder Highway became Fremont Street, the main drag into downtown, three lanes across and one way only, heading up towards the pulsating lights of Glitter Gulch. There were people everywhere. In the heat of the desert night, they milled around, gathering outside the souvenir shops or the even brighter lights of the casinos. They jaywalked all over the road, crossing from the casinos on one side to those on the other, barely glancing to see if there was any traffic. Except for the constant screech of the slot machines and the lights flashing '25-cent Craps', it could have been a midsummer promenade in a respectable family seaside resort.

Horace stopped the car on the corner of Fremont and Fourth Streets, beneath an enormous statue of a kneeling cowboy panning for silver with a platter in his hand. 'There they are!' He pointed ahead, to where lights of every colour cascaded down the sides of the buildings, turning the night into day. 'The Four Queens. The Golden Nugget. Binion's. The Union Plaza. I can't take you any further.' He gave her a shy smile. 'I dropped so much money in the casinos when we first lived in Vegas that my wife walked out on me. She only came back if I promised never to play again. If I went further, I couldn't trust myself.' He held out his hand to Frankie. 'Good luck. Don't get hooked.'

She thanked him. He was a nice little man. As he drove away, she felt bereft.

Finding Tucson was no longer Frankie's primary concern. She needed money. She walked on, towards the bright neon lights and another giant skyline statue, of a beckoning cowboy and a white-booted, high-kicking cowgirl. The noise was deafening. The electronic scream from the slots, the human shrieks from people hitting the jackpot, the clatter of coins, Frank Sinatra singing *My Way*, and the distant wail of a police siren. Her father would have revelled in it.

She reached the bulbous gold crown of The Four Queens. The casino stretched the whole of one block. People wandered in and out and along the front, then back in again at the next corner. Inside, it was bright and white with rows of slot machines reflecting up into a mirror-patterned ceiling. The machines were being played by people whose robotic concentration never wavered, never once distracted by the crowd which milled around in the aisles behind them. They remained, hour after hour, eyes glazed, unspeaking. Some played one machine. Others played two, or even three, their eager hands reaching simultaneously for both handles. It was hard to tell where the human ended and the robot began.

Unlike Monte Carlo, where Frankie had been once with William, there was no dress code in Las Vegas. No membership. No discreet ejection of a dust-covered girl in grubby shorts and a T-shirt. Everyone was welcome. There were solitary young men, pasty-faced from all-night gambling. Pensioners with plump wives, supplementing their pensions. Young women on their own, shoulder bags clutched across glittery bosoms as they teetered towards the slot machines. Women in shorts. Women in jeans. Women in flouncing silk and flowers, dressed up like Carmen Miranda. Old couples, one pushing the other in a wheelchair. Young couples with children. Students without money, sharing an ice cream. Middle-aged couples, steeped in a lifetime of respectable avarice, settling their rayon-covered bottoms at the roulette wheel. Old ladies on walking frames, fighting to reach their favourite slot machine.

300

Frankie made her way through to the back, past the blackjack tables and the roulette, to the ladies' room, where she washed her face and arms and neatly plaited her hair. Back in the bright lights of the casino, she watched an inscrutable Chinese woman in a baggy black cotton shirt and trousers win a thousand dollars at blackjack.

A cocktail waitress, tray in hand, smiled at Frankie. 'Cocktails?'

'Do you have milkshakes?'

'Sure.'

'How much?'

'If you're playing, they're free.'

She ordered a banana milkshake and sat down at one of the slot machines, pretending to work it. When the milkshake arrived, the waitress hovered. Frankie knew she was expected to tip, but she couldn't afford it. So she looked away.

The milk pacified her gnawing hunger. She moved on to watch a game of craps where a group of South Americans were betting heavily on the dice. One player was peeling off hundred-dollar bills as if they had no value. Nothing in the casino was real. Money was only paper. Coins were merely metal. There were no clocks. No sense of time. Nothing to remind the players of the real world outside.

Towards the back of the casino, Frankie found the poker room. There were some half-dozen tables railed off, with a manned desk at the entrance. The tables were full. People were hanging around, waiting for a seat. Frankie stood by the rail to watch. The players were mainly men. They watched the dealer shuffle the cards, with the dead-eyed look she knew so well from her father. It filled her with horror. It reminded her of the mornings when she'd had to walk to school because there was no money for her bus fare. On one table the pot was five hundred dollars. Not a lot, but a fortune to someone who had only twenty-eight dollars to her name.

The girl behind the desk gave her a friendly smile. 'If you want to learn to play poker, we have free lessons at lunchtime. Seven Card Stud and Texas Hold'em. Cost you nothing. Just a $20 buy-in, if you stay on to play.' She picked up the tannoy, and called out, 'Seat on $5–$10 Texas Hold'em.'

An old man in a cowboy hat pushed forward. He took the spare seat, bought a hundred dollars in chips, arranged them in five piles, then expertly riffled two piles into one. The other players at the table watched him apprehensively.

Frankie turned away. She was dropping with exhaustion. She had to sleep somewhere. Anywhere. But the cheap motels were two miles away. She was too tired to walk that far. In any case, she needed her money for food – and tomorrow's poker.

The heat hit her as she left the air-conditioned casino. It was midnight, but there was no relief. No breeze. She walked down Fremont, away from the brightest lights, then turned off the main drag and followed a side street round to a ground-level car park. The gate was manned. She hesitated, but the desire to sleep was overwhelming. Nodding to the security guard, she walked straight past him, across the tarmac to the wall on the far side. Two parked cars formed a shelter. Oblivious to the dirt, she sank to the ground, her back protected by the wall, and closed her eyes.

She was woken almost immediately by a torch in her face. 'You can't stay here,' shouted the guard.

She picked up her shoulder bag and moved on. Her feet hurt. Her limbs ached. Her mouth tasted bitter and parched. She wondered if there was a British Consul in Las Vegas, and what time he opened in the morning.

Her wandering took her down more streets to the back of a multi-storey car park. A flight of concrete steps led up from a wired gate, closed but unlocked. She opened it, paused, listened, then hurried up. On the first floor, a car was being reversed. On the second, she heard voices. On the third, the cars stood in their silent rows, gazing out towards the city lights.

She heard the noise of an engine. A car was coming up. Panicking, she hid behind a pillar as the headlights swept the floor. A young man dressed in the black trousers, white shirt and black bow tie of a dealer stepped out. She watched as he bent to lock his car. Another car arrived, a red Datsun. Its driver was young and slim, with Latin features and a small moustache. He, too, wore the outfit of a croupier. He called out cheerfully, 'Hey. Are you on the graveyard shift as well? Let's have breakfast when we finish.'

They clattered off to work, talking and laughing. Francesca waited five minutes. Then she approached the red car. The front was locked. But not the back. For a moment, she hesitated. But the soft upholstered back seat beckoned. She slipped inside and curled up. As she drifted into an uncomfortable sleep, she thought of William. He'd sneer to see her now, but, bad as things were, she was still glad she'd escaped.

She woke with the daylight, feeling even stiffer and dirtier. There was a can of Coke on the floor. Again she hesitated. But her parched throat drove her to take it. As she did so, she understood for the first time how people like Lindsay Dault – and even Jack – had turned to crime.

It was early morning, but the sun was already fierce. She walked up Fremont Street. The casinos were open. They never closed. As she passed The Four Queens, she remembered the poker lesson. All her life, she'd sworn she'd never gamble, yet here she was, thinking of risking everything, just like her father. But what else could she do? She watched the cocktail waitresses weave in and out of the morning gamblers, dentally perfect smiles cemented to their faces. No casino would employ a grubby foreigner with no green card, no address and no clothes.

She went into Binion's Horseshoe. Horace was right about its atmosphere. It had the honky-tonk of the Old West in its casual, friendly smokiness. The interior was the dichotomy of a respectable Victorian seaside hotel confronted by unrestrained Las Vegas glitter. There were sedate wood-panelled walls alongside opulent mirrors of brass and glass, an unintrusive burgundy carpet beneath battalions of shrieking, flashing slot machines, and blackjack tables covered in dark green felt, whereas some other casinos had succumbed to more durable but hideous vinyl. Even at this early hour, Binion's was buzzing. There was big money on the green baize tables. Serious money.

Along one wood-panelled wall was the Poker Hall of Fame, rows of black and white photographs of those who had made poker great. Men like Nick the Greek, known for his astronomical bets; Johnny Moss, the first World Champion; 'Corky' McCorquodale, who had introduced Texas Hold'em to Las Vegas in the early Sixties; Edmund Hoyle, the eighteenth-century British barrister who had laid down the rules for card games; Wild Bill Hickok who was shot in the back when holding a pair of aces and a pair of eights, subsequently known as 'the dead man's hand'.

Again, Frankie had to use the ladies' room as her bathroom.

303

She sponged the dust from her face and the grime from her arms and hands. She longed for a shower, but that was impossible. In the loo, she stripped off her filthy clothes, put on her last set of clean underwear, slopped deodorant all over herself, then decided that the previous day's dirty T-shirt and denim shorts were less dirty than those in which she'd slept in the car park.

Hunger was making her faint. Lack of salt was sapping her energy. Breakfast in the Coffee Shop was one dollar ninety-nine. She settled on to a green and pink tapestry-covered bench and ordered ranch eggs and bacon. The Coffee Shop, like much of the casino, was wood-panelled Victoriana, with a sensible dark green carpet and comfy chairs. It could have been a respectable hotel in Eastbourne, were it not for the keno numbers flashing up on the screen and the solitary betters filling in their cards.

At one o'clock, Frankie returned to The Four Queens and took her place at one of the blue vinyl-topped tables. There were eight men and three women at the poker lesson, all older than herself. A bubbly blonde dealer took them through the rules. She showed them how to cup their hands around their cards and how not to lift them from the table. She explained about string-betting, which was not allowed: the total wager must be placed in the pot in one move. She told them it was forbidden to reach into bags or pockets for more money during a hand: their stack must be on the table in front of them, in full view.

'Poker's a game of skill and bluff.' She gave them an encouraging smile as she expertly shuffled a pack of cards. 'We play two variations here: Seven Card Stud and Texas Hold'em. I'm gonna teach you Hold'em. It's a form of stud. Your aim is to make the best five-card hand out of the seven cards. The best possible hand is a Royal Flush, an ace-high straight in the same suit. But you ain't gonna have that, unless you're very lucky. The next best hands are: a straight flush, five suited cards in sequence; four of a kind; a full house, three of a kind and a pair; a flush, five cards of the same suit; a straight, five consecutive non-suited cards; trips, three of a kind; two pairs; and a pair. A high pair beats a low pair. A player holding one of a pair and a high kicker, such as an ace, will beat a player holding one of the same pair and a lower card. There are four rounds of betting. On this table, we play low-stakes poker, $1–$3. That means the minimum bet is one dollar and the maximum is three dollars. First, we'll have a couple of trial hands.'

They each bought twenty dollars' worth of chips. The dealer placed the button in front of the player on her left. 'This button moves clockwise with each hand,' she explained. 'In theory, the player with the button is the dealer. The button used to be a buckknife. You all know the expression "to pass the buck".'

They smiled and nodded.

'The player on the left of the button opens the betting before the deal with a blind bet, known as "the blind". You're dealt two cards each, face down. These are "in the hole", as we say.' The dealer gave them another bright smile. 'You assess your cards. It's worth staying in the hand if you hold high cards, cards of the same suit, connected cards such as a nine and a ten, an ace with a high kicker like an ace with a jack, or a pair. You always play in a clockwise order. When it's your turn, if your cards are good you bet. If you hold trash, you fold and pass your cards face down to me. You're then out of that hand. The only time to play a trash hand is when you've put up the blind, because you're in the game anyway, unless another player raises. In which case, if you hold trash you should then fold. If you have a so-so hand, you can check by rapping the table. You remain in the game unless another player bets. In those circumstances, you have to call the bet, which means to match it, or fold. Hold'em is a game of patience and aggression.'

Frankie cupped her hands around her two cards, a five and a queen, both diamonds. She remembered her father explaining that the queen on the playing cards was Elizabeth of York, wife of Henry VII, mother of Henry VIII. He'd gone on to tell her gruesome stories of Anne Boleyn's ghost chasing after Henry with her head under her arm. In her terror, Frankie had thought Henry had also cut off his mother's head, and that was why it appeared on the cards.

For the sake of the lesson, they turned their cards face upwards. The man on her right had a pair of aces. The woman on her left held two jacks. The dealer asked each person how they would play.

'I'd stick with it in the hope of picking up a flush,' Frankie replied, adding her dollar chip to the pot.

305

'You've played poker before?'

'Oh, no!' It was a lie, but she needed money. The more of a sucker that other players thought her, the more they'd bet against her.

'Now we have the Flop,' said the dealer, laying two diamonds and a heart in a row in the centre of the table. 'These are dealt face up. They're communal cards. The essence of Hold'em is whether your two hidden cards make a higher hand with the communal cards than your opponents', and whether your opponents think they do. That's why you need a poker face!'

There was another round of betting. Three players folded but the rest stayed in. The dealer added a fourth card – known as Fourth Street – to the Flop. It was a diamond. Frankie raised the betting to three dollars.

'You have to remember that none of you would know what this young lady has in the hole,' said the dealer, adding the fifth and final card – known as the River, or Fifth Street. It was an ace. It gave Frankie's neighbour three of a kind. But Frankie had won with a flush. Or rather, she would have, had it not been a lesson. They played another hand. Again she won.

'Some beginner's luck!' The dealer gave her a knowing look.

Frankie smiled enigmatically.

When the lesson ended, some of the players slipped away to the slot machines. Others joined the table, including a huge grizzly bear of a man who sat down unsmiling, and a tiny, emaciated pensioner with a miniature portable fan. Frankie stayed put, her chips on the table in front of her. They played on in a supervised game, which meant that they could pass their cards face down to the dealer for help. But the difference was that if they won they kept the money.

Frankie's first hand was trash. She folded. So was her second. Again she folded. On the third hand, she had to put up the blind. She was dealt a pair of twos. The Flop produced a king, queen, jack. The man on her right bet three dollars. Frankie folded. She didn't dare continue in case he had a high straight.

She was down to nine dollars when she was dealt a pair of tens. She caught another on the Flop. That gave her three of a kind. She bet two dollars. She'd have gone higher, but she was running out of money. Everyone folded, except the grizzly bear on the far side.

Fourth and Fifth Streets produced a pair of fives. Now she had a full house. She bet two dollars. Grizzly raised her three. She had to match him or fold. Clenching her fists with nerves, she hesitated. She had a good hand, a strong hand. She matched him and, with a little flourish of triumph, turned up her cards. There was a pause. She looked at Grizzly. His face was completely without expression as he flipped over a pair of fives.

'Four of a kind wins,' said the dealer, pushing the chips in Grizzly's direction.

Frankie sat back, white-faced, sick. She felt as though she'd been punched in the stomach. In hindsight, she should have bet the maximum after the Flop and hoped to chase Grizzly out of the game. By not doing so, she'd allowed him to improve his hand. That was her mistake.

She had one dollar left on the table and fourteen in her pocket. Slowly, she extracted twelve, keeping one back to place that call to the British Consul and another for the bus fare to his office. On the next hand, she was shaking so much she could barely cup the cards on the table: a two and a nine. She folded. She couldn't risk it. The next hand gave her a six and a ten. Again she folded. Her nerve had gone, she was scared. She tried to psych herself up. Poker was a game of skill and bluff, and confidence. No wonder she was losing.

The next hand gave her a five and a four, unsuited. She was first to bet, the worst position, 'under the gun'. Cautiously, she pushed out one dollar. So did everyone else. The Flop brought six, seven, ten. She bet another dollar. Grizzly called her bet and raised two dollars. So did the little man with the portable fan. Everyone else folded. Frankie had to match or fold. She added two dollars. Fourth Street produced a three. Now she had a straight, but a low one. She felt the sweat run down the back of her neck. She bet three. The Fanman matched. So did Grizzly. Fifth Street was an eight. She bet three again. The Fanman folded. But not Grizzly. He matched her and raised three. Frankie felt her nerve go. She was sure that Grizzly had the nine. His high straight would beat her low one. But she couldn't bring herself to fold now, not when she had ten dollars in the pot. She had to match him. She pushed forward her remaining three dollars, saying, 'I'll see you.'

Grizzly turned over his hand. Everyone leaned forward.

307

Frankie's eyes were so blurred that she could hardly focus on his cards. 'Pair of sevens, pair of tens,' said the dealer.

Frankie couldn't control her cry of excitement and relief. She'd won forty dollars. It was the most valuable money she'd ever possessed. She didn't even mind tipping the dealer.

Confidence bred confidence. She played on, and won the next hand. Now she had sixty dollars on the table. The cocktail waitress brought her a black coffee. It woke her up.

The dealers changed. Frankie played on, losing some and winning some. She fell back to twenty dollars and went as high as eighty dollars. Of course she should have pulled out when she was ahead, but she didn't. She was on a roll. It ended when her high straight was beaten by the Fanman's diamond flush. After three hours of playing, she stood up. She had forty-two dollars: twenty for tomorrow's buy-in, twelve for a motel, and ten for food. She walked out of the casino exhausted but exhilarated. The British Consul could wait.

Thirty-Four

The first cheap motel Frankie could find was nearly an hour's walk from Casino Center. It consisted of a group of one-storey cabins strung out behind a drugstore. There was one larger cabin, with a small reception area attached. Inside was a desk, two chairs, a cool-drinks machine, and a notice saying: *Prentice and Loretta welcome you. Ask for anything except credit!* Underneath the sign sat a buxom redhead with heavy black make-up and a skin-tight silvery T-shirt. Frankie wondered if it was a brothel, but she was too exhausted to care.

'Ah'm Loretta,' said the woman with a broad smile, as she took Frankie's money and handed her a key. 'If you need anything, call me. There's an icemaker by the drinks machine. The drugstore sells just about everything you could want. Within two blocks you'll find hamburgers, ribs, Tex-Mex, Chinese.'

'Thanks.' Frankie bent to pick up her shoulder bag.

'A city of half-broken dreams, Las Vegas,' said the woman, sympathetically.

'Why only half-broken?'

'If it broke people's dreams completely, they wouldn't come back. Vegas leaves 'em with just a little hope.'

Frankie smiled. She wished she could come up with a clever reply, but she was too tired.

Her cabin was small and bare but surprisingly clean. It had a sparkling shower, a new bed, a chair and a television. Frankie stood in the doorway, the heat behind her, luxuriating in the cold air which rushed out to greet her. Stepping inside, she closed the door on the day, relishing the first blissful moments of solitude, silence, shadows and cool. She stripped off her dirty clothes, tossed them into the basin and turned the water on to them. It gushed out, cold and clear. Naked, she stepped into the shower, turning on the water full blast so that it beat down on her head, her hair, her face and her limbs, pummelling the dirt from her. There was a tiny sachet of shampoo. She squeezed it on top of her head,

309

allowing the suds to run from her hair to her body. She washed away the dust of the road, the grime of the car park, the cold sweat of losing, the heat of winning.

Only when she'd washed herself, her hair, and all her dirty clothes, stringing them out along the curtain rail and across the back of the chair, did she permit herself to stretch out on the bed and sink into the safety of the clean white sheets.

She woke in the early evening, starving. Her clothes were already dry. She pulled on her shorts and a top, and opened the door. As always, the heat stunned her with its ferocity. She crossed to the drugstore to buy a carton of milk, a loaf of bread and the cheapest cheese she could find, carefully counting out five dollars. There was no one around. She must have been wrong about the brothel. Back in the room, she lay on the rumpled bed, eating her picnic, and flicking the television from channel to channel. But she couldn't concentrate on the outside, she was too busy trying to survive in her own world.

The cards were kind to her the next day. Not all the time, but enough. She played aggressively, betting to the maximum on a good hand, betting equally high on some trash ones, to bluff the other players. She remembered her father saying, 'It isn't just the cards you hold which count, it's those which other players think you hold.'

She left The Four Queens fifty bucks up, crossed the road to Binion's to quell her hunger with a steak sandwich, then crossed back to The Golden Nugget, which was bright white and gold like a sultan's seraglio. The Fanman was already seated at a low-stakes game. He nodded to Frankie. She smiled. Grizzly was leaning against the manager's desk, telling bad beat stories – where good hands had been beaten by opponents' sheer luck – to one of the off-duty dealers. 'So there I was, with four kings and, goddammit, he turns up a straight flush.' He grunted at Frankie. 'Haven't seen you around before yesterday.'

'I haven't been here.'

She bought her chips and followed the manager to a seat opposite the Fanman. She played carefully. Most people did on low-limit tables. They were the rocks – tight players who never varied their game. That evening, when she walked back to

Loretta's, she had seventy dollars, split three ways, hidden about her person. In her right pocket, she had her nail scissors. She had no intention of losing one cent to another Tucson.

For several days her luck was in. She didn't make much, the stakes were too low, but there was never an evening when she left with less than fifty dollars. At the end of the week she moved up to a $3–$6 table. The pots were bigger, but so were the blinds. She was apprehensive, although not as nervous as that first day when she'd been down to two dollars. She won the first hand with three aces. There was sixty dollars in the pot. She tipped the dealer and piled the rest in front of herself. The next hand gave her a king-high straight flush – the nuts, the best possible hand according to the cards face up on the table. Only a player holding an ace could beat her. She won.

By late that night she was up three hundred dollars. She left the table and sauntered down Fremont, humming the tune of *The Man Who Broke the Bank at Monte Carlo*. In a few more days, she'd have enough to repay Miss Tomasina. After that, she'd put some aside for Blue: she was already behind with his kennel fees. She pictured his beautiful tawny eyes and the sleek top of his head where she had kissed him and whispered goodbye.

It was late. Much later than usual. She was tired. But she had money. She hailed a cab. As she settled into the back seat, she decided that tomorrow she'd check out room prices at the hotels on Fremont. Next morning, she took a cab back up to Casino Center. The walk in the heat was too tiring, especially now she could afford a ride. She returned to The Golden Nugget, the scene of last night's triumph. But there was no free seat in the $3–$6 game and a waiting list for the $10–$20 table. She cursed inwardly. She was psyched up to play. The game was about confidence, and hers was brimming. After barely a moment's hesitation, she changed all but twenty dollars into chips, and settled down at a $20–$40 game.

The players were of a different calibre. They were tougher, harder. They had heart, which in poker terms meant guts. There was a very blond, sullen German whom Frankie nicknamed Sauerkraut, a large, bearded man in a baseball hat with 'Oil Slick Dick' written across the front, and a tiny, dainty old lady with a face like the Angel of Death's grandmother.

311

Frankie's first couple of hands were trash. She folded. The button moved to her right. The blind cost her twenty dollars. She went two rounds with a pair of nines, but folded when a king appeared on Fourth Street and Oil Slick Dick bet heavily. For half an hour, Frankie never went beyond the Flop. She was down a hundred dollars without having got near a pot. She began to have second thoughts about this table.

As if in answer to her prayers, she was dealt an ace and a king, both clubs. Sauerkraut was first to bet. He pushed out forty dollars. So did Death's Grandma. Everyone seemed to have a good hand. Frankie had her first high hand. She bet. The Flop brought a queen and ten of clubs and six of diamonds. She tried to hide her excitement, but the prospect of a royal flush blurred her focus. All she needed was the jack of clubs. The odds against it were high. But so was the pot. Sauerkraut folded, but Grandma bet a further forty dollars. Frankie tried to figure out what the old lady held, but the wizened face gave nothing away. She added her forty dollars. Fourth Street produced a nine of clubs. Now she had a flush. But she still needed that jack. Grandma bet forty. Frankie equalled. Fifth Street produced a six of clubs. Frankie was disappointed. She'd tried to fill an inside straight, and failed. But she still had a high flush. An excellent hand, although not a dead cert. Grandma bet a further forty. Frankie was pretty sure the old lady held a lower flush or possibly a straight. In either case, her high flush would win. She matched the bet. There was silence, as everyone craned forward. Slowly, Grandma turned over her hand. She had a pair of queens in the hole, and the last card on the table, the six of clubs, had given her a full house. Frankie felt sick. She could only sit and watch as her chips were swept away. She'd lost nearly all her money in less than an hour.

'It's a tough way to make an easy living,' cackled the old crone, using a well-worn expression as she clawed up the chips.

Frankie rose from the table and reeled out of the poker room, crashing into people without seeing them. Last night she'd had three hundred dollars. Not a fortune. Nothing compared with what she used to earn, in that other life. But this was a new life where money meant food and board. Lack of it meant a night in the car park.

She staggered out into the biting sun, down Fremont Street,

312

bumping against other pedestrians. They shouted abuse. She shouted back. What a fool she'd been to move to a higher-stakes game. Who the hell did she think she was, hitching into town one day and playing $20–$40 Hold'em the next? She leaned against the window of a pawn shop. Behind the bars were rows of gold watches and gold bracelets, many with names inscribed, all souvenirs of good luck followed by bad. She glanced at her own watch, the Piaget she had inherited from her mother. The idea of parting with it was abhorrent.

She followed a side street to the Post Office, and sat down on the wide white steps, grabbing as much shade as she could find. This was how her father had lived, lurching from hand to mouth, exhilaration to pitfall. She wanted to throw up, but she clamped her mouth tight against doing so in public. She longed to lie down, but if she went to the motel, tomorrow she'd have no buy-in. The thought of Tucson, floating around with her four hundred dollars and her clothes, made her wild with rage.

She forced herself to return to Fremont Street, where she walked up one side and down the other, going in and out of all the casinos, asking the cocktail waitresses if they knew of a girl called Tucson. They didn't. They told her to try the many big casinos out on The Strip. But that was a mile away. Frankie was too hot and too exhausted to walk any further. She looked at her watch again, and reluctantly removed it.

The first pawn shop offered her eighty dollars. 'But it's worth at least five hundred,' she protested.

'Not in Vegas. Here it's worth what I can sell it for.'

'I'll be back for it next week.'

He indicated the trays of watches. 'That's what they all said.'

The next shop offered seventy. She walked on. After an hour of thudding around on the hot sidewalks, Frankie returned to the first shop. As she parted with the watch, she felt as if she were selling her mother's memory at a knock-down price.

She felt guilty about using this money to play poker, but she saw no other way of making money. Before her eyes kept wafting the three hundred dollars she'd won, and lost. Returning to The Four Queens, she settled down to the timidity of a low-limit game. But her nerves were shot. She couldn't forget the fear of losing. Even with a good hand, she bet cautiously. If anyone raised, she folded.

313

Only when she had an unbeatable hand did she go all the way. Then everyone else folded. They'd got the measure of her game. Clenching and unclenching her fists, she watched her stack reduce. All she needed was one good hand. Just one, and her confidence would come flowing back.

At two in the morning she stood up. She had five dollars left. Not enough for tomorrow's buy-in. Barely enough for a cup of coffee and a phone call to the British Consul. She'd lost her watch. She'd lost everything. She wanted to crawl away and die.

She reeled out into the night. Fremont was crowded. It was always crowded. She'd never felt so alone. For the first time since she'd arrived in Las Vegas, she craved someone to talk to. Someone who'd commiserate. As she followed the cross-street to the car park, she passed other lonely people. Some shuffled in the shadows. Others walked briskly, psyching themselves up to make that begging call home: a collect begging call. Frankie had no home.

Of course, she could have swallowed her pride and telephoned Robert and Priscilla, or Steven, or Melanie, but she couldn't bring herself to admit defeat. Not yet. As she climbed the concrete steps to the car park, she thought of the love she had shared with Jack. The warm sense of belonging, of being cherished. She recalled her mother's voice, that perfect English. The cosiness of White Oast, Steven calling her 'dear', Blue chasing squirrels. Gossiping on the telephone with Mel. Poor old Big Ears. Marius chewing on his pipe. And, always, Jack. The passion and the laughter. If only she could put back the clock.

The red Datsun was parked in its previous position. The back doors were unlocked. Crying with gratitude, Frankie crawled inside. Something on the back seat scratched her. It was an envelope, unsealed, with 'Fabrizio' scrawled across it. The dealer must be Italian. It seemed funny that he knew nothing about her, whereas he was such an important part of her survival. She opened the envelope. Inside was a note wrapped around a fifty-dollar bill. It read: *Thanks for letting me stay in your apartment. I made a call to Sydney. This should cover it. R.*

In the morning Frankie woke feeling very ill. Her eyes stung. Her body ached. Her throat was sore. She eyed the envelope on the back seat, half opened it, then closed it again. It was out of the question that she should take money. People like her didn't steal.

She left the car, closing the door quietly, and started to cross the car park. But her eyes wouldn't focus. The rows of vehicles swam across her vision. Sweat pouring from her face and body, she clutched at a concrete pillar. She needed liquid, food, salt. She hurried back to the car and, with shaking hands extracted the fifty-dollar bill. As she closed the door, she heard voices on the slipway. She ran.

The two ranch eggs and toast at Binion's, paid for from the stolen money, should have choked her but they didn't. With every mouthful she expected Fabrizio to arrive, shouting, 'Thief!' Or the police with handcuffs, saying, 'Come quietly and it'll count in your favour.' But no one came, except the waiter with more coffee.

How Jack would laugh. And Tucson. She was no better than either of them. She remembered how she, and other barristers, had talked pompously of the criminal type. In those days she hadn't known what it meant to be desperate.

With trepidation she returned to The Four Queens and joined a low-stakes game. The Fanman and Grizzly were already in place. She was convinced that God, if He existed and could find His way around Las Vegas, would deal her the worst possible cards.

The first couple of hands were trash. She folded. The next gave her a ten and a nine, unsuited. She bet carefully. The Flop produced another ten. Everyone folded, except the Fanman. Fourth Street gave her a third ten. The Fanman folded. She'd won. The pot was twelve dollars, her motel money. Yesterday, she'd been playing for hundreds. Today, she was grateful not to have to sleep in the car park.

By mid-afternoon her stack had increased to sixty dollars. Not enough to recover her watch, but sufficient to pay for her bed, food and tomorrow's game. She went back to the motel to sleep.

During the next few weeks, Frankie continued to play in $1–$3 games, resisting the temptation to move to higher stakes. Most nights she returned to Loretta's in profit. The walk in the heat was a killer, but she refused to succumb to a cab. Last time a cab had heralded bad luck.

She existed in a strange and solitary world. She spoke to no one, except for a few words to Loretta when she checked in each night.

In the casinos, she exchanged no more than the odd phrase with other players. At the bar, when she ordered her evening sandwich, she sat alone. Her emotions were on hold, except when she was involved in a game. Then they ran high. All her life she'd needed people. Now, she didn't. At least, she tried to persuade herself she didn't. If she began to think of Jack or her mother or Melanie, or of anyone she cared for, she forced herself to stop. Or rather, she tried to.

For Frankie, poker wasn't just about money, although she certainly needed it. The game was about risking and winning. It was life in a tiny capsule. It was the modern-day equivalent of the shoot-out at the OK Corral, and many of the people Frankie played against looked like Wyatt Earp or Doc Holliday. They were yesterday's cowboys in tomorrow's world. Money was the sole barometer of success. If Frankie won, she was exhilarated. If she lost, she felt sick. Frequently, it took her several hours to wind down enough to sleep. But the chips bore no relevance to real money, once she'd covered her bed, a sandwich, and the ten dollars she set aside each night towards her debts. In this way she was unlike her father. He'd had no self-control. She was relieved to discover this difference. At the same time, when she lost she felt very close to him. The car park was her great fear. Poverty had snapped at her heels. She still bore its teeth marks in the moment when she'd stolen the fifty dollars.

There were no reminders of reality in Las Vegas. Frankie's perimeters shrank to Fremont Street, the casinos, the long walk, and the motel. She bought postcards to send to Robert and Priscilla, and to Steven. For several weeks they lay unwritten on the television. What could she tell them? How could she explain her life? In the end, to appease their concern, she wrote: *Will be in touch. Don't worry, Love, Frankie.* To Eamonn, she wrote that she would send money for Blue as soon as she could: she knew she was taking advantage of his love of dogs, but she had to repay Miss Tomasina first. To Mel, she wrote the truth. Or almost. She left out that she had stolen fifty dollars.

Melanie wrote back, full of concern. William had told everyone that Frankie had had a breakdown, run off with a drug addict, and no one knew where she was. *I'm so glad to hear it isn't true,* Melanie wrote. *I've been so worried. William refused to give me*

316

Robert's address and I didn't like to bother poor Steven in case he didn't know you'd left William again. The rest of the letter was full of gossip. Mel was very pregnant and stopping work in December. Nailbag had fallen downstairs. Hugo had finally found a girlfriend. William had been to the palace to be knighted by the Queen. Frankie was thankful she hadn't changed her passport to Lady Eastgate. It was bad enough being Eastgate.

One morning, as she was leaving the motel, Loretta called her into the reception. 'Why don't you take the room by the week instead of checking in every night?' she said. 'I'd give you a discount. Seventy bucks a week, in advance.'

Frankie hesitated. It was tempting. Then she shook her head. 'I couldn't spare that much. I need it for my game.'

'You play blackjack?'

'Poker.'

The redhead lowered her knitting in respect. 'You gotta have a lotta heart to play high-stakes poker.'

Frankie laughed. 'That's what everyone says. But I don't play for high stakes. Not yet.'

'I used to work in the casinos. We both did.' Loretta jerked her head towards a closed inner door from where the sound of a television ball game could be heard. 'When we married, we bought this place. But I miss the casinos. It's a way of life. We were happy then.' There was a choke in her voice, and she added quietly, 'My husband, Prentice, has multiple sclerosis.'

'That must be very difficult for you,' said Frankie, sympathetically.

Loretta's eyes filled with tears. 'You're nice. Pay me what you can spare now, and the rest by the weekend.'

'Thanks. I'll stay.' Frankie counted out forty dollars.

Loretta folded the money into the pocket of her skin-tight trousers. 'Tell me, do you think Prince Charles and Princess Diana are going to divorce? I hope not. I just loved their wedding. When I feel low, and Prentice is very sick, I watch the video. It's a fairy tale. It takes me away from my problems. I don't want to hear that fairy-tale people have problems too.'

She was cut short by a croak of 'Lorrie!' from behind the closed door. Frankie's last view of Loretta was as she bent her plump sympathy to a crumpled figure in a wheelchair.

317

When Frankie retrieved her watch, she told the pawnbroker triumphantly, 'I told you I'd by back.'

He shrugged. 'That's what they all say.'

Leaving his shop, Frankie passed a news stand. There was a picture of the Princess of Wales on the cover of *Vanity Fair*. She bought a copy for Loretta, who hugged her and said, 'That's the first gift I've received since Prentice got too sick to go out.'

Loretta offered Frankie a nicer room. It was bigger, with a table and chairs in an alcove, and a second door which opened on to the tiled back yard surrounding Loretta's small, private swimming pool. 'This will be my sister's room when she comes to help nurse Prentice, at the end.' Loretta spoke with the courage of someone who was trying to accept the inevitable. 'Till then, you can have it. And you can use the pool. Prentice used to swim twenty lengths every morning.'

Once Frankie had retrieved her watch, she moved to a $3–$6 game and began to save up Miss Tomasina's five hundred dollars. It took time. There were other urgent demands on her money. Her two pairs of shorts and two T-shirts were falling to pieces with constant washing. The soles of her trainers were worn from her long walks on hot tarmac. She couldn't use the pool because she had no swimwear. With her next big win, she bought a black bikini, some pretty cotton underwear, a pair of beaded sandals, and three soft cotton sundresses: white, ice pink and ice blue.

Shorts had been more practical for the long walk, but it was lovely to wear a dress again. She wore the pink on the first evening. She felt feminine and dainty. She fluffed out her hair and added coral gloss to her lips and a little scent behind her ears. Accustomed to her scruffy, sometimes grimy appearance, the dealers stared at her in amazement. As she crossed the poker room, even the men at the Seven Card Stud looked up, for just one second, before returning to their cards. When she took her place at her table, Grizzly gave the nearest he could manage to a broad grin. That night she won three hundred dollars.

'When a woman wins a hand, she makes more money than a man,' an attractive blond-haired man told her, as she left her table just after midnight. He was leaning against the desk, waiting for a seat in a $20–$40 game.

She laughed. 'Why do you say that?'

'Because a man can't believe he's going to be beat at poker by a woman.' He gave her a lazy smile, which matched his lazy drawl but was at odds with his flinty green poker-player eyes. 'Especially by a young, pretty woman. And a foreigner! Don't you realise that poker is the last bastion of the American male?'

'What a chauvinist!'

'Show me the woman who wants a wimp.'

She laughed and walked on, replying over her shoulder, 'This woman doesn't want any man. They're too much trouble.'

He called after her. 'And women aren't?'

He was the first man for months whom she had found attractive and he was clearly attracted to her. It wasn't the intense magnetism of that moment when Jack had cupped her hand in his, but he gave her a warm glow. She was tempted to turn round to see if he was still watching her, but she didn't. The next evening, she took even more care with her appearance, wearing her white sundress and painting her toenails scarlet for the first time since she'd lived with Jack. But the blond man didn't show. After three days, she reverted to shorts. They were easier to walk in.

Her days at Loretta's followed a pattern. She slept till noon, swam in the pool, and ordered coffee and blueberry muffins from the drugstore, breakfasting in the shade of Loretta's gaudy pink parasol.

Sometimes Loretta joined her. 'Frankie, it's time you found a nice man,' she said one day.

'I'm better alone.'

'You've had bad luck.'

'No, Loretta. Prentice has bad luck to have multiple sclerosis. I made bad judgements.'

'Don't you want to go home? See your family?'

'I only have a stepfather and a stepbrother.' She thought of her mother, sitting in the garden at White Oast, surrounded by a luscious green lawn and succulent nodding daffodils. Las Vegas couldn't have been more different. Perhaps that was why it was her perfect escape. Nothing jogged her memory. She could block out the past. Or, at least, she could try to.

It was mid-September before Frankie telephoned Robert and Priscilla. She would have done so earlier but she couldn't face Robert's barrage of questions. As soon as he heard her voice, he shouted, 'My God, Francesca! We've been worried to death. How could you do this to us? How could you run away in the middle of the night? Where are you?'

'Las Vegas. I sent you a postcard. Didn't you receive it?'

'With no address! Have you forgotten, we move to San Francisco next week? Give me a telephone number. As soon as we're settled, I'll drive down to fetch you. I expect I can manage to take a few days off work for a family emergency.'

'Robert, I don't need fetching. I'm perfectly all right.'

'You don't have any money. How are you living?'

She longed to say she was on the game, just to hear the shock in his voice, but she replied, 'I'm playing poker.'

'You're gambling! I'll leave tonight. You always do get in with the wrong sort of people, Francesca. But I blame myself. I haven't been much of an older brother, I admit it. I intend to start now.'

'Robert!' She interrupted his flow. 'I appreciate your concern. I'll come up to San Francisco at Christmas, then you'll see I'm very much alive. I'm sorry I left you to deal with William. But I don't need looking after any more. I'm a big girl, not a child. I may have come to freedom late, but I'm learning. I made mistakes in the past. I expect I'll make many more in the future. But they must be my mistakes.'

Thirty-Five

Towards the end of the month, Frankie flew back to Dallas. At the airport she hired a car. On the drive in, she stopped to buy a large bouquet of pink and white carnations, exquisitely tied with a pink bow. Miss Tomasina was stitching a patchwork quilt when Frankie opened the front door. She gave a small cry of pleasure, 'I knew you'd come, girl. Zeb and I said you wouldn't forget us.'

Frankie laid the carnations on the old lady's lap. Then she produced an envelope containing ten crisp, new fifty-dollar bills. 'Thank you,' she said.

'I don't want it.' Miss Tomasina tried to hand it back. 'It's enough for me to see you again.'

'It's my debt. I have to pay it.'

'Did you meet my cousin?'

'I meant to, but I never reached there.' She didn't tell Miss Tomasina about being robbed or she'd have refused to take the money.

'But you must have found work,' said the old lady, indicating the envelope.

Frankie smiled. 'Of a kind.' She settled into the opposite chair. 'I've been playing poker in Las Vegas.'

'You don't say!' Miss Tomasina gave her tinkling laugh. 'Why, my old pa used to play poker every night, except Sundays. Zeb! Zeb! Come in here.' The Comanche appeared in the doorway. He smiled at Frankie. 'She's been playing poker.' Miss Tomasina laughed again. 'Can you beat that!'

Frankie remained with Miss Tomasina for two days. She went to bed early and rose early, and spent her time listening to the old lady talk of her childhood, or sitting in the rocking chair on the shaded deck. One afternoon she walked down the road to Robert and Priscilla's old house, retracing the steps she'd taken on the night of her escape. She slowed as she reached the house. A woman was carrying groceries in from the boot of her car whilst two children rode their bicycles up and down the short drive. They

321

were the new people who lived in the house. Their guests slept in Frankie's igloo home beside the swimming pool. She wished she could see it again but she sensed the woman wouldn't like it. She walked back to Miss Tomasina.

When the time came to leave, it was an effort to drag herself away from the warmth and affection of the old lady and Zeb and to launch out on her own. She wasn't so much afraid, as afraid of losing her nerve.

It was evening when she flew into Las Vegas. Long before they landed, from the aircraft window she could see the lights along The Strip bouncing up into the sky. In the airport, the shriek of slot machines drowned the tannoy. A part of her still longed for Miss Tomasina and safety. The other side screamed, 'Don't be scared. Not now!' By the time she had collected her bag, the Las Vegas Frankie was in ascent. She grabbed a cab and went straight to The Golden Nugget. Five hours later, and a hundred dollars richer, she reached Loretta's. By then, she'd lost her fear of fear.

Summer had passed. The sun no longer burned with the same intensity. Frankie was restless. Although she tried not to think about Jack, memories of him filled her half sleep. One night she started a letter to him, begging him for another chance. In the morning, she ripped it up. She wrote long letters to Melanie and received equally long replies. She wrote to Steven. He answered in his spidery writing, begging her to return to White Oast. She sent a thousand dollars to Eamonn, apologising for her outstanding debt. When she won, she no longer retained only Blue's kennel fees, ploughing the rest back into her stack. Now she saved for some unknown future.

One night she was woken by voices. One was Loretta's. Then the telephone rang. Not long afterwards, a car drove up and doors slammed. She rose, threw on some clothes, and hurried across to Loretta's house. All the lights were on. She knocked. Loretta answered. She'd been cryng. 'It's Prentice,' she said. 'He's taken a turn for the worse.'

'Can I help?'

'Oh, no. The doctor's here.' She squeezed Frankie's hand. 'Thanks.'

Several days later, Loretta joined Frankie at the swimming pool. She didn't beat about the bush, that wasn't her way. 'I need your room for my sister,' she said. 'I can't manage Prentice on my own any more. And I can't even offer you another room, because we're leasing them all to one of the other motels.' She paused. Tears sprang into her tired eyes and rolled down her plump, exhausted cheeks. 'I'm going to miss you, Frankie.'

'I'll visit you often.' There was nothing Frankie could do to comfort Loretta, except to put an arm around her shoulders and listen as she talked of the day she'd married Prentice.

Frankie moved into Binion's, because she liked its old-fashioned honky-tonk atmosphere, and if she was going to live in the centre, she might as well be right in the swim. Rooms at the back, looking eastward, were eighteen dollars a night. Those overlooking Fremont were more expensive. Frankie was happy to be at the back. From her window she could see the mountains.

Binion's Horseshoe was home to the World Series of Poker, the championships. Any player with the ten thousand dollars buy-in could pit his skill against the world's best. But apart from those three weeks in May, there was no poker room, not at that time. Casinos made more money from blackjack, roulette and the slot machines – games played against the house.

Compared to Loretta's, Frankie's room seemed enormous. The bed was king-size, the bathroom huge. Large windows looked out east, to the mountains. She unpacked her clothes, then lay on her bed, watching the light die on the distant peaks. She felt disjointed. She missed Loretta's company, even though they had not talked of much but Prentice or the British Royal Family.

The lights and sounds of the street brought her back to reality and poker. She dressed carefully in her pale pink sundress, fluffing out her hair and touching her lips with coral. Whenever she took trouble with her appearance, she invariably won, at least to start with. Looking good gave her confidence, and that was a major factor in her game.

Tonight she felt confident. Tucking a hundred dollars inside her purse and another hundred in her pocket, she locked the rest, along with her passport, in her room safe. Then she locked her door and set off down the corridor towards the lift. She pressed the button and waited, humming to herself.

The lift arrived. It halted with a jolt. Its doors drew back and she stepped inside. The only other occupant was the blond-haired man from The Golden Nugget. 'Don't tell me you're still rooking fifty bucks off old-timers in low-limit games,' he said, smiling.

'There's no law against it.'

'At least play for high stakes, so it's worth my while to beat you.'

'I might win.'

He laughed. 'I doubt it.'

He was very good looking in a clean-cut, boyish way, though his skin had the subterranean pallor of someone who never went outside, except after dark. He was no taller than Frankie. In fact, he could even have been slightly shorter. His blond hair was thick and he wore it brushed back, which gave him extra height. She suspected that he was a few years younger than her. What made him so attractive were his large, green eyes with their dark rings underneath. They gave him the look of a degenerate angel.

The lift stopped.

'You haven't answered me,' he said.

'I only started playing Hold'em in the summer.'

'A beginner!' He followed her through the maze of slot machines to the exit on Fremont Street, adding, 'You'll never improve your game if you're scared to play against better players.'

'I like to win.' She started to cross the road to The Four Queens, convinced he would follow.

'See ya!' he called, and walked away.

Not that Frankie cared. He was just some poker bum trying to make her lose her money.

The same old crowd, plus a couple of tourists, were in the low-stakes game. She played steadily. One of the tourists was spectacularly drunk. The other was scared to death. They were both on tilt – playing badly and losing heavily. At the end of two hours, her stack had tripled. She cashed in her winnings and moved on to The Nugget.

The $3–$6 dollar game was full and there was a waiting list.

'There's a seat on $20–$40,' said the girl behind the desk.

Frankie hesitated. Then she thought of what the man had said and she raised her chin. 'I'll take it.'

Death's Grandma was firmly entrenched at the table, with a couple of hundred dollars stacked in front of her. The other players included a gangster in dark glasses who looked like everyone's idea of Al Capone; a young, snappily dressed Syrian known as Damascus Joe; and a long-haired, balding Mr Tambourine Man in a psychedelic kipper tie and a purple Sixties shirt.

Only Grandma spoke as Frankie took her place. 'How ya doin', honey?' She riffled her chips to emphasise her victories. 'Not gone back to England yet? Can't say I blame ya. When I wanted to play poker in London, the goddamned casino made me wait forty-eight hours to gain my membership. And then they wouldn't let ma husband in without a tie.'

'And they wouldn't let me drink my bourbon at the card table,' growled Al Capone.

Frankie smiled. She tried not to show her nerves, telling herself it was only a game and she could leave the table any time she wanted to. Her first hand was rubbish. She folded. On the second hand, it was her turn to put up the blind. It cost her twenty dollars, so she went to Flop with a pair of sixes. Then an ace made her think twice. Someone might have its pair. She folded.

The next hand gave her a jack and a ten, suited. Grandma bet twenty dollars. Al Capone called and raised to forty dollars. Damascus Joe matched him. Everyone else folded. Frankie, who had her best hand of the evening, pushed forward forty dollars. She thought Grandma would fold. She didn't. She matched. The Flop produced eight, nine, seven. Frankie had a straight. Excitement bubbled up inside her. She gritted her teeth to keep a straight face, clenching her fist on the table so that she wouldn't fiddle nervously. Grandma looked at her, smiled, and folded. So did Damascus Joe. Only Al Capone went on to Fourth Street. Then he folded. Frankie had won. She'd added over a hundred dollars to her stack, but it wasn't the victory she'd expected: the pot should have been bigger.

Winning gave her courage. She played on. Over the next few hours, she won more than her share of hands. But her pots were small. At three in the morning, she glanced up to find the blond man watching her from the rails. He winked. She smiled coolly. But her concentration had disappeared. She played two more hands, lost, and left.

He joined her as she passed the desk, taking her elbow proprietorially, which both pleased and annoyed her. 'Do you want to know why they all fold when you have a good hand?' he asked.

'Of course I do.'

'You have a "tell". You know what a tell is?'

'A sign which a player unconsciously makes if he or she has a good hand – or a bad one.'

'Right. Come on! Let's have breakfast in Binion's.' He walked ahead of her.

She had to run to catch up with him. 'Aren't you going to say what my tell is?'

'Why the hell should I?' He barged onwards, through the slots, and down the wooden stairs to the wood-panelled Coffee Shop.

This time she didn't catch up with him until he was already seated on one of the tapestry-covered benches, elbows on the table, drinking a glass of milk. 'It's considered good manners to wait for you guest,' she said icily.

'I have an ulcer. If I forget to eat, like tonight, I'm in pain.' He paused. 'I'm sorry.'

She sat down and watched as he gulped his milk like a thirsty child raiding the fridge after school. 'Well? What's my tell?'

'I'm not going to say.' He ordered ranch eggs and toast for both of them, and another glass of milk for himself. 'I watched you. You're good. One day I might find myself playing against you. I want to be sure of winning.'

'Please!' she said with a smile.

'Going to make it worth my while?'

'I don't pay bills with my body.'

He held out his hand. 'Don't be so uptight. I was only kidding. The name's Scott. I didn't mean to offend you.'

She shook his hand. 'Frankie Tiernay. Apology accepted.'

He blotted up his fried eggs with a hunk of bread. 'So, tell me how you ended up in Vegas.'

'I was . . . umm . . . travelling around the States. I came here. I had a poker lesson in The Four Queens. I played. I won. I lost. I won again.' She repeated the well-worn Vegas saying, 'It's a tough way to make an easy living.'

'No husband?'

'Not any more.'

He gave her his lazy, sleepy smile. 'My wife lives in Nashville,

326

Tennessee. At least she did two years ago, when we last spoke. My pa owns a smallholding, fifty miles from Nashville, right next door to her pa's. I guess that's why we married. Poor Noelle. She could never understand why I preferred playing poker to tending the cattle. Pa's convinced the whole of Vegas is built with mafia money earned from dice, drugs and hookers. He could be right. But at least it's more fun than tending cattle in Tennessee.'

'Is your mother alive?'

'I dunno. She walked out when I was six. She went without a backward glance and never even said goodbye.' Scott acted as though he didn't care, with all the bluff bravado of a small boy desperately hurt.

Frankie warmed to him. She recalled how often she'd acted that way about her father, until finally she'd believed she didn't care.

The waiter brought her some more coffee. 'You shouldn't drink that stuff,' said Scott bossily. 'That's why you're so uptight.'

'Don't bully me! I spent ten years married to a dictator.'

He saluted. 'Yes, ma'am.'

They both laughed.

It was five in the morning when they stepped into the lift. Her room was on the fifth floor, his on the sixth. When the lift stopped at her floor, he moved forward. 'Of course they all think we're off to have sex.'

She blushed. 'We are not!'

He laughed at her embarrassment. 'I'll see ya around.' The doors closed and he was gone.

Frankie walked along the corridor, telling herself she didn't really like him. She was merely flattered at his attention.

She woke early next morning and lay in bed, wondering if Scott were thinking about her. She telephoned Loretta to ask after Prentice. He'd had a bad night. Frankie promised to visit soon. At midday she took the lift up to the rooftop swimming pool on the Westside Tower and stretched out in the sun. It was hot. She dozed.

She woke to find Scott adjusting a parasol to shade her. He was wearing dark glasses. 'Sunbathing's bad for you. You'll end up with a face like a cowboy's saddle.'

'Thanks. You know how to make a girl feel great.'

He cupped her chin in his hand and bent to kiss her, very quickly and very gently on the mouth. 'You're too pretty to be saddle leather.' He picked up her sun lotion and bent to smooth it over her back. His hands were firm on her skin. His fingers ran down the bumps of her vertebrae. She tried not to show that his touch disturbed her. Suddenly, he stood back. 'I hate the heat. I'll catch you later.' He walked away.

Frankie expected to see him at The Golden Nugget, but he didn't appear. Instead, he slunk up to the pool on the following afternoon to tell her he'd lost five thousand dollars. She commiserated. Her own game was going well. Scott had been right about improving against better players. In higher-stakes games, they seldom went all the way to Fifth Street. The knack was to steadily accumulate other players' opening bets by raising aggressively before the Flop to frighten them into folding. She learned the psychology of the seating: to be sweet to the man on her left so he would think twice about stealing her money, and to be aggressive to the one on her right, the player whose bet she coveted. They were nearly always men. She preferred it that way. It was easier to sucker them along.

A week later, she lost two thousand dollars. Her biggest-ever loss. She reeled from the table, straight past Scott who was standing near the rail, and out into the street. He followed and took her arm, protectively. 'You'll get run over.'

'I'm flattened already.'

She felt too sick to face breakfast. He understood, and accompanied her to her room, leaving her at the door, unthreatening. She remained there for thirty-six hours, during which time she plumbed the depths, imagining that her mother could see her gambling, and knowing how horrified she'd be.

When she could bring herself to face the world again, she was handed a note by the reception desk: *Am in the Plaza*. She wandered up to the top of Fremont. Scott was playing Omaha, another variation of Seven Card Stud. He was on a roll. He didn't even see her. She still couldn't face the poker tables, so she mooched around Binion's, dropping twenty-five cents into the slots. Scott was no company. He was still on a roll. She was angry with herself for having expected more from him.

Boredom and necessity drove her back to poker. And, she had to admit it, a craving for its excitement. She joined a low-limit table at The Four Queens. By midnight, she was sixty dollars up. She kept looking for Scott among the railbirds. But he didn't come.

There was no sign of him the next day, or the next. Four days passed. She longed to ask at the desk if he'd checked out, but she was embarrassed. In the Coffee Shop and in the bars, she found herself talking to strangers. Scott had raised a hunger in her: for romance, for sex, for company.

Her concentration went, because she kept thinking about him. She lost consistently. By mid-week, she had less than a hundred dollars, and her hotel bill was due. The car park snapped at her heels. She felt faint with fear. How could she have let herself run so low? She had to force Scott out of her mind and think poker. She kept away from The Nugget, where the stakes were higher, and returned to The Four Queens, winning steadily over several evenings until she had accumulated her hotel bill. Only then did she transfer to The Nugget, and a higher game.

Death's Grandma was the only familiar face. Again, the old crone folded each time Frankie had a high hand. But a tourist on tilt helped her recoup. By Saturday, six thousand dollars was neatly stacked in her safe. She felt like a millionairess. What did she care about Scott? He was just a handsome, uncouth poker bum. She didn't need him. Or anyone!

She took a day off, mailed a thousand-dollar bankdraft to Eamonn, rented a car, visited Loretta, drove up to The Strip, had lunch in Caesar's Palace, had a massage, a facial, a haircut, and spent five hundred dollars on new clothes. Coming out of the shopping mall, weighed down by packages, she crossed to the casino with whose valet parking service she'd left her car. As she tipped the boy who'd fetched it, and stepped inside, a chubby, curly-haired blonde in valet uniform walked out of the office. It was Tucson.

Frankie wanted to shout, 'Thief! Where's my money?' but instead she drove off as though nothing were amiss. A hundred yards on, she turned into a car park, swinging the car around to face the valet's office.

For the next two hours she waited patiently as Tucson fetched cars, parked cars, chatted to clients, joked with colleagues, and pocketed tips. Frankie watched the friendly smile which had reminded her of Melanie. The casual saunter. The cheeky confidence. At six o'clock, another girl arrived. A moment later, Tucson came off duty. She walked straight down the car park, across the back of Frankie's car, to a battered yellow Volkswagen.

It was easy for Frankie to follow Tucson, because the Volkswagen stood out like a rusty can amongst the shining, gleaming vehicles of Las Vegas. They drove along The Strip away from town, past Caesar's Palace, past Dunes, past the airport, until Tucson turned off into the parking space of a motel so scruffy and run-down that it made Loretta's look like a palace. She got out of her car, unlocked one of the cabins, and disappeared inside.

Frankie wasn't scared. She was too angry for fear. She knocked on the door of the cabin. There was silence. Then it opened cautiously, and Tucson peered out.

Frankie stuck her foot into the gap, forced the door open, and pushed Tucson back into the room. 'I want my four hundred dollars,' she shouted, making the most of the element of surprise.

Tucson stared at her in disbelief. Then she babbled, 'Oh, hi, Frankie. I'd never have recognised you! I was going to mail your money to you in England, but I lost your address.'

'Balls!' Frankie took a step forward. 'You left me without a cent. You took my clothes. You even took my bus ticket. I want it all back, or I'll call the Arizona police!'

'You can have the clothes.' Sullenly, Tucson pointed to a heap of Frankie's now grubby clothes lying on the floor beside her leather suitcase. 'But I ain't got four hundred dollars.'

'Then I'll make do with what you have – for now.' Frankie seized Tucson's bag. Inside was a purse.

'That's my rent!' Tucson made a grab for it, but Frankie was too quick. 'I'll kill you, you bitch!' screamed Tucson, suddenly producing an open penknife and lunging forward. 'I'll fucking kill you.'

Instinctively, Frankie defended herself. She seized Tucson's wrist and somehow managed to twist it backwards. As she did so, the knife raked Tucson up the inside of her arm. Not hard, but enough to draw blood. She screamed, 'You knifed me. My God, you knifed me.'

Frankie was horrified, but she couldn't let herself show sympathy. She pushed Tucson on to the bed, saying, 'Sit down, or I'll hurt you again!'

Tucson slumped against the pillows. 'I liked you, Frankie,' she whined. 'I'm sorry I took your money. But don't leave me broke. Please!'

'I'm only taking what's mine.' Frankie opened the purse. Inside was ninety dollars. She took it all. Then she tossed her clothes into the suitcase, closed it, and straightened up. 'If I have any trouble from you,' she said, 'I'll tell your casino that you're wanted for theft. If you come near me, I'll call the police.' She didn't want the knife, but she didn't dare leave it. So she took it. She walked to the door, hesitated, then drew out a five-dollar bill. 'Here's something to phone that elusive brother of yours. It's more than you left me.'

She marched out, slammed the door, got in her car and drove away. At the first cross-street, she had to stop. She was shaking so much that she couldn't drive. Not that she regretted what she'd done. She felt justified. It had been self-defence, Tucson had got what she deserved. Frankie had retaliated for herself, and for all the silent victims of crime. Nevertheless, she was shocked to discover such violence in herself. She wondered what her colleagues in chambers would say if they knew she'd stabbed another girl. What would she herself have said, two years ago? She remembered how often she'd nodded as a judge told a defendant that it wasn't for the public to take the law into their own hands. But what did anyone know about the jungle until they had walked alone in it?

When Frankie had calmed down, she turned her attention to the knife. She wouldn't put it past Tucson to make an anonymous phone call tipping off the police. Feeling like a criminal, Frankie wiped the knife carefully with a tissue, removing all trace of blood or fingerprints. Then, holding it in the tissue, she closed it, got out of the car, walked to the nearest garbage bin and dropped it inside. As she did so, she thought of Jack. How he would have laughed!

Thirty-Six

Frankie was lying by the pool, her eyes closed, wondering whether or not to tell Melanie about the penknife. She'd just decided not to when something tickled her bare stomach. She opened her eyes to find Scott standing next to her. He was stroking her skin with the petals of a red rose. 'I won ten thousand bucks,' he crowed. 'Ten thousand!'

'Where?'

'The Bicycle Club, Los Angeles. I won the last hand with a pair of nines against a pair of eights.' He paused. 'I was afraid you might have checked out.'

'Don't they have telephones in LA?'

'I was on a roll. You understand, you'd be the same.' He bent to kiss her, very gently, brushing her mouth with his. 'Will you have dinner with me tonight? We'll go to Caesar's Palace. Take in a show. Do all the things that tourists do.'

'I'd love to.' She smiled up at him.

He stroked her cheek. 'I'll see you at seven, in the bar.'

As Scott walked away, Frankie's mind raced through a thousand questions. Did she want him? Did her desire spring from loneliness? Did she want someone close to her, with all the heartbreak which intimacy brought? What should she do about so-called safe sex? Could she wait till tonight before they made love, when every nerve in her body shivered? Should she ask him to use a condom? What should she say? What did other girls say?

By evening, she was in a frenzy of agitation, shimmering up and down in front of the bathroom mirror as she attempted to apply lip gloss with a shaking hand. She was wearing a new outfit, a black, stretchy skirt with a wide gold belt, and a black bustier under a glitzy red and gold sequined satin bomber jacket.

The telephone rang. She grabbed it. 'Hi, Frankie,' said a strange woman's voice. 'I'm calling from the poker desk at the Union Plaza. Scott asked me to tell you he's in a game.'

'I see.' She replaced the receiver. Poker bum! She clenched her

332

fists. Then unclenched them. It was her own fault for depending on yet another no-good man, as Miss Tomasina would say. She slipped a wad of dollar bills into her jacket pocket and hurried out.

There was a seat next to Damascus Joe on a $20–$40 game in The Nugget. He gave her his neat, polite smile. 'How are you, Frankie?'

'So-so.' She riffled her chips like an old hand, deciding that he was really quite attractive. Rumour had it that he spent a thousand dollars a week on cocaine. That, Frankie didn't like, although she knew many players took it to stay awake. Loretta said you could usually tell which, by those who were still buzzing after twenty hours of play. Tonight, Frankie didn't care what Damascus Joe's habits were. If he asked her out, she'd go. She might even spend the night with him. It would serve Scott right.

She played aggressively and won her first hand with nothing but bluff. Bugger Scott! Bugger the lot of them! She'd been playing about an hour and her stack was up three hundred when the manager tapped her on the shoulder. Scott was standing by the rail. He raised his eyebrows, she shrugged. She had no intention of running into him. She played another couple of hands, whilst he waited by the desk. He didn't apologise for keeping her waiting. He'd lost and was in a bad mood. They took a cab to The Strip. He was silent. Frankie kept to her corner of the back seat, wondering why she'd bothered to come.

They drove up the avenue of brightly illuminated fountains and cypresses to Caesar's Palace. There were people and cars everywhere, milling around under the golden-roofed entrance.

'Boxing tonight!' shouted their driver. 'Should be a helluva good fight.'

'That's where we're headed.' Scott paid the fare. Then he jumped out and started to walk away. Frankie followed, battling her way through the crowds, the cars, and the hot night. She didn't want to see boxing. She hated it. She wanted to go back to Binion's. But Scott barged on out of earshot, through the entrance of the hotel, across the casino and out the back.

'Scott!' she yelled eventually. 'You're on your own. I've had enough.'

He turned and walked back to her. 'I'm a bad loser.'

'You're a terrible loser. Don't take it out on me.'

He took her hand in his. 'I won't. I promise.' He drew her closer, so close that the buckle of her belt rubbed against his. His mouth was level with hers, his eyes level with her eyes. He moved against her. She trembled. He ran his hands down her thighs to the hem of her short skirt, his fingers circling on her bare skin. She bit the lobe of his ear. He squeezed her hard. She chuckled. He smiled.

The desert sky was sultry purple. The stars were sharp. Lights from The Strip bounced up and round. People hurried past them.

'Come on,' said Scott. 'The match has started.'

He took her hand and ran with her, through the entrance and up the steps to their seats. In the ring, two powerful black men sized each other up, whilst the referee jumped away from them like a frightened grasshopper. The bell rang. The crowd cheered. The boxers jigged around each other. One lashed out, then the other. They pummelled. The crowd screamed. Young girls jumped up and down in a frenzy of excitment. A little old lady in the front row fainted.

Although Frankie disliked boxing, she couldn't help but be affected by the atmosphere. There was something both sensual and brutal about the fight. Something animalistic in the baying crowd. Scott ran his hand up her leg. She leaned against him. He kissed the corner of her mouth. Her lips parted.

The fight went five rounds before one man received a split eye and the referee called halt. 'Come on!' said Scott. 'We don't watch any more.' He hurried her out of the stadium and into Caesar's Palace. Frankie had only been there once, on the day she had confronted Tucson. It was an enormous extravaganza of red and gold and glitter, with hostesses dressed like Queen Cleopatra and men in centurion mini-skirts who said, 'Hi there. Howyadoin?' At the Café Roma, Scott gulped down a glass of milk, whilst Frankie waited to tell him that she intended to go home to Binion's.

He put down his glass. 'I wanted this to be a terrific evening and I've ballsed it up,' he said. 'I always do, when things are important to me.'

She warmed to him again. He drew her close, as he had before and whispered in her ear, 'Let's stay here, at Caesar's. We could order up dinner. Champagne. Lobster. Strawberries.' He ran his hand down her back. 'What do you say?'

Before she had time to hesitate, he was at the reception desk, booking them in.

Their suite was luscious pink, with an enormous heart-shaped bed and a mirrored ceiling. There were pink curtains, pink flowers, and a pink carpet. Scott and Frankie stood in the centre of the room, gaping. Then they looked at each other and giggled. Frankie reached for a strawberry from a gilded plate on a gilded trolley and popped it into Scott's mouth. He handed her a glass of ice-cold champagne.

'Pa would have apoplexy if he saw this,' said Scott, throwing himself on to the bed and bouncing up and down like a small boy playing on a trampoline. 'He thinks a two-bit motel is extravagant. I expect that's why Ma left him. But she could have said goodbye. She needn't have gone without a backward glance.'

'I'm sure she didn't mean to hurt you.' Frankie tossed her jacket to one side and joined him on the bed. 'We all hurt people without realising it, until it's too late.'

'Did you hurt your husband?'

She thought of William. 'I thought so once. He certainly hurt me. But the one I hurt most of all was another man. Because I hurt him, I hurt myself.'

'Your lover?'

She nodded. 'I left him to return to my husband. My worst judgement!'

'Do you still love him?'

'If I'm honest, yes. But it's long finished.'

They lay quietly side by side, holding hands, looking up at themselves in the disjointed sections of mirror. Then, slowly, they turned to face each other, drawing nearer so they could kiss, gently, tenderly. He wrapped his arms around her. 'I've wanted to make love to you since I first saw you,' he whispered, running his mouth down her neck, to the soft mounds of her breasts visible above the black bustier.

He reached for the strawberries, laid them in a line down her cleavage, and leaned over her, eating them one by one, his mouth on her skin sending shivers of excitement through her body. She reached up to him, wanting his weight on her and his strength in her. She wanted to be held, surrounded, protected, loved. He unclipped the bustier and dropped it on the floor. She unrolled her skirt from her hips. She reached for the buckle of his belt. He smiled into her eyes, tasting the champagne from her mouth. They kissed deeply, slowly, He held her hands above her head and lay along her, caressing her body with his, taking her slowly and with the utmost control, just as he played poker, until he reached a point where he could not hold back, and she didn't want him to.

They made love. They talked. They ate. They watched television. They made love again. When Scott fell asleep, he was still cuddling Frankie. She lay awake, listening to his breathing, and wondering if she wouldn't be happier with a man like Scott whom she might love but was not in love with. It freed her from being hurt.

In the morning, he turned on the television. Against a background of one of the never-ending quiz shows, they made love in the jacuzzi, splashing water everywhere, laughing. When it was time to leave, Frankie linked her arms around his neck. 'It's been fun,' she said, nuzzling him. 'Thanks for bringing me here.'

'My pleasure, ma'am!'

'Now you have to say what my tell is.'

He was shocked. 'You didn't stay with me just to discover that?'

'Of course not!' She kissed him tenderly. 'But I deserve to know.'

'I'll think about it.' He squeezed her. 'After tonight!'

'You rat!'

They argued all the way down in the lift and across the casino. As they passed the poker room, a game was in progress. Scott slowed. 'Looks interesting,' he said.

'I'll see you later.'

'You don't mind if I stay?'

'Not if you say what my tell is.'

He raised his fist, clenched it, then unclenched it. For a moment she watched him, frowning. Then she said loudly, 'Damn!'

That evening, Frankie joined Death's Grandma at a high-stake game. She kept her hands on the rim of the table resting casually, even when she held the nuts – the best hand according to the cards visible on the table. Several times she caught the old lady eyeing her hands and she had to stifle a giggle. When she joined Scott for breakfast in the Coffee Shop, she was four thousand dollars up.

'I trust you'll be showing your gratitude to me tonight,' he joked, as Frankie buzzed with excitement.

'I'll show it to you now.' She grabbed him under the table.

He gave a yell and dropped his milk. They looked at each other, and laughed.

A week later, the Dow Jones fell twenty-two per cent, and the London stock market crashed. People talked of 'Black Monday'. A few faces disappeared from the poker tables, but these disasters didn't affect Frankie or Scott. They lived in their day-for-night world.

Frankie enjoyed being with Scott. He was both friend and lover. They kept their separate rooms on their separate floors. It suited both of them. There was no anxiety in their relationship. No *angst* if they didn't meet. No obsession if either failed to phone. He was moody and a bad loser, but he had no malice except when he played poker. All his deviousness was channelled into cards. Outside the casino, he was like a little boy.

Loretta was delighted to hear Frankie had found herself a man, and one who'd keep her in Las Vegas. She invited them both for Thanksgiving dinner. It could have been a gloomy occasion because Prentice was so ill, but Scott kept them laughing with stories of his childhood in Tennessee. On the way home, in the taxi, Frankie squeezed his hand. 'Thanks,' she said. 'You were terrific.'

He smiled. 'I like them. They're simple, kind people. They remind me of the folks back home.'

One evening when Frankie was playing Hold'em at The Golden Nugget, the manager tapped her on the shoulder. 'Your brother wants you to join him in the restaurant.'

'Robert!' Astonished, she looked up.

Robert and Priscilla were hovering near the desk, looking awkward and out of place amidst the glitter and the noise. She finished her hand and hurried to their table.

'I couldn't believe my sister was sitting in a casino with all those hard-nosed men,' Robert spluttered before she had time to say hello. 'You looked like a gangster's moll.'

Frankie laughed out loud. 'Their money's as good as anyone else's.' She pulled up a chair and sat down, her elbows resting on the table.

337

'But you had five thousand dollars in front of you,' Robert went on.

'Oh, Robert, don't be such a bear!' exclaimed Priscilla. 'Frankie looked terrific. I think she's very brave.' She was pink with excitement. The colour of her cheeks matched her pink dress.

They were interrupted by Scott, who appeared at Frankie's side. She introduced him. He smiled and shook hands. 'I'll catch you later,' he said, and kissed her on the mouth before leaving.

Robert stiffened. 'I suppose it's not my business to know who that man is.'

'He's just my lover.' Frankie tried to keep a straight face, but she couldn't. Robert reminded her of an overstuffed toy panda. She started to giggle.

'I'm glad you think everything's so funny,' he snapped, 'but we had a hell of a time with William.'

'Yes. I'm sorry.' Frankie took a deep breath to quell her mirth. 'I just couldn't face him. I was afraid.'

Priscilla patted her arm. 'We understand. He was awful. Such a prig! He never once said he was partly to blame. As he left, he told me you'd beg him to take you back one day.'

Frankie rolled her eyes. 'Never! The next time I see him will be in a divorce court.'

They went on to talk of Steven. 'I was at White Oast last week,' said Robert. 'He's trying to come to terms with your mother's death but it's hard for him. He loves your letters. He keeps every one. Of course, he longs to see you. When are you going back to England?'

Frankie shrugged. 'Not yet. Not till I'm strong enough to withstand whatever William might try to throw at me. Mel says he put it around that I ran off with a drug addict and am now in a clinic being detoxified.'

'You can always rely on us to back you up.' Robert squeezed her hand and smiled. 'Well, girls, shall we take in a show? Will you accompany this middle-aged raver out on the town?' He rose and held out an arm to each of them.

They didn't talk about her mother again, but their presence brought back the past for Frankie. The memories remained with her, as vivid as ever, even after Robert and Priscilla had left Las Vegas.

In December, Melanie had a baby daughter, Rachel Francesca. As soon as Frankie received Mel's letter asking her to be a godmother, she telephoned her. It was the first time they'd spoken since she'd left London, but it seemed like only yesterday.

At Christmas, she flew up to San Francisco to stay with Robert and Priscilla. Their children Dwight and Susan were home. Dwight was large and, to Frankie's mind, dull. Susan was fifteen and giggly. They were living in a ranch-style house in Walnut Creek, beyond the Berkeley Hills. The house was similar to the one in Dallas but smaller and with no guest igloo in the garden. House prices, as Robert told Frankie several times each day, were very much higher on the West Coast. Before returning south, Frankie went on up to Canada because she needed to renew her US entry visa.

At New Year, she flew to Atlantic City with Scott. There was no poker, but they amused themselves playing at tourists on the blackjack tables and walking along the boardwalk. On the way home in the aeroplane, he reached for her hand and said, 'Let's take an apartment together. It's crazy to pay for two hotel rooms.'

She laughed. 'Scott, you are so unromantic.'

He held her closer and kissed the tip of her nose. 'I'll never meet another lady who suits me like you do.'

She drew back very slightly. 'I like things the way they are.'

'Are you turning me down?'

'I was married for ten years. It took me a long time to escape. I couldn't give away my freedom. Not now. Maybe never.'

'Or maybe not for me, but for another guy, like the one you left to return to your husband?'

She thought of Jack. What was he doing now? Who was he with? Who'd been by his side on New Year's Eve, as she had been that first year when they'd gone to Brighton to watch Jet race. 'I told you,' she said. 'That's all over.'

'Do you still think about him?'

'Yes. I do. I'm sorry, Scott, but I'm too fond of you to lie.' She linked her fingers through his to comfort him. After a moment, he pulled his hand away.

Although they didn't talk any more about living together and outwardly their relationship remained the same, Frankie was aware that Scott had retreated from her. She was sorry, but she didn't blame him. She would have done the same. They were both in the survival game.

The spring made her restless again. She flew to Dallas to stay with Miss Tomasina and Zeb. From there she went to Aspen to catch a little skiiing. In the early years of their marriage, she and William had always taken a skiing holiday. From Aspen she went on to Reno, to recoup her expenses at the poker tables. In any case, after weeks away from the game, she was longing to get back. She enjoyed Reno but after a while she'd had enough. It wasn't Las Vegas. At least, not for her. She ended her travels with a few days on Lake Tahoe. Then she flew home to Vegas. It had done her good to get away.

That summer Binion's acquired the adjacent Mint Hotel, knocked down the intervening wall, doubled the casino's gaming capacity, and opened an all-year poker room beneath the black and white photographs of the Poker Hall of Fame. At the same time, The Nugget closed its poker room and began work on a new hotel, The Mirage, out on The Strip. It was to be the most extravagant hotel in Las Vegas, with Siberian tigers playing in the reception area, and an erupting volcano in front of the entrance. Of more interest to Scott and Francesca was their high-stake poker room.

As soon as the worst of the heat was over, Frankie took off again, up to San Francisco for Thanksgiving, over to Lake Tahoe with Scott for New Year, over to Los Angeles on her own, to the Bicycle Club, the biggest card room of them all, several weeks later. She returned to Las Vegas to find Scott had bought a car. Not that he intended to drive it. His perimeters did not extend beyond Fremont Street.

'It's for you,' he said, when he met her at the airport. 'I thought if you had wheels, you wouldn't keep travelling. I miss you when you go away.'

She hugged him. 'I miss you too, Scott.'

'But not enough to move in with me.'

'We're happy as we are. Why spoil things?'

'You're like a cat on a hot tin roof,' said Loretta, when Frankie drove out to visit her. 'Poker used to be enough for you. Is Scott playing you up?'

'He's fine. It's me!'

For a few weeks, the car did make a difference. Frankie drove out to the Hoover Dam, up and down The Strip, out to Loretta's. Then her restlessness returned.

One morning, very early, when Scott was still at the tables and Frankie couldn't sleep, she drove out west, to Red Rock Canyon, following the dirt track between the briliantly coloured sandstone hills. There was no one around. Just silence and the red rocks. Sitting in the car, her elbows resting on the steering wheel, she watched the sun come up on yet another day. Only today was different. She knew why she was restless. She wasn't sure that she had the answer, but she had to try.

Fabrizio came off the graveyard shift. He hurried along the sidewalk to the multi-storey car park. It had been a hard night. He was tired, his shoulders ached from dealing cards. He took the lift to the second floor. As he walked towards his car, a woman stepped out of a nearby vehicle. She had a tousled, glossy mane of brown hair and was expensively dressed in a cream linen skirt and a cream silk blouse.

He'd seen her before, from a distance, when he'd dropped by to see a friend, a dealer at The Nugget. She'd been playing high-stake poker. He remembered thinking her attractive. She was even more attractive now, because she looked very determined, but also strangely vulnerable.

'I owe you fifty dollars,' she said, offering him a crisp new note.

'You have the wrong man. I've never met you.' He grinned. 'Unfortunately.'

She drew closer. He could smell her light. lemony scent. 'Eighteen months ago I took some money from an envelope in your car.'

He was still puzzled.

'I was broke,' she went on. 'I had nowhere to stay. I slept in your car. You always left the back door unlocked.' She pushed the bill into his hand. 'I'm sorry I took your money, but I was hungry.'

'If you'd asked me, I'd have given it to you.'

She smiled ruefully. 'I was too desperate to ask.'

He watched her walk back to her car. He'd have liked to know her better. But she gave him a little wave and drove away.

Loretta was preparing Prentice's milkshake when Frankie burst into the motel, saying, 'I'm going back to England. I've come to say goodbye.'

'Oh, Frankie! Don't go!' Loretta lowered the milkshake. 'What does Scott say?'

'I haven't told him yet. He's in the middle of a game. In any case, I've only just decided. There's a flight out, via Dallas, this afternoon. I plan to be on it.'

'He's going to be so upset. I know, 'cos I'm upset.'

Frankie sighed. 'I don't want to leave either of you, but I have to go back. I've been so restless, you said so yourself. I realise now that I'm nervous because I know I have to face the past. When I left England, I was running away. As I told you, my mother had died and I'd lost the man I loved by returning to a disastrous marriage. I came to Las Vegas with nothing. It was sink or swim, and I learned to swim. This town gave me a fresh start. It taught me that I can survive on my own if I have to. It's made me strong. Now I want a divorce. I'm determined to make all those people who've listened to my husband's lies realise how brutal he was. I want to see my stepfather. I owe it to my mother to spend time with him. I want to see Melanie, my friend, and Blue, my dog.' She paused. 'And I have to see the man I loved. Just once. Perhaps by seeing him, I'll bury the ghost and accept that it really is over. But until I do, he'll always be in the back of my mind.' She thought of Tucson, the penknife, and Fabrizio's fifty dollars, and added, 'There are many things which I didn't understand before, but I do now. Las Vegas has taught me a lot about myself.'

Loretta smiled. 'You will come back and see us, with or without this man?'

'Of course.' Frankie hugged her. They both had tears in their eyes. 'Keep in touch with Scott for me,' she said, 'just to make sure he's OK. Look after yourself, you and Prentice. I wouldn't have survived here without you, Loretta.'

'Sure you would. You're a poker player. You've got heart.'

Frankie walked to the door. There she stopped and added, 'I'll always have a soft spot for Las Vegas. It's vulgar and glitzy and tacky, but it's also gutsy. It taught me not to be afraid of being afraid. It's made *me* gutsy.' She gave Loretta a thumbs-up and walked out into the bright morning sunshine.

She returned to Binion's. Scott was no longer at the poker tables. She buzzed his room, but he didn't answer. She went up and knocked on the door. There was no reply. She asked the dealers, but none had seen him. She had him paged, while she booked her flights, paid her bills and packed. She called all the other casinos. He wasn't in any of them. The morning ticked by. She searched up and down Fremont Street, leaving messages with everyone who knew him. An hour before her flight departure, her cab arrived. She kept it waiting as she had Scott paged one more time.

In desperation, she telephoned Loretta. 'Scott hasn't come back,' she said. 'I have to leave now. Will you tell him that I did everything to find him? I know he'll never forgive me, but I want him to know I didn't walk away as his mother did, without a backward glance, without trying to say goodbye.'

Thirty-Seven

It was raining when Frankie landed at Heathrow, just as, that day in Phoenix, she 'd imagined it would be. Water bounced up from the oily runway and the smell of wet fuel hung in the damp air. This same rain was falling on Jack. Cold hit her as she stepped from the plane. She'd forgotten what it was like to be cold.

She took a taxi into London and checked into Blakes. It was a more expensive hotel than she had intended to use, but she needed a good address. Not just to impress others, but for her own confidence. Vegas had made her punchy. She mustn't lose that. She unpacked. She didn't have that many winter clothes, but those she'd bought were good. Again, for herself as much as for anyone. She might not always feel confident, but she had to look it. Poker had taught her many things, not least to bluff.

It was a relief to shower away the night flight, retouch her make-up and slip into warm clothes: black tailored trousers and a cream cashmere sweater. She stood by the window, looking out at the rain-soaked slate roofs of South Kensington. It was strange to be back in London, once her city, but in an area where she had never lived. She felt as if she'd been away for decades. Simultaneously, now that she'd left Las Vegas, she found it hard to believe such an outlandish place existed.

She reached for the telephone and began to tap out Melanie's number. Then she thought better of it, replaced the receiver and asked the porter to order a taxi. As she left the room, she picked up a large, exquisitely wrapped parcel.

The bright white façade of Simon and Melanie's beautifully restored house had weathered in the past years. London grime had settled in the cornices. Birds had made their nests up under the roof. The steps leading to the elegant porch were no longer pristine. The brass doorbell had mellowed.

Frankie pressed it. Immediately, deep inside the house, she

heard a clanging. Then footsteps. A young pink-faced girl opened the door. 'Can I help you?' she asked, with a hint of Melanie's Welsh accent.

'Is Mrs Rosenmann at home?'

There was a shout from the landing. 'Sophie, who is it?'

Before the girl could answer, Frankie walked straight in, calling, 'Mel! It's me – Frankie.'

Melanie was standing at the top of the stairs, with a very blonde and very pretty toddler clutched in her arms. 'Frankie!' She stared in disbelief. 'Is that really you? My God, you're so glitzy and glamorous. Oh, it's lovely to see you. Come up! When did you arrive?'

'This morning.' Frankie ran up the stairs two at a time. Laughing, they hugged each other with Rachel in the middle. 'This is for you,' she said, holding the parcel towards the litle girl, whose podgy fingers reached excitedly for the enormous pink, glittery bow.

Melanie led the way into her bedroom and settled Rachel on the rug. Kneeling on the floor, Frankie handed Rachel the parcel for the second time. It was as big as the child. She squealed as she tried to unwrap it. Surreptitiously, Melanie loosened one end to help her. At last the parcel was open. Inside was a life-size walkie-talkie doll, just like the one Frankie had been given by her father, only this doll had fair, curly hair, like Rachel, and was dressed in pink not red.

'Did you bring it all the way from Las Vegas?' asked Melanie.

Frankie answered in an exaggerated southern drawl, 'You bet I did.'

'You are kind to have remembered her. Now you're back, we can have her christening. We've been waiting for you. Oh, I'm dying to hear about all your adventures.' Melanie stopped and laughed. 'Here I am, babbling away as usual and not giving you a chance to speak.'

They were interrupted by Sophie calling up the stairs that lunch was ready. 'You will stay, won't you?' said Melanie.

Frankie put an arm around her. 'I'd love to. And for a gossip afterwards, if you've time.'

'Time! I have all day.' Melanie picked up Rachel and kissed her downy forehead.

Over lunch they talked of impersonal things such as Wales, Melanie's mother and the poll tax. Afterwards, Sophie took Rachel out for a walk. As soon as they had left, Frankie and Melanie curled up in armchairs in front of the drawing-room fire, with a bottle of wine, a pot of coffee and a box of bittermint chocolates. 'I'm taking two years off,' said Melanie, eating two chocolates at once. 'Before Rachel was born, I said I'd be back at work within a month. But everything changed once she arrived. Sophie's sweet, but I don't want to leave my baby with someone else all day. I want to hear her first word. I want to be here if she needs me. I'm her mother.'

'Why go back at all, if you don't want to?'

'Oh, I couldn't stay at home, not indefinitely. I enjoy the law too much. So I shall join all the other working mothers, racked with guilt because I can't be in two places at once.' Melanie added another shovel of smokeless fuel to the fire. 'Now, come on, Frankie, tell me what you've been up to. You look stunning. Are you in love?'

'Oh, no! Never again. I told you in my letters, I've been in Las Vegas playing poker.'

'I've been so worried. You're not hooked, are you?'

'Mel, you are funny. Anyone would think I'd confessed to being an opium addict. Of course I'm not hooked, not in the way you mean, and not as my father was. I love the challenge and the risk, as he did. I want to win. It isn't just the money, it's pitting my wits against my opponents. But if I lose, unlike my father, I don't get drunk. I crawl away until my battle scars have healed. Then I come back fighting. Poker has taught me many things. Like life, it's a mixture of lucky timing, skill and confidence. It's about being pushy at the right time and being patient at other times. It's about self-control, which is something my father never had.' Frankie described her past two years. Much of it she had already written in her letters, but Melanie wanted to hear it again. She listened wide-eyed to Frankie's escape from Dallas, her meeting with Tucson, being robbed, the long, hot hitchhike, the early days in Las Vegas and the slow climb out of poverty. Frankie even told Melanie about Tucson attacking her with the penknife, and how she'd cleaned the blade before throwing it away. 'I felt like a criminal,' she said.

'It was self-defence. What else could you do?'

'I know. She deserved it. But I still felt bad.' Frankie didn't add that she'd also stolen fifty dollars. She didn't want to risk Melanie not understanding.

'Weren't you frightened to gamble with the only money you had?' asked Melanie, pouring more coffee.

'I was past fear. I was in the gutter.'

'What are you going to do about William? He's still telling everyone that you ran off with a druggie. I tell them it isn't true. But he's a judge. They believe him.'

'I'm going to divorce him for cruelty. That's why I couldn't come home before. I had to wait till I was strong enough to take everything he'll throw at me.'

'You mean Jack Broderick?'

Frankie nodded.

'Of course that won't count, not in the law,' said Melanie. 'After all, he had you back. But he'll find some way to discredit you. A High Court judge as a wife-beater! Frankie, have you any evidence? Simon and I saw him shout at you but we never saw him hit you or saw your injuries.'

'Other people saw my bruises, such as Blue's trainer. I refuse to let William get away with what he did to me. And there's another thing, Mel. I'm going back to the Bar.'

'To chambers?'

'Heavens, no! They wouldn't have me, and I don't want them. I shall set up on my own, in the Inn. I'll specialise in cases of medical negligence, like the case of that little boy Alexander Swaffield.'

Melanie put down her coffee cup. 'Frankie, you're brave. I don't think you'll succeed. William will do everything to keep you out of the Inn. But I'll do anything to help you.'

Frankie stood up. 'There'll always be a place for you in my chambers. Think about it. Now I have to get some sleep. I've been travelling for fifteen hours.'

'Stay here with us. Why pay a hotel? At least I'll know William hasn't bumped you off.'

'Thanks, but no.'

'Is it because you think Simon disapproves of you?'

That was in part the reason, but Frankie shook her head. 'It

347

wouldn't be fair on Simon. After all, he shared a chambers with William.'

Melanie followed her to the front door. On the hall table was the previous week's *Sunday Times* business section. 'Read this!' She turned to an inside page. 'I was planning to send it to you.'

Frankie wasn't prepared for the shock she felt on seeing a photograph of Jack. The caption read:

Jack Broderick, the prodigal with a past. Chairman of Richmond Racing and chief investor in three new greyhound tracks and leisure centres. Broderick, described as charismatic, dynamic and ruthless, has never tried to hide a fourteen-year gaol sentence.

She lowered the page. 'It's strange, isn't it?' she said in a tight voice. 'He used to be the night person, the shady one, and I was the day person, the respectable one. Now it's the other way round.'

'Do you still love him?' asked Melanie.

'I love the memory.' Frankie went out into the rain.

Back at the hotel, she telephoned Steven. He was thrilled to hear from her. His voice quavered with emotion. She arranged to rent a car and drive down to see him on the following day. After that, she fell asleep.

Steven was standing on the doorstep at White Oast when Frankie drew up. She was shocked to see how stooped and thin he had become, even more so than before. But his eyes burned fiercely with the pleasure of seeing her. They lunched beside the drawing-room fire: he felt the cold. Mrs Broom bustled around tucking his rug around his legs as though he were a child. Afterwards, Frankie drove him into the village to buy some freesias, then up to the graveyard to visit her mother's grave: he could no longer walk that short distance. When Frankie had last visited the grave, there had been no gravestone. Now there was a beautiful white marble headstone across which was carved, in simple lettering:

Dominique Hartington
1932–1987
beloved wife of Steven
and mother of Francesca

'She shouldn't have died first,' he said. 'She was twenty years younger than me. It doesn't seem fair on her.'

'Or on you.' Frankie knelt beside the grave to arrange the freesias in the marble vase.

They returned to the house, to tea and crumpets by the fire. Later, in the frosty dusk, Frankie walked alone around the garden. It was tidy, a gardener saw to that, but it wasn't quite the same as when her mother had tended it. She passed the spot where the first Big Ears was buried. A small square of white stones still marked his grave. She paused beside the bench where she'd sat with her mother in the spring sunshine and talked of France. The daffodils were pushing up beside the crocuses, just as they had been two years earlier when her mother had finished the chemotherapy and they'd believed her cured. The memory of those last days of hope brought tears to Frankie's eyes. She brushed them away before she went inside, so as not to upset Steven.

She spent the night at White Oast. It was lovely to be back in the old house again with its familiar creaks and smells and sounds coming in from the garden. Her bedroom was just the same. The red doll was on the top shelf, the books were all in order. But perhaps, like the garden, it wasn't quite the same now her mother was no longer there to add her touch.

In the morning, she telephoned the kennels. Eamonn answered. 'How's Blue?' she asked eagerly.

'Oh, he's . . . er . . . all right.'

'Is something wrong? You don't sound very sure.'

'I'm busy, Frankie.' He put the phone down.

She was stunned. She nearly rang him back. But she didn't. Instead, she went into the drawing room, where Steven was reading the newspaper. 'I'll come down for lunch on Sunday,' she said calmly, as though nothing had happened. 'We'll take fresh flowers to the grave.'

He patted her hand. 'I wish you'd stay here. I realise you can't. You have your own life. But I haven't felt so happy since your mother died. Let's go to her favourite restaurant on Sunday, the one where I always took her on her birthday. We can order our special menu.'

Frankie bent to kiss his whiskery hamster cheek. 'I'd love to go. I'll be here by midday.'

349

The calm she had exhibited to Steven disappeared as soon as she was clear of White Oast. She roared up the A21 towards London, her foot flat on the accelerator, her speed seldom dropping below ninety. There was no sign of life when she reached the kennels, except for the yapping of the dogs. She crossed to the kennel gate and turned the handle. For the first time she could remember, it was locked. She rang the bell.

It was a few minutes before Eamonn opened the gate. 'I knew you'd come,' he said, his round face completely expressionless.

'Of course I have. Where's Blue? Is he dead? Is he hurt?'

'I'd have told you if he was.' He held out half a dozen airmail envelopes, each addressed to him in her large, scrawly handwriting. 'Here's your money back.'

She brushed aside the envelopes. 'Eamonn, what is going on? Blue's my dog. I have a right to know. Please tell me!'

He shook his head. 'I told Jack you wouldn't give him up without a fight.'

'What do you mean? Has Jack got Blue?'

'He'll kill me for telling you.' The old trainer sighed. 'I don't own these kennels, Frankie. Jack does. You debt wasn't to me. It was to him.'

'Then I'll pay Jack. But I want to see Blue. Is he here?'

'I'm sorry, Frankie. You'll have to speak to Jack first.'

It was useless to argue. Eamonn wouldn't let her in. There was nothing she could do but drive away. Of course, she'd dreamed of meeting Jack again. One day. Somehow. She'd imagined meeting him looking her best, her most seductive. Now she didn't give a damn about looking good for a man who banned her from seeing her dog.

She drove straight to Richmond. There was a new security guard at the entrance. He didn't know her. She had to give her name and wait whilst he checked with Jack, which made her even angrier.

'Mr Broderick's secretary will meet you at the far end of the grandstand,' he said, rising to show her the way.

'I know where that is.' She didn't mean to snap his head off.

The grandstand was alive with the mid-morning bustle of cleaners, secretaries, caterers, and kennel-staff, all hurrying to prepare for the evening meeting. She wondered how Marius was.

And Nicoletta? She'd barely thought of them whilst she was in America. She'd blocked out everything and everyone associated with Jack. Or at least she'd tried to.

An efficient, smart blonde woman was waiting for her on the terrace. She gave Frankie a professional smile whilst taking in her red snakeskin cowboy boots, tight jeans and glittery Las Vegas red sweater. 'Mr Broderick has a meeting in twenty minutes,' she said.

'Twenty minutes is more than enough.'

The Paddock House was the same endearing muddle of Edwardian home and hi-tech office. She could hear a telex and a telephone chattering in the back room, and the honky-tonk sound of 'The Entertainer' coming from the office. It reminded her of Binion's, and she knew then why Binion's had appealed to her.

The secretary opened the office door ahead of Frankie. 'Miss Tiernay.'

'Show her in.' It was Jack's voice, that mix of late nights and night streets.

He was sitting at his desk, leaning back in his leather chair, a pen balanced between the tips of his fingers. Frankie stepped into the room, and they stared at each other in silence, whilst the secretary closed the door and slipped away.

Like the stadium, Jack hadn't changed. There was no reason why he should have. Two years was not long. But somehow she'd expected him to be different, because so much had happened to her. Perhaps his dark hair was a little less unruly, and he wore a suit, something he'd never done except in the evenings, but his blue eyes were as brilliant and as beautiful. How silly! Eyes didn't alter. He started to smile, that lazy, half-amused, half-quizzical smile she used to love.

'Where's Blue?' she demanded.

'He belongs to me, in lieu of payment.'

'I sent money.' She thumped the airmail envelopes on to his desk.

'You were late. The kennel's terms are that owners whose fees are more than three months late risk forfeiting their dogs.'

'But you never apply that. Not if they're paid eventually. No kennel does.'

'I did this time. You were three months and one day late.'

'But you don't even like Blue!'

'That's not the point. In any case, I've become very fond of him.'

Tears of anger and frustration came into Frankie's eyes. 'I want Blue, Jack. He's my dog. I love him. I'll pay whatever you want.'

'Blue isn't for sale. Now, if that's all you came to see me about, our meeting is over. I have a business to run.'

Suddenly, Frankie felt nothing but cold dislike. There was no spark of rage or love or anything. No avid hate, the aftermath of passion. Every emotion drained out of her as she stood there, looking down at the man who had haunted her half-dreams. 'I'll get him back one day,' she said. 'Whatever it takes!'

She left before he had time to answer. As she walked back through the grandstand, she came face to face with Marius. He reached up his gnarled hand to stroke her cheek. She took it and held it against her face. 'I've missed you, Frankie. It's not been the same since you've been gone,' he said. 'I'm sorry about Blue. I told Jack it would break your heart, but I'm afraid that's what he wanted.'

'Oh, he hasn't heard the last of it,' she replied. 'He may have won that round, but I don't get beat that easily. Not any more!'

Thirty-Eight

'I don't know how I'll get Blue back, but I'm determined,' Frankie told Melanie, as she paced up and down the kitchen of the Kensington house. 'The bastard! Stealing my dog. And to think I believed that I still loved him!'

'How can you get Blue back if you're not allowed to see him?' asked Melanie, settling Rachel into her highchair.

'I'll break into the kennels.'

'No! You'll be arrested.'

'It's all right, Mel. I was only joking.' Frankie was glad she hadn't told Melanie about the fifty dollars.

Melanie handed Rachel her lunch, a bowl of mince, diced carrots and peas. 'We saw William at a party last night,' she said. 'No, don't worry. We didn't say you were back, and I'm sure he doesn't know, or he'd have indicated. When are you going to tackle him?'

Frankie winked at Rachel, who was now lining up her peas in preparation for throwing them on the floor. 'I'm biding my time. I have to choose the right moment. Well, Rachel.' She bent her face to the child's. 'What would you like for your christening present? How about an antique silver dressing-table set for when you're a big girl?'

Melanie beamed. 'That would be lovely. You are clever at thinking of presents.'

They fell silent, both remembering the baby which Frankie had lost.

'I used to want Jack's children. I loved him so much that I wanted part of him,' Frankie said quietly. 'Something his and mine. I'm such a fool.' She picked up her bag and jacket, and walked out of the kitchen, saying, 'Thanks for listening. I'll phone you tomorrow.'

Melanie called after her, 'Frankie, be careful! Please!'

Back at the hotel, Frankie counted her money into piles on her

353

bed. In the few days that she'd been in London, she'd spent over a thousand pounds, nearly two thousand dollars. She still had money, around twenty thousand dollars, but at this rate it wouldn't last long. She kept thinking of the car park in Las Vegas, and wondered if the fear of being destitute would ever leave her.

Scott had talked of The Hertford Casino in Mayfair. Along with The Victoria in the Edgware Road, it was among the few London casinos with a reasonable-sized poker room. When Frankie telephoned The Hertford, their first question was, 'Are you a member?'

'No, but I play regularly in Las Vegas.'

'Perhaps you have friends who are members?'

'No, I don't. What's the problem?'

'There's a membership rule. It applies to every British casino. You'll have to sign on, then wait forty-eight hours before you can enter.'

It was another planet from Las Vegas.

The Hertford Casino was off Brook Street. From the outside, it seemed just another imposing, white-painted Mayfair building, with steps up to a porch and a black-painted front door. Except that at The Hertford, the doormen looked tougher than at other buildings. They were fully trained security guards. Inside was a battery of glamorous receptionists, all with flicked-up hair and toothpaste smiles. Behind them, a magnificent wrought-iron staircase led up to the gaming rooms.

It was late afternoon when Frankie went in to sign her membership form. The club was waking up for the evening. Two men in dinner jackets were walking upstairs. Two women in lamé trousers were leaving their coats at the cloakroom. They had a prowl in the way they moved. For the first time in her career as a professional poker player, Frankie was conscious of being a woman on her own in a casino, and therefore what some men would consider fair game.

On her way back to the hotel, she stopped at an estate agent in South Kensington to enquire about short-lease flats: something furnished and serviced, and cheaper than the hotel. The agency windows were full of pictures of houses for sale, all at discounted prices in the current falling market. Those who'd failed to sell were being forced to rent.

By lunchtime on the following day, she'd seen six properties and had signed a two-month lease on a small but well-appointed furnished flat in a large block just off Kensington High Street. It had one large bedroom, a double sitting room and a balcony. It was anonymous and well protected. That afternoon, she moved in.

The first person she telephoned from her new home was Melanie, who came straight round with a bottle of champagne to celebrate. 'I'm so pleased you've taken somewhere,' she said. 'It means you're here to stay. At least for a bit.' She looked around the flat. 'It's very smart. It must cost a thousand a month. And you're renting a car. Frankie, how can you afford it?'

'Poker.'

'That was in Las Vegas.' She hesitated. 'You're not gambling here, are you?'

'Life's a gamble.' Frankie poured them each a glass of champagne. 'Drink up!'

'Stop changing the subject!'

'If you don't approve, why ask me?'

'I'm a nice girl from the Welsh valleys brought up to believe that gambling is the work of the devil. You thought so too, once. Look what it did to your father. Oh, I'm sorry, I shouldn't have said that, but I'm terrified you're going to lose everything. And you should be frightened, too. But you're not. You used to be so cautious.'

'It was time I changed.'

'But how can you risk your money when you want to start your own chambers?'

'Mel, how do you think I'm going to find the money to start? From poker!'

'When you work full time, will you stop playing?'

'I'll cut back. I'll play for fun.' Frankie looked at Melanie's anxious face, and added more seriously, 'If I were truly a professional player, I wouldn't go back to the law. Poker would satisfy me. I wouldn't need another life, I wouldn't want it. But although I love to play, it's partly a means to an end for me. I want more from life – and I want to give more.' She kissed Melanie's cheek. 'Thanks for worrying, but there's no need. I won't dine with the devil.' She grinned. 'At least, not too often!'

355

On her first evening at The Hertford, Frankie dressed discreetly in black trousers and a plain jacket. She plaited her hair and wore little make-up. Her only jewellery was the Piaget watch she'd once pawned. She did all of this on purpose. She didn't want to draw attention to herself, either inside the club or out of it.

By London standards, The Hertford was big. Compared to the casinos in Las Vegas, it was tiny. That wasn't the only difference. Frankie was used to the wail of slots, the hustle, the glitz, the crowds, and the friendliness. She was used to people in shorts and halter-tops, stetsons and cowboy boots, all good enough to enter so long as they had money. The Hertford prided itself on exclusivity. Every man had to wear a tie: members who arrived without were lent one. Women were expected to dress up. The light from the huge Waterford chandeliers flattered diamonds and low necklines.

The poker room was on the first floor. It had the quiet atmosphere of the smoking room in a gentleman's club. There were a dozen tables, occupied mostly by men. Of the two women present, one was an elderly, inscrutable Chinese lady, dressed in black silk. She had gold rings on every finger and a huge stack of chips in front of her. The other was young and brittle, a spiky redhead. Her name was Dilys. She was the only person to smile at Frankie.

The minimum buy-in was fifty pounds. The highest was five thousand. Unlike Las Vegas, all games were pot limit – you could bet, call or raise to the limit of what was already in the pot on the table. Frankie bought a hundred pounds' worth of chips and settled down at a low game. She was nervous. The silence made her feel as though she were playing cards in a morgue.

Her first hand was a nine and a two unsuited. She folded. Her next hand was rubbish. Again, she folded. For an hour, she won nothing. The blinds were depleting her stack. At last, she was dealt a pair of queens. She kept her nerve through the Flop and Fourth Street to catch another queen on Fifth. The pot was ninety pounds. It felt good to win. Four hours later, and three hundred pounds richer, she took a taxi back to her flat.

Frankie was asleep when Melanie telephoned, early on Sunday morning. She'd been out at The Hertford till the small hours. It had been a bad night. She'd finished a thousand down.

356

'You sound terrible,' said Melanie. 'Are you ill?'

'Oh . . . I've just got a bit of a sore throat.'

'Were you out late last night?'

Frankie struggled to sit up in her bed. 'Quite late, Auntie Melanie.'

'You're being cagey. That makes me worried. But I won't question. I rang to ask if you'd seen the *Mail*? There's a picture of Jack Broderick on the gossip page.'

'There is? Thanks. I'll buy a paper and phone you tonight. I'd better dash, I'm late for Steven.'

Frankie was showered, dressed, and out of the house in twenty minutes. On her way to the car, she stopped at a newsagent's. Before driving down to White Oast, she hunted through the pages. At first, she thought Melanie was mistaken. None of the photographs looked like Jack. Then she read the caption: *Leaving the Environmental Ball, Mr Jack Broderick of Richmond Racing and Miss Felicity Plaistow of the well-known horse-racing family.* The girl was blonde and handsome, with a long, haughty, aristocratic face. It enraged Frankie to think that this girl could pat Blue, whereas she could not.

Steven was waiting anxiously in the hall at White Oast, afraid she was going to arrive late. 'I booked for twelve thirty,' he said. 'They get so busy. I asked for our special table, the one your mother preferred, by the window overlooking the garden.'

For both of them, the restaurant brought back bittersweet memories. As in the past, Steven ordered mushrooms in garlic and steak au poivre. Frankie would have preferred something less rich, but she didn't say so. They ate slowly, talking of her mother, sadly, fondly, quietly. Frankie couldn't help remembering the last time they'd come here, when she'd found her mother afterwards in the kitchen, complaining of indigestion. They hadn't realised then that it was the beginning of the end.

After lunch, they drove up to the churchyard to lay freesias on the grave. Walking back to the car, along the narrow and slippery path beneath the yew trees, Steven took Frankie's arm and said, 'Your mother would be pleased to see us here today, together.'

'Oh, I'm sure she can see us.'

'You know,' he went on, 'if I'd had a daughter I'd have been very happy for her to be like you.'

357

Frankie felt tears prick her eyes. She was too choked to answer. In that moment, she realised that in Steven she had the father she'd searched for. Her own father had been wild and amusing, but he'd never possessed Steven's quiet reliability. She'd never felt completely safe anywhere but at White Oast.

It was late by the time she left for London. Clouds were scudding across an otherwise clear sky, cutting off the light when they passed in front of the moon, letting it through again when they raced on. Frankie drove thoughtfully, still thinking about Steven. When she reached the M25, the orbital ring around London, she slowed. Central London was straight ahead. Blue was twenty minutes to the west. She had to see him.

The pub at the entrance to the lane was packed. Laughter and light spilt out into the night. But the lane itself was deserted. Frankie parked long before she reached the kennels, pulling off the road into the shadow of a holly tree. She stepped from the car, closing the door quietly, and walked as softly as she could across the tarmac to the main kennel door. She turned the handle. The door locked. She'd thought it would be. Following the high security wall around to her right, she came to another, smaller door. It led to Eamonn's house. He only locked it when he went to bed. She took a deep breath, counted to ten and slipped inside.

Keeping to the shadows and praying that none of the retired greyhounds who lived in his kitchen would hear her, she crept across his lawn and down the side of his house. He was in the kitchen, cooking his supper, talking to the dogs as he moved around. The light from the room threw his tubby shadow across her path and on to the wall. She ducked below the window as she passed into the kennel yard.

There were two kennel-maids in the office. They were listening to the radio and talking. From time to time their chatter was interrupted by a man's voice. Frankie thought he must be one of the assistant trainers. It was their job to take it in turns to watch over the kennels at night.

Tiptoeing across the yard, Frankie managed to reach the first covered row of kennels. Immediately, the nearest dog jumped up. It yelped. So did another. She heard the office door open. The man called out, 'Eamonn? Is that you?'

Frankie didn't answer. She hurried down the aisle between the

358

kennels, searching in each for Blue, desperate to find him before she was discovered. Dogs woke and jumped up and down. They yelped joyfully. There was nothing she could do to prevent them. They didn't understand the need for secrecy.

She had almost reached the end of the first aisle when a figure stepped in front of her, blocking her exit. She darted backwards into the shadows, but the flash of a torch revealed her face.

'Who are you? What do you want?' demanded the man from the office.

She stepped forward. 'Please don't call Eamonn. I don't mean any harm. I came to see Blue.'

'This is a National Greyhound Racing kennel. No one's allowed in without permission. Come on! I'm calling the police.'

'Please listen! Blue was my dog until Jack Broderick took him because I fell behind with my fees.'

'Are you Frankie Tiernay?'

She nodded.

'You still have to leave. I'm sorry.'

'Let me see Blue. Just for a minute. I promise I'll never tell anyone and I won't get you into trouble.'

'I can't. I'd lose my job.'

'I haven't seen my dog for two years. I was only one day late with the payment. Please!'

The young man hesitated. The whole kennels knew the story of Jack Broderick sequestering his girlfriend's dog whilst she was abroad. He couldn't help being sympathetic to Frankie. He loved dogs. He'd be devastated if someone took his dog away. 'One minute. That's all,' he said.

'Oh, thank you. I won't forget this.'

He hurried her into the second aisle, to the larger kennels at the back. 'In here,' he said, unlocking an inner door. 'Quick!'

Blue was lying on a raised bed, covered with his favourite blanket. His legs were draped indolently in the manner she knew so well. He looked up as the door opened, surprised to be disturbed during the night.

'Blue!' Frankie whispered. 'It's me.'

In a huge bound he was off his raised bed and into her arms, yelping and slobbering with excitement. 'Sssh!' she hissed, bending down to him and hugging him. Then she took his face in

359

her hands and gently kissed the top of his sleek head, as she had done when she'd last said goodbye.

'All right! That's enough!' The man hustled her out. 'I have to get back or the girls will come looking for me.' He locked the door and hurried her down the aisle. When they reached the yard, he said, 'You're on your own. If you're caught, don't drop me in it. Please!'

She touched his arm. 'If I can ever help you, I will.'

A voice shouted from the office, 'Daniel! Are you OK?'

'Fine,' he replied.

Frankie waited until he had reached the office, then she slipped across the yard, back through Eamonn's garden to the gate in the wall.

By the time she reached London, it was far too late to telephone Melanie, but they spoke the next morning. 'I should have warned you that Jack was pictured with a girl,' said Melanie.

'Oh, I don't give a damn about her. My only interest is in getting Blue back.'

'Frankie, I'm sure Blue is well looked after.'

'That's not the point. He's my dog. I love him.' Frankie reached across to her jacket and picked one of Blue's steely taupe hairs from it.

Her first step towards divorcing William was to consult David Jarrow. 'It's wonderful to hear from you,' he said when he heard her voice on the telephone. 'Nicoletta and I often talk of you. Where have you been?'

She told him, adding, 'I would have written, but I cut out the past until I could face up to it.'

They went on to talk of William and the evidence she would need to divorce him for cruelty.

Her next step was to list that evidence. Robert and Priscilla would testify. So would Eamonn, if forced to. But none would count as much as the policeman who'd seen her battered face on the day she'd collected Blue. Armed with that date, she went to the police station, fully expecting a long, arduous struggle to find the policeman's name. But fate was kind. He was not only on duty but he remembered her well. 'We don't have many judge's wives with black eyes,' he told her kindly.

That evening, she telephoned Geoffrey Culmstock at his home.

Virginia answered. 'Francesca? Good heavens! You want to speak to Geoffrey! Well, I'll . . . er . . . just see if he's in.'

As she waited, Frankie calculated the odds on the likelihood of Geoffrey coming to the phone, and decided they were seven to three against.

'Francesca!' he boomed down the wire. 'You have a nerve ringing me.'

'Would you have lunch with me, Geoffrey? We'll meet wherever you say.'

'What do you want?'

'Your advice.'

'That's up-front of you.' He hesitated. She could almost hear him thinking. Eventually he continued, 'I'm busy until a week on Friday. Meet me for lunch in Hall. That is, if you have the courage to show your face.'

'I'm a barrister and a member of the Inn. I'll be there.'

Of all the places to meet Geoffrey, Inner Temple Hall would have been Frankie's last choice. There, she ran the risk of meeting William, and she didn't want to confront him yet. But she couldn't argue with Geoffrey. She was surprised he'd even agreed to see her. She wore her one smart black suit, although a side of her longed to shock them all in Las Vegas sequins. But she needed to mirror Geoffrey and the lady barristers he felt comfortable with. It was a lesson she'd learned from Tucson.

The Inn was gloriously familiar. Spring sunshine lay across the green velvet lawns, which were freckled with pale pink blossom. It was magnolia time. Frankie felt the warmth of nostalgia as she walked up the uneven pavement beside Makepeace Buildings, where the branches of the magnolia trees reached through the black iron railings. Barristers hurried past, on their way back from court. Others talked earnestly in twos and threes. Doors inside Makepeace opened and closed. Footsteps hurried up and down the stone stairs. Familiar noises. Familiar sights and smells.

She crossed the top of King's Bench Walk and slipped through the alleyway behind the library. A couple of barristers in the courtyard stared at her in amazement. As she reached the steps up to the Hall, two of them overtook her. One said, with little attempt to lower his voice. 'Good heavens! You know who that is? Eastgate's wife!'

Frankie flushed and hurried up the steps.

Geoffrey was seated at the far end of the Hall, his huge bulk eased into a corner, his large red face bent to examine a large, juicy steak. She knew he'd chosen that table on purpose, to make her run the gauntlet of the whispers and the stares. She took a few steps forward. Eyes swivelled in her direction. To her relief, there was no sign of William. She took another step. Voices fell silent. She clenched her fists. Then, slowly, she relaxed them, as she had learned to do in front of Death's Grandma's, and sashayed across the floor towards Geoffrey, giving them all her fuck-you stare, as though she'd just won the entire Inner Temple in a game of poker.

Geoffrey didn't stand up, as if to emphasise his opinion of her. 'I'd have thought I'd be the last person you'd turn to,' he launched in, omitting any greeting or pleasantries.

'You're the best head of chambers. And you don't like me, so you'll tell me the worst, not some story you think I want to hear.' With one graceful movement, she pulled out her chair, sat down and ordered a salad and a glass of mineral water: she could have done with a glass of wine but she needed her wits.

'Well, that's honest.' Geoffrey looked at her with grudging admiration. 'I respect William. He was a brilliant barrister. He's now an excellent judge. He's also a cold fish and a snob. No one blames you for leaving him, it was how you did it. He didn't deserve to be made a fool of. Twice!'

'Are you sure you know the facts, Geoffrey?' she asked. 'Shouldn't you consider the evidence and not listen to hearsay?'

'What are you talking about?'

'William beat me up and raped me. He hit me so hard that I couldn't attend an interview. I may have run off with Jack Broderick the first time, but the second time I ran because I was scared of William. I didn't go off with anyone, drugged or otherwise, and I certainly haven't been drying out in a clinic. I ran to escape another vicious beating. If you don't believe that William mistreated me, ask Sanjiv if he didn't find me sleeping on the floor of chambers one morning. Ask my brother what happened when he telephoned from Dallas. How I was crying for help. Ask Eamonn O'Donnell, dog-trainer, what my face was like after William had worked me over.'

Geoffrey was shocked. He ate in silence, frowning, his big jowls munching over his steak. 'Melanie told me that William wasn't the saint towards you that he appeared in public,' he said eventually. 'But I still don't understand what you want from me.'

'Your advice. I plan to divorce William for cruelty.'

'What's wrong with a two-year separation?'

'Why should I let him get away with it? Don't tell me I should because he's a High Court judge.'

Geoffrey sat back, wiped his fleshy mouth with his napkin, and pushed his plate to one side. He studied Francesca's sensuous glamour, her full red lips and her golden suntan enhanced by the white silk of her camisole, and was certain she'd found herself a rich lover. Or several. Not that it was any of his business. But he couldn't help being disturbed by her, and by her story. He didn't like William and never had. He'd never felt close to Francesca either. He'd found her too reserved. Virginia had thought them marvellous. That was because they were attractive, and she liked decorative guests. He didn't think his wife would like this new Francesca. She was a bit too decorative.

Frankie's mind was racing, although her face showed none of it: her hands on the table were relaxed, her fingers unclenched. All these months she'd planned to make William suffer. Now she assessed the odds and saw they had changed. To drag William through the mud would ruin her own chances of a chambers in the Inn. She'd cut off his nose, but spite her own face. She remembered Jack saying how he refused to allow the past to ruin the present. There were other kinds of victory, just as conclusive but more subtle. As she sat, outwardly calm, in front of Geoffrey, she listed her options and worked out her strategy, just as though she were playing in a high-stakes game. For these were high stakes, the very highest. 'There's something else,' she said. 'I want to practise law again. I want to return to the Inn. No, don't panic, I'm not asking for a place in chambers. I'd like to set up on my own, to specialise in cases of child injury, particularly medical negligence.'

Geoffrey exploded. 'You don't stand a chance in hell. The Inn wouldn't give you premises, and certainly not if you wash William's dirty linen in public. We protect our own, or have you forgotten?'

'No, I haven't. That's why William should take note.'

He pushed back his chair and stood up. 'Are you threatening to blackmail the Inn?'

'Not the Inn, Geoffrey. I love this place. I was proud to be a member. I still am.' Her face softened. 'I'd forgotten how much I loved the Inn until this morning when I walked through the mellow courtyards where all those ancient, legal feet have trodden, then up past Makepeace Buildings, beside the magnolia trees. Whenever I think of the Inn, I think of it in magnolia time. No, Geoffrey, I'm talking about William. So long as he's bad-mouthing me to the Inn, I'll never be able to rent rooms. I'm not asking for favours. But I might change my mind about the messy public divorce if William agrees to publicly retract the lies he's told about me and to promise never to impede my career.'

'If you drag him through a messy divorce, you certainly won't get rooms.'

'Exactly. So unless he agrees, I have nothing to lose. And there's nothing so dangerous as an opponent who has nothing to lose.'

Geoffrey couldn't believe this was the same reserved, madonna-like Francesca Eastgate, his hostess at numerous rather-too-formal dinner parties in Islington. Without saying goodbye, he turned and marched down the full length of the Hall to the exit, where he bulldozed his way through the crowd around the door. Frankie followed. Again she heard the whispers. At one table she saw Rupert and Charlotte, their heads huddled together. At another she saw Simon. He was on the far side, with his back to the panelled wall. Their eyes met. She looked away.

'Hello, Frankie.' He spoke loudly and clearly. 'It's good to see you back.'

She stopped. 'Thank . . . thank you.' She smiled. 'Thank you, Simon.'

She was still reeling from the surprising warmth in Simon's words as she went down the steps and into the courtyard. To her amazement, she found Geoffrey waiting for her. 'It took courage to come here today,' he said gruffly. 'You knew I didn't want to meet you. But you came into the lions' den! I admire you for that. And I respect your ability to reason. Desire for revenge can bring a life sentence, not to the aggressor but to the aggrieved. You were a good barrister once, Francesca, but you lacked compassion and understanding. You'd make an exceptional barrister now.'

Frankie held out her hand. 'That's the best compliment you could have given me, Geoffrey.'

He took her hand in both his, covering it completely. 'Goodbye, Francesca.'

'Will I hear from you?'

'I'll think about it.' He walked off towards Makepeace Buildings.

Frankie went in the opposite direction. She ran up the alleyway to Fleet Street, to the first public telephone she could find. From there she called Melanie. 'I was wrong about Simon,' she confessed. 'He's the nicest man alive. He stood up for me in public.'

Thirty-Nine

Simon and Melanie agreed that Frankie was wise to forgo her public revenge in exchange for William's retraction and future silence. They discussed the matter at length over supper that evening. 'You must have something in writing,' said Melanie, dipping slivers of raw fennel in the remains of the salad vinaigrette. 'William's very powerful. There are so many subtle ways he could harm your career at some later date.'

Simon looked horrified. 'Darling! William wouldn't go back on his word.'

Frankie and Melanie exchanged glances. 'Being a judge didn't stop him beating me up,' Frankie pointed out.

'I know. I'm being idealistic. But I always wanted to be a barrister. I thought of them as being . . . oh, not perfect at all . . . but at least knowing the difference between right and wrong. Otherwise we're no better than the criminals we prosecute or defend.'

Frankie thought of Jack growing up on the streets and of William, moneyed and educated. In spite of everything, Jack had a raw, inherent morality. He'd stolen for *himself*, he'd killed the man who'd grassed on *him*. But he wouldn't take money to defend causes he didn't believe in or people he didn't like. 'We are no better,' she said. 'But we've had finer opportunities.' She remembered the fifty dollars. 'And less desperation.'

Over Brie and grapes, they calculated the expense of Frankie setting up in chambers on her own. 'I know it would be tough,' she said. 'I'd have to have at least two rooms, one for me and one for a clerk. I'd have to persuade solicitors to give me work, without touting! I might go weeks before my first brief. But it's what I want to do.'

'Geoffrey must believe in you.' Simon reached for a second slice of Brie. 'Ummm. This cheese is delicious.'

'Frankie bought it from that place in Jermyn Street.'

'Paxton & Whitfield.' He took a third slice. 'Where were we?

366

Oh, yes. Geoffrey might put up some of the money. He makes near on half a million a year. That's why he turned down becoming a judge. He told the Lord Chancellor that he couldn't afford the wage-cut – or so rumour has it.'

'I don't want to borrow money,' said Frankie. 'If I go it alone, it must be all mine. And Mel's too, if she decides to come in with me. But for the time being, it would be just me. My decisions and my responsibility. My success or my failure.'

Melanie fetched the coffee from the kitchen. 'You could practise from home, once they change the Bar rules,' she shouted through the hatch.

'No. I want to be in the Inn. I love the atmosphere. In any case, I'd still have to buy a house and hire a clerk and secretary.'

Melanie returned to the dining room. 'Paid for by poker, I suppose. Simon, we have to stop her. She's going to lose everything.'

'You must be very good!' Simon winked at Frankie. 'I used to play at university. You must take me with you one night.'

Melanie puffed up like a threated hedgehog. 'You're not risking our money! We have Rachel to consider. Frankie, you're not to take him.'

Simon reached across and squeezed her hand. 'It's all right, darling. I'm teasing.'

It was late when Frankie left Simon and Melanie. At least, late by their standards. She went straight to The Hertford. Several hours later, as she was leaving the poker room, Claud, her favourite among the poker-room managers, handed her a big, glossy Binion's brochure. On the cover was a picture of Benny Binion, grinning out from under his giant stetson. 'World Series of Poker,' said Claud. 'No Limit Texas Hold 'em. You should enter.'

'Not when the buy-in is ten thousand dollars. I'm saving for my future.'

'Poker players don't save.'

She smiled. 'This one does, now.'

'You can enter via satellite. We'll be holding a couple of games here next month. The buy-in is a thousand dollars. That's about six hundred and fifty pounds at today's rate. Ten players per table. Winner takes all. Hey presto, you have your ten thousand dollars.'

Frankie flicked open the brochure and smiled at her memories of Vegas, that Glitter Gulch in the desert. On the first page was a picture of Johnny Chan, nicknamed the 'Oriental Express', last year's winner, and two-times champion. 'I wouldn't stand a chance against a player like that,' she told Claud.

'They don't only pay the winner. Prizes are on a sliding scale, down to number thirty-six.'

'You have to be good even to get in the top hundred.'

'You are good.'

'Not that good! And don't flatter me that I am.' She hesitated. Then she laughed. 'What the hell! I'm up a thousand tonight. Vegas would be fun.' She took a roll of notes from her jacket pocket and peeled off seven hundred. 'Here's my satellite buy-in. No, Claud, keep the change. I'm feeling lucky.'

Frankie didn't discuss her entry into the World Series with anyone. Poker was her secret life. In it, she became the Frankie Tiernay who stuffed a roll of notes into her pocket and went out at a time when most people were going home to bed. She was a player who could bet a thousand pounds without flinching. Who could win or lose, and not show her loss except to herself. She was a woman who needed no one. Who had no fear, except of being afraid.

To explain a possible absence from London, she mentioned to Melanie and to Steven that she might go to Paris for a week, to meet some American friends. She didn't like to tell a lie but the alternative was to worry them.

She heard nothing from Geoffrey. Her hopes began to fade. Perhaps she'd misread him, and he'd never intended to help her. She bought an answering machine so as not to miss his call if she were with Melanie or down at White Oast or at The Hertford. But there was no message. When she wasn't out, she wrote long letters to Miss Tomasina, Loretta, and Robert and Priscilla. She continued to play poker every couple of nights, but it alone could no longer satisfy her. She needed other challenges. She craved a sense of purpose.

She was composing a letter to Jack, demanding access to Blue, when Geoffrey telephoned. It was three weeks since they'd met. 'Lunch with me tomorrow,' he said. 'It must be near the Inn. You choose the venue.'

'What's wrong with the Hall?'

'Brave lady!'

Again he made her run the gauntlet to his table at the far end of the room. 'We should be meeting William at two o'clock in my chambers,' he told her as she sat down. 'Isn't that what you wanted me to do, Francesca? To witness your agreement with him.'

'Yes. Of course, Thank you.' She smiled serenely, but her heart was thudding in her ears.

The waiter took their order. Geoffrey had steak and kidney pie. She asked for a salad. When it arrived, she could barely face a single lettuce leaf, but she forced herself to eat.

Geoffrey tucked his napkin under his chin and ate his pie with gusto. He didn't speak again until he'd finished. Then he pushed his plate aside. 'I read that article about Broderick in the Sunday papers,' he said, almost as though he wanted to shake her. 'I take my hat off to him. I came up the hard way. I know how difficult it is, even without a prison record. Do you still see him?'

'That all ended when I returned to William.' She laid down her fork. 'You haven't told me how you persuaded him to meet me.'

'He may not turn up.' Geoffrey reached for his pudding, an extra-large helping of apple crumble doused in hot custard. 'I merely hinted that you planned to divorce him on grounds of cruelty and had a witness to a beating, but I thought you might be persuaded to back off. Naturally, he denied having touched you. But now he's had a week to think about it, if he's guilty he'll want to buy your silence.'

'And if he doesn't come?'

'Either you've told a pack of lies or we have a psychopath as a High Court judge.' He carried on eating, relishing his pudding.

They left the Hall with five minutes to spare. Frankie followed him out. This time she was too nervous to notice if anyone was whispering about her. Her knees knocked as they crossed the courtyard and walked down the alley. It seemed strange to return to chambers at Geoffrey's side when he had helped to force her out. Not that she bore him ill-feeling any more. On the contrary, she liked him better than she ever had. She only wished he had a nicer wife. As they approached the shiny black street door, she couldn't help glancing up at the board beside it. Her name had been removed long ago, but it was still a shock not to see it there.

Geoffrey went up the stairs ahead of her. 'How's your poker?' he asked.

She stopped dead. 'How do you know I play?'

'You won five thousand pounds from an eminent member of the judiciary. He was outraged.'

'Oh, that surly man. I thought he was familiar but I didn't realise he knew who I was.'

'He did. He came storming up to chambers to tell me.'

Frankie threw back her head and laughed out loud, her throaty, raunchy laugh. She was still laughing when they entered the reception. Nailbag looked up from his desk in astonishment. Rupert and Charlotte, near the mailboxes, gaped. Hugo, pouring his coffee, sloshed it on to the floor. Only Sanjiv, who was leaving for court, gave her a broad wink.

'Hello,' said Frankie, smiling brightly as she followed Geoffrey to his room.

'That's set them all twittering,' he said, closing the door.

She took a seat opposite his desk. 'Do you mind?'

'I'm only sorry I can't help you more. I like a fighter.'

'Geoffrey, you have helped merely by being seen with me in Hall and here.'

The clock in the corner of his office stood at one minute to two. Frankie watched the hand move round. In a minute, William would walk in: the man who'd hit her, the man who'd raped her. Would she feel anything for him? Fear. Sorrow. Nostalgia. Hate. The clock hands moved on to the hour. She took a deep breath to calm her nerves, and listened for William's footsteps. The minute hand moved on. She swallowed hard. It went round again. And again. Five minutes passed. She looked at Geoffrey. He shrugged.

'I promise you that he hit me,' she said, choking with anger and frustration. 'I didn't make it up.' She stood up. 'What can I do to convince you?' As she pushed back her chair to leave, the door opened and William stepped inside.

He'd put on weight. That was the first thing Frankie noticed. He'd always prided himself on being slim and straight and fastidiously dressed. Now he was paunchy. It made him look unhealthy and brutish. His hair had turned completely grey. It was very flat on top from being squashed by his judge's wig. His pale eyes flitted around the room as though expecting someone else. 'What's all this rubbish you've been telling Geoffrey?' he demanded.

'She's told me the truth, William,' said Geoffrey.

'Where's the so-called witness?'

'Her brother confirms that he telephoned when you were attacking her.'

'She could have made up any story. He couldn't see down the telephone wires.'

'Her dog's trainer saw her face.'

'A man who trains greyhounds for criminals! Who's going to believe his word against mine?' He looked at Geoffrey with contempt. 'I told you she was a liar. I'm surprised you fell for it. Cruelty has to be substantiated by a doctor's report or an independent witness.'

'Or a policeman?' asked Frankie, wondering how she could ever have loved this man.

'A policeman. Of course. That goes without saying.'

'You should have remembered that before you let Blue into the street,' she said, with unrestrained triumph. 'I had to collect him from the police station. The policeman saw my face.'

William hesitated. Then he saw that Geoffrey was equally surprised by this information. 'That was two years ago,' he said. 'He'll have forgotten, unless you registered a complaint.' He gave a mocking laugh. 'And I know you didn't or I'd have heard about it.'

'You're wrong. I've seen the policeman. He remembers me well. They don't get many judge's wives with black eyes and split lips. His statement will count as evidence.'

'Unless I agree to retract what I've said about you and never to impede your career?'

'Exactly.' She couldn't stop herself from smiling. Everything was going her way. She'd get her chambers. She'd come back to the Inn. She'd never be afraid of William again. 'And I want it in writing,' she added. 'Witnessed by Geoffrey.'

William looked from her to Geoffrey. 'I'll never agree to any such thing,' he said, and walked out of the room.

Frankie was stunned. She turned to Geoffrey, who shook his big head. 'Why the hell didn't you tell me about the policeman?' he demanded.

'I didn't want to play my best card first.'

'Francesca, I can't help you if you don't trust me. William

371

realised I knew nothing of this witness. He jumped into the breach. You're a bloody fool. We could have had him.'

Crestfallen, she reached for her bag. 'I'm sorry. It was stupid of me.'

'You're right. It's been a waste of my time.'

'Then I mustn't take up any more of it.' She rose. 'Thanks for trying for me, Geoffrey. I'm sorry I blew it.' She went out as fast as she could. She didn't want anyone to see her disappointment.

The World Series satellite game at The Hertford took place on the following Saturday. After her blunder over William, Frankie was in no frame of mind to play, but to pull out would mean forfeiting her buy-in. In an attempt to give herself more confidence, she wore her punchiest outfit; her stretchy black skirt and glitzy satin jacket.

Some thirty players were milling around the poker room at The Hertford, trying to look unconcerned. Frankie was surprised to see Damascus Joe among them. He greeted her like a long-lost friend. 'You're beautiful,' he told her, kissing her on both cheeks, his pupils even more dilated than usual.

She remembered that in a fit of pique she'd considered having sex with him, just to annoy Scott. No wonder she made such a quagmire of life. 'Let's hope the cards are beautiful,' she said, collecting her buy-in from the cashier.

'We've missed you in Las Vegas, Frankie.'

'Thanks.' She didn't want to talk. She preferred to psych herself up in silence.

'I saw Scott last week in Reno.'

He was trying to throw her concentration. It was all part of the game. 'You must tell me.' She smiled sweetly. 'Later!'

He grinned. She'd been right.

Once the players were all present, Claud drew their names out of a hat, dividing them into tables of ten. Damascus Joe was on the second table. Frankie was called to the third. On her right was a tiny Scotsman known as Wee Free. On her left was a tight-lipped banker called Sebastian. She'd played him before and won. Opposite was Dilys, the spiky redhead, the only other woman in the satellite. Next to Dilys was Tubby, a second-hand car dealer from South London. There were five other men, all of whom Frankie knew by sight.

She told herself she wasn't nervous, although of course she was. The World Series was the biggest tournament. Her first hand gave her a two and an eight, unsuited. She folded. Wee Free won. The second hand gave her a pair of nines. She went all the way to Fifth Street, to be beaten by Sebastian with a pair of tens. On the next hand, she played too carefully. She won, but the pot was small. A couple of good hands gave her more pots. Her play became more aggressive. Slowly, her stack increased.

Tubby was the first to be knocked out. After three hours, five other players had joined him. Wee Free, Sebastian, Frankie and Dilys were the only ones left. The chips were evenly distributed. They had around fifteen hundred pounds each.

It was Frankie's turn to put up the blind. She pushed forward the minimum, a hundred. She was dealt a pair of jacks. Wee Free called the bet. Sebastian raised to two hundred. Dilys hesitated, then equalled. Frankie was forced to match or fold. She matched. She caught another jack on the Flop. Now she had three of a kind. She bet eight hundred. They all called. Fourth Street produced an ace. The muscles of her stomach tensed with nerves. If any player held a pair of aces, she was beaten.

Wee Free went all in. Sebastian hesitated, then matched. Dilys pushed her chips forward. Frankie puzzled about what they could possibly hold to make them so confident. Did someone have two aces? She hesitated, her fingers lying casually on the table. Then she took a deep breath and bet her whole stack. The others had to match her. They went all in.

Fifth Street turned up another ace. This was a disaster. Anyone who held a pair would now have four of a kind. Because no one had any chips left, there were no more rounds of betting. Frankie had paid to see them. Sebastian laid his cards face up on the table: he had a pair of kings. Dilys shook her head and passed her hand face-down to the dealer. Frankie waited for Wee Free. She was convinced he held the two aces. She steeled herself to lose the game. Wee Free hesitated, then very slowly he pushed his cards across the table to the dealer. He'd been bluffing.

With a triumphant flourish, Frankie turned up her hand. She held a full house: three jacks and two aces. She'd won her satellite. She had her ten thousand dollars entry to the World Championship. She wanted to jump up and down with excitement, but she didn't. That wasn't done in poker circles.

The other players shook her by the hand. They did their best to look pleased for her, but her victory meant their defeat. Claud hurried over to congratulate her. Across the room, Damascus Joe gave her a thumbs-up. He too had won his game. The railbirds discussed her strategy and wished her luck in Las Vegas. Stacking the six thousand pounds in chips into turrets on the table, Frankie casually riffled two stacks into one. As she did so, she glanced up at the spectators along the rail. Then her smile froze. Watching her with a mixture of disbelief and admiration was Jack Broderick.

They stared at each other, not speaking, not moving. He was alone and wearing a dinner jacket, as he had done at gala nights in Richmond. She had no idea what he was doing at The Hertford, or how long he'd been watching her, but the more they looked at each other, the more she felt the old magnetism return. The electricity, the frisson, the challenge. And the laughter. She forgot that this was the man who'd taken Blue from her, the man for whom she'd felt nothing but dislike. He forgot the hurt when she'd returned to William, the times he'd sworn he'd never forgive her, the times he'd wanted to kill her. She smiled, not her tough, poker-player smile, but her own funny, vulnerable smile. He took a step towards her. She rose to meet him.

At that moment, a girl appeared in the entrance to the poker room. She was blonde and handsome, with a long, haughty face. Frankie recognised her from the newspaper. 'Jack,' she called, 'aren't you coming?'

He didn't answer her.

'We're all waiting for you downstairs.'

His eyes held Frankie's. He hesitated, then turned away.

Frankie slumped back on to her chair as Jack walked out of her life with another woman.

Forty

The heat haze and the screech of slot machines hit Frankie as she landed at McCarran airport. The flight had been full of journalists in town to cover the championships, fat tourists in Bermuda shorts, and solitary pale-faced men carrying little luggage but a change of clothes and their money. They were professional poker players, the modern gunslinger. For the first time since Frankie had seen Jack, her dark mood lifted. It felt good to be back.

Binion's was packed. People fought to get in from the scorching sidewalks. There were journalists, cameramen, television crews, tourists, spectators and players, all fighting to see the action. The events had been taking place for some weeks: Seven Card Stud, Omaha, Deuce to Seven Draw. But the No Limit Texas Hold'em, with a $10,000 buy-in was the big one, the championship.

The hotel staff greeted her like a long-lost friend. The doormen said they'd missed her. The cocktail waitresses waved. The receptionist smiled and said, 'We've given you your old room. We thought it might bring you luck.'

'Thanks. I'll need it.' Frankie signed the register. 'Many people I know around?'

'Just about everyone.'

'Scott here?'

'He's not staying at Binion's. He checked out right after you left.' The girl lowered her voice. 'I guess he was kinda cut up. Not that it's your fault. These things happen. It's life.'

Frankie slipped her twenty dollars. 'Thanks for telling me. If you see him around, I'd like to know.'

She registered her ten thousand dollars with the tournament cashier, then took the lift to the fifth floor. Her room welcomed her like an old friend. She unpacked, showered, and stretched out on the bed, watching the light on the familiar mountains turn from white to yellow to red. It had been a long journey. The

375

tournament began in thirty hours. She needed rest. But although she closed her eyes, sleep would not come.

She thought of Jack. She didn't want to, but he crept into her mind now, as he had done continuously since she'd seen him at The Hertford. She wondered if he'd thought about her. Once, she'd have known. They'd had telepathy. Now it was gone. She wished the magnetism had gone too. She could still see him as he walked away from her to the girl with the horsy face. A girl whose features spoke of money, breeding and respectability. Everything Jack had once mocked. A girl who reminded Frankie of the convent girls to whom she'd lied about her own father. Frankie wished she hadn't seen Jack in the casino. It had been so much easier when she thought she was indifferent.

In the morning, she telephoned Loretta, who shrieked with pleasure 'Come on over. Right away! I'm dying to see you.'

Half an hour later, Frankie was being embraced by the plump, red-headed motel-owner. 'I brought you a present,' she said, producing a large illustrated book about the Princess of Wales. 'I hope she's still your fairy tale.'

Loretta stroked the glossy cover. 'I need her more than ever now.'

'How's Prentice?'

'Not good. Come and see him. He knows you're here.' She ushered Frankie into the sitting room and laid a protective hand on her husband's hunched shoulder. 'Prentice, honey, Frankie's come back from England.'

Frankie tried not to show her shock, but Prentice had deteriorated further than she thought possible in a living person. Only his eyes moved, flitting backwards and forwards, as if the life lost from the rest of his body had concentrated in them the same way that the blind hear more acutely than the sighted.

They talked in the air-conditioned sitting-room, sitting close to Prentice so as to include him in their conversation, although he could no longer speak. Frankie described how she'd won her satellite and they discussed her chances in the World Series.

'We'll be watching on the TV,' said Loretta.

'I just hope I'm not the first to be knocked out. That would be so humiliating.' Frankie grinned nervously. 'Oh, I wanted to ask you about Scott. He's not at Binion's and I checked his name on the tournament board, but he's not down yet.'

376

'He lives two blocks away, in one of the motels. He wanted to rent your old room, but the buildings are still leased.' Loretta smiled. 'We see a lot of him. He's a nice boy. The kid brother I never had. You haven't come back because of Scott, have you?'

'No, but I was very fond of him and I'd like to see him.'

'I'll ask him to call you.'

'You don't think I could drop by his place?'

Loretta shook her head. 'He was so cut up when you left. I explained that you'd tried to find him, but it made no difference. He told me about his mother, how she'd walked out without saying goodbye. He's kinda come to terms with losing you. It's only fair to let him decide if he wants to see you again.'

The press tournament was in progress when Frankie returned to Binion's. All the journalists covering the championships pitted their prowess against each other. She watched from the rails. Later, she checked at the reception to see if Scott had called. He hadn't. She returned to the poker room but she couldn't concentrate. She was restless. She kept looking for Scott amongst the crowd, and wondering if Jack was in love with the horsy girl, and if she, herself, would be knocked out tomorrow in the first hour. Finally, she gave up watching and took the lift upstairs. In the corridor she passed Sauerkraut, the big, blond, surly German. He ignored her.

Frankie woke at dawn shivering with apprehension at the prospect of playing in the tournament. She rose, showered, dressed, ordered breakfast, then didn't eat it. Instead, she drank black coffee and paced the room, clenching and unclenching her fists against a background of Las Vegas television news. Coverage alternated between the poker championships, student riots in Tiananmen Square, and a drug-related murder in North Vegas.

Nerves and air conditioning made her cold. She slipped on a jacket over her silk camisole. She rolled up the cuffs, rolled them down again, then rolled them back up. She changed her yellow culottes for white trousers, then changed back again. She plaited her hair and put on a little make-up. She drank more black coffee. Finally, she could bear it no longer. She left her room and took the lift down to the casino. As soon as she stepped into the mêlée, she felt better, punchier.

There were a hundred and seventy-eight entrants for the No Limit Texas Hold'em that year. The first prize was eight hundred and forty-four thousand dollars, the second was three hundred and thirty-seven thousand, six hundred. The remainder of the prize money was graduated down until the thirty-sixth player, who merely covered his buy-in. The unluckiest player was the thirty-seventh, who survived the longest of the players to get nothing.

Scott still wasn't listed amongst the tournament players, nor was there any sign of him in the crowd, although Frankie recognised other faces. Damascus Joe, winner of his London satellite, gave her his neat smile. Death's Grandma and Oil Slick Dick waved to her. Dick was wearing a new, clean shirt for the occasion. Al Capone was near the rail, in a new white stetson and his usual dark glasses. He grinned when he saw Frankie. Even the little Fanman, his portable fan clutched to his chest, waved cheerfully to her.

A hand landed on Frankie's shoulder. She turned, expecting Scott. It was Grizzly. He, too, was looking smart. 'I heard you won your satellite,' he said. 'It's good to see ya back. Ah've missed your pretty face. There aren't too many like you around the tables.'

She smiled. 'Thanks. It's good to be back. I'd forgotten how friendly Las Vegas is.'

The organisers drew the names of the players out of a blackjack shoe, seating them randomly at tables of nine. To her horror, Frankie found herself on the same table as Death's Grandma and Grizzly. Some demon chance had drawn her against two people who habitually beat her. The satellite had been a shoot-out: they'd played until one person on each table held all the chips. The early stage of the tournament was a freeze-out – tables were combined as players fell by the wayside and seats became vacant.

When everyone was seated, Jack Binion, Benny Binion's son, called for quiet and read out the names of all the contestants. Each player rose, nodded and sat down again. The big names and the local boys were cheered wildly by the railbirds, and the TV cameras moved in for close-ups. Eventually, Frankie heard, 'Frankie Tiernay, London, England. She looks sweet but she's gotta lotta heart.' She stood up, smiling. There were whistles and catcalls. She blushed and sat down.

It seemed an eternity before the game began. The other players joked of bad beats and being on tilt. Frankie started to clench her fists, then noticed Grandma was watching her. So she stopped and drummed her fingers to release the tension. Then forced herself to keep them still. At last, the dealer took his place. The chatter fell away. Frankie tried to tell herself that the tournament was just another poker game.

But it was different. There was no second chance. Once her ten thousand dollars had gone, she'd be out. And there was no limit to the betting, except the size of a player's stack. For the first two hours, the blinds were $25–$50. Frankie had to bet aggressively on a good hand to make up for the trash ones. She kept getting garbage. Within an hour, fifteen players had been eliminated. The first to go was from her table. He slunk away. She felt very sorry for him. Another hour, and the blinds doubled. The field was down by thirty. Three tables were broken up to fill the vacant seats. On Frankie's table, Grizzly was in the lead. He kept raising. She felt sure he was bluffing, but her cards were so bad she couldn't afford to challenge.

After six hours, of the original table only Frankie, Grizzly and Grandma remained. The rest came from elsewhere. The blind was now $100–$200. Grizzly had thirty thousand dollars. So did Grandma. Frankie's stack was the lowest: five thousand, and decreasing with every round. At last she was dealt a reasonable hand, a ten and a jack, both diamonds. Grandma put up the blind, $200. The other players matched. Frankie frowned and hesitated, as though she was holding rubbish. Then, with a sigh, she matched and raised. Three players folded. But not Grandma or Grizzly. The Flop produced the four and six of diamonds and seven of spades. Frankie cursed in silence. There was a good chance someone held a straight. Grandma bet. So did Grizzly. So did the remaining three newcomers. Again, Frankie hesitated, long enough to look as though she might fold. Then she called, and raised another five, hoping to scare them out of the game. But they stuck with her.

Fourth Street produced a ten of clubs. Now Frankie had a pair with a high kicker, but that wouldn't beat a straight. The newcomers folded. But not Grandma or Grizzly. Frankie was too far in to fold. She'd had the smallest stack on the table, and much of it was now in the pot. She bet. Fifth Street gave her no help.

Sweat dripped down her back. She felt sick with disappointment. She looked at Grandma, who gave her the nearest thing to a smile. She glanced down at her cards. Then, deliberately, she clenched and unclenched her fists. Grandma saw her. So did Grizzly. They hesitated. The railbirds sensed the tension. They craned forward. Frankie held her breath as Grandma folded. Then Grizzly. She'd won. She didn't have to show her cards. She'd bluffed them with a reverse tell.

She was pink with excitement as the dealer scooped the pot in her direction. Her hands shook as she stacked the special tournament chips in neat turrets. They were still shaking as she cupped them around her cards at the start of the next round. She had to force herself to concentrate. But winning gave her confidence. On the following hand, she bluffed all the way without even a pair. She won that pot. And the next. Twenty minutes later, Jack Binion announced the end of play. It was a gruelling eight hours since they'd started. Of the hundred and seventy-eight entrants, half had been eliminated. But not Frankie.

Laughing with relief and elation, she reeled across the poker room, thanking strangers for their congratulations. Grandma and Grizzly were also through. So was Oil Slick Dick. He was calling for champagne. Damascus Joe was out. He was crushed by disappointment. Frankie sympathised. She'd have felt that way too.

She intended to go to bed early, but it was long after midnight by the time she staggered up to her room, still buzzing from her triumph. Forgetting she'd told Melanie she was going to Paris, she dialled her number.

'You're where? You've done what?' Melanie gasped. 'Oh, my God! I'm going to book you into Gamblers Anonymous.

She telephoned Loretta, who shrieked with joy.

She called Miss Tomasina, who gave a tinkling laugh of appreciation.

She rang up Robert, who was for once speechless.

She telephoned Geoffrey, who chuckled his congratulations. 'You might have some other good news soon,' he said.

'William's agreed?'

'Not yet. But he's touched on the subject.'

'Geoffrey, I don't know how to thank you.'

'Come back to the Bar. That'll be enough for me. But a word of warning, if you want to return to the law you'll have to cut back on the poker, or at least play in private games. Three nights a week in a casino is too public.'

She laughed. 'Don't worry, Geoffrey, I'll stick to Scrabble when I play against members of the judiciary.'

She ordered up a bottle of champagne and drank half of it. Sitting on her bed, she cradled the telephone, hesitating. She started to tap out the code for England. Then she stopped and replaced the receiver. A few minutes later, she picked it up again. This time she went to the penultimate digit of Jack's number before stopping.

On the second day of the tournament, they had to continue until only twenty-seven players were left. At noon, Frankie was seated at her table. This time she'd been drawn with different players. Not nearly as nervous as yesterday, she joked and laughed with the other players, informing them that the bright red of her catsuit was her lucky colour. Nearby, and luckily not at her table, she could see big names like Johnny Chan, 'the Oriental Express', with his famous lucky orange in front of him; bearded Don Zewin, dressed in black; a new face, a lanky college drop-out called Phil Hellmuth Junior; and a big Irishman whose voice reminded her of her father. She wished her father could see her now, playing poker against the champions. He'd have been speechless with pride.

The dealers took their places. The railbirds jostled for position. Suddenly, Frankie was so jittery that she could barely cup her cards on the table. Her first hand was a four and an eight, suited. She folded. Of course, she should have called the bet, but her nerves were shot. Her second hand was rubbish. So was her third. She went a whole round without playing a hand. Again, it was her turn to put up the blind. She pushed forward the minimum, $200. Immediately it was raised to $400. She had to equal, or lose her money. She matched and went to Fourth Street, then lost her courage and folded. On the following hand, she held a pair of sevens, but a large, bald man opposite, whose head shone like a cathedral dome, raised to the maximum, so she folded again. He went on to win with a pair of sixes. She cursed herself for folding. Her stack was being drained by trash hands and bad nerves. At this rate she'd be first out of the game.

With her next good hand, a pair of tens, she bet aggressively. Fourth Street produced an ace. Dome-head bet hard. She reckoned he was bluffing: he'd done so last time. She went all the way to the end, only to find he held three aces. He scooped the pot, which included two thousand dollars of Frankie's money.

Two hours into play, a man at the far end went all in on a straight, but lost to a flush. He was out of the tournament. At least she wouldn't be the first to go. The next hand killed off two more. A table behind her broke up. Three players from there joined her table. They each had twenty thousand dollars in their stacks. She had less than ten.

Two hours later, she was down to three thousand when she was dealt a pair of jacks, her winning hand in the satellite. Frankie was last to play, the best position. She kept her face blank and her eyes down so as to reveal nothing. Three players folded. Frankie raised by three hundred. The remaining players matched. There were six now in the hand. The Flop produced another pair of jacks, one of which was a club, and a seven of clubs. That gave her four jacks. From the cards on the table, no one could beat her. She began to sweat with excitement. The catsuit stuck to her back. The first player checked. So did the next three. Dome-head frowned, hesitated, then bet the minimum. Frankie wasn't sure if he was trying to sucker her along by pretending he had a moderate hand. Whatever he held, she was practically undefeatable, but she didn't want to go to Fourth and Fifth Streets, giving him a chance to improve his hand. She bet hard. If he held trash, he'd fold and she'd win the pot. The other players folded. But to her surprise, Dome-head equalled without hesitation.

She tried to calculate what he held to give him such confidence. It had to be a flush or a straight. Beneath her plaited hair, her scalp itched. But she didn't scratch it. That might show him she was worried. The railbirds sensed the tension. They craned towards her table. Fourth Street was a ten of hearts. Dome-head bet to the maximum. Now she felt sure he held a straight. He'd be in for a nasty surprise when he saw her hand. She raised. He matched. Fifth Street was an eight of clubs. Again he bet to the maximum. She raised. He equalled and raised again. She couldn't believe it. However high his straight was, it couldn't touch her jacks. He must realise she had a good hand. Or maybe he thought she was bluffing, as he had done. To stay in the hand, she had to match him. The pot was now nearly ten thousand dollars. It would give her the break she needed. But to equal, she had to go all in. On four jacks, it was worth it. She pushed forward her chips to see him.

Dome-head turned over his cards. There was a gasp from the rail. Frankie stared in disbelief. She'd been so exhilarated by her four precious jacks that she'd failed to notice the potential connecting clubs. He held the nine and ten of clubs. The last card on the table, the eight, had given him victory. Until that moment, she'd been winning.

'Straight flush beats four jacks,' said the dealer. He gave Frankie a sympathetic shrug and scooped the chips towards her opponent.

She'd lost. She was out of the tournament. She'd been beaten by an outdraw – by the last card, the worst kind of defeat. She rose and staggered through the crowd, who muttered brief sympathy. No more. If she couldn't face losing, she'd no business to be playing poker.

The slot machines swallowed her up with their screeching and flashing lights. She pushed her way down the aisle, elbowing tourists out of the way, heading for the lift, and solitude. Someone said, 'Bad luck, Frankie.'

She shrugged. Tomorrow she'd feel better. Today she felt like hell.

When the lift arrived she stepped inside, thumped the fifth floor button, and leaned against the back wall, her eyes closed. The doors began to shut. Then someone pushed an outside button and they reopened. She turned to face the corner, wanting no company, sympathetic or otherwise.

'Hello, Frankie.'

Standing in the doorway, framed by the babble and lights of Binion's, was Jack Broderick. She stared at him, too drained by her defeat to register surprise. 'What do you want?'

He stepped inside and pushed the button to her floor. 'I came to see you play.'

'You mean, to see me lose! I'm surprised you didn't cheer.'

He studied her white, tired face and the dark rings under her eyes. 'I couldn't believe it when I saw you at The Hertford. Oh, I know your father used to gamble, and Marius always said you'd beat me at cards, but I had no idea you were so good. It takes nerve to play high-stakes poker. I admire that. You played a good game today, though not as good as yesterday.'

'You were here?'

'How could I miss it!'

They had reached her floor. She stepped out of the lift and began to walk away.

'I'll challenge you to a game,' he called after her. 'Name your stakes.'

She didn't answer. She just kept walking. Meeting Jack again was the last thing she needed today.

There was no sign of Jack when Frankie finally surfaced next morning. Of course, he could have checked out, but instinct told her he hadn't. Not that she cared. At least, she told herself she didn't. But his presence in the same hotel, the same city, made her jumpy.

She ate breakfast in the Coffee Shop with Grizzly and Damascus Joe. They talked 'if onlys', of cards they should have played and bets they should have called. Every time someone clattered down the wooden stairs to the Coffee Shop, Frankie couldn't help turning her head to see who was coming. After breakfast she wandered up to the pool and stretched out in the sun, but within half an hour she was restless. She went downstairs to watch the tournament with Oil Slick Dick and Al Capone, but the cards couldn't hold her attention. She grabbed a cab and headed downtown to see Loretta.

'Scott hasn't been in touch,' she said.

'Give him time.' Loretta paused. 'Is that why you're upset, or is it being knocked out of the tournament?'

'It's neither, although of course I was sick at losing.' Frankie pulled a face to hide a deeper emotion. 'You remember the man I left my husband for. Well, he's here. At Binion's.'

'Oh no! What are you going to do?'

'I wish I knew.'

'Do you still love him?'

'I don't know.'

'I though that was what you went to England to discover.'

384

'I saw him in England and felt nothing, except anger. Then I saw him again and I wanted him. But he had someone else.' Frankie stood up. She'd only just arrived at Loretta's but already she was twitching to get back to the hotel.

She spent the afternoon mooching around the casino, dropping quarters into slots, whilst the tournament reduced the players to the final six for tomorrow's game. The Fanman and Grandma were into a high-stakes side-game. She joined, but her mind was elsewhere. Five hundred dollars down, she said good night, left the table, and went upstairs to bed. The message light on her phone was dead. No one had called. She fell asleep with the television on, the sound low.

When she woke, it was mid-morning, and one of the interminable game shows was on the screen. Three shrieking couples were trying to guess the weight of an elephant in order to win a heart-shaped bed. She switched it off and lay in blissful silence, thinking of Jack. If there was such a thing as fate, it had brought him to Las Vegas, to her.

She rolled over and picked up the phone.

Jack took a long time to answer. As Frankie waited, she wondered if he was with a woman, the horsy girl from London, or someone he'd picked up in Vegas. It wasn't her business, but she didn't like it. Finally, he picked up his phone.

'Do you still want to play poker with me, Jack?' she asked softly.

'I haven't changed my mind, but you're leaving it very late. I fly home tomorrow.' His voice was brusque, almost hostile.

'I'll play for Blue,' she said, still friendly.

'What are you offering?'

'Seven thousand dollars. It's all I have left.'

There was silence. She thought he'd fallen asleep. Then he said, 'I don't want your money. I want to make love with you. Just once. I want you to put on your slave-girl act and beg my forgiveness for all the hurt you caused me. That's the only stake that interests me.'

She was shocked by the venom in his voice. Of course, she knew she'd hurt him, but she hadn't expected a desire for revenge as strong as her own against William. It took her a minute to reply. When she did, her voice had lost all gentleness. 'I accept,' she snapped back. 'I'll come at six. Phone Eamonn. I'll be collecting Blue next week.'

Forty-One

As soon as Frankie came off the telephone to Jack, she made another call. This time it was to the hotel shop, to order two packs of cards.

She was up and dressed by the time they were delivered. Leaving one pack sealed, she opened the other and started to deal, but not in the normal way. She held the cards in her left hand, with three fingers along the outside edge and her index finger on the right corner. Then she practised dealing the second card first. Initially, she was slow. But she persevered until it was almost impossible to tell that she'd retained the top card for herself. Her fingers had found the old routine, the one her father had taught her, the mechanic's grip. Except that her hands were nimbler than his. They always had been. He'd tended to fumble. That was why he'd been caught, and the men had come to the stadium to smash his face on the railings.

Once Frankie had perfected the deal, she practised peeking at the cards. This she found harder. She managed to view the top card as she dealt, even the top two. No more than that. But she'd have the advantage: she'd know one of Jack's hidden cards.

In the late afternoon, she showered and dressed, selecting a plain white T-shirt and white culottes, nothing fussy to distract her from her game. She ordered up sandwiches and black coffee, and nibbled as she smoothed her hair into a neat ballerina plait. She wasn't nervous. The hostility in his voice had dispelled her nostalgia. All she wanted from him now was Blue.

Jack's suite was on the top floor. He opened the door as soon as she knocked, standing aside to let her pass. She crossed to a table near the huge plate windows which looked west towards Fremont and The Strip. The sun was setting. It threw its red and orange light across the desert town, casting the sidewalks into deep, dark shadows. 'Where's your horsy girlfriend?' she asked, glancing around.

'In London.'

'I suppose Vegas isn't quite her style.'

'She didn't come, because I didn't invite her.' He walked towards the bar. 'Would you like a drink?'

'No thanks.' She produced the sealed pack of cards. 'We'll play no limit, a thousand dollar buy-in, and no re-buys. Winner takes all.' She stacked a thousand dollars on the table in front of her. Then she unwrapped the cards, shuffled, and passed them to Jack to cut. 'I'll deal. We're playing Texas Hold'em.'

'Oh, no! We play Dealer's Choice.'

'No. Hold'em.'

'The game you're best at? Forget it!'

She hesitated. 'All right. Dealer's Choice. And as I'm dealing, we're playing Hold'em.'

She held the cards as she'd practised all day, as her father had taught her, and dealt Jack a two and a nine, unsuited, and herself a pair of queens. She won the hand and a hundred dollars. With a satisfied smile, she stacked the money in front of her and passed the cards to Jack.

'Seven Card Stud,' he said.

It wasn't that different from Hold'em, except that each player received two hidden cards and one exposed before betting. As the holder of the lowest exposed card, Frankie had to bet first. Hidden, she had a pair of eights. She bet fifty. Jack matched. They played on to the last round, by which time they each had two hidden cards and four exposed. Frankie was trying to make a full house. The seventh card was dealt face down. It gave her three eights. But Jack won with three queens.

On her deal, she reverted to Hold'em. This time he beat her full house with four kings. His hand was a chance in a million. She told herself his luck couldn't last. But Jack was on a roll. Regardless of how Frankie dealt, he won. He was drawing unbelievable cards. Aces and kings. Four of a kind. A full house. A straight flush. Frankie was down to her last hundred dollars. She clenched her fists and scowled.

Jack leaned back in his chair. 'What a run of bad luck,' he mocked.

'Shut up and play!'

It was her deal. She gave herself two aces. The Flop produced another ace and two fives. Now she'd show him! She pushed forward all her money.

He raised an eyebrow. 'Aren't you being rash?'

'Come on, Jack. Play or fold.'

He hesitated whilst she waited, masking her impatience, then with a sigh he matched her.

Fourth Street was a ten. Fifth Street a seven. Triumphantly, she showed her cards. 'That one's mine. At last!'

Jack turned over his hand. He also held two aces.

Frankie stared in disbelief. 'Something's wrong. There are five aces on the table.'

He laughed out loud, unashamedly, and shook three kings and a queen from his right sleeve. 'I told you once that I play clean, and if that doesn't work I play dirty. You're a better poker player than I am. I couldn't risk losing.'

'You cheat!'

'Takes one to know one. I too know the mechanic's grip.'

'All right. I admit it. I cheated.' Frankie pushed her chair back from the table and stood up. 'But you know I only played to get Blue back. I suppose you find it funny to have dangled that prospect in front of me, only to snatch it away.'

He threw the cards on to the table. 'I'd never have taken Blue if you'd written, just once, to say you were sorry. But you never stopped to think how hurt I'd be. After all the promises, the love and the laughter, you went back to that cold-blooded hypocrite.'

Tears prickled Frankie's eyes. 'Don't you think I regret it?'

He took a step towards her, and asked with a quiet, pent-up anger, 'Why did you leave me?'

'I was afraid of you and your world. You'd become so secretive. So violent. I don't mean just the time you hit William on the doorstep, but you were angry towards me. At first I thought you had another woman. Then I became afraid you'd gone back to crime. Don't you remember the morning when you came home, dishevelled, with the pistol. When I questioned you, you lost your temper. It reached a point where every time I heard a police siren, I thought they were coming to arrest you.'

'Fat Dudley wanted the track. He threatened to hurt you. I had to silence him. That business with your mother's car was a warning.'

'Jack, it was village boys playing a prank.'

He seized her by the wrists and shook her hard. 'Why the hell didn't you tell me?'

'I didn't know till later. Why didn't you tell me about Dudley?'

She thought he would take her in his arms, but he didn't. He pushed her away from him. 'You didn't want to know there was still a dark side to my life, so I did my best to hide it because I was afraid of losing you. Marius told me what happened when you were a child. How you couldn't speak for a week after your father was beaten up. Knowing that, how could I frighten you with Dudley? It wasn't easy for me to go straight. People I'd known in the past put pressure on me or asked for favours. But I resisted, mainly for you. I wanted you to be proud of me. I shouldn't have bothered. You left me anyhow.' He turned to look out of the window. Night had fallen whilst they had been playing. The neon lights from the casinos bounced up into the sky.

Frankie thought of Tucson, the red Datsun and the fifty dollars. If she'd understood when she was with Jack what she knew now, things might have been different. 'I tried to believe in you,' she said, wanting him to understand that he'd driven her away. 'I did believe, until that night. Even after that, I tried. But Mother was dying. I felt so vulnerable. I longed for your comfort, but when I telephoned you wouldn't even speak to me. You became a stranger. William offered safety. Security. I went back. It was the worst mistake of my life.' Leaving the cards and her money on the table, she picked up her room key.

Jack stood very still, watching her. 'He beat you up. Marius told me. I was glad.'

She flinched.

'I also wanted to kill him for hurting you.'

Their eyes held each other, as they had done in the stadium car park. A current passed between them.

'You've changed,' he said softly. 'You're not so disapproving.'

She gave him her tender, crumpled smile. 'I've seen the gutter too, Jack.'

He shook his head, half in amusement. 'To think that I'm now the one's who's respectable, written up in the Sunday papers, and you're the one who sits up nights playing poker.'

She chuckled. 'I thought that funny too, when I read your profile.'

His voice became hard again. 'You stayed away two years. Why didn't you come to me sooner?'

'I had to get away, on my own. I had to escape William, and come to terms with the past. Oh, not just you and me. Lots of things. My father. My mother. The mess I seemed to make of my life. I came to Las Vegas and learned some hard lessons, not least about myself.'

'And you didn't think to write?'

'Not a day passed when I didn't think of you. I began hundreds of letters, only to rip them up. There seemed no point in writing when I knew you wouldn't answer.'

'You never gave me a chance.'

'To make me live like a prodigal, constantly apologising for my past sins? I'd been through that with William.'

'I'd never do that to anyone!' He bought his fist down on the table, causing the cards and money to jump. 'I may have many faults, but I'm not a hypocrite.'

In the heat of the moment, she'd forgotten they were both prodigals. She started to apologise but he turned his back, and said, 'Go away, Frankie! It's too late to say you're sorry.'

'Jack, we all do and say things we regret. It's part of life.'

He didn't answer. He stood very straight, staring out at the bright lights. She longed to run to him and put her arms around him, but she was afraid he'd push her away. She walked to the door and opened it. He still didn't speak. She hesitated. He didn't turn round.

'Goodbye, Jack,' she said.

'Goodbye.'

She wasn't going to beg. She walked out. He didn't call her back.

She went down to her room and lay on the bed, running backwards and forwards through their conversations, wishing she'd said some things and hadn't said others. She alternated between being angry with Jack for taking offence, and being angrier with herself for giving it.

At midnight, the television news told her that Phil Hellmuth Junior, the college drop-out, was the new No Limit Champion. He'd beaten Johnny Chan, 'the Oriental Express', with a pair of nines over an ace and a seven, suited. Once, Frankie would have

391

sat up, eager to watch the closing moments of the tournament. Tonight, she didn't.

On the following morning, she rose early, pulled on her old cut-off jeans and a T-shirt, rented a car and drove down to Loretta's. She wanted to be away from the hotel when Jack checked out. 'Scott never called me,' she said sorrowfully, her arms resting on the kitchen table as she watched Loretta twist her knitting wool in and out of the needles.

'He's met a new lady and doesn't want to upset her or himself.'

'He deserves someone nice.'

'So do you. What's happened with that man?'

Frankie pulled a face. 'I upset him. I didn't mean to. I always seem to say the wrong thing. Even when I rehearse my speech, I never get the words out straight.'

'Or maybe the man doesn't stick to your script?'

Frankie laughed. 'You're right. Damn him! I wish I could marry a pack of cards. A nice new pack, all wrapped up in Cellophane. At least I know how to handle cards.'

Loretta shook her head. 'You say the craziest things. That's what I like about you. Don't give up on fairy tales, Frankie. Some of them do come true. Ask yourself what that man was doing in Las Vegas.'

'He came to watch the World Series.'

'He came to see you. Go back before it's too late.'

'It's too late already.'

When Frankie left Loretta's, she didn't go back to the hotel. She couldn't face seeing Jack leave. Instead, she drove out to Red Rock Canyon. She stopped the car well beyond the handful of houses, where the only sign of human existence was the dirt track weaving between the sandstone hills, and watched the burning daylight dance along the red horizon. She loved this place. It had an eerie, desolate beauty which reminded her of her hitchhike journey up from Phoenix. For the first time in months, she thought of little Horace. Had he kept away from the casinos and saved his marriage? She hoped so.

She'd had nothing that day when she'd arrived in Las Vegas. No money. No future. No one to love or be loved by. She'd never forget the hunger and the heat. The nights when she slept in the red Datsun. The desperation of stealing that fifty dollars. Now she had money. Not a fortune, but she could make more. Only money wasn't everything. It didn't fill the void where love and laughter used to live.

She had to give Jack one more shot. She turned the car and raced back to Las Vegas. As she reached Binion's, Jack was stepping into a limousine. She jumped from her hired car, leaving its doors open and engine still running, and hurried to him. 'I . . . ummm . . . came to say goodbye,' she told him, suddenly shy of saying the other things, the ones she'd rehearsed out at Red Rock Canyon.

'Climb in. I've been waiting for you all morning.'

She hovered by the limousine door. 'Jack, we need to talk. I can't just come away with you. It may not work. We're different people now.'

'We'll talk on the plane.'

'I want to return to the law. I decided that when I was in England.'

'Did I ever try to prevent you? No. You stopped yourself.' He glanced at his watch. 'Our plane leaves in thirty minutes.'

She was assailed by fear. Of giving and loving, of being vulnerable again. 'I plan to specialise in child injury cases. My work will take a lot of my time. You won't like that.'

'Do you think I want to be your gaoler, as William was? Oh, I admit there were times when I was suspicious, but I was never jealous of your work. I was proud of you.' He tapped his watch. 'One minute, and I drive on.'

She threw up her hands. 'What about my clothes, my suitcase?'

'They'll send them on.'

'I've six thousand dollars in the safe.'

'Stop making excuses! If you don't want to leave Las Vegas with me, why have you come back to the hotel?'

Her face crumpled. 'I do, but I'm afraid.'

'Frankie,' he said, with finality. 'I love you. But if you don't come with me today, I'll never ask you again. We both made mistakes. We have one more chance. This is it. Get in!'

She had no jacket or sweater. Her passport and her driving licence were in her bag: she'd needed them to rent the car. Everything else was in her room. She didn't even have a toothbrush. She hesitated, clenching and unclenching her fists.

393

Then she said, 'Oh, what the hell! They're only possessions. I won't be the first person to leave Las Vegas with less than I arrived with.' And she slipped into the back seat, next to Jack.

He cupped her hand in his, and said, 'What? No bitten fingernails?'

She smiled and leaned against him. 'No, but we were arguing in a kind of car park.'

She didn't know if it would work, if they would last. In poker, she'd have known the odds. In life, she didn't. But she couldn't let Jack go. Her mother had said everyone should know great love. Jack was hers. He made her laugh. He made her cry. He made her proud. He made her rage. He was the only man in whom she could ever confide that she'd once stolen fifty dollars, and know that he'd think no less of her. For that, and so much more, he was worth the gamble.

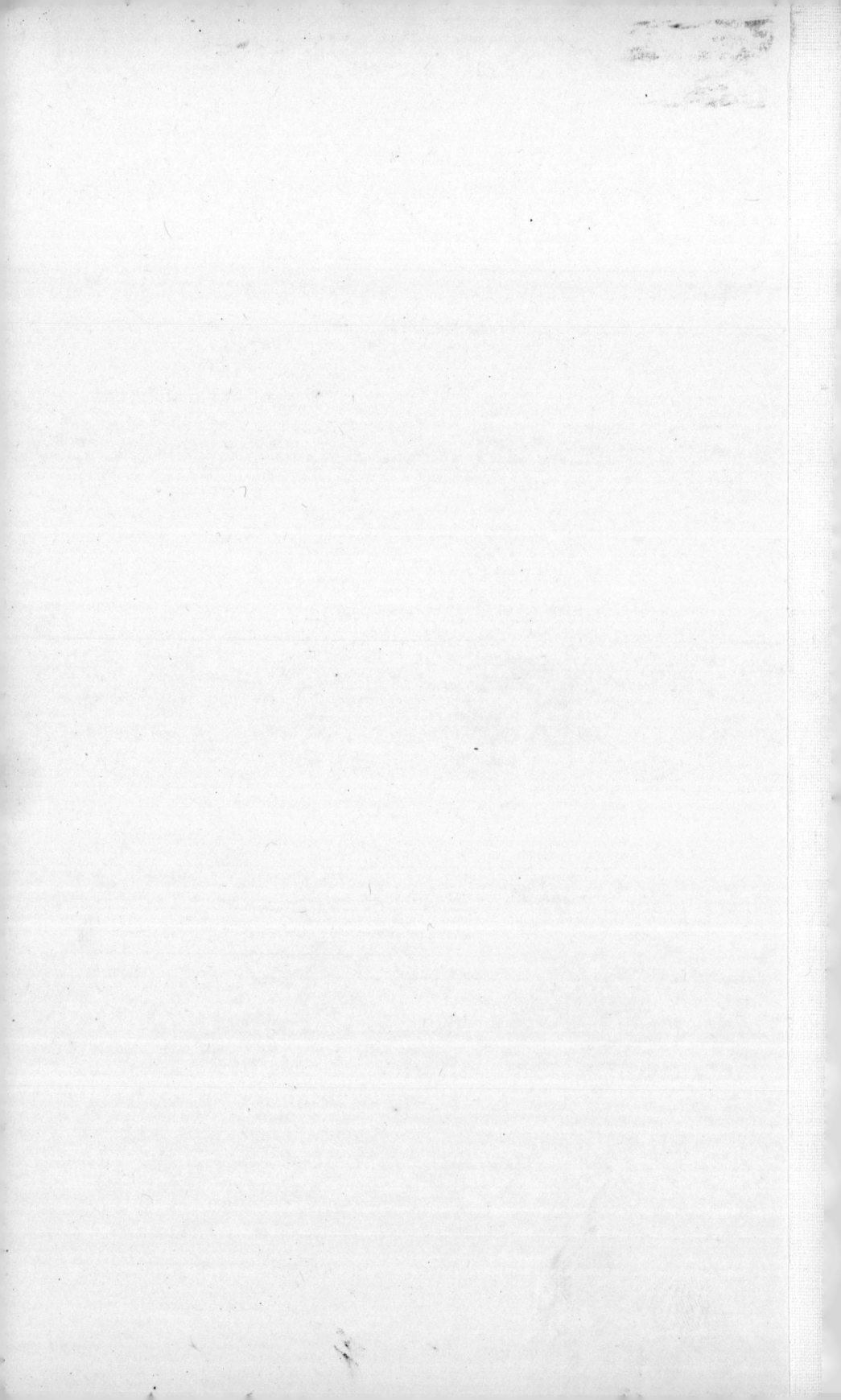